Boost

A Haunted Addiction #1
D.A. Paul

To Maxx,

for being so amazing.

Chapter 1

It was halfway through the summer of my junior year, and I was completely convinced that I had sleep apnea. It was only a matter of time before I was hooked up to one of those breathing machines that would make me look like Darth Vader. Despite the warnings I found while doing internet research, I refused to tell my parents about the constant night terrors. I was just vain enough to prefer the risk of dying in my sleep from choking on my own throat, than having to use a breathing mask.

I took another sip of coffee and stared out at the vacant suburban street. A golden retriever trotted through my mother's lavender plants.

"Hey Bubba," I called.

Bubba's ears perked up, and he came racing up the porch steps towards me. The lime-green fuzz of the tennis ball that he was mouthing, swirled together under a thin layer of drool. He dropped it on my lap.

"Ew, Bubba, did you get out again?"

He wagged his tail harder in response and nudged the tennis ball with his nose.

Every so often, Bubba would escape from Mrs. Peterson's yard to go vandalize rose gardens and terrorize stray cats around the neighborhood. I couldn't really blame him. Mrs. Peterson was a cranky old woman who always smelled like Windex.

I picked up the ball with two fingers, and threw it into the small patch of grass that made up our front lawn. Through the screen door behind me, I heard the sound of bacon hitting the frying pan, which meant my mom had finally come downstairs. I was a semi-vegan, so the bacon was probably being made for my older brother, Ryan. The sound of a crinkling newspaper meant my father was also up, ignoring my mother at the kitchen table as he read business economics in the Oregon Roseville Times.

"Bubba!" Mrs. Peterson ambled slowly down the street in a pink floral nightgown, her rollers trapped in a mess of white hair. "Bubba!" she cried. Beside me, Bubba thumped his tail harder, bowing his head guiltily.

"C'mon punk, let's go home." I used the tennis ball to lure Bubba to Mrs. Peterson before making my way back to the front porch.

"Lidia!" My mother's muffled voice sounded from the kitchen.

I sighed and went inside.

"Morning geek," Ryan greeted me as I slid the screen door shut.

"Morning asshole," I shot back.

"Watch your language." Dad flipped a page of the paper without looking up.

My mother turned to me. She was still in her bathrobe, but makeup already smothered every inch of skin on her face. "Honey, why aren't you ready for camp?"

"I'm going to get ready right now."

"Why aren't you already dressed?"

Experience told me not to roll my eyes.

I rolled my eyes anyways.

"Lidia-"

"What?" I shuffled past her, but she followed as I walked quickly down the hall. My bare feet were still a little wet from the dew outside and they left footmarks on the polished hardwood floors.

"Lidia!" Her manicured hands flew up in frustration. "Ethan's going to be here in half an hour! You're not even dressed, or showered, or have your makeup-"

"So?"

"Ethan-"

"He's not dating me just because I wear makeup, mom."

"I know that honey, but-"

"So, I think our relationship will survive me looking like a dirty hippy for one day."

"Everyday!" shouted Ryan from the kitchen.

"Lidia that attitude-" she was cut off by my bedroom door slamming shut.

Heaven forbid my boyfriend see me without makeup.

I stormed over to my closet. My mother was the only person in my life who frustrated me beyond comprehension. Maybe it was the fact she was so shamelessly desperate to be young again, or maybe it was the fact that she was so stubbornly blind that my dad was cheating on her. I didn't know what it was, but we didn't get along. Ever.

I had already packed for the trip. This year, I decided to spend the summer away from my family by volunteering at a summer camp with Ethan. A warm bubble filled my stomach at the thought. Both of us in geeky camp gear away from strict parental supervision- it was going to be awesome.

Ethan and I had met last year when he was assigned the seat next to mine in trigonometry class. He was the new student, just moved to Oregon from Lake Chelan in Washington. Two months after meeting him that first day in class, we were officially dating. Though I wasn't big on dating in high school, Ethan was the exception. He had been my first, and as far as official boyfriends go, he was the only.

I shimmied into a pair of tight, slightly ripped jeans, and a loose white T-shirt. I glanced at my makeup bag, debating whether or not I wanted to put any effort into my appearance. I decided *not*. Mostly just to spite my mother.

I didn't really feel like I needed makeup anyways. Looking in the mirror, I saw my soft features and arching brows. I liked my face. Ethan liked my face. A lot of people liked my face. Besides, makeup was really just glorified face paint.

I started shaking out the strands of my long messy brown hair before throwing it into a loose bun. A splash of my favorite vanilla body spray and voila, done. I skipped downstairs with my backpack and almost ran straight into Ethan.

"Oomph," I sputtered as we collided.

He caught me before I fell off balance and wrapped me in a warm embrace. I could feel his wide toothy grin on my shoulder and pictured the genuine expression of excitement plastered across his freckled face.

"Are you ready?" he asked, releasing me and exposing the exact face I had just pictured. His pale blue eyes gleamed and he ran a hand through cropped copper-brown hair.

And all those freckles.

I smiled. "Born ready."

Ethan took the duffel bag from my shoulder and brought it to the front door. My mother, brother, and grumpy-looking dad were already in the entryway. My father was looking back down the hall towards the kitchen table where his paper was, and Ryan had his arms crossed in a *mom-made-me-come-out-here* way.

Mom beamed at me with watery eyes as she gave me a quick hug. Then, after letting go of me, wrapped her arms around a bemused Ethan for a much longer embrace.

Cougar.

"Be safe you two," she said after finally releasing my boyfriend.

"We will!" I hopped off the porch and practically ran to Ethan's Jeep. As soon as I touched the warm metal of the handle, the locks popped up with a click.

"Hold on, it might be locked," shouted Ethan as he wobbled toward me carrying the small amount of luggage. He started to dig the keys out of his pocket, but I was already pulling the door open.

"I got it," I said with a cheerful smile. "Your car is malfunctioning." I disappeared into the passenger side.

"Oh," Ethan's eyebrows knitted together, but eased up quickly as he threw the bag into the back and slid in front of the wheel. He turned the key in the ignition and the engine roared to life. "Get ready for the best summer of your life."

I had already stuck my head out the window. The cool summer breeze whipped past my cheeks as he backed out of the driveway.

"To Camp Tanka!" I shouted, pumping one fist out the window. My mother shot an uneasy glance toward the neighbor's house before giving a shy wave and closing the door.

"To Camp Tanka!" Ethan echoed.

· ·

"I have to pee."

"You just went pee." Ethan turned his horrible hip-hop music down as we passed another exit.

"I have to pee so badly."

"Lidia, you just went pee. You can hold it for, like, thirty minutes. We're almost there," he said, ignoring my deep breathing as I struggled to retain my urine.

"I have to pee!" I shifted. "Another exit, look!"

There was a small nasty gas station just beyond a large mossy stump. We had been driving deeper, and deeper, into the woods for the past hour. Sunlight was barely visible through the thick evergreen canopy.

"I'm not kidding," I said, cradling my lower abdomen. "Please."

Ethan didn't respond.

"My bladder is going to explode."

Still no response. He looked as if he was thinking about passing the exit.

"Well fine, but I feel sorry for your jeep, these seats are fabric and-"

Ethan sighed loudly and took a sharp right into the rough gravel of the decrepit square building.

"Oh thank God!" I opened the door and leapt out of the Jeep before he had even come to a full stop. I ran as quickly as I could into the station while keeping my thighs pressed tightly together.

I finished up in the bathroom as quickly as possible, it wasn't exactly somewhere you'd want to hang out. The tiles were cracked and grimy, white lights overhead flickered, and the entire restroom smelled horrible.

The walls and floor of the rest of the store were a smoke-stained white, and filled with shelves of non-perishables in crinkly bags. I walked along the lines of humming refrigerators on the back wall. The lights inside the glass flickered. Slowly, a cool tingle etched its way through my skin until my bones prickled.

It was the same feeling I got every time I woke up suddenly in the middle of the night.

The reason I couldn't sleep.

Is this awake apnea?

I grabbed two green energy drinks and went to the little register to pay.

"Hi," I said as the toothless man scanned each can.

He was wearing a cowboy hat that hid most of his balding head, but it did nothing to distract from the few tangled wisps of white hair that leaked from the sides in patches.

"Four, eighty seven," he said.

I handed him my card.

Behind the man, an older woman was leaning against the wall of lottery tickets and cigarette packs. Most of her round body was covered by a modest floral nightgown, but her entire face was an array of black and blue. Red patches where she had sustained her injuries swelled and purpled around the darker echo of knuckles that had buried themselves into the side of her face.

Who had beaten her?

I looked back at the man waiting for me to enter my pin. A trickle of fear shot through me as I leaned down and punched in a few numbers.

"Uh," I swallowed and looked up. "Are you okay?" I asked the woman.

She glared at me through swollen eye sockets.

"Just fine, ma'am."

I turned to the cashier who had just spoken.

"Have a nice day," he said and slid the cans over the counter to me.

"Well-" I looked back toward the women, but she had disappeared. I took the two cans and looked around the store once more before I left. The bone-chilling creepiness didn't subside until I had crossed the lot and climbed into the cab next to Ethan.

"You got more liquids?" he asked.

I took a deep breath and popped the lid to my drink. It fizzed loudly.

"Don't complain, I got you one too." I handed him the can and he smiled a big goofy grin.

"You look good drinking that." Ethan leaned over and kissed my cheek sweetly. "The green matches your eyes."

I turned the embellished can around my hands, studying the neon green swirls. My eyes were not that green.

"Thank you." I took a sip and Ethan reached over to take my other hand.

"I'm a lucky guy," he said. "I've got a hot girlfriend."

As we drove, I focused my attention on the passing nature scenery. *Those bruises, that face.* I wanted to mention it to Ethan, but as we continued to drive, the more it felt like I hadn't seen it at all.

It wouldn't be the first time.

Mysterious non-drug-induced hallucinations had been freaking me out for weeks. Usually just shadows, or flashes of something I thought I saw but weren't really there. I couldn't even count the number of times I had swerved on the road while driving in an attempt to avoid hitting a mangled raccoon or dog, only to have it disappear two seconds later.

Ultimately, I blamed the lack of sleep.

I shook my head, trying to clear my mind. It didn't work so I tried for distraction. "So, what's your friend's name again?"

"What friend?"

"The one who's going to be at camp with us. His name's Andrew or something?"

"Ander," Ethan corrected me with a smile. "Don't call him Andrew, he'll get pissed. He's really cool, I'm excited for you to meet him... I haven't seen him since Christmas."

Ethan's parents had split up. His dad had moved down to Oregon while his mom stayed at the old place in Lake Chelan. Apparently, Ethan and Ander had been neighbors in a very tiny neighborhood. Naturally, they became best friends, and the two households were like family.

"I was thinking, maybe you could come up and visit my mom this Christmas... if you're up for it. You haven't met her yet."

My eyes lit up. "Really?" I bounced a little in my seat. "Yeah, I would love to. If my parents let me go."

"Great!" Ethan smiled in silence for a moment before his good mood faltered and a flash of concern etched itself into his expressive features. "I hope he's doing okay."

"Who?"

"Ander. I told you about his sister, right?"

He had. She was fourteen, and battling leukemia. Ethan never really told me how bad it was, but I assumed any type of cancer was really, really, bad.

"Yeah. Is she doing any better? "

"I don't know. She didn't look too good last year." Ethan let out a heavy breath. "I feel horrible. He's my best friend and like, two months after she was diagnosed, my dad left, and I moved, and that stupid private school he goes to doesn't allow him to have a phone so it's hard to keep in touch."

"He doesn't have a phone?"

"No, he goes to a snob boarding school where they don't have computers, or phones, or like, anything."

"Not even computers?"

Ethan shook his head. "Nope."

"Hmm," I pulled the trigger to my seat. It swung back and I felt the rocking of the car over the broken road like a cradle. "I've heard of places like that."

"You have?"

"Yeah. It's called Amish... How do you ever talk to him?"

A tight smile stamped around the corner of his lips. "Letters."

There was a beat of silence as I pictured Ethan bent over a table, scribbling his inner most thoughts and passions onto a little piece of paper using a quill pen.

"How romantic," I laughed. "Do you guys write in code?"

"No," Ethan scoffed, spouting a little bit of his energy drink as he did so. "I can't wait to see you two together... It'll be, like, ten minutes before you piss him off." He thought for a second. "Or he pisses you off."

"I thought you said I would like him!"

"You will," Ethan reassured me. "Just watch your sarcasm."

I scrunched my face and looked out the window.

"You're so cute." Ethan reached over to give me his hand. I refused, but, after sticking my tongue out at him, received it.

I sat back in my seat and smiled as we turned to enter onto a bumpy dirt road. Slits of sunlight peaked through the openings in the trees overhead. After a few minutes, we passed under a large wooden sign that read **Welcome to Camp Tanka**.

This was going to be a good summer.

Chapter 2

This was going to be a horrible summer.

As Ethan and I climbed out of the Jeep, we were immediately met with an onslaught of screaming seven-year-olds. They rushed us, armed with sticky fingers and battle cries. I fell backwards against the car, but after the kids saw that we had no authority, they continued running towards the nearest adult.

This was a terrible mistake.

There were two yellow school buses parked in the circular ring of the camp center. In the middle was a dying garden and a flagpole with an orange and blue symbol printed on the fabric swaying in the warm breeze. Around, behind, and everywhere between, were children. Somehow, it seemed like every single one of them was screaming.

I shot a worried glance at Ethan who smiled nervously. We grabbed our bags from the car and started walking past the parents, camp counselors, and the small munchkins winding their way around our knees.

On the far side of camp, there were lines of small cabins in front of the dark backdrop of cedar trees. The gutters were filled with pine needles, and there was a sparking bug zapper hung on each porch. To my right, I saw a larger wooden building, which I assumed would be the cafeteria. Behind it, in a clearing through the trees, was a glossy blue lake that sparkled under the sun. It made the distant mountains look dark and ominous in comparison.

"It's pretty," I said. "I didn't know we were going to have a lake."

"That way." Ethan nodded at a group of awkward looking teenagers huddled together in front of the cafeteria. "Did you bring a swimsuit?"

"Yep, I did. Not the blue one though, just the yellow one."

He slumped his shoulders.

"Sorry," I laughed. "It wasn't child appropriate."

As we neared the group, a booming male voice shouted Ethan's name. A tall dark-haired boy in a grey T-shirt emerged from the crowd.

He was taller than Ethan by an inch, and he had shaggy dark brown hair that hung casually in twenty different directions. He was definitely fit, and attractive, but it was his confident walk that made him stand out.

I stared a little longer than I meant to. I looked back at Ethan and took a step closer to his side. "Is that your friend?" I whispered.

The guy stopped just short of us and playfully threw up what looked like a gang sign and scrunched his lips. Ethan started laughing and mirrored the boys greeting.

You have got to be kidding me.

The two boys embraced each other briefly. Ethan looked ecstatic.

"Ethan! How have you been?"

"I've been good," he said. "How have you been? I haven't seen you since Christmas."

18

"I've been alright. School sucks, my brother's still a dick."

The boy shot a thumb behind his back towards the crowd of teenagers. I saw a taller, equally attractive guy standing haughtily next to a small blond girl. His dark hair had a reddish hue in the sunlight and he looked a few years older than Ander, despite the fact that his face was scrunched up in the pouty expression of a two-year-old.

"Hi."

I looked back at the boys and saw that Ander's blue eyes were pointed in my direction. *Sweet campfire s'mores.*

"I'm Ander... You must be Lidia?"

The image of Ethan's and Ander's faux ghetto reunion was too fresh. I couldn't help myself.

"What's up playa?" I replied.

Ander's mouth tweaked into a half smile, not sure if he was supposed to laugh or not.

"Yep. This is Lidia," said Ethan. I swear I could hear sarcasm in his voice, but he still reached down and took my hand.

"Hah, so, uh..." Ander looked back at me, eyes twinkling slightly. "Why are you dating this loser?"

Ethan punched Ander's arm and the two of them laughed. I just stood awkwardly, waiting for them to calm down. Finally, they did, and we started walking again.

"What's with the pow-wow?" asked Ethan as we got closer to the crowd.

A few more scared-looking teenagers piled out of their parent's cars and sprinted toward the gathering in front of us. Once they reached the crowd of people, most just stood there, too afraid to ask what was going on.

"We're supposed to sign in and get our cabin number." Ander elbowed Ethan playfully. "Not co-ed."

"Bummer."

"I know!" Ander sounded exasperated as he stared blatantly at a busty blond near the front of the crowd. "It's supposed to be the teen equivalent of Vegas. What happens at camp, stays at camp. I've come prepared."

Ethan, your friend is a douchebag.

Ethan laughed. "Twenty bucks says you won't get any."

Good job babe.

"Twenty bucks says I do."

"Technically," I interjected. "Twenty bucks can't say anything."

The two boys stared blankly back at me.

"It doesn't have a mouth," I said. *Duh.*

"Twenty bucks says that's stupid," Ander muttered as he looked back at the crowd.

I turned and saw Ethan watching us with an eyebrow raised. He shrugged, silently conveying- *I told you so.*

"I hate it when you're always right," I said.

"Right about what?" Ander asked, still scoping the blond.

"I bet Lid that you guys would piss each other off within ten minutes of meeting."

"What?" Ander looked back at me. "You didn't piss me off."

"Oh good, I was so worried!"

He looked a little offended. "You don't like me?"

"Oh, I like you just fine, *Andrew*."

"Ander," he corrected sternly.

Ethan busted up laughing and a few people turned to look over at us.

Just then, a small round women with fiery red hair came shuffling out of the cafeteria through a set of rustic wooden doors. Two gawky guys followed her carrying a plastic fold up table and a chair like Egyptian slaves preparing the throne. Her royal highness waited patiently as the boys set up the table and chair before she sat delicately onto the small plastic seat. It quivered slightly under her weight and her large bottom curved over the edges as she flattened a piece of paper on the desk.

"Welcome to Camp Tanka," she squawked. "Everyone needs to sign in. Next to your name will be a cabin number. Volunteers may drop off their belongings in the cabin, and then you will meet the camp leader that you will be helping this summer. Dinner is at six, which is about two hours from now. We will all be meeting in the cafeteria."

My stomach rattled. *I hadn't eaten since... I haven't eaten today!* It was an unfortunate realization because after I remembered that I hadn't eaten, I got twice as hungry.

A line started to form in front of the table and everyone took turns signing their name and receiving a cabin key before dispersing. After I signed and received a key, I lagged behind, waiting for Ethan and Ander.

"Which cabin did you get?" I asked as they stepped over to the bare patch of dirt where I was waiting.

"Four." Ethan held up a key.

"Fifteen." Ander shrugged his backpack on. "You?"

"Sixteen."

"Oh," he smiled down at me. "We'll be neighbors."

"Joy."

Ethan handed me my duffel bag. "I'll see you at dinner?" He leaned in for a quick kiss.

Ander rolled his eyes, but looked too happy to fool anyone into thinking he was annoyed.

"Yeah," I said. "See you at dinner."

Ethan waved as Ander and I strode toward the last few cabins, nearest the dark part of the woods. *Great.* My stomach grumbled. *Maybe I can forage some nuts and berries.*

I took a deep breath, the air smelled like moist soil. The sun had started to set behind the mountains and trees behind us, casting long shadows at our feet.

"I wonder if anyone's been attacked by a bear out here."

"Probably." Ander looked like he was staring at something through the trees behind our cabin.

"You weren't supposed to agree. Now all I am going to be thinking about is becoming bear meat."

Ander smiled but said nothing.

"Look!" I glanced back at the rest of the camp that was still in sunlight as we walked further into the shadows. "They're exiling us! We are the bear sacrifice."

At this, Ander laughed. I realized with a slice of guilty pleasure, that he had a very nice laugh.

"Don't worry, I'll be on watch for you. I promise to jump in front of a bear before he tries to eat you."

It would've been a sweet promise if it sounded genuine. Ander was more likely to shove me in front of a carnivorous animal. Head first, no doubt.

"Yeah, you're big enough," I said sadly. "You'd probably fill him up before he could get to me." I pictured myself helplessly flailing my arms as my head got quickly eaten.

"Yeah probably." Ander ran a hand across the top of his head, haphazardly attempting to flatten its wildness.

When I stepped up to the porch of my cabin, Ander stood at the bottom and looked up at me.

"At least it wouldn't eat all of you," he said. "Maybe just your legs." He smirked and I smiled sarcastically back, waving goodbye as I yanked the door open to the dark cabin.

It took a minute for my eyes to adjust to the dim light. As far as I could tell, there was no light switch on the wall, or bulb in the ceiling. Everything smelled like old wood- a musty, waterlogged cedar.

I claimed the bed with the quilt that was absent of puke stains and looked the least scratchy. The creaky bed springs poked my butt as I sat and looked around the cabin, not that I could see much. There were three other sets of bunk beds clustered into the room, but other than that, it was pretty bare.

A few heavy seconds ticked by before the door suddenly opened with a flourish. A short, black-haired girl with heavy eyeliner stepped into the room. She held a glorious battery-powered lantern in her hand.

"Oh," she said flatly. "There you are."

Her monotone voice didn't make it sound like she was looking for me at all. In fact, with all the gothic makeup and lack of chipper camp spirit, I wondered if I was still at summer camp. *Have I accidently wondered off into Wednesday Adam's cabin at Camp Cippewa?* She bore her lackluster eyes into mine.

Probably.

Behind the gothic girl, followed four young campers. The girls, including the camp leader, were all wearing vibrant orange T-shirts. The gothic girl placed the light on the bed and withdrew an orange shirt from the large backpack she had just swung onto the mattress neighboring mine.

"I'm Amber, but you can call me Trina."

"Hi. My name's Lidia."

"I know."

The rest of the room was better lit now, functional at least. Amber, or Trina, turned from me and started feeling around the splintered wood panels of the wall nearest the window. Her hands found a switch, and with a quick snap, warm light filled the room from little circular bulbs that were protruding from the cedar walls. The lights hummed and flickered as they pumped out electricity.

The younger campers bickered over the bunks in high pitched voices, but I was relieved that none of them were screaming. *This group is obviously mature for their age.* Just as the thought crossed my mind, one of the girls withdrew a stuffed unicorn from her backpack and threw it at another girl who had just claimed the bed she was going for.

Trina watched them vacantly for a minute before she swung herself onto the bunk.

"So, I saw you with those two boys during sign up. Are they your boyfriends?"

Boyfriends? Plural?

I choked on some spit, trying not to laugh. "No, no," I coughed. "Just the freckled one."

"Oh," Her face remained blank as she started rummaging through her bag again.

"Why do you ask?"

Trina shrugged, "I guess the tall one is pretty sexy. I was going to try and hook up with him, if you don't mind."

Oh my God, it is Vegas.

"Go for it. He's pretty rude though."

Trina shrugged again, undisturbed.

"Well," I looked around the cabin for something to talk about. "So, how much longer until dinner?"

"We still have an hour." She looked back at the giggling girls.

One of them was shouting something incoherent to the others.

"Hey girls," Trina commanded.

To my surprise, they all stopped and turned toward her. I didn't have a lot of experience with kids, but apparently, gothic horror makeup and a monotone attitude could gain you insta-authority with the youngsters.

"We have an hour before dinner. Do any of you want to paint your nails?"

There was a stampede of little ballerina feet as they all circled around her.

"Okay. Lidia and I will do it for you."

I raised an eyebrow as one girl with missing teeth scrambled onto my lap. "What's your name?" I asked.

"My name is Mellissa. I have a brother and his name is Jorden, but he, but he, but he can't go to camp because he's too little," Mellissa took a breath and continued. "I want blue nails. Blue is my favorite color because it's the color of my dad's car and he likes blue and I like blue too."

"Ha, Okay," I said. "I think blue will look very pretty."

Trina glanced over at me. "We have to do it for them so there's less mess."

I nodded and told the girls to go choose their color from the bag of polish that was sitting on Trina's lap. As the girls bickered over who would get the only pink in the pile, I looked back at Trina.

"So, Trina, uh, what brings you to camp?" *Sadistic rituals in the woods?*

She answered with a nonchalant shrug, one I was quickly becoming very accustomed to.

"I love kids."

She could've just admitted to dropping a pencil for all the enthusiasm she showed, but I smiled. Trina was strange, but, I think I sort of liked her.

Sixty minutes later, our little gang of girls filed down the cabin steps. The girls delicately held wet finger tips out like baby bird wings, waiting for them to dry in the night air.

"Girls, keep in line," said Trina.

The girls fell into line behind her and continued to skip, fingers dancing excitedly. I had decided to paint my own nails a fire hydrant red. The glossy cherry color reflected light in lines as our cabin group merged with at least half a dozen others, all marching into the cafeteria.

According to the rules that Trina had explained to me as we sat painting nails, camp leaders were required to sit with their cabin group. The volunteers however, usually sat at their own table with other volunteers.

My cabin group dispersed inside the crowded cafeteria, orchestrated wonderfully by Trina's skillful rule. I grabbed a plastic tray and took my place in line behind two younger boys making rude sounds and pulling each other's hair. The tops of their heads came up to my waist, making me feel like a towering lunch bully.

A moment later, the blond-haired girl Ander had been staring at earlier, sidled up behind me. She had a nametag that read- *Hello, my name is Whitney Carman,* and she was grimacing as a set of boys shot invisible guns at her face.

Yeah... she is loving this.

I slid my tray against the cool metal bars of the service line. The round, redheaded lady whom had coordinated the sign-in sheet earlier, was now serving heaping spoons of ground beef onto dry taco shells.

She smiled at my sour expression under her white hairnet. "Here you go sweetie."

"Thank you." I looked down at the heap of crushed animal flesh on top of the dry taco. A little further down the line were the condiments.

Condiments! Maybe I won't starve after all!

I shuffled over to the table and loaded my tray with an obscene amount of shredded lettuce, avocados, and diced tomatoes. I made my way happily to a table where I saw Ethan and Ander already scarfing down their food. Ethan laughed when I sat my tray next to his.

"Oh no, babe," said Ethan, still chuckling at the sight of my plate. "I didn't even think about the food here."

"Did you even get any meat?" Ander peered down at my plate, horrified. "All you got was rabbit food."

"Lidia's a hard core vegan," explained Ethan.

"Not hardcore. I'm a semi-vegan."

"What's a semi-vegan?" Ander reached over to prod my lettuce pile with his fork, but I swatted it away with my own.

"I'm mostly vegan, except on occasion...I had cream in my coffee this morning!" I smiled proudly. "Cream is not vegan."

Ander raised an eyebrow. "Why the hell would you want to put yourself through that torture?"

The pretty brunette girl with a nametag that read-*Emily*, snickered at his comment.

"You know, Ander," I said, popping another slice of tomato in my mouth. "I would ask any of your ex-girlfriends the same question."

"Burn!" Ethan oohed as Ander's lips tweaked into a reluctant smile.

"I love meat," said Emily. She took a large messy bite of her taco to emphasize the point. Pieces of ground beef cascaded down her chin.

"Lidia hates anything that's dead," Ethan said. "It's hilarious."

I nudged his arm but he ignored me.

"I tried getting her to watch a zombie movie with me, and she kept gaging every time the zombie-"

I stomped on Ethan's foot, hard. It was true, I didn't like death, though Ethan didn't know why.

When I was twelve, my grandma was kicked out of her retirement home for acting violently towards the other patients, and came to live with my family. I was old enough to understand the gist of Alzheimer's, and Grandma's history of mental illness, but still, hearing an adult chatter to imaginary people was creepy. My room was next too hers, and night after night, she would scream at nothing, telling it to get out of her room, to leave her alone, then she would cry like a small girl until my mother finally came in to comfort her.

A month after Grandma had started living with us, my family left for a short weekend vacation. My mom had asked the neighbor to check up on Grandma once or twice during our trip, but considering what we came home to, we guessed that she never did.

I was the one who found the body.

I opened the door and caught a waft of a strange sweet-sick smell. Instead of turning around to go back outside, I rounded the corner into the living room. Grandma's lifeless body lay crumpled in an uncomfortable position on the floor. Her neck was bent way back, making her slack-jaw mouth gape. Her empty eyes bulged from the sockets, staring at me like a doll, and her stiff body had looked swollen.

"So," Ander said. "You don't eat meat because it's dead?" He was still looking at my plate like it had personally offended him.

"I saw a documentary on YouTube a year ago about factory farming," I explained as I threw a thin slice of lettuce at Ethan's face. "They do horrible things to those animals... I just don't want to eat it anymore."

"Oh," Ander nodded at my lettuce heap. "So, aren't plants dead after you eat them?"

I rolled my eyes as Ethan laughed. I let the boys delve into conversation as I finished the last of my plate, minus the beef. It wasn't until I saw Trina staring absently into her taco shell that a brilliant idea popped into my head.

"So, Ander-"

Ander turned his gaze to me. "Hmm?" He was mid sip of the Kool-Aid served to us instead of water.

"My bunkmate wants to bang you."

He choked and slammed his glass on the table, little droplets of red juice dribbling off his chin.

"Who?" asked Ethan.

"Yeah," Ander looked thrilled. "Who is it?"

I gave him Trina's famous nonchalant shrug, and panned a red fingernail across my cheekbone. "I'll introduce you if you want to stop by my cabin on our way back."

"Is it the hot blond?" He scanned the room for his admirer.

"Twenty bucks richer." I smiled.

Ander raised an eyebrow and after a second with no reply, a mischievous smile passes over his lips. He no doubt spent the rest of the dinner hour dreaming about raunchy activities with the hot blond who was still being shot at by invisible guns.

■ ■

"Behave yourself," whispered Ethan as he kissed me goodnight. We didn't have a chance to really, really, kiss. There were little eyes everywhere as the rest of the camp filed out of the cafeteria doors just as noisily as they had come in.

"Lidia!" called Trina from the front of our small cabin group.

"I'll see you tomorrow," I smiled against Ethan's lips as he kissed me again. "You'll have to ask Ander about his hot date."

Ethan looked at Trina, and then back at me. "I will."

I ran back to Trina and fell into step with her and the other girls. Two of the girls, Melody and Angelica, were holding hands and singing a cheerful song with toothless grins. They were radically off key, but I smiled since they were so cute.

31

Once we were in the cabin, I cornered Trina next to her bed. She looked at me, dead eyes and a lot of makeup.

"So, the hot guy, the one that you-" I dropped my voice so the other girls couldn't hear, "want to hook up with."

"Yeah?"

"Well, I told him I would introduce you guys tonight."

"You did."

How did she keep her voice so flat? I casually wondered what would happen if I slapped Trina. *Would she show any emotional reaction?*

No, she would probably just burn my bed in the middle of the night while I slept.

"Uh, yeah. If you wanted to meet him," I said.

"I guess." She went back to fiddling with the straps of her bag. She moved a variety of black objects into different sections. "But maybe you should warn him, I don't do relationships," she said. "I don't believe in love. Only full forced physical devotion... and never to the same man," she sighed heavily. "It's a curse, I guess. Most men don't understand it."

"Uh-" I heard footsteps climb the stairs outside. "I'll make sure he gets the message."

I tiptoed to the door and stepped onto the porch. Ander smiled as I waved him up to the door. "So, you want to meet my roommate?" I asked.

"That's why I'm here."

I peeped my head into the cabin. "Trina, he's here."

Trina walked over slowly, sulking through the crack in the door with no enthusiasm. Ander's face paled for only a minute before he forced himself to smile again.

"Trina, this is Ander," I gestured to the two of them. "Ander, meet Trina."

"Hello Trina," Ander's expression was still forced, but I appreciated his effort to be polite. "It's nice to meet you."

"Hi."

There was a stinging stretch of awkward silence where I tried very hard not to laugh.

"Would you like to go for a walk?" Ander asked.

Wow, he's handling this so well.

"I guess," Trina shrugged. No smile.

Ander ushered her down the steps into the darkness, but before he left, he leaned down to hiss a threat in my ear.

"It. Is. So. On." I could feel his breath against my neck. "I'm going to get you back, Lidia." Ander pulled back and smiled like he already had something planned.

"You two have fun now!" I said as he stepped off the porch. "No glove, no love!"

Ander's middle finger waved goodbye as they disappeared into the darkness.

Chapter 3

I sat in one of the uncomfortable fold-up office chairs, waiting my turn for interrogation. I shifted unpleasantly, allowing the sticky wetness of my skin to peel from the seat. The thick melted ice cream that had been dumped on my head an hour ago was starting to smell like sour strawberry milk.

"Miss Powell," hiccupped the round redheaded women. It was the same lady who had organized the sign-in sheet the first day of camp. I had since discovered that she was in charge of Camp Tanka. I thought her name was Mrs. Duffus, which sounded insulting, so I tried to be vague.

"Yes ma'am?" I asked softly.

"You may come in now."

I peeled my legs from the chair once more, and shuffled through the door. As I did so, Ander and Ethan came filing out. Their heads were bowed in shame, a poor attempt to hide their silent laughter. Ander winked at me as I stepped into the room.

The small wood room was bare except for the large window that let in the warm August sun. It had been so hot the past few days. The sun had practically cooked the cabins, turning them into musty saunas.

"Well, Miss Powell. Have a seat."

I sat.

Mrs. Duffus took the seat opposite me from behind a small desk. "The two boys who were just in here seem to have no idea *who* could've been responsible for this prank."

I nodded, trying to convey my confused innocence.

"Do you think *you* could tell *me* who might of stolen three cases of strawberry ice cream from the camp cafeteria, melted it, and set it in a bucket above your cabin door?"

"No ma'am."

"Mmmhm." She pursed her lips, looking severely pissed off. "And you and these boys have been playing cabin pranks all summer from what I understand."

Crap.

"We were just joking around with each other," I shrugged. "Soap in Gatorade bottles, hiding things, putting meatloaf in PBJ sandwiches..." I inwardly cringed as I recalled taking a bite of my PB&J and getting a hefty serving of mystery meat. "It was just some fun between me and some girls."

Trina and Whitney had helped me accomplish a few innocent pranks these past few weeks. Though, to be honest, Ander and Ethan's ice cream bath had topped the list.

After one of the boys had hidden the majority of my underwear in the wilderness, I had gathered the girls for a prank of our own. We snuck into their cabins to paint their nails as they slept. Ander had looked especially upset during breakfast the next morning when examining the neon pink that coated each finger on his large hands.

It was a wonderful bonding experience for us ladies.

"I see," said Mrs. Duffus. "As you know, camp ends in three days. I would hate to send some of our volunteer helpers

35

home so close to the end. However, I want to make it very clear to you, as I did with the boys, that camp pranks, of any sort, are not tolerated here."

I nodded.

"Do I make myself clear?"

I nodded again.

"Okay, you may go."

I stood and scurried out of the office as quickly as I could.

I need a shower.

My clothes and face had started to dry in the warm air. It was creating a sticky shine of crystalized sugar that formed an adhesive layer to my skin. I licked the side of my arm on my way to the girl's locker room by the lake. I probably looked ridiculous, but I tasted delicious.

I got into the shower stall and began washing away the candied sugar, pulling little chunks of thawed strawberry out of my hair as I did so. I had enjoyed the excitement of getting pranked, and was a little disappointed we had gotten caught. I finished rinsing the conditioner and shampoo from my hair, dressed myself in the yellow bikini bathing suit, and put on a fresh set of camp gear. I would've worn underwear, but since Ethan and Ander had scattered most of mine around the woods, I was missing a few vital pieces.

As I left the girls locker room, a pair of hands caught me around the waist.

"Ethan!" I gasped.

He greeted me with his goofy smile and a kiss. "Hey trouble maker."

"Hey... you," I said, fumbling for a sassy reply.

"Do you have a suit on?" His hands traced the bulging lines of my bikini straps.

"Yep."

"Ander and I are going out by the lake, you should come hang out with us. I promise no pranks."

"You promise?"

"Yeah, I promise." Ethan lowered his mouth to mine again. "I've missed you," he murmured. "I was hoping you could, like, sneak out tonight and come see me. I feel like I haven't gotten any time to be with you." He kissed me again. "I know it feels like I'm ignoring you but-"

"No, don't think that. I'm glad you've got to spend time with your friend."

"I know," he said, gaze trailing down to the hem of my shorts. "I want you guys to be friends though."

"We are already well established frenemies."

I took his hand, and we walked together to the lake. It was mostly empty. A few kids were taking turns flinging themselves off the dock edge in life jackets while Ander's older brother stood by as lifeguard. As always, he looked irritated.

We reached the part of the dock where Ander was stretched out on his back, his bare chest tanned and sun kissed. Ethan whipped his shirt off and took a place on the dock next to Ander. Mirroring Ethan, I removed my outer layer and sat down.

I thought I caught Ander peeking up at me, but pretended I didn't see.

"So, why is your brother doing this again?" I asked, genuinely curious since Ander's brother hadn't smiled once during camp.

"Extra credit."

"What kind of extra credit? If I could get math points for watching a bunch of kids, I would be thrilled."

Ethan cooed and slid his iPod towards me. "You get girlfriend points though."

"Thanks babe."

Between us, Ander groaned and turned over.

I took Ethan's iPod and plugged myself in. The sun felt good on my skin. I could feel a pleasant sting as the warmth evened out the slight farmers tan my camp T-shirt had given me. The air was fresh, cool, and smelled only slightly swampy from the lake sloshing beneath the dock. Everything was perfect. Everything except one little thing...

"I can't do this." I pulled the headphones out of my ears and slid the iPod back to Ethan. "It's too horrible."

"Oh my God," Ethan let out an exasperated sigh. "You are such a music snob."

"I'm sorry, but you have the music taste of a thirteen-year-old girl." I wasn't lying. Everything was loud, simplistic, and happy. If Ethan's music was a color, it would be bright bubblegum pink.

"Dude," Ander immediately started laughing. "She is so right." His back heaving up in great muscular spasms as he snickered into his folded arms

Ethan swore at him under his breath and scowled in my direction. I shrugged and leaned back against the rough wood of the dock.

"What about my music?" Ander asked. He set an old-school portable CD player next to me.

"Retro," I turned the device around in my hands. "Cool."

"Listen to it."

Ethan glared at him. "Stop fishing for a compliment dickwad," he snapped.

Ander looked at Ethan in mock surprise. "Let the lady speak for herself!"

Ethan went all prickly and watched as Ander handed me his headphones. I put one in my ear and winced as a blast of heavy metal raped my eardrum. I took them out.

"Well?" Ander said, obviously pleased with himself. "Was that girly music?"

"No," I answered slowly. "But... I wouldn't really call that music at all, so-" I trailed off as Ethan started laughing at Ander's revolted expression.

After a second, Ander choked out a short laugh too. "You suck!" He grabbed me playfully and I squealed an apology. Ander ignored my cries and hoisted me up in his arms just before he flung me off the dock and into the lake.

Hitting the water felt like breaking through glass.

Tiny droplets shattered around me in a swarm of bubbles and I momentarily lost awareness of which way was up. It was silent underwater, I could only hear the muddled throb of my own heart. The bubbles and foam subsided, and I pushed off the murky bottom towards the glossy light that was shining through the veil of blue.

But I was stuck.

Swallowing a gulp of water in surprise, I whipped my head around. A decrepit waterlogged hand was gripping my ankle. The hand shot out from under the brown muck of the lake bottom where a half buried boy stared up at me through empty white eyes. His flesh was swollen from soaking in the dingy lake for what looked like weeks.

I screamed but only bubbles flowed from my mouth.

He's dead.

He's dead!

I kicked against the water, thrashing my legs as hard as I could, but I didn't move. I kicked harder. My lungs screamed, shriveling without air. I could feel panic. Sharp terrified stabs of pain coursed through my chest, and my throat choked on nothing as it struggled to obtain air through my shut mouth.

Large hands grasped my midsection. I turned just in time to see a swirl of dark hair behind me. Ander gaped at the floor of the lake and thrust his hand toward the boy in the water just before everything went black.

■ ■

"Lidia, Lidia, wake up!"

There was a patting on the side of my cheek. The sound of wet flesh against wet flesh.

"Wake up." The patting ceased to be gentle, and it felt like miniature slaps.

A gush of water erupted from my lips and I hurled myself onto my side to spit up putrid remnants of the lake. It tasted like rotten plants. Coughing possessed my body, rattling my esophagus until it was stripped raw.

"Jesus, you scared the hell out of me."

Hands were yanking me this way, and that.

"What happened down there?"

Someone was slapping my back gently now. I looked up at three flesh-colored figures blocking out the sun. My eyes were watering and they stung, making everything look blurry. My head pounded like a bass drum.

"I-I don't know." I coughed again, wincing in pain. When I spoke, it was raspy and choked. "I saw a boy in the water."

I had somehow inhaled water through my nose and I could feel the pressure behind my eyes. It hurt to breath.

"What boy?" This voice was different, and I looked up to see Ander's older brother.

"I saw a boy-"

"Alex," Ander shot a glance at his brother, who nodded wordlessly. Then Ander stood over me, and put a gentle hand on my shoulder. "Are you okay, Lidia?"

I coughed harder. "Fine-" I choked.

Ander looked at me with concern. He was serious, and really worried. It was weird.

"I'm fine," I told him. My voice was so broken, I sounded like a man.

Ander lifted me by pulling on my elbows and, confused, I complied. He handed me over to Ethan who draped me over his arm.

"Did you see it?" I asked Ander.

"No." The concern etched deeper into his expression. Ander's hair was still wet from the lake, it dripped water down his face and little droplets clung to his nose and eyelashes.

"But," I shook my head. *Had I been hallucinating? Again?*

"Take her up to the nurses," said Ander as Ethan nodded and hoisted me up.

"I'm fine," I slid out from under him and I took a step closer to the dock edge.

Ethan was behind me. "Come on babe. Let me help you."

I peered over the edge into the water. Every light particle reflected the muck that made up the rotting bottom of the lake. Through the disgusting water, I saw nothing. There was nothing but rocks and some floating green plants where the boy had been.

I'm going crazy.

"You must've tangled you're foot on the seaweed stuff." Ander took a hesitant step near me. "I'm sorry I dropped you in like that, I didn't know." He reached out and pulled me closer to the center of the dock. "I have to watch over these guys." He shot a glance at the small gathering of kids that had watched my near death experience.

I hadn't even noticed them.

"Ethan, you should take her to the nurse."

"I'm fine," I croaked through my beaten lungs. Other than sounding like a man, I really was fine... I almost felt good. I shook my head.

Oxygen deprivation?

"What's wrong?" asked Ander.

"Nothing...I feel, like, high." I laughed because it was ridiculous. "Is that normal for drowning?"

Ander's eyes widened. "Get her to the nurse." He spoke to Ethan, but Ander was looking at me.

"Yeah," Ethan muttered, "Sorry." Ethan led me to the nurse's station in silence. It was only after the nurse, a large woman with a shock of red lipstick, had deemed me healthy, did Ethan start speaking again.

And then he didn't stop.

I endured a rush of questions and apologies from Ethan as we left the nurse's cabin. Even though it was sweet of him to be concerned, I just wasn't in the mood to listen to his emotional rambling. I wanted some time to figure out what to do. To figure out what was wrong with me.

The few things I had imagined in the past were disturbing, but they had never actually hurt me. This though, it was way too real. I thought I had felt it. I would've drowned if

Ander hadn't been there. *But then, he saw it too... or had I imagined that as well?*

I'm losing my mind.

I excused myself from Ethan by telling him I was tired, and I went back to my cabin. I powered up my cellphone, scrolled through a few missed messages, and then tried to connect to the internet.

No service.

I stormed out of the cabin with my phone. I walked aimlessly around large groups of kids playing basketball, throwing Frisbees, and tie-dyeing t-shirts, while I held my phone in the air like I was presenting the Holy Grail to God.

"Come on, come on." I continued to wander while my phone twirled the little waiting for signal sign. I lifted it a little higher, arm fully extended. I had just gotten one bar, when I ran into something solid and fell to the dirt ground.

Ander's older brother, Alex, turned slowly as I brushed the dirt from my hands and stood up. He watched me rise to my feet slowly.

"Feeling better?" he asked.

"Yeah," I said, mirroring his expression of bored indifference. *Jerk didn't even offer to help me up.*

"Cool." He gave a small salute and strode past me back toward the more populated area of camp.

"Weirdo," I muttered as he left.

Once Alex was gone, I held my phone up again. *Come on, come on.* I got another bar...Just before the screen flashed four times and shut off.

"I just charged you!" I shouted at the black screen. It sputtered to life again. And died. Again.

Frustrated, I went to find my camp group. Trina was coaching the girls through craft time. They were all carefully beading multicolored bracelets.

"What's wrong with you?" she asked as I sat next to her on the long wooden bench.

"My cellphone is busted."

"Oh." She threaded two navy blue beads. "That sucks."

"Yeah, it does... Plus, I almost drowned in the lake two hours ago. Ander rescued me after I blacked out underwater."

"You can't swim?" Trina threaded a brown bead. The dark blue and brown reminded me of the lake bottom, it made something feel rotten in the pit of my stomach.

"I can, I just-" I took a piece of string and started threading random colors. "I've been, like, hallucinating."

I waited for a response but she just continued making her bracelet.

"I've been seeing creepy stuff lately. Like, sometimes I'll be walking into the library and a lady with her head on fire walks right past me. Then she's just gone and I look like an idiot because I'm freaking out, and people have to ask me if I'm on drugs." I slumped my shoulders. It was a true story. "It sucks...I thought I saw a boy holding my foot in the water, but nothing was there."

"Weird." No emotion. *Amazing.*

"I wanted my cellphone so I could look up whatever type of schizophrenia I have, and a good doctor who can fix it."

"You can go to my therapist."

I couldn't help how my eyes wandered across her flat, expressionless face, masked by a hefty layer of makeup. I wasn't sure if Trina's "therapy" was working.

"Her name is Alice, and she's, like, super into all of that hallucination shit. She did acid as a teenager." *Great.* "Only, she's pretty old. Which isn't really cool. She, like, makes me sit there and drool over the pictures of her kids. They're super goofy looking. I'll give you her number."

No Thanks.

"Thanks Trina." I finished my bracelet and slid it over to Mellissa. She opened a wide toothless mouth and gave me a giddy smile.

∎∎∎

Later that night during dinner, everyone at the volunteer table was talking about me. Whitney asked a million questions while Ethan hurriedly answered all of them.

I sat between the two and picked at some very poor quality spaghetti. All the noodles were mushy, and the vibrant red tomato sauce resembled ketchup more than it did marinara. It probably was ketchup.

The only person who seemed to notice my effort to avoid the entire conversation, was Ander. He was as moody as I was, shoveling mouthfuls of camp Italian into his mouth before excusing himself to take a seat next to his brother at one of the cabin tables.

I watched them curiously as the people around me talked. Ander and Alex looked like they were conspiring. Maybe

46

they could tell that I was secretly insane. At least Ethan hadn't noticed yet.

I stabbed a long noodle angrily. *Insane, great.* I slurped it up and then decided I wasn't hungry enough to eat gross camp food, so I shoved my plate away. *Well Lidia, admitting it is the first step.*

"Hey," Ethan whispered in my ear. "Meet me behind the building after dinner."

I gave him a puzzled look. "Why?"

He grinned mischievously.

Oh, that's why...

I felt a little guilty because I wasn't really in the mood for a hormone-induce sexcapade on camp property. I didn't really know how to turn him down though.

"Okay," I whispered back.

He kissed my cheek, then turned back to eating the rest of his pasta. I sat there in silence for the rest of dinner. I was brooding, and ultimately, felt a lot like Trina.

Dinner finally ended, and Ethan steered me away from the crowd as we all began piling out of the building. We ran across the damp grass along the wall of the cafeteria, only stopping when we reached a sheltering cluster of bushes in the back overlooking the lake.

Ethan's freckled grin came closer, and he began kissing me the way he only ever kissed in private. I felt a rush of adrenaline. I could still hear the fading laughter of campers making their way to their cabins, and Ethan's hands were getting very friendly.

Behind Ethan's shoulder, the moonlight created rippling stripes of silver light on the lake surface. A breeze swept up the murky swamp smell of the water. It brushed past my skin, and the cool air seeped through the fabric of my clothes.

There was a snapping of twigs in the woods near us. The campers had made it back to their bunks, and the night should've been silent. I listened again as Ethan's lips traced patterns along my neck. There was another snap, and a low murmur of hushed voices.

"Shh!" I hissed in Ethan's ear.

He stilled, his mouth partially open on the base of my neck. "Is someone coming?" He looked around, blind in the dark.

"You didn't hear that?"

"Hear what?"

"Something in the woods," I said. Cold dread rushed through my body.

"No."

We stood still and listened a moment longer. Hearing nothing, Ethan bent back down and continued his exploration of my mouth.

I pushed him off.

"What?"

"I can't. Not tonight."

"Why not?"

"Because I almost died today and I'm really freakin' tired!" I said. Something in the shadows of the trees caught my eye. I stared, but couldn't see anything.

"Okay," Ethan's voice was flat, childish disappointment etched into his obvious frustration.

"I'm sorry." I kissed his cheek quickly, keeping my eyes on the woods.

"It's fine." He wrapped two arms around me, and held me for a moment. "I'm glad you're okay. You really scared me today, Lid," he sighed. "I thought I was going to lose you."

His words caught me off guard and I wrapped myself tighter in his arms. "I'm okay."

He kissed my cheek. "Do you want me to walk you back to your cabin?"

"No." *Yes, I really do. I'm hallucinating and will probably see a zombie as soon as you leave. It will probably eat me too.* "I'll be okay."

"I love you."

What?

Ethan and I, though dating for almost a year, had never actually said those three special words. My breath caught in my throat as my pulse quickened.

"I love you, too."

The moonlight revealed his freckled face as it split into a relieved grin. He kissed me again. "Goodnight."

"Night." I waved and sauntered off, dazed, but happy.

I was almost to my cabin when I heard shuffling in the bushes again. I froze as every muscle in my body tensed, ready to run.

Not another hallucination... anything but that.

"Who's there?" I whispered.

Please be a bear, please be a bear.

A long, pinched, kissing noise came from the cluster of trees on my right, followed by unfamiliar laughter.

Chapter 4

"Alex, knock it off."

There was a slapping sound, and a gruff cry of pain.

"Ander?" My voice wavered embarrassingly.

Two flashlights switched on and I was flooded like a deer caught in headlights. One of the lights whirled up, illuminating Alex's face from below his chin.

"Did we scare you?" He smiled with mock menace. Alex looked more animated then I had ever seen him at camp, excited even.

My heart rate returned to normal as I took a few steps into the tangled thickets where Ander was standing.

"What are you guys doing out here?" I pushed past a hanging blackberry vine and it caught on the sleeve of my shirt. "Ouch," I pulled it off and cursed as Alex swung his flashlight around the woods wildly.

I still couldn't see Ander in full light, but thankfully, he let the beam from the flashlight make a pathway through the ferns and branches as I climbed deeper into the woods toward them. When I was only a few feet away, I saw that they weren't alone.

Two small children, both with pale skin and a shock of albino-white hair were standing between Ander and his brother. They stared blankly back at me from under the hooded bill of Camp Tanka baseball caps.

"What are you guys doing out here?" I turned to Ander. "What are they doing here? It's way past-"

"Extra credit." Alex's answer cut me off and he smirked at my horrified expression.

"What type of extra credit is this?" I asked.

Not only was it against camp policy to have campers out of bed in the middle of the night, but I was pretty sure that it was illegal. Every part of this situation screamed sketchy, and I didn't trust the smartass smile on Alex's face.

"I'm taking these kiddos hunting for extra credit," said Alex cheerfully. "Ghost hunting."

As if that explained anything.

"What the *f-fudge?*" I looked at the small girl. "What is going on?" I hissed through clenched teeth.

"We know them," said Ander hurriedly. "This is Kyle and Rachel, we go to school with their sister. This is sort of a favor."

"Their sister wants you to take them off camp property, in the middle of the night, as a favor?"

"We're going to the shack!" said Kyle excitedly.

"Yeah!" chimed the little girl. "Can we still go?"

"Sure thing." Alex turned his flashlight to the thick black woods and started making his way into the unknown.

I stood dumbfounded. *Are you kidding me?*

"Lidia, you coming or what?" shouted Alex from somewhere in the dark.

I stared daggers at Ander who continued to look sheepish. After a minute under my glower, he shrugged, and turned to follow the group.

"Hey!" I plowed my way through another tangle of bushes to catch up. "I can't let you guys do this. Seriously, what are you thinking? This isn't even legal."

"Why don't you just come along?" asked Ander, attempting to keep the mood light. "It's just for fun."

"You're sneaking kids off of camp in the middle of the night, and bringing them to a shack out in the middle of the woods."

"Yeah," his cheerful demeanor faltered but he continued walking. "I know it looks kind of bad."

"Bad?"

"But you don't know the situation." He held up a branch for me to climb under. "And really, we've known Kyle and Rachel for years, and we promised we'd take them ghost hunting."

I scowled sourly at the back of his head as we continued walking.

"Do you want to hear the story about the shack?" Ander eased as much sugar into his voice as he could muster.

I didn't answer.

"A man named Anthony Front turned his house into an old military hospital for wounded soldiers during war. It was a middle way for injured soldiers who couldn't get to a real hospital. And the doctor was, like, messed up in the head."

I swatted a low hanging spruce branch out of my face, but I still got wacked with sharp pines.

"His wife died in childbirth, and his son was born deaf, so he got obsessed with ways to fix his hearing. He started doing experiments on animals in the basement, and then he started trying to do experiments on the soldiers he was taking care of. He would sometimes take the patients, usually just the ones that were going to die anyways, and cut their ears open. He used these long tongs with blades at the end, to get to the eardrum, and then he used knitting needles to move stuff around," Ander sighed. "Nasty stuff. It's one of the most haunted places in America."

The images Ander called to mind made me want to vomit. "Great story." I let the branch in front of me swing back and hit him in the stomach with a *thwack*.

We finally reached a small clearing. The moonlight shining overhead illuminated the overgrown patch of weedy grass, and in the middle of the field was a small decrepit house. The windows were boarded up with large black pieces of plywood. Graffiti covered the left side of the house, though swarms of ivy and blackberry bushes were trying to swallow the entire building, obscuring most of it.

"Home sweet home," sighed Alex with a smile. He pulled something out of his pocket and gestured the group forward.

My breathing became scattered and a bone tingling cold leaked through my skin as we all stepped onto the porch of the house. The floorboards were rotten, making them feel soft underfoot.

"Here we go," Alex pushed the door open with a loud creak, allowing the smell of neglect to pollute the fresh night air. The smell was faint, but sharp, something like rat piss and mold.

"You okay?" whispered Ander from behind me.

"Fine." I felt the blood drain from my face.

This place feels wrong.

"C'mon." To my surprise, Ander wrapped his hand around mine. "Follow me." He dragged me inside behind Alex and the two kids, all of whom looked eerily excited.

The inside of the house was pitch black, except for the spots of white light where Alex and Ander's flashlights danced across the broken walls. I could see that the walls had once been covered in floral wallpaper, but now, long strips were torn and molding, leaving bare patches of fleshy wood exposed. Everything smelled horrible.

"Your hands are freezing," said Ander.

I withdrew my hand from his quickly and crossed my arms.

Alex lifted the small rectangular object he had pulled out of his pocket, and raised it above his head. It was a tape recorder.

"Is there anyone here?" he asked the empty room.

Is he really doing what I think he's doing?

The silence that followed his question was deafening.

"Can you tell me your name?" Alex asked.

There was a thump from somewhere upstairs. My heart jerked and I tried to swallow, but couldn't. My mouth had gone dry.

"I heard something!" said Kyle.

"Shh," Alex hissed. Ander shone his light on him, and I watched as Alex pressed a button on his tape recorder. It replayed his voice in a loud static rerun.

"Is there anyone here?"

There was nothing, just the silent crackle of the tape recorder before something barely audible whispered through the static.

"....Yes." The crackling sound replied.

"Can you tell us your name?"

"....W-in-sto-n..." It rasped, almost indistinguishable.

Alex replayed the answer again. After the crackling static became white noise, I could hear that the voice had clearly said *Winston*. He switched a button and the heavy silence of the house thickened.

Alex looked excitedly around at the beaming faces, then his gaze settled on me. I was on the verge of blacking out. I felt like my entire body had frozen over into ice, and I had stopped breathing.

"She okay?" Alex shot a questioning look at Ander who mirrored his concern.

Ander came closer and draped an arm around my shoulders. "Hey, you alright?"

"I want to leave." I felt like ghosts were leaking out from shadowed corners of the room. Everything that wasn't touched by the flashlight's glow felt cold and heavy. "We should go."

Ander sighed, but didn't answer. He just left his arm around me.

Alex lifted the tape recorder again. "Can you identify yourself with anyone here, Winston?"

Silence.

"We are trying to identify some new mediums."

What is that supposed to mean?

"Will you please contact the energy you feel in this room?"

Silence.

Alex twisted the machine in his hand, turning up the volume and hitting play.

"Can you identify yourself with anyone, Winston?"

"...g-irl...she has... t- ha.." The faint reply rasped through the speakers.

I buried my face into Ander's shoulder. "I don't want to be here," I said again.

Ander held me a little tighter and hushed me softly.

"We are trying to identify some new mediums."

Static.

"Will you please contact the energy you feel in this room?"

".......It c-...." It cracked.

Alex switched the recorder off and jiggled his shoulders in pleasure. Rachel skipped up to his side and tugged on the corner of his shorts.

"Do you think he meant me?" she asked hopefully.

"Maybe, I guess-"

I was suddenly ripped out from under Ander's arm, and landed face first onto the soiled wooden floor. A humming buzz erupted through every entwining muscle in my body, and the marrow of my bones stung with a frostbite-like cold. It was painful.

So painful.

I whimpered. I lifted my head slightly at the sound of a male voice breaking through the thick stagnant silence. A dark image slowly leaked out from the wall in front of me. The blood that dripped from the gaping holes on the side of the man's head stained the front of his uniform a black crimson. His form flashed, and was gone.

An unseen force began lifting me up off the floor by my shoulders, pulling me to my feet and dangling me in the air like a puppet.

"Holy shit," muttered Alex, staring up at me.

Up at me.

I was in the air.

I was floating.

The pain was gone.

I felt nothing but the freezing air, suspending me with its thick nothingness. The cold fear that had reduced me to a shuttering victim moments earlier coursed through my veins, filling me with a rush of hot adrenalin.

I shut my eyes, and I screamed.

I screamed as loud as I could. Expelling all the energy coursing through my veins in a long, piercing outing of air.

My feet hit the ground and crumbled beneath me. I splayed my hands out, catching the floor. Particles of dirt and gravel cut sharply into the soft skin of my knees and palms.

No one spoke. Alex, Ander, Rachel, and Kyle all stared, speechless, as I knelt on the cold rotten floorboards.

"Lidia...are you okay?" Ander's voice was calm, controlled.

The shaking had returned, along with a wonderful buzzing sensation. My head felt like a balloon, and my body, though it was now securely on the ground, felt lighter than air. I briefly registered hands lifting me up, and laughter coming from Alex's direction.

"Oh my God," Alex gasped between barreling laughs. "Did you see that?"

He continued to laugh as he followed two disgruntled-looking children out of the shack. I thought someone picked me up and carried me out of the house, but I wasn't sure. We stopped in the open patch of grass, not twenty feet from the building. As weird as it was, it felt very similar to how I had felt after I was pulled out of the lake. I felt high. I felt good.

"I thought he was talking about me," Rachel pouted.

"Talk about some serious extra credit!" choked Alex, still laughing hysterically.

"Alex, shut up!"

I turned my gaze over to Ander's handsome face. My vision wasn't blurry, but everything was... shiny.

"Are you okay?" he asked.

I reached out to touch his face, trailing my cool finger tips along the corner of his jaw. He even felt shiny.

Alex doubled over, rolling around on the grass with hysteria. "Oh man. Hah, she got it good. She'll be shooting fireworks tomorrow."

"It's not funny, Alex." Ander studied me, concern evident in his deep blue eyes. "She's not used to this. That could've fried her." He searched my face again. "Look!" he said, gesturing Alex closer.

Alex crawled over to me from his spot in the grass to look at my face. I felt my lips twist into a reluctant smile.

I feel good.

Alex chuckled, softly this time. "Nah, she's fine." He stood up and switched his flashlight on. "You should stay with her for a while though, she's going to be coming down pretty hard," he said. Alex gestured toward Rachel and Kyle. "You guys ready to go?"

"I want to go back in!" said Kyle.

"Next time. Molly didn't start training until she was thirteen."

"I'm almost twelve!" Rachel said.

"Stop complaining, or I'll leave you out here," Alex snapped. "Come on," he nodded towards the woods. They began walking into the darkness, disappearing completely until there was just a little orb of light.

"Can you walk?" asked Ander.

I nodded and shuffled clumsily to my feet. He turned his flashlight back on, and led me towards the woods. I followed him numbly, gazing around at the world, the sparkling forest under the stars shone like diamonds.

The numbness didn't last though. Each step closer to camp sobered the humming buzz pulsing through my brain and vision. As we reached the final stretch of woods, the camp clearing became visible behind a thin veil of trees. The entire reality of what had just happened rushed back to me, and fear broke through the last of my high like an oceanic tidal wave crashing onto the beach.

Floating.

The voice whispering in the static.

The thrusting push that pinned me to the dirty floor.

Floating.

Floating.

The panic rushed through me, possessing my body and driving me forward. I raced past Ander, thorns raking at my skin and clothes. My steps matched my accelerated heart rate.

"Lidia!" Ander called after me.

I broke through the trees and into the camp clearing. I heard Ander curse, and suddenly he was chasing after me.

Please no, just leave me alone.

I went faster, but I had nowhere to run. Unless I wanted to dive further into the dark woods, cabin sixteen was as far as I could go.

"Lidia!"

Floating.

My lungs began to burn and my legs ached.

Floating.

I reached the side of cabin sixteen and stopped. Hot tears stung the sides of my cheeks. I took in a huge gulp of cold night air.

"Lidia," Ander came to a stop, slowing as he approached me. "Lidia?"

A hand brushed softly against my shoulder, and Ander turned me slowly to face him. He wrapped his warm arms around me and I collapsed against his chest, sobs escaping my effort to cling to the high.

"It's okay," he murmured into my hair as I sobbed harder.

Floating.

"It's okay, Lidia." His hand cupped the back of my head. "Shh, it's okay. You're okay." His chanting reassurance finally subsided my tears. When I could form coherent sentences, I pushed away from him.

"I-I want to see Ethan," I choked.

Ander nodded, "Okay, but you can't tell Ethan."

"Why?"

He tilted his head to the side, his meaning clear. *Ethan wouldn't believe me, and Ander wouldn't back my story.*

"What happened?" I whispered.

"You had a supernatural encounter," his lips twisted slightly, trying not to smile. "You did well though. That was a hell of a boost."

"A what?" *How often does he do this?* "What are you talking about?"

"Uh, just-" he fumbled for words and raked a hand through his hair. "Yeah, usually first encounters aren't that powerful."

I recalled scattered parts of Alex and Ander's conversation. The disappointment of Rachel and Kyle.

"What's going on?"

"It's pretty complicated. It's- It's actually really complicated, and I can't explain it all tonight." Ander tried to look reassuring, but it only made him look condescending, as if I was the weird one. "I can tell you that you had an encounter with a ghost tonight, and that you're safe now. I know you're still probably really confused, but, I'll explain it later. You should try and get some sleep tonight."

"I can't sleep," I said. I hugged my sides. "Did you see that boy in the water?"

"Yes."

A mix of relief and fear twist along the corners of my insides.

"Do you still want to see Ethan?" he asked.

"I don't know." I shook my head. "No, I just want this day to be over."

"Go get some sleep."

I nodded.

Ander watched me as I ascended the porch steps. I looked back nervously at him standing in the grass, waiting for me to step inside.

I opened the door and made my way blindly through the darkness to my bed. I heard the soft breathing of the girls sleeping soundly in their bunks.

Ghost are real. I can see them, I've felt them.

I peeled back the covers and climbed into bed, fully clothed, and just stayed there until the sun came up.

Chapter 5

"You look awful."

"Thanks Whitney." I took another bite of my breakfast.

The cafeteria was crammed with campers packed noisily on the long rectangular tables. Ethan wasn't there, he had to help his cabin group with a small boy that had gotten the stomach flu. I wasn't too focused on his absence though, I wanted to talk to Ander. I kept scanning the cafeteria, trying to catch his eye, but he was sitting with his brother across the room.

Is he ignoring me?

The entirety of last night felt so surreal. I was still shocked, and totally exhausted.

Ander looked up from his table and our eyes locked. He stared for only a second before turning away to participate in the conversation at the table. He laughed coolly.

As if nothing had happened at all.

"What did you do last night?" Whitney asked curiously.

"Well, I can tell you what I didn't do."

"What?"

"Sleep."

"Yeah, I can see that." She pushed back a long strand of hair and looked sadly at her plate of camp pancakes. The pancakes were more like hockey pucks, made of a bread-like substance and drowned in a substantial amount of maple flavored corn syrup.

"So, did you see Ander last night?" she asked.

"Err," I froze mid-bite of my pancake puck. "Yeah, I sort of ran into him and his brother last night after seeing Ethan."

She nodded but didn't say anything.

"How did you know I saw him last night?" I asked.

"I heard him yelling- *Lidia,* when he chased you past my cabin."

"Oh."

"Did you guys have a fight?"

"He just, uh, him and his brother scared me, so I got pissed... I think he came after me so that I wouldn't rat him out to Ethan." I gave myself a congratulatory mental pat on the back for my almost truthful lie.

"Oh." She took another bite. "Did he mention anything about me?"

"No Whitney, he hasn't."

She sank deeper into her seat.

"Whitney, he's a-" I searched for the right words. Somehow the term man-whore sounded too crude. "He's not *that* type of guy. You knew it was going to be a one night thing, I don't know why you keep torturing yourself."

"Well, I just, I don't know if I should give him my number or not. I mean, we had sex, so, isn't that what you're supposed to do? It's not like he was hooking up with anyone else. Trina said she ditched him that first night because-" Whitney rolled her eyes, "her lunar spirit told her to."

"Yeah, he tells Trina to do a lot of things."

"So, should I give him my number?"

"I don't think her lunar spirit has a cellphone."

Whitney gave me an annoyed look.

"Ander doesn't have a phone either," I said. "Remember?"

"Well, maybe I can give it to him and he can use a friend's phone or something."

Doubt it.

"Sure," I sighed. "Maybe that would be a good idea."

When breakfast ended, I split away from Whitney and pushed through the moving tangle of orange-clad campers. It was like swimming, waist deep, in a sea of Oompah Loompa's.

"Ander!" I shouted over the noise.

Ander looked back, smiled slightly, and then dodged me by swinging a pair of small children onto his shoulders and shuttling the laughing boys to the next cabin group activity.

"Son of a b-"

"Lidia!" Trina gestured for me to join her and the rest of the girls.

Sullenly, I trudged over to her side and she led us to the tennis court. I watched the giggling girls quietly. They were moving around like crabs on wheeled scooter boards. It would've been fun to watch if I wasn't so exhausted.

The sun's warmth stung the bare skin of my exposed neck. It hypnotized me into a soft dozing state.

Ghosts didn't come out into sunlight.

I told myself this, and other lies, but each time the word "ghost" shot through my mind, I remembered the previous night. I remembered the shack.

I'll explain later- is what Ander had said. But, how much later, was later?

A hand came down on my left shoulder and I jerked back. My arm jabbed the chain link fence that I had been leaning against and the metal thundered with the cold jingle of disturbed steel.

"Whoa," Ethan said as I clambered to my feet. "Jumpy."

"Hi." I reached back and used the fence for support.

"What's up?"

"Nothing."

"Hm," Ethan scanned the tennis court. "Have you seen Ander? I was supposed to meet him before lunch, but I can't find him."

I shook my head. "No, I haven't. He's probably somewhere with Alex. They were together at breakfast this morning."

"Uhg," Ethan let out an aggravated noise. "I hate Alex. Alright, I'll go find him." He leaned over to kiss my forehead. "Love you," he said softy.

"Love you too." It was so weird that we were saying that now. I pondered the subject for a few seconds as I watched him walk away. Walking toward the lake. Toward the ghost boy.

68

The uneasy feeling at the pit of my stomach returned, and I sank back onto the ground. All I had to do was wait for the opportunity to talk to Ander.

But it never came.

Ander managed to avoid me for the last two days of camp. The only time Ander allowed himself within speaking distance of me was right before we left.

All of the kids had gone home, and there was no one left except the counselors and a handful of volunteers, all circled in little cliques around the dusty parking lot. Whitney had already given everyone a slobbery farewell as she cried her goodbyes. Trina had merely slipped me a little piece of paper with her therapist's phone number written on it, before disappearing without saying goodbye to anyone.

"You know," said Ethan speculatively. "I'm actually going to miss this." He had just spent the last sixteen hours getting puked on, so this fond attachment was incomprehensible to me. I couldn't wait to leave.

To just leave, and hopefully leave the memory of the shack too.

Alex separated from our semi-circle of friends and disappeared into the driver's seat of a decrepit old Chevy. It had rusty red paint and a long leather bench seat with patches of yellow foam peeking out from holes in the interior.

"Yeah," said Ander. "It was a pretty good summer."

"Yeah," agreed Ethan. "I'm glad I got to see you man."

The Chevy engine clicked and sputtered to life. White smoke poured out of the exhaust. Alex pulled out slowly from his parking spot, easing his way past volunteers walking toward their cars, and stopped in front of our small group.

"Ander!" Alex leaned over to yell out the open passenger window. "Hurry up!"

"Later," mumbled Ethan into Ander's shoulder as they quickly embraced in a man-hug.

"Yeah man, see you soon," said Ander. They clapped each other on the back once, and let go. Ander's smile turned to me and he took a step closer, arms extended.

Taken aback, I allowed him to wrap his ginormous arms around my slender frame.

"You never explained," I whispered gruffly.

"I will."

I was just about to ask *when*, and *did he plan on using his nonexistent cell phone*, when he pulled away. I couldn't go after him and demand answers, not with Ethan right there.

Ander turned back to wave at each of us before holstering up his backpack, and jumping into the car with Alex. The engine roared as smog clouded over the bumper, and then they were gone, driving away into the deep shadows of the trees.

■ ■

"I'm home!" I trudged into the entryway with my duffel bag. I heard Ethan's Jeep crunching over gravel as he pulled out of the driveway. "Hello?"

No one was home.

Not for the first time, I was reminded of how similar my house felt to a museum. Large, pretty, cold, clean, and if you got dirt on the creamy white carpet, you die.

I hitched the bag further up my shoulder and made my way up the stairs towards my bedroom. I dropped the bag on the floor and flopped onto the bed. Reaching over, I turned the stereo on, blasting something to numb whatever feelings of unease I wanted to shake off. I decided on dub-step. I laid back and let the deep, erratic swirling bass, drown my brain as I studied my chipped nail polish absentmindedly.

Out of the corner of my eye, I saw my bedroom door slowly shut.

I sat up.

The window could've let in a draft.

I looked over to the window. It wasn't open.

Huh...

I got up and turned my music down, then sidled over to the door and opened it to peek outside. My parents' bedroom door was open, but it slowly crept shut as I stood there watching.

"Hello?" I stepped forward. The hallway had become unpleasantly cold, despite the late summer heat streaming in through the windows.

Slam! The bathroom door across the hall from me smashed shut with a deafening force.

Slam! The door to Ryan's room banged close.

Slam! My bedroom door, not three inches behind me, pushed out a gush of cold air as it violently swung shut.

71

I leapt down the stairs and ran out of the house like my hair had caught fire. Once I was safely in the front yard, I turned around to see my home towering above me. My conscience whispered at the back of my mind- *Ghost.*

I sat cross-legged on the cool grass of the front lawn, and hoped it just looked like I was trying to tan as I steadied my breathing. Thoughts of Ander and the shack kept creeping back.

What's happening to me?

■ ■

"Honey!" my mother cried as she swung one bare leg out of her shiny white car. "What are you doing out here?"

"Getting skin cancer."

"With your T-shirt on?" She was carrying two white bags that smelled suspiciously like teriyaki. "Gosh Lidia, you're getting burned. You're going to have a farmer's tan." She stomped her heels on the pebble stone walkway next to me. "Get inside. You look ridiculous."

Thanks mom.

I followed her wearily into the house. It was sunny and warm again. I couldn't see what was going on upstairs, but I wondered if the doors were still shut.

My mother set the bags on the kitchen table. "People will start thinking you spent your summer plowing corn on a farm."

Someone has to do it.

"Your father will be home soon, I want everyone downstairs in twenty minutes for dinner. We have something very important to discuss with you."

"Okay."

She strode away, but continued to speak. "I brought home your favorite teriyaki from Ming's."

I don't eat meat.

"I also got the new sushi rolls. I hope-"

I stopped listening and veered off to the immediate right while she continued her speech. I tiptoed upstairs and gently shut myself into my bedroom without her noticing. Vaguely, I registered how messed up it was that I would rather face an angry door-ghost than spend the next half hour with my mother.

Twenty minutes later, the entire family was seated at the dining room table. The white Styrofoam boxes of teriyaki were set out in the middle and we were each taking turns serving ourselves the food. I filled my plate with white rice, some vegetables, and three of the four fresh salads of roman lettuce that came with the dishes.

"Don't you want any teriyaki chicken, honey?"

"Lidia doesn't eat chicken," said Ryan. He slid the last piece of the grilled chicken onto his plate before smirking at me from across the table.

"You don't eat chicken?" My mother sounded surprised, the way she always did when I told her I was semi-vegan. "Since when?"

"Since I saw that documentary on factory farming, so-" I counted my fingers. "About a year ago."

My father grunted and took another bite. "Don't get enough protein."

I rolled my eyes.

"Hank," my mother said. "Do you want to tell Lid about the phone call we received yesterday?"

"Yesterday, Lidia, I received a phone call from the Dean of Admissions Office at Mountain Heights Academy in Washington."

"What's Mountain Heights?"

"It's one of the top ten schools in the Pacific Northwest, higher ranked then Roseville, that's for sure." He sat up stiffly, thrusting his nose into the air. "We were informed that you had a meeting with some scouts from the art department at Mountain Heights in April."

"Well, I don't think they had the right number then. I didn't meet any scouts." I took another bite of salad. "What type of dressing is this? It's really good."

"I didn't know there were scouts," Ryan pouted, almost inaudible.

I rolled my eyes. "There weren't any scouts, Ryan."

"How did you get a meeting with them?" he asked, ignoring my previous comment. "You don't even do anything. You're not in a club."

"I didn't meet with anyone."

"We have also received an acceptance letter from the school," Dad continued without listening to either of his children. "You filled out an application last spring."

"No I didn't."

"Why didn't you tell us sweetie?" my mother cooed.

"Lidia, you have been admitted and offered a full scholarship with tuition assistance. Together, it adds up to being more then it would cost to board you there."

Board me there? Are you kidding?

My mother reached over to pat my hand with her wrinkled orange one. "We're so proud of you honey."

"Board me there?" I set my fork down. "I told you, I didn't have any meeting with a scout." I felt the blood begin to pump through my cheeks, my temper threatening to break the surface.

My dad smiled. It looked weird, he never smiled. "Lidia, I received an official letter in the mail. I want you to consider this opportunity. With the money they're offering us, you could easily save enough to have the first year of college paid for."

"I did–"

"Maybe they were watching you, and you didn't notice." My mother tried to rationalize, taking a delicate bite of rice. "Meetings, don't always mean traditional meetings."

I steamed.

Considering the only adult that walked into my art class last semester was the batty Mrs. Longfield and her lilac jumpsuit, a "nontraditional meeting" with a scout seemed fairly impossible. *Why can't they just listen to one frickin' thing that comes out of my mouth?*

"I don't want to go to Mountain Heights." I tried to breath, "not only is it a stupid name for a boarding school, but–"

"That's not the way we talk in this house young lady." My dad wasn't smiling anymore.

"What? *Stupid*? Dad! It sounds like a one way trip to Po-dunk Community College, or Fop University, c'mon!"

Ryan snorted and a little bit of sauce dripped from the side of his mouth.

"There's no need for your attitude at the dinner table," my mother snapped.

My father clasped his hands in front of him and looked at me like the Devil getting ready to strike a deal. "Now Lidia, you are a grown adult."

No dad, I'm seventeen. If you really thought I was an adult, I wouldn't have a curfew.

"And as an adult, your mother and I-" he gestured to my mom who beamed at his moment of recognition, "have to respect your choices. But I want to stress the importance of this opportunity for yourself, and your future."

I nodded, completely defeated by the pointless argument. They could sit in whatever delusional dreamland they wanted. As long as they didn't try and force me to go, everything would be fine.

Chapter 6

Ethan and I laid in his bed quietly. His bare freckled chest glowed golden from a block of sunlight streaming in through his window.

"We should go out soon," he said. "My dad gets home at seven."

I shifted in the sheets next to him and crawled out of the covers to retrieve my shirt that had fallen on the wood floor. "What should we do?" I asked, pulling the grey V-neck over my head. "I don't see why you sneak around like this."

"I just don't want to get shit from him about being at home alone with my girlfriend."

I rolled my eyes. "Yeah, he might actually suspect you're doing *exactly* what you're doing."

"Exactly," he confirmed.

I walked around his bedroom and gathered up all my missing pieces of clothing. I had just pulled a leg through my jeans when Ethan's phone rang. He grabbed it off the nightstand, checked the id, then scampered out of the room in his baby blue boxers and white tube socks.

Curious, I peeped my head around the corner. He was smiling, talking animatedly to someone on the other line.

"Hey, hold on. I'm with Lid...Yeah, that sounds great-huh? No I haven't...No ...Yeah. Okay man, see you in a bit."

"Who was that?" I asked innocently as he came back in.

"You'll see," Ethan smiled. "How do you feel about bowling?"

"Bowling's good."

I searched for my left sock as he dressed quickly in a branded shirt and jeans. Downstairs, the doorbell rang and a jolt of panic rushed through me.

"Is your dad home already?"

"Nope." Ethan turned and rushed out the room. "Be right back!" he shouted from the hall.

"Okay."

Things had settled down the two weeks since camp had ended. My parents were still trying to ship me off to boarding school, and I did see a man with a bleeding bullet wound standing outside of my usual coffee shop, but other than that- things were pretty normal.

I spent most my time with Ethan, leeching to his side constantly to avoid being alone. My biggest fear was coming in contact with another ghost while I was by myself, so I just always hung out with people. I wasn't sure if I would survive another supernatural encounter, but for now, I was at least assured that my house wasn't haunted. Besides the one incident with the doors when I got back from camp, my house had been quiet.

I stood in front of Ethan's floor-length bedroom mirror, pulling at a piece of clothing so that it fell at a particular angle. It was stupid, really. Of course my shirt wouldn't stay like that, but I wasn't really paying attention to what I was doing anyways.

Ander had never bothered to contact me, and in a way, I was glad. The more it became a distant memory, the less I felt like the experience at the shack ever happened.

"Lidia, come down here!" called Ethan from downstairs.

I slid my bracelet onto my wrist and pinched the latches of my earring as I lumbered down the stairs and into the entryway. In the open doorway was a tall figure blacked out by the intense apricot sunset behind him.

"Hey Lidia," Ander's voice greeted me from the doorway and I froze. He sauntered forward, closing the door behind him and cutting off the light.

My stomach sank like a rock and a nauseating nervousness bled through my body. "What are you doing here?" I asked.

Ander peered at me through hooded eyes. "Ethan invited me to visit before I head back to school tomorrow." He looked different then he did at camp. He was freshly showered, in jeans and a black sweater, even his shaggy hair wasn't as wild as it had been.

"Oh," my throat was dry. *Go way, go away, go away, go away.*

"You want anything to drink?" Ethan asked. Without waiting for an answer, he led us into the kitchen, and retrieved three purple sodas from the fridge. I snapped the metal cap of my drink open with a fizz.

Was I going to start seeing things now that Ander was around?

The boys were talking, but I was only half listening.

What if Ander is some sort of spirit magnet?

"Hey, Lid, you can invite Sammy tonight if you want," Ethan said.

"Okay," I pulled my phone out of my pocket to text one of my best friends.

Sam, want to come bowling with E and his bff?

Okay :) What time?

"What time are we going?" I asked, interrupting the conversation.

"Probably in half an hour," estimated Ethan as he took a final gulp of soda and tossed the can in the recycling bin. "Two points!"

Thirty min? Want to spend the night? I need a girl's night!

K, see you there!

I let out a huge sigh of relief. Even if Ander did bring weird ghost stuff with him, at least I wouldn't be alone tonight. I slung the phone back into my purse and covered my face with both hands as if to wash away the stress. When I looked up, both Ander and Ethan were staring at me.

"Should I be worried?" asked Ethan.

I shook my head. "No, we should go soon though, there's always traffic."

■ ■

The Roseville retirement home was having a competition at Sandy Slick's Bowling Alley that night. They took up all but two lanes, and despite my youth, I felt a little intimidated by their color-coordinated team jerseys.

We got our shoes and then sat down on the empty plastic chairs surrounding our lane. The smell of deep-fried sugar was rich in the air that was otherwise polluted with the pungent smell of old people. It at least masked the smell of feet as I leaned down to switch my clean shoes for tattered leather ones.

Ethan fiddled with the buttons on the middle console, typing out our initials on the TV screen hanging overhead. "Okay L.P. you're up first!"

I shot up quickly, one shoe barely tied in an attempt to avoid Ander as he took the seat next to mine. I went over to the rack and chose a pink ball. After picking it up, I immediately regretted my decision. It must've been twenty pounds. I heaved the ball towards the slippery lane, not bothering to strain my muscles enough to actually lift it up. It hit the waxed wood with a heavy thump.

"Come on, Lidia!" shouted Ethan, clearly annoyed at my lack of enthusiasm.

The ball rolled two feet before sinking into the gutter.

"Alright, alight," I muttered. I went back to the rack and picked out a pretty orange ball. It was a little lighter. I lifted it up to my shoulder and shuffled to the top of the lane. "Okay," I took a deep breath and released it with a swing of my arm.

The ball rolled steadily towards the left gutter. It was going to sink in before it hit the middle of the lane so I turned back to the boys without bothering to watch it roll.

"It's not my fault that I suck... I blame bad genetics." I held up both hands to say- *oh well*.

"Whoa!" Ethan stood up and extended a long finger toward the lane behind me. "Dude! It just spun out! How did you do that?"

"What?" I turned back to see every single white pin on the floor. The television above me showed an animated cartoon of red collared pins being smothered under the weight of a bowling ball.

Ethan came over to give me a high-five. "Good job babe! How did you get that spin?"

"I-I don't know." My eyebrows knit together in confusion. Behind Ethan's shoulder, Ander lounged against the plastic bench and grinned at me.

"A.M. you're up!" Ethan directed.

Ander rose easily to his feet and sauntered over to choose a ball. Ethan and I sat back down and watched as Ander bowled two perfect strikes.

"My turn!" Ethan got up and went to the rack as Ander sank into the seat next to me. I didn't look at him. Instead, I chose to focus all of my attention on Ethan.

"So, you're avoiding me?" Ander asked quietly over the sound of music and shattering pins.

"No."

God Ethan, just pick a ball. He was balancing two, one in each hand, judging the weight.

"Good, because I want to talk to you about what happened at the shack."

"No thanks."

"No thanks?" he laughed.

"I don't want to talk about it anymore. I don't want to know who, or what, or how. I'm good with being blissfully ignorant."

"Lidia," Ander scoffed and his voice took a more demanding tone. "We're going to talk about it tonight."

I didn't say anything. I could feel Ander boring his eyes into the side of my face, but I just watched Ethan as he practiced his bowling swing with an invisible ball.

I'm dating such a meathead.

Ander made an irritated sound and leaned closer. When he spoke, it was practically a whisper. "You don't understand how dangerous it can be when-"

"Lidia!" Two small hands covered my eyes.

I breathed in a massive waft of strawberry scented shampoo. "Sammy!" I squealed.

Sammy swung two tiny arms down to give me a hug.

"I'm so glad you came!" I said.

"I know girl, I feel like I haven't seen you all summer." She took the seat next to me, her short legs dangled a few centimeters from the ground. As usual, Sammy was wearing a short jean mini skirt and a bow in her hair. She spotted Ander and her mascara eyes raked the length of his body, which was now slouching sulkily in the seat next to mine. "Hi," she extended an arm towards him. "I'm Sammy, Lid's friend."

Ander smiled and granted her a curt nod, but he didn't take her hand. Surprised, Sammy looked back at me and mouthed- *rude.* I responded by mouthing- *I know.*

"Strike!" Ethan threw up both hands. "Who's the man?"

I rolled my eyes as he came over to us. There weren't any seats open, so Ethan pulled me up before taking my seat, and then pulled me back onto his lap.

"What's up Sammy?" Ethan gave her a high-five.

"Hey E, me and your girl are having a sleepover tonight."

Ander's head turned toward us as Ethan nuzzled his face into my neck.

"Oh really?" Ethan asked. "You guys going to get naked and start a pillow fight?"

Sammy faked offense. "You know, movies aren't actually real."

Ethan shrugged. "I thought that's what girls always did at sleepovers." He turned to Ander. "Didn't you?"

Ander shrugged stoically. He was biting the inside of his lip as he watched a wrinkled man in an old-fashioned hat shuffle his way through the crowd of elders. "Yeah," he said absently.

Sammy sighed. "Ethan, your mistaking sleepovers for slumber parties."

"What's the difference?"

"Slumber parties are bigger, and usually involve truth or dare." She pushed her long brown hair behind her shoulder. "You're up, Lid."

I groaned and went to pick out another bowling ball, this time blue with opalescent swirls of pearl.

"Go Lid!" Sammy cheered. "Get it!"

"Don't get your hopes up!" I shouted back at her. "A polar bear could beat me at this game... and they don't have

84

thumbs." She continued to cheer as I threw the ball. As it had done previously, it rolled, making a beeline for the gutter, until...

What the-

It suddenly ricocheted off an invisible wall and started moving diagonally towards the pins. They smashed into a dozen white pieces and the sound shattered through the music.

"Oh my God," I whispered to myself.

Ethan swore his surprise. "Lidia! How did you do that?"

I looked back at the group. Sammy was doing a happy dance in her chair, Ethan was walking towards me, and Ander was sitting relaxed, an impish smirk plastered across his face.

"Okay, okay," Ethan grabbed a ball and came up beside me. "Show me how you get that spin."

"I have no idea how that happened. I think the lane's off balance or something. Maybe a miniature earthquake hit and moved the ball... I have no idea. "

"Come on, show me."

"Ethan, I don't know."

"Don't be a poor sport, just show me."

I groaned and stormed over to the rack, grabbed a ball without even looking to see what color it was, and shot-put it onto the lane. It hit the wood with a hard thud, then moved only a few inches before it started gliding toward the gutter. Just before it was about to sink in, it suddenly went plummeting toward the pins for a strike.

Ethan stared, completely shocked. "Okay, okay. Let me try." He ushered me out of the way before winding up his perfect form and shooting the ball onto the lane in a straight line. Just as it reached the middle, an invisible force spun the ball, sending it into the gutter with a *thunk*.

I heard Ander laughing behind us.

"Ethan you suck!" Ander stood to take his turn. "Do we need to get bumpers?"

I walked back towards the seats, making an effort to veer away from Ander who was grinning at me in silent laughter.

"Come with me." Sammy grabbed my arm and dragged me away from the lane. She led me past a group of meandering old couples and straight into the girl's bathroom. She swung around, cornering me against the cold tile. "Okay, don't get mad."

"Okay-"

"I have to ditch on our plans tonight."

"What?"

"I'm sorry," she said. "Ander asked me to a movie with him."

"Tell him you'll do it tomorrow."

"He leaves tomorrow!"

I let my head fall back against the bathroom wall in exasperation.

"I'm sorry Lid, you know I don't ditch on girls night, but come on." She looked at me with a hard stare, one eyebrow lifted. "He's hot. You can't expect me to pass that up." Sammy pushed out her lower lip and turned to the dirty mirror to fix her makeup. "I won't go if you don't want me to."

"No, it's fine."

Not fine.

"Really?" she squealed, turning from the mirror and embracing me in hug.

"Yeah."

No. No. No.

Ghost.

Chapter 7

When Ethan and I pulled onto my street later that night, a summer storm had already flooded the neighborhood. Every pothole became a puddle, and the sound of thunder boomed from outside of the Jeep as he pulled into my driveway.

"Lidia?" Ethan asked.

I snapped out of my daze at the sound of my name. "Hmm?"

"I was asking if you wanted to go to Ashley's party tomorrow night." Ethan took the key out of the ignition and turned to me, his face slightly annoyed. "What's been up with you tonight?"

"Nothing, I'm just tired."

"Well, do you want to go then? It might be fun to see some people before school starts."

"Yeah, sure."

"What's wrong?" he asked.

"Nothing."

"You've been acting weird all night."

"I told you, I'm just really tired."

"Okay." Ethan could tell I was lying, but he wasn't one to beg for information. Instead of pressing for details, he put the key back into the ignition and the Jeep rumbled to life. It idled gently as rain pattered against the roof and a flash of lightning shot through the sky.

"I better get home, my dad's probably wondering where I am," he said.

I opened the door and hopped out. The rain hammered my skull, and I was drenched within seconds. Before I shut the door, I turned to Ethan. "Love you."

He sighed and leaned over so that I could reach back in and give him a kiss. "Love you too. Text me tomorrow, okay?"

"Okay." I shut the door and ambled up the pathway.

Lights were on inside, illuminating the porch with a dim orange glow through the stained glass windows framing the entryway. I fiddled with the keys before opening the door, and then stepped inside.

The first thing I heard were two male voices that oohed and guffawed in manly baritones. Ryan had one of his friends over, and from the sound blasting through the living room, I guessed that they were watching something violent on TV.

"Extreme wipeout! Stay tuned to see if Roger has the balls-" The narrator on the television was interrupted by a comical crash, *"or the brains."*

I raked through my damp hair as I entered the living room. Ryan and his friend, Justin, were taking up both of the sofas, a feast of junk food wrappers and empty pizza boxes littered the coffee table in front of them.

"Hey! There's the genius!" Justin, a large quarterback with bad acne and a head that looked like an under developed turnip, greeted me. "Congratulations!"

"Congratulations for what?" I asked.

"For being a snobby hypocrite," said Ryan without taking his eyes off the TV.

I looked back at Justin, confused. "What?"

"You got into Mountain Heights. That's awesome."

"Seriously," I rolled my eyes.

"I'm taking your bedroom." Ryan took a sip of soda. "And I'm selling all your old Pokémon cards on Ebay."

"For the last time, I'm not going to boarding school."

"Tell that to mom," Ryan said as he looked over at me. "She left a note on the kitchen counter." His eyes returned to the TV and he was immediately distracted by a skateboarder's nearly fatal fall.

I went into the kitchen and found a note written on a yellow piece of paper.

Lidia!

I tried calling your cellphone, but the call wouldn't go through. We are so proud of you for making the responsible choice! I know you have been reluctant to do what we thought was best, but we're proud of you for making the right decision. We only wish you would've told us sooner. I put out some of your cute clothes on your dresser so that you can pack tonight. The person I talked to on the phone said you signed up to take their student service bus to school, it will be here at eight tomorrow morning. PLEASE dress to impress. This is an important step in your future and you need to put your best face forward in order to make good friends! Your father and I have gone out to celebrate. Call me back if you want us to bring home anything.

-Mom

I finished the letter, then read it through again. My mother could be so *dumb*. The entire school thing, including this call, all must've been from an elaborate scammer. I just hoped she didn't give them any credit card information.

90

A sudden chill wrapped around my body. It felt like I had been drenched in a veil of icy cobwebs.

Ghost.

Keeping my eyes plastered to the floor, I ran out of the kitchen and burst into the living room. Justin and Ryan stared at me for a moment in surprise. I tried to compose my face into something casual, but I could feel the unnatural stretch of my fake smile.

"What's your problem?" asked Ryan.

"Nothing." I stood stiff and white behind the couch Justin was lounging on. I started chipping my nail polish nervously. "It's a scam. I never accepted anything, they're probably just trying to get her bank information."

I walked over to the side of the couch and Justin kindly removed his giant feet from the cushion. His white socks were stained brown on the heel with lint littering the fabric like Styrofoam packaging beads. I took the farthest corner of the couch away from him, and wrapped myself in a blanket. There was a cold that still lingered in the room like a fine mist. I felt watched.

More ghosts... I brought a hand up to my face. The tip of my nose was cold. *I hate Ander. He's a ghost magnet that infects everyone around him and-*

"I saw your acceptance letter, it looked real to me," Justin said conversationally.

Ryan laughed at something on the TV. "Yeah," he said, finally ripping his gaze away and looking at me. "It's a real school. I don't know why they want you."

"They don't!" I wrapped my arms around myself and watched the TV screen without actually seeing it. "It's fake."

"No it's not," said Ryan defensively. "Look it up. Their football team sucks, but college admission rates are pretty good." His face crossed into a slight scowl. "I don't get it. You don't do anything except read, and make out with Ethan."

"Well, at least I know how to read."

They didn't ask me to leave, so I stayed and watched bikers smash their faces into pavement to crunching sound effects. If I tried, I might've been able to enjoy it, but the stench of Justin's dirty socks distracted from almost everything else.

"Dude!" Justin looked up at Ryan from the limelight of his cellphone. "Karolyn texted me. Do you want to go to a party at Jakes?"

"Hell yeah." Ryan stretched his arms behind his head before he clicked the TV off.

I sat awkwardly on the cushion as the two boys got up and walked around me toward the stairs. The black screen of the TV still fizzed with static electricity, it sounded loud in comparison to the silence that suddenly filled the room.

"Can I come?" I spat impulsively.

Ryan looked at me like I had grown an extra head. "No," he scoffed. He turned and followed Justin up the stairs.

The doorbell rang.

Please be mom or dad, please be mom or dad.

It wasn't mom or dad.

It was Ander. He stood on the front porch, kicking his sneaker at the corner of the welcome mat. His dark hair was wet from the rain and both hands were buried in his jacket pockets. Ander looked up, warm hues of indoor light illuminated his blue eyes so that they shone bright against the darkness of the stormy night behind him.

I slammed the door shut in his face.

I was barely two feet out of the entryway when I heard Ander's knuckles knocking against the hardwood door again. *Nope.* I turned the corner towards the stairs. *Not tonight, ghost boy.*

"Whoa," Ryan rounded the corner, nearly smacking into me. "Have you seen where mom put her car keys?" He zipped the fresh sweatshirt he was wearing.

"I think they're by the calendar in the kitchen."

He nodded and walked away. Just as his tall figure left my frame of view, I saw a faint translucent woman standing what had been only two feet behind him. I sucked in a breath of sharp cold air.

The spirit drifted closer like she was riding on wind. Her pale frame was thin, airy. Small lines were etched around the corners of her mouth and eyes where she must've had wrinkles when she was alive. She opened her mouth and her voice sounded like a million whispering echoes, suffocated into a single confined space.

I spun and raced back to the entryway. I yanked the front door open and pushed myself past Ander who was standing with a fist raised, ready to knock again. I slammed the door behind me.

"Ghost." My body shook as I covered my mouth, attempting to breathe through the gaps in my fingers.

"Lidia?" Ander asked hesitantly. "What–"

I spun towards him and pointed an outstretched finger toward the door like it had bitten me. "There, in there! I saw one!"

"One what?" he asked.

"Ghost!"

"Oh, for Christ sake," Ander rolled his eyes and pushed past me. He opened the door and went inside. The door closed behind him with a gentle snap.

I waited.

The rain beat down on the roof covering the porch, and the blackness of night suddenly felt very dense. I waited, and waited. It was probably no longer then a few seconds, but it felt like forever.

The door opened again and Ander's hazy smile greeted me. "Oh, hello," he said, feigning surprise at the sight of me standing on the porch. "You can come in now." He opened the door just wide enough for me to pass through.

I didn't move. "Are you sure?"

Ander nodded, a wobbly grin plastered across his face.

I took a step forward tentatively.

"Ah," Ander raised an arm and rested it against the doorframe, blocking it completely. "Only if you promise one thing."

"What?"

"You have to agree to listen to what I have to say." Ander raised an eyebrow, his expression sobering. "About ghosts," he said.

I ignored his request and pushed past his outstretched arm. "Is it-" I asked looking around the entryway. "Is it gone?"

"Yes. I checked your closet, under your bed, and I chased all the little monsters away."

I glowered at him. "If you think this is funny, then you're insane."

"Said the girl who can see dead people."

"So can you!" I hissed back. Ryan and Justin were laughing as they exited the back door.

"Yeah," Ander cocked his head to the side. "But unlike you, I actually know how to get rid of them."

"Fine! Let's talk." I turned and stomped upstairs.

As Ander entered my bedroom, I stood with my arms crossed and surveyed his tall figure with a scowl. He looked around, failing to hide a smirk of amusement. Secretly, I wished I had put my pile of laundry away earlier, and made my bed, and just cleaned in general. There was a small pile of folded dress clothes that my mother had retrieved from my closet and sat on top of my dresser.

Suddenly, it clicked.

My eyes widened and my mouth opened, shut, and then opened again.

"You okay?" Ander asked slowly. "What?" He flattened his hair nervously as I continued to stare.

"What school do you go to?"

95

Comprehension dawned across his features and his eyes turned somber. "Mountain Heights Academy in Washington."

"You-"

"It's a school for mediums, that's why it's so exclusive... It's for people who see the dead."

"What?" My stomach sunk and I stepped backwards towards the bed. I tried to sit, but missed the edge of the bed and slid down onto the carpet instead. "What did you do?"

"I got you in." When Ander saw my look of desperate confusion, he sighed and came to sit beside me on the floor. "There's a lot to explain." He studied me for a minute. "Are you ready to listen?"

I wasn't, but that didn't stop him from talking.

Ander told me that ghosts were real. When someone dies, they either pass on to the afterlife- whatever that may be, or they remain a spirit. Most spirits are categorized as phantoms, a manifestation of residual energy of a soul that left the body, but not this world. Many people experience some sort of supernatural encounter once in their life, but only mediums can see the spectrum of energy a spirit might produce as an apparition. These apparitions can appear as an orb of light, a mist, and even a corpse.

The ability to see the dead is linked genetically, usually popping up every few generations. Due to the large time gap between mediums in families, most parents of young mediums are unaware of their abilities, and the kids are commonly diagnosed with schizophrenia and anxiety disorders. It was because of the rising rates of misdiagnosed mediums that Mountain Heights Academy was established thirty years prior by the Federal Department of The Gifted. The school was built for the purpose of training young mediums and arming them with the ability to function normally in modern society, despite their ability to see the dead. Since the school started, misdiagnosed teens and suicide rates have dropped drastically.

"It's called a boost," Ander said.

"What is?"

"It's the high, the rush after you absorb a spirit. Part of being a medium is learning how to take in the spirit energy and use it... It's why you levitated in the shack. It's sort of like a drug, but the high only lasts for a few seconds. And the stronger the spirit, the stronger the boost." Ander took a breath and continued. "There are also dangerous spirits. You can't absorb all of them."

I let out a breath of air that I didn't know I was holding. "This is so weird." My thoughts kept returning to Grandma. *Was she a medium?* "You said it usually skips a few generations?"

"Yeah, most of the time. It can show up anywhere in the family though. I've never met my mom's parents, but I know that on my dad's side, everyone is pretty much normal," he shrugged. "Except for my cousin Lenny. He collects turtles or something." Ander shook his head. "Weird dude."

"I-" I swallowed. I had never really talked about finding my grandma dead on the floor, or her screams in the night. "My grandma, she died a few years ago. She had Alzheimer's, but I don't know. What if she was actually a medium?"

"She might've been." I could see him on the cusp of asking what happened, but he didn't.

I pulled my knees up and closed my eyes for a second. *If my grandmother had been a medium, what sort of tortured life did she lead?* Grandma had been mentally unstable throughout her entire life. Either she could see dead people, or she was just flat out psycho like my mother. Both seemed equally plausible. I opened my eyes again. Ander was watching me with a gentle expression on his face, waiting for me to calm down before continuing.

"Were you close with your grandma?" he asked after a minute.

I shook my head. "I barely knew her." *If she was a medium, the doctors wouldn't have diagnosed her with Alzheimer's disease. There's science involved in that stuff.* I nodded to myself, trying to navigate my thoughts elsewhere. "So," I said. "Can spirits kill you?"

"Uh, I guess." He saw my face and continued in a rush. "They don't try to. A poltergeist can be dangerous because sometimes they transfer their energy and mess with physical objects. Only really dark spiritual energy would kill, but that doesn't happen a lot."

Is that what happened to Grandma?

"But that's why you need training, because it's dangerous being a medium! Mountain Heights is a school for people like us... It's not like, a freak school or anything," he added seeing the look on my face. "It's just state certified to train and do testing. Every registered medium needs to pass the National Test. You need to be able to block the Spooks and control your boost."

"Spooks?"

"Dark spirits. The dangerous ones."

"Right." I had a headache. I half believed everything Ander said, he obviously believed what he was saying, but my other half was having trouble believing I had the sixth sense.

98

"So," I tried to form a coherent question. "So, what happens if I don't pass my test?"

"You take it again."

"And if I don't take it at all?"

"Once you're registered, you have to take the test. The Department usually keeps an eye out for new mediums if they have a record of other family members that are mediums... Maybe you were the first in your family, or maybe your grandma went unregistered."

"So, I'm not registered. They don't even know who-"

"Uh," Ander cut me off. "Alex registered you the night we found out you were a medium. Right after the shack. I thought you might be after what happened at the lake, but, we wanted to make sure."

I gave him a look.

"Sorry," he said, not sounding sorry at all. "There's no way around the test. But I mean, for good reason. An unlicensed medium is dangerous to everyone. Plus, the test really isn't that bad. It's really basic."

"But what if I don't take the test?" I asked. "Is the government going to come drag me out of my house and have me arrested?"

"They won't have you arrested." Ander was pulling strings out of the carpet. "But someone else will come and find a way to get you to school, and then-" he trailed off. "And then we don't get the extra credit."

My eyebrows shut up. "Extra credit?"

"Yeah," Ander's blue eyes met mine. "Most mediums don't know that they're mediums. The Department finds most of us in insane asylums... Alex was." Ander's voice had grown soft, raw. "Alex started having hallucinations when he was eight, and by the time he turned ten, he had already tried to commit suicide twice. He didn't know what he was seeing, and there was a while when he was just nuts. He didn't get hurt by any Spooks, but still–"

"What can they do?"

"Spooks? Anything. If they're strong enough to hurt you physically, they will. Most Spooks just want to feed off your energy, they're like the spiritual parasites. Eighty percent of the time, they just want you as a host, and it's scary, because mediums can't get possessed like normal people can. If you let a Spook in, it'll change you." Ander bit the corner of his lip. "Some Spooks, some people think they're demons, but they can become a part of you. Once they're inside there's no way to fix it."

"What do the demons look like?"

Ander shrugged. "Don't know. Technically, angels and demons aren't human spirits, so mediums can't see them."

"But they're real?"

"I guess. I believe they are, but I can't prove it... we only see the energy of people that have died."

Great.

Just excellent.

"I don't want to go to Mountain Heights," I said.

"It's not that bad, Lidia."

100

"What about Ethan?" I forced myself to look at him. "I have friends here. I'm not leaving Ethan."

"I could try and talk to him-"

"No," I snapped. I didn't want Ander talking to Ethan about this. There wasn't much to say. Either he told Ethan I was a freak who saw dead people, or he made up a lie as to why I had to go to boarding school. Either way, it sucked.

Ander let me sit there in silence. I chipped my nail polish as I tried to calm my racing thoughts. I had four million questions to ask, but my mind had gone blank and I couldn't think straight.

"What happened to Alex at the asylum?" I asked.

"Professor Short volunteers at asylums every summer, and he was the one who found Alex. Alex was diagnosed with," Ander scrunched his brow together, trying to remember. "Something to do with acting violently towards his" -he made air quotes- "imaginary friends." Ander smirked, though his eyes were still gentle. "Anyway, they got him out of there, and offered him a place at Mountain Heights. Once Alex finally noticed that I had started seeing, he got me into school too. Though, I did have to do a little bit of therapy because my mom got freaked out when I started talking to myself."

"Who were you really talking to?"

Ander shrugged. "I don't know, some kid who got stabbed six times in the back by a soldering iron."

"Wow."

"Yeah," Ander said casually. "He always messed with my Legos. It was so annoying."

I rubbed my face with my hands, attempting to wash away everything he was saying. "I still don't get it."

"Which part?"

"Every part." I shook my head. "You said you get extra credit?"

"Extra credit is the term used for new kids at Mountain Heights. We thought Molly's little brother was starting to see, so that's why we went to camp this year. We were going to get him in." Ander raked a hand through his hair. "If a student returns with a newly registered medium they get an extra credit bonus from the school."

I looked at him blankly. "You want to rip me away from my friends, my boyfriend, my home, and send me to a haunted boarding school, just so you can get a higher GPA?" Even I could hear the scathing tone in my voice.

Ander went back to pulling at the carpet. "Not exactly."

I stood up and paced around the room. *This has to be a joke. A really sick joke.*

"This is stupid." I shook my head. I didn't believe him.

But I did.

And didn't.

Either way, I wasn't going to volunteer myself to go to boarding school. I had Ethan here. I had a life here. I had friends.

"What do you mean, not exactly?" I asked.

Ander was standing now too. He watched as I walked in circles, his eyes sympathetic, but steady. "The extra credit is a ten thousand dollar check to whoever found the unregistered medium," he said.

"Money? You think I'm going to leave just because someone's giving you money?" I barked a quick laugh. "Good luck with that."

"We already talked to your mom."

"You can't sell me to your school!"

"It's a good school!"

"I don't care! I'm pretty sure that's illegal!"

"Your parents think it could get you into a better college."

I rolled my eyes. "Oh no. What will Harvard say if I can't absorb dead people?"

"We're picking you up at eight tomorrow."

"No, you aren't."

Ander turned and stepped towards the door. "Call Ethan tonight, and tell him you're going to school with me tomorrow."

The bedroom door flew open and revealed the empty hallway on the other side. It had opened on its own. I felt a choked gasp get stuck in my throat, but Ander seemed undisturbed.

"And pack your stuff." His gaze trailed across my face before he turned to leave the room. "I'll see you tomorrow."

"I'm not going!" I shouted after him, but he ignored me.

A second later, the front door slammed.

Chapter 8

I stood dazed in the middle of my room.

I knew I wasn't going to Mountain Heights, but it was going to be super awkward getting out of it. My parents wouldn't be happy to find out that I hadn't changed my mind, and there was going to a whole lot of confusion when Ander came to pick me up in the morning. He would probably show up, pretending like everything was planned and I would kindly let everyone know that I was staying at Roseville High. There might be some heated words from my parents, but unless they had Ander drag me out of the house kicking and screaming, I was staying put.

I took a deep breath. So much information, stress, and confusion had been jammed into the past hour, that I didn't even feel it anymore. It had been a lot to take in, and I still wasn't sure I believed everything Ander had said. All I knew was that I was very tired.

I changed into a pair of grey sleeping shorts and a white tank top before crawling into bed. I laid there for a long time while mental reruns of everything Ander had said played through my mind. The more I thought about it, the more I realized that I didn't really know who Ander was.

I turned to my side so that I faced the bedroom door. I watched the empty half lit hallway before drifting into an uneasy sleep.

I was still facing the empty hallway when I woke up. I heard footsteps downstairs and I felt a rush of warm relief. *Parents are home.* I closed my eyes. *Everything will be okay, I just have to get through tomorrow morning.*

The pair of footsteps slowly ascended the stairs.

Thump, thump, thump.

Those weren't my mom's footsteps.

I stopped breathing and listened.

Thump, thump.

Ryan?

A faint whisper was distinguishable in the silent house. "What do you mean, you forgot it?"

"It's fine. We just have to get her in the car. I have enough."

"Alex, I told you she won't go, why didn't you grab it?"

"Oh, you gonna go cry about it?"

I was listening to Ander and Alex walk towards my bedroom. I rolled out of bed and stood dumbfounded in the middle of the room.

He said eight!

He had said tomorrow at eight!

I knew I didn't have enough time to run into my parent's room, if they were even home yet. I tried to do a mental recap of how long I had slept. *An hour? Less than an hour? More?*

One of the boys swore. They were only seconds away from my bedroom. I frantically ran to the crack between the open door and wall. I held my breath, trying to subdue my erratic heartbeat as I watched two black figures block out the hall through the sliver of light between the hinges.

"Shh!" Alex hissed. I heard their booted footsteps across my white carpet. *Thump, thump, thump.*

Ander swore. "She's not here."

"Where is she?"

"How the hell am I supposed to know?"

Thump, thump, thump.

Alex's voice called in the darkness. "Oh, Lidia...Where are you?"

Ander went over to the dresser to look in the closet. *Please God no, please.* He turned abruptly as if he heard my thoughts and saw me hidden in the shadow of the door. Without assistance, the door began to slowly swing shut until it latched with a soft click in the doorframe.

I felt naked as I stared at the two strangers in my room that had just stripped me of my hiding spot.

"There she is," said Alex. "I didn't know people older than five still hid behind doors."

"We're leaving early." Ander's voice was sharp. "You ready to go?"

"I told you I wasn't going."

"Yeah," he sighed. "I thought you might say that."

"Which is why we're leaving before your parents get home. Where's your bag?" Alex shoved past Ander who was watching me coolly and began rummaging through my closet. Ander's eyes were unnerving as I tried to concentrate.

Okay... Okay...

Fight or flight.

My body automatically tensed, ready for flight. I leaned my back against the door and moved barely an inch toward the knob.

"You can't make me go," I said. My mind had gone numb in panic, and I sounded bolder then I felt. "I'm not going to your haunted boarding school." I scooted another inch. "And I'm telling Ethan about you, and the police."

Ander didn't answer, he just watched me as I slid another inch closer to the door knob. *Just a little closer now.* My fingers brushed cool metal.

"Stop," said Ander.

"Stop what?" *One more inch.*

My body was suddenly immobilized. I tried telling my arm to move forward but- it couldn't. I tried screaming, but my mouth wouldn't open and the sound only came out as a loud ugly hum.

What is he doing?

Ander's eyes were still fixed on me and I couldn't turn to look away. My heart started to throb and my breathing became scattered. My chest wouldn't move with the sudden panic induced need for air.

"Girls have so much crap," Alex muttered as he threw random pieces of clothing and bottles of cosmetics into my duffel bag. He squinted and held up a pink bottle to read the label. "Vanilla bean bliss. The alluring scent of vanilla, raspberry, and dark amber." He scoffed and threw the bottle into the bag.

"Alex!" Ander barked. "Hurry up, I can't hold this."

"Calm down." Alex threw a bra into the bag.

Something salty and warm dripped into my open mouth. Tears.

"Don't tell me to calm down!" Ander snapped back. "If you had just told them what you were supposed to say, then we wouldn't have to do this."

"Then let her go." Alex inspected a sparkly feather puff before throwing it into the bag and covering my clothes in glitter.

Ander's heated expression was still fixed on me. After a minute of staring, he broke my gaze and turned to glare at Alex, who was still sifting through my dresser drawers.

My body released and my constricted chest heaved as I gasped for air. I doubled over, half wheezing, half trying to choke back terrified sobs.

Ander sighed and raked a hand through his hair. "Don't cry... Come on Lidia, don't cry." Sympathy laced Ander's otherwise irritated voice.

Alex snorted. "God Ander, you're such an asshole."

"Shut up Alex!"

I closed my eyes. *Calm down, Lidia.* Slowly, my breathing returned to normal and I stopped choking on air. At the sound of the bag zipper being shut, my eyes flew open.

"Let's go," Alex reached behind me and opened the door.

Run.

My legs started to move, but I could barely feel them. I raced past the two shouting boys to leap down the stairs, tripping slightly on the steps. Before I could get far, large hands wrapped around my waist. I could feel Ander's disgruntled voice on the back of my neck. "Lidia, stop!"

I jerked my body ferociously, trying to escape his grip.

"Lidia, stop it! Why do you have to make this so fucking difficult?"

"Why?" I writhed uncontrollably. "Because screw you! That's why!" It wasn't the time nor the place to be answering rhetorical questions, but I had surpassed flight and was ready to fight. I let out a scream of anger which sounded like a mutilated cat.

Ander's hand flew up and clamped tightly against my open mouth, muffling the scream. I could taste the flesh of one of his fingers, so I brought my teeth down, hard.

"Ahg!" Ander's hand dropped from my mouth and I took the opportunity to swing around, whirling my arms wildly.

I buried a clenched fist into the side of his face. Ander cried out in pain and his arms fell away. I leapt forward, but only got two steps ahead before another set of hands grabbed me and pressed something soft and dry against my nose. It smelled sharp, and deep. The scent hit the back of my skull painfully, and it slowed me down. It took only seconds before my muscles got too heavy to move, and my eyelids were too heavy to open, and the darkness became too soothing to resist.

Chapter 9

I could smell smoke and leather mingling with a gush of fresh air. The breeze whipping past my face tossed my hair against my cheek, and the seat beneath me rocked gently. I opened one of my eyes just enough to see that I was in the backseat of an old car with tattered leather seats.

I closed my eyes again, trying to keep calm.

Where am I?

Soft acoustic music hummed from the radio, but I didn't hear anyone talking.

I opened my eyes again. Ander was in the passenger side of the leather bench seat, looking bored. He had a black eye blooming with violent colors of red and purple. *That must've been from me hitting him...*

It looks painful.

Good.

"Where are we?" I asked.

Ander swiveled his head back towards me, one eyebrow furrowed in displeasure, the other eyebrow stayed stationary due to excessive swelling. "Oh, she lives."

"Where are we?" I looked out the window at the foreign landscape of a small town I had never seen before. "Oh my God. You-" I couldn't even form coherent words. "You took me."

Ander turned back to face the front. "We're on our way to school."

Alex snickered and fiddled with the radio until it hit a station playing static reruns of classic rock.

"Where are we?" I tried to sound stern, but my voice faltered involuntarily.

"The hell if I know." Alex looked down at the dashboard. "I'd say, about four hours away from Mountain Heights."

I leaned back in my seat as the reality of my current situation washed over me. I wasn't tied up. *Should I try jumping out of the car?* We were slowing, just barely, as we passed through a stop sign. I reached over and tried the door. It was locked.

"Child locks are staying on," Ander said. "Especially after you freaked out last night."

"Freaked out?" I was about two seconds away from freaking out at him all over again. "You kidnapped me!"

"Did you listen to anything I told you last night?" Ander asked. "Did you want us to leave you until a Spook found you?"

"Yes!"

Alex chuckled. "Oh, words." He turned onto a new road and the town disappeared behind us.

My head clonked against the cool glass of the window. *This can't be happening.* The landscape became a blur of green, brown, and gold as we drove on half-broken roads through the flat marshy underbelly of wherever we were. After Alex replayed the same song for the third time, I rolled my eyes and finally noticed my attire. I was still in the short grey sleeping shorts and the thin white tank top. The *very* thin white tank top. I folded my arms over my chest.

"Where's my phone?" I asked.

"You don't need it." Ander didn't even bother looking at me.

"Ethan doesn't know where I am, my parents don't know-"

"Yes they do." He sounded exasperated. "I sent Ethan a text, and left a note for your mom."

Shit.

"What did you say to Ethan? I told him I wasn't going to Mountain Heights. Are we even still in Oregon?"

"Nope!" Alex turned the volume up to an oldies rock song and started singing along to the high-pitched wail of an electric guitar.

I leaned forward, shouting over the music to Ander. "What state are we in?"

"Washington." Ander still wasn't looking at me.

"And you're going to make me walk into school on my first day wearing this?" I held out my protective arms to display my current attire.

You kidnapping, life ruining, jerk. I hope your eye stays like that forever.

This time, Ander turned to look at me. His eyes hovered only momentarily on my practically see-through shirt before turning back around.

Alex laughed, and I saw his eyes peering at me through the rearview mirror. I brought my arms back to my chest.

"You're extra credit, Lidia," said Alex. "Wearing pajamas is going to be the least of your worries."

I glared at the back of both of their heads. "Right. You guys must be so proud of yourselves. Enjoy the money you get for ruining my life," I seethed.

Alex turned to Ander. "Did mom get the check?"

"Yeah, she'll start chemo next Thursday."

"Any questions?"

"Mr. Dodger said it was a gift of appreciation from the school for your tutor job."

Alex nodded, "Nice."

I followed their conversation vaguely. The word chemo rang a bell, and I remembered Ethan saying something about Ander's little sister. They were using the money to pay for her chemotherapy. A twinge of sympathetic guilt struck my heart, but it disappeared quickly. As noble as it was for two brothers to earn extra money for their sister's cancer treatment, I couldn't help feeling like they had crossed a major freakin' line.

"What did you use to drug me?" I asked. "I can't believe you drugged me."

Ander took a sip of the Coca-Cola that he held between his legs. "I can't believe you flipped out like that."

"Whatever it was, it gave me a headache. What if it had killed me?"

"Then you'd be less annoying."

"My head hurts."

"Well, I have a black eye, so tough."

I kicked the back of Ander's seat as hard as I could. The leather made a dull *thunk* and pain shot through my toe.

Worth it.

Ander muttered something that sounded offensive under his breath but didn't turn around. Both of them ignored me after that. We rode in silence through the wild landscape for another hour before Ander finally spoke.

"Alex, pull over." He pointed to a small white building that looked like a bus stop just off the side of the road.

"You don't need to tell me twice." Alex swung the car onto the side of the road. The old Chevy creaked and whined as it came to a stop on the gravel. The two boys got out of the car first. Ander walked over to my door and pulled it open. I got out as gracefully as I could while still keeping my arms crossed.

Alex walked away from us and into a thicket of bushes, disappearing behind a tall alder tree. A second later, I heard a relieved sigh as a stream of liquid came trickling through the dirt from the place where he was standing. *Boys.*

Ander strode past me and I noticed his eye looked even worse than it had before. He pulled the trunk open and began sifting through the luggage stuffed inside. After a minute, he retrieved my duffel bag and handed it to me.

"Here. You can get some real clothes."

"Thanks," I looked around at the vast openness of where we were standing on the side of the road. "Where can I change?"

"Wherever you want." He shrugged, a small smile tugged the corners of his mouth as he turned and started walking towards the woods.

Wherever I want. I looked around at the nature engulfing half the road. *Home, I want to change at home.* But that wasn't an option. The small white building on the opposite side of the street had an old broken sign that read, Raspberry's $5.50. It was obviously out of business, but it was at least shelter.

I could change in-

Ander had left the trunk open. I dropped my duffel bag on the gravel and began rummaging. *My phone might be in here!*

The top of the trunk abruptly slammed shut, missing my fingers by inches.

Alex smiled. "What chya' looking for?"

"My phone."

Alex tsked liked an old woman but said nothing. He moseyed over to the driver side of the car and pulled a pack of cigarettes from his pocket. He lit one and smoked it quietly as I silently flipped him off and then jogged across the road to change.

The raspberry stand was empty. The white paint of the cheap wood walls was etched with grime, and something smelled rotten. It was also freezing in the cool shade of the stand and I shook myself as I opened the duffel bag and withdrew a pair of jeans and my favorite lavender shirt. Some of the cosmetic bottles Alex had thrown into the bag the night before had opened, and a small patch of bronzer stained the side of my jeans. It looked like sparkly dirt.

116

"And it keeps getting better, and better," I growled as I scrubbed fruitlessly at the fabric.

"Lidia!" I heard Ander shout from the street. "We're ready to go, where are you?"

I ignored his call and decided to search for something that might help get the stain out of my jeans. Crouching behind the counter of the stand, I looked inside one of the shelves. There was a lot of old trash lodged inside. A few metal food wrappers, four decaying cardboard boxes, needles. *Needles?* There were six needles hidden in the back of the shelf, covered in dirt and dried blood.

"Lidia?" Ander called again.

I whipped my hand back from the shelf and rubbed it furiously against the knee of my jeans. "Gross." I hoped Alex had hand sanitizer in his car, but I knew he probably didn't. "Yuck, yuck, yuck." I brushed my hands together, as if the germs would fall like dust particles.

A wet choking sound came from behind me. My back thumped against the counter wall as I tipped over in surprise. There was a girl my age sitting in the opposite corner of the stand.

Vile burbled from her mouth, leaving a pastel streak of puke along the straggly ends of her long black hair. She was wearing extremely short shorts, exposing pale bruised legs that were curled underneath her as she hunched over, letting the sick trickle into a thick pool on her lap.

My heart stopped and my stomach turned unpleasantly. I watched helplessly as she heaved and gagged. I could smell the sick that fell from her mouth and I knew she was dying. Again.

She was already dead.

117

"It's not- too much." Her saliva and vomit stringed her mouth together as she spoke. Her teeth were brown, rotten. "It's not too much." The girl rose to her feet slowly, supporting herself on the wall as she took a step toward me.

"Ander!" I screamed, heartbeat returning with savage intensity. I pressed my back against the wall. "Ander!"

The girl staggered forward until she was standing right above me. Thick globs of puke continued to burble from her mouth and splatter in the dust of the stand floor. Her eyes were vacant as they stared at me, dazed. "I'm fine," she choked. Her chest contorted with a heave and she stepped forward again.

"Ander!" My own ears rung with my shrill scream.

Ander rounded the corner of the stand, looking alarmed. Without hesitation, he thrust his hand forward and it sank deep into the girl's chest. A vacant expression washed through her face as white light glowed from the spot in the middle of her rib cage where Ander's arm was half buried. The cool air became static. It almost felt fuzzy on my skin.

And then she was gone.

I stared openmouthed up at Ander from the corner where I was still cowering. I couldn't form words, but as I watched him examine his hand with a pleased expression on his face, I noticed that the air was warm and smooth again. It still smelled rotten though.

"Tah-dah!" Ander half bowed.

"Was that a Spook?"

"No." His lazy smile and hazy eyes watched me for second. "Just a ghost."

"What was she trying to do?"

"Nothing." Ander cleared his throat and shook his head. When he looked at me again, he seemed more serious. The smile had faded and his deep blue eyes had cleared from the momentary fog. "She was reliving the last few minutes of her life. It's pretty common."

I swallowed, attempting to regain control over my vocal chords. "She overdosed."

"Yeah," Ander brushed a hand through his hair absently. "It happens... C'mon." He extended a hand toward me. I took it, still noticeably shaking.

"What'd I miss?" Alex came sidling over to the stand, puffing smoke into the air lazily.

"Lidia found a ghost."

Alex scowled. "Uhg," he threw the cigarette to the ground and stomped out the glowing particles with a thick boot. "Smells like it's still here."

"Yeah, it does." Ander turned and left the stand.

Alex and I followed, which was hard because my legs still felt like jelly. As we neared the borderline of trees and bushes on the side of the road, the rotting smell became more prominent. It stank like the sickening sweet scent of rotting flesh. It smelled like Grandma.

"Found it!" Ander yelled from the bushes.

"Found what?" I asked.

Ander emerged from the trees and took my arm, pulling me in the opposite direction. "I found the body."

"You- you what?" My stomach dropped.

119

Alex ran into the bushes behind Ander, and I tried to follow but Ander kept a firm grip on my arm as he led me back toward the car.

"Come on," he said as we crossed the deserted asphalt. "You don't need to see that."

"She died? Nobody found her? No one was looking?" *Is this normal for him?* I felt the back of my eyes burn with fear. "I can't do this, Ander."

"Do what?" Ander released my arm as we neared the car.

"Please take me home." I was begging. It was in my voice, it was in my face. I just wanted to go home.

"Do you think you can deal with this stuff on your own at home?"

No.

"That wasn't even a Spook, Lidia... A Spook is worse, and it puts not only you, but Ethan in danger too. I'm not letting you put him at risk like that."

I didn't answer. There was nothing I could say. Ander watched me leaning against the car door for a minute before he retrieved something from his back pocket. It was my phone.

He dialed a number and then brought it up to his ear. "Hi, uh, yes, I'd like to report a possible poacher dumping spot near a raspberry stand off the corner of Highway nine in Eatonville. My brother and I were driving and we just smelled—yeah. That's what we're guessing...Yes...Bernie Mackleson...Okay, thank you, bye." He hung up. "They'll be here in ten minutes, we better head out."

"You didn't report the body."

"If you report a body, you have to stay for questioning and we have to get to school. The smell will lead them to her anyways. Guaranteed."

Behind him, I saw Alex exiting the woods with a sour look plastered onto his face. From what I could discern, it sounded like he muttered *nasty.*

Ander turned to me, and our eyes locked for a moment. Even the eye swelling with a dark purple bruise held my gaze. "I'm not doing this to scare you," he said. "I know it sucks, but I'm helping you survive. It's better than being institutionalized, and you'll need to be able to deal with this stuff. "

I knew he was right, though I wished he wasn't.

I'm going to Mountain Heights Academy.

Ghosts are real.

I'm a Medium.

I won't see Ethan for- God knows how long.

The last thought shot a sharp pain through my heart. "Can I call Ethan?"

"Uh-" Ander scrunched his noise.

"Please."

He sighed and pulled my cellphone out of his pocket. "You can call him in the car...If you dial anyone else," he raised an eyebrow and pointed to the phone. "This little baby is going for a swim."

Chapter 10

"Ethan, please, I meant-"

"I can't believe you just left like that! What the hell?"

I was back in Alex's car again. The car was driving further and further into the dark forest of the mountain while I sat in the backseat with my cellphone plastered to my ear. I had called Ethan, desperate for the chance to explain my situation, but when he had finally picked up, I found that I didn't really have anything to explain. I simply told him I changed my mind.

It was hard to keep my voice straight as I told him lie after lie. That I wanted to get into a good college someday, that this school was going to be really good for my future, and how I had arranged a ride back to school with Ander and Alex weeks ago without telling him. I couldn't tell him the unbelievable truth, and lying to him was the least hurtful thing I could do. It was better than telling him I left because I could see dead people- he would've taken that worse than if I had just slapped him in the face. At least he thought this was the truth.

"Ethan, I'm so sorry." Tears threatened to escape my eyes, but I didn't want to cry in front of Alex and Ander. "It was the best thing. I can still see you Thanksgiving, and Christmas, and I'll be home for the entire summer."

"You didn't even say goodbye!" Ethan yelled, channeling all his hurt into the volume of his voice. "How could you do this, Lidia? Sam didn't even know you were leaving!"

"Ethan, I-I'm so sorry," my voice cracked. *So much for not crying.*

"How could you?" he bellowed. "Just leave, like, I can't believe it! Why would you do that?" His voice softened for a moment. "I thought you loved me."

"I do!" My heart ached and I felt the hot tears roll down my cheek. *He's going to break up with me.* "I do love you." I felt sick.

"Give the phone to Ander!"

I gave Ander the phone and he sighed before bringing it to his ear. "Hey."

I couldn't make out what Ethan said through the other end, and Ander wasn't saying anything at all. *He's going to break up with me…. can I blame him?* I wiped a tear from my eye and tried to compose my face. This wouldn't have happened if Ander and Alex hadn't kidnapped me. If they had just let me figure it out on my own. *I didn't need them, and now I have nothing. Even if we turned back right now, Ethan wouldn't want me after this.* No one would.

"It's, look-" Ander spoke sternly into the speaker. "No man, I- , Ethan! I convinced her to go." There was more yelling from the phone speaker and finally Ander turned to hand the phone back to me. "Here."

"Lidia," Ethan's voice was calmer, but no less angry. "Look, I don't know-"

"Ethan, I'm sorry!"

"Whatever! Whatever… look, I don't know where this leaves us. I-I love you." A thick painful knot formed in my throat.

"But maybe we just need a break." There was finality in his voice.

"Don't do this," I whispered.

The car bumped as we drove over an uneven patch of road. Alex and Ander were silent in the front seat, avoiding eye contact.

"I didn't' sign up for this!" Ethan said. "I just think it's better, that if you're going to leave without even telling your boyfriend that you're switching schools, that maybe, we need a break. You obviously don't care about me the way I thought you did."

He hung up.

I stared at the black screen of my cellphone and tried to keep my face from collapsing into a fit of tears. I took long, slow, breaths of air as I looked out the window. The trees sped past in blurs.

"Are you okay?" Ander shot a sidelong glance at me through the eye that wasn't swollen shut.

"No." *And it's your fault.*

No one spoke after that, and the rest of the drive passed quickly. I tried focusing on the developing mountain landscape outside, and wallowed in the cool chill that blew in through the window as we drove by lingering patches of dirty snow hidden deep within the rocky forest.

We had been driving uphill on a narrow cliff road for the past hour. Finally, we turned a corner and the hill peaked, sending us onto a secluded gravel road. We moved steadily down into what looked like a crater valley. It was practically a hole nestled into the surrounding forested hills of the mountain.

It was blanketed with a flat grassy field and a large three-part building. The dying sun reflected bright orange light off the windows that made up most of the school, and I squinted to get a better look as we neared.

Each of the three buildings that created the entire structure of the school were square with deep oak paneling that made up what wasn't covered in glass. It was a modern building, but due to the wear it had endured from the harsh mountain weather, it didn't look new. The fourth floor of the main building had a triangular A-frame peak, and the centerpiece of the large front window was beautiful stained glass. The middle building was the biggest, and looked like it held the majority of the school. I assumed the other two buildings were dorms.

Alex turned the Chevy into the parking lot near the edge of a small patch of evergreen trees. The parking lot was already packed with student cars and even a few Greyhound shuttle buses. There were people everywhere. Most were carrying boxes and luggage across the lawn to one of the two side buildings.

All of these kids can see ghosts.

Once the car was parked, we all got out while silently avoiding eye contact. As we began unloading the trunk of our luggage, Ander swung my bag over his shoulder. I reached over and tore it off of him immediately.

"I can carry it myself," I spat.

Ander looked a little confronted but didn't protest; I followed him and Alex across the lawn and into the grand entrance of the main building.

The inside of the school matched the rest of the building, though it looked more polished than the outside. Most

125

walls were paneled with warm oak that was lit by the dying sun blazing through the floor length windows lining the hallways. There were a few banners tastefully placed throughout the school, featuring a crescent of dark evergreen and red with a grey wolf logo in the middle. *Mountain Heights Academy – Home of the Timberwolves.*

What's a timber wolf?

Stupid.

I thought the mascot would've been something ghost related. I had pictured a green and red football team walking out onto the field with a bloodied corpse logo plastered onto the front of their jerseys.

The boys led me up a flight of stairs and into a short hallway lined with trophies and shiny silver medals. We passed by a few doors, each with name plates- *Dr. Shorts, Mrs. Suzanne Waters, Mr. Frank Radford...* We reached the end of the hall and then turned the corner into the main office.

The main office overlooked the dark forest near the back of the school. There were lots of little cubical and filing cabinets littering the room behind the front desk.

"Can I help you?"

"We need to get the schedule for a new student," said Ander.

"Oh," the receptionist's eyes looked at me for a moment in surprise. "She's a little older than I expected."

"Late bloomer." Alex was picking through the candy bowl. "I already talked to Mr. Dodger, we just need to pick up her schedule." He found a red mint and unwrapped it without looking at any of us.

"Okay." The receptionist pulled a manila folder out of a drawer and sifted through the papers. "What's her name?"

"Lidia Powell," Ander said.

"Mmmhmm." She continued searching.

What did she mean older? How old am I supposed to be?

"Okay, here it is." The women scanned a document. "She didn't attend this morning's orientation, did she?"

I shook my head.

"Alright, well, why don't the three of you pop into Mr.Dodger's office for a moment." She smiled at me. "I just want to make sure you're all caught up."

Alex looked severely put out, but Ander took the folder she handed him and led us back down the hall until we reached a door with a sign that read- *Mr. Dodger, Dean of Admissions.* Ander knocked twice.

"Come in!" prattled a happy male voice from inside.

Ander opened the door and I was immediately met by a heavy waft of cinnamon scented air. It was a sweet spice, but the strength of the scent made my eyes water slightly as I entered the room.

A small grey haired man with a plaid polyester suit the color of rotten oranges and melted chocolate came prancing over to us from behind a large desk. The room was well lit by a fireplace and a window that took up two of the walls. The rest of the room was lined with books. It was like a mini-library.

"Ah, there they are! Very good." Mr. Dodger beamed, grasping each of our hands in both of his. "Mrs. Dodger," Mr.

Dodger threw his arms up excitedly and addressed a middle-aged woman sitting quietly in the corner. "Will you please send for student assistance to come help these lovely young people with their luggage?"

The woman stood to her feet. "Yes." She sidled past us out of the room.

Mr. Dodger winked at me and leaned in closer to whisper behind a thick wrinkled hand. "She's my wife."

"Oh," I didn't know what to say. "Cool."

"Sit down, sit down." Mr. Dodger walked over and took the chair closest to the empty fireplace as Ander, Alex, and I, all piled uncomfortably close onto a plush green couch opposite him. "You missed orientation," he said.

"It took us longer than we thought to get back," said Ander. He reached over and handed Mr. Dodger my folder.

"Not a problem... I'm assuming these two handsome men filled you in on why you've been accepted into Mountain Heights?"

I nodded.

"Excellent. Well, we are very pleased to have you." Mr. Dodger's eyes scanned over the papers inside the folder. "May I ask how long you've had your gift?"

"Uh, I don't know... since April."

"April!" He smiled, or, at least I think he did. It was difficult to make out his mouth under his bushy mustache. "Well, you will be in a first-year introduction course with other recruits. They will be much younger than you, is that alright?"

I nodded.

"Very good. I see that you are a junior, correct?"

"Yes."

"All you're other classes should be with students closer to your age. The training will be a little difficult, but it's never too late to learn how to be a successful medium. Never too late!" He beamed silently for a moment, retaining a long stretch of awkward silence.

Alex cleared his throat and it seemed to snap Mr. Dodger back into focus. He retrieved a thin copper wire and a small battery from his coat pocket and set them on his knee.

"Miss Powell, we are surrounded by the energy of the dead at all times," he said. "They linger in their memories through the natural world, and most are harmless, but often-" he shook his head sadly. "Often, there are darker spirits imprinted on this world by an untimely death, or a particularly gruesome act of violence, and some are simply evil."

"Like demons?"

"In a way, yes. We often call them demons for lack of a better term. Mediums, like you and me, and your two handsome escorts here-"

I growled inwardly because I longed to throw my two handsome escorts out the window.

"Are able retain this energy and use it." Mr. Dodger held up the copper wire. "Most people come in contact with the spirt world, and it just-" he swept his hand past the copper wire. "*Woosh*. The energy flies right through them!" Mr. Dodger placed the wire back in his pocket and held the battery. "Mediums, however, are more like this rechargeable battery. We are able to capture, and release this energy in different forms."

"Ander told me a little about absorbing ghosts."

"I prefer the term spirits, and yes, you will." Mr. Dodger smiled, thoroughly enjoying himself. "Here at Mountain Heights," he continued, "we have training courses that every student must attend until they pass their Standardized Energy Transference Test, SETT. Most students are able to pass within their first year, and we have a test offered each quarter. After you pass the SETT, you are free to attend any school you wish."

I stopped listening for a moment.

I don't have to stay here?

"We simply prefer to prepare student mediums for the world ahead. It's a rough road for those who go undiscovered," said Mr. Dodger. "Many don't make it."

"I don't have to stay here until graduation?"

I could go back home. Back to Ethan... if he'll still have me.

Mr. Dodger nodded solemnly. "Most student prefer to finish their academic career here. We have excellent records, and many students find it difficult to leave the friends they've made during their stay."

"I've already left friends."

Ander shifted uncomfortably on the couch next to me.

"I understand," said Mr. Dodger.

"Uh," his gaze made me uncomfortable so I continued. "I do appreciate the help I can get here though."

"And it's happily given, Miss Powell!" Mr. Dodger folded his hands in his lap as he looked at the three of us. "It will be difficult to get caught up at first. I would greatly appreciate if your two escorts would be so kind as to tutor you over the first semester?"

Neither of the boys moved. Alex looked severely annoyed, while Ander just looked mildly horrified.

"Gentlemen?"

They nodded.

"All part of the extra credit business." Mr. Dodger giggled to himself, giddy with the prospect of my new tutors. "Ander, I believe you are a senior this year, is that right?"

Ander nodded.

"And Alex here was a star graduating pupil last year. He has kindly retuned this year as a trainer for field experience and active training. As this is the area you most need to develop, I would prefer if you held your extra field training sessions with Alex, and had at least one night a week to study school material with Ander here. You will find that our institution is a bit more rigorous than most high schools, and I want you to be thoroughly prepared for graduation, wherever you may choose to stay for your senior year."

"Thank you," I said. The sun had set during our short talk in the office, and the sky outside the window was now navy blue scattered with bright stars.

"Now!" Mr. Dodger jumped from his seat and clapped his hands together. "For the technicalities. This way, this way."

We got up from the chair and I stretched stiffly before following Mr. Dodger to his desk.

"I am, unfortunately, going to ask for any cellular devices, or other electronics you have in your possession."

A brief echo of Ethan's voice went through my head, *no technology allowed.* Sadly, I retrieved my phone from my pocket and handed it to him.

"Why can't we have cellphones?" I asked nimbly as he covered it with a sticker, and placed it in a drawer with Alex's phone.

"I simply don't understand today's generation," Mr. Dodger tsked, fumbling through a stack of unorganized papers splayed across his desk. "So dependent upon technology... You'll understand that due to the nature of the students at this school, communication with the outside world is limited. For the protection of students and their privacy agreement- have you received one of those yet?"

I shook my head.

"We filed her for family privacy when we had her registered," said Ander. He turned to me and shrugged. "It just means your parents won't find out that you're a medium through mail, or anything."

Mr. Dodger nodded, "very good."

"So, they'll always just think this is a normal school?" I must've looked horrified because Mr. Dodger turned a kind smile my way.

"It's very common to have family privacy, my dear."

"Are there ghosts at school?" I asked.

"Oh, my goodness no!" Mr. Dodger handed me a folder of papers. "That would be just too distracting." His bushy mustache bounced. "Can you image history class interrupted by a Vietnam solider? It would be educational, but no, no.... we have Ultrasonic Spirit Meters." He pointed to the corner of the room where a small black box flashed a red light from the shadows. "They disrupt the energy waves so that spirits aren't able to manifest themselves on school grounds. Which reminds me of perhaps the most important rule here on campus." He looked at me seriously, and then to Alex and Ander. "You are not to use any sort of boost on campus. That is a part of field training, and it will stay at field training." He looked pointedly at Ander. "We don't want a repeat of last year, now do we?"

"No sir," Ander said as Alex stifled a laugh.

"Very good," Mr. Dodger nodded. "I'm not sure the chemistry department can deal with another situation like that again this year. There would be serious repercussions."

Ander nodded, pretending to be serious. "Right. It won't happen again."

Mr. Dodger turned to me. "Classes start day after tomorrow, and I'm sure these two young men will aid you in getting to know the campus before then."

Doubtful.

"I just gave you a packet with a list of school policies and rules, along with a dress code, and a list of required books. All books can be purchased in the library on the main floor. Your school uniform should be waiting in your dorm room, along with the rest of your luggage. The uniform only has three sizes, so if the medium doesn't fit, we can find you something smaller."

"Medium will be fine, thank you." I hadn't even noticed our bags had disappeared.

"Now, your dorm number should be on the first page there."

I opened the folder and saw my name typed above a long list of rules and policies.

Lidia L. Powell

Junior.

Level: A

Residence: 403G.

Mr. Dodger took my hand again. "It was a pleasure to meet you, my dear." He turned toward Alex and Ander to shake their hands gruffly. "And you boys. The funds have already been transferred into the desired account. I take it one of you would like to show Mrs. Powell to her room tonight?"

"I will," Ander said.

Ugh.

"Ah, lovely." Mr. Dodger led us out the door. "Goodnight, I look forward to a wonderful term!" Before he shut the door, he turned to Ander and pointed to the swollen black eye. "And try to put some ice on that."

Chapter 11

The sound of a ringing alarm clock woke me up the next morning. I could see my roommate's blond head in the bed beneath me as she reached over to turn it off.

I had met her the night before, sort of.

After Ander, Alex, and I had left the main building, Ander led me through the halls towards the girl's dormitory and up to the third floor. He pointed me down the hall, mentioning briefly that he would meet me for breakfast the next morning. Then he left.

My roommate had watched me without greeting as I shuffled inside. The first thing I noticed when I entered was that the room was roughly the size of a large coat closet. There was a long dresser taking up an entire wall, two desks placed near the large window overlooking the forest, and a bunk bed stuffed into whatever space was left. My roommate had already decorated the left half of the room with band posters and portraits of shirtless men.

"Hi," I had said as I went over and pointed to my duffel bag sitting on the top bunk. "So, I'm top?" The bottom bunk was already clothed in a patterned purple spread, so I guess the question was moot.

"Yeah." She had two-toned blond hair, a very curvy figure, and heavy eyelids over large brown eyes. She would've been a lot prettier if she wasn't looking at me like I had tattooed the word *loser* across my forehead.

"I'm Lidia," I said. "What's your name?"

"Molly."

"What grade are you?"

"Senior." She turned back to the bag she was unpacking. "What are you?"

"Junior."

"Oh."

When she didn't answer any more of my questions, I concluded that Molly was a total snob, and that I hoped her overly large boobs suffocated her in her sleep. Still, I was at least grateful that she looked like a clean roommate. The room had already started to smell like perfume and bubblegum. The rest of the night was spent unpacking in silence and eventually going to bed.

■ ■

As the early morning light streamed through our large open window, Molly lethargically dressed in our school uniform. It was a hideous button up white blouse paired with a red and green plaid skirt. To make matters worse, we were given the choice of tights or stockings to go with the flat black shoes that were also required. The fact that girls had to wear skirts at all seemed a little sexist and old-fashioned, but I wasn't about to boycott the uniform. Not on my first day.

Molly scrunched her blond curls and applied a thick layer of black makeup to her already dark eyes. Even Trina would've been proud. When she was finished, she turned and caught me watching her through the confines of my blanket.

Molly surveyed me like a dying slug. "Breakfast is in fifteen minutes."

"Thanks."

"Yeah." She shrugged and left the room.

I sighed and got up. *They better serve coffee here.* I brushed my hair and tucked it back with a headband before digging into my makeup bag. All the silent crying I had done the previous night had left my eyes puffy and a little red. I did what I could, which wasn't much, and then left for breakfast.

I had absolutely no idea where the cafeteria was, so I just followed the stampede of plaid skirts. Groups of giggling girls ranging from the ages of twelve to nineteen, all rushed down a flight of stairs and into the second story glass hallway leading into the main building.

The sea of plaid was joined by a tidal wave of black slacks as the gentlemen- boys, came bombarding toward us. The stampeding crowd jostled me slightly before we all entered into a large cafeteria.

Wow, how many people go to this school?

The cafeteria had high ceilings and a lot of natural light. The far wall was made up almost entirely of windows overlooking the mountains, and a school banner on the other side of the room was hanging above a large buffet table. The high ceiling of the cafeteria was supported by multiple wooden post that broke up the scattered tables into different sections.

Most of these sections were divided by age. The youngest students sat farthest away from the giant glass windows, while the faculty, older students, and some people that looked like students but were dressed entirely in black, sat around the tables with the best view. Amongst the black clad students, was Alex.

I shuffled to the side, allowing the others to spill from the door beside me without getting caught up in the crowd as they streamed into the cafeteria. I stretched my neck around the different tables, looking for Ander.

This sucks.

I felt so out of place. I felt invisible, yet, I still felt like everyone was watching me. At one of the tables facing the window, I saw Molly laughing with a stocky boy wearing a woven beanie.

"There you are."

I turned to see Ander standing casually with his hands in his pockets. Even with the black eye, Ander looked really good in the school uniform. Of course, the guys had a better outfit all together. While Ander's well-fitted slacks and school sweater made him look like a Ralph Lauren model, I was stuck looking more like a deranged version of Gogo Yubari.

"Here I am," I answered with a tight smile.

"So, what do you think?"

I looked around the room again. "Well, it's definitely the fanciest cafeteria I've ever been in."

Ander gestured me to the nearest table, which was unpleasantly close to the back wall next to a group of gawking tweens. I assumed the younger boys were also new to Mountain Heights, and I seriously doubted this was Ander's usual table. Still, at least the table was somewhat hidden, and I didn't feel so exposed.

"Um," Ander continued standing as I sat down. "I'll go get us some food."

I waited as Ander sauntered over to the buffet table and loaded a tray with food. He was interrupted a few times by people coming over to him and pointing at his eye.

Great. I haven't even started school and I already have a reputation as the girl who punched someone in the face. The people Ander talked with laughed, and then a new set of students came up to greet him. I ripped my gaze away from Ander to study the rest of the room. Students, particularly the ones my age, were all ogling at me as they ate.

I felt naked.

Ander returned to the table a few minutes later and slid a red plastic tray between us. It was piled high with an obscene amount of fruit and bread.

"Uh, I didn't really know what vegans eat, so-" Ander trailed off, picking up a plate of scrambled eggs. "You like apples, right?"

"Yeah," I took one of the apples. "Thanks."

He watched me for a second. "So," he said slowly. "Do you have questions about school and stuff?"

"I have a million."

"Shoot." Ander smiled good-naturedly, some of his uneasiness seeming to fade.

"Well," I scowled and sunk my teeth deep into the fleshy red skin of the apple. "Why do some people have a family privacy policy and others don't? How many people tell all their friends and family they can see ghosts?"

"Not many."

"And I still don't get why I have to do testing. I mean, I get it, but what about the people who never get found, and then go nuts? Are there laws?"

"Oh yeah, there's a whole government division for special medium-related cases. Sometimes, someone who is never found will get in with a Spook, and that usually results in crime or murder, mostly. They do an assessment and then they get neutered and put in jail."

"Neutered?" I raised an eyebrow, waiting for him to continue, but he didn't. "How do you neuter a medium?"

Ander pointed to his plate of scrambled eggs with his fork. "Imagine this is your brain."

"That's messed up."

"So is murder," Ander shrugged. "That's only for really extreme cases, it's the only way to get rid of a medium's abilities. Usually, if someone goes off the grid and then does something big, like, I don't know, levitate a car."

"You can levitate a car?"

"No, but some people can. Anyways, if you're not hiding it under the pretense of being a magician, or Chris Angel, or something, then the authorities will usually find you and you'll get time at Plymouth Penitentiary." Ander took the last few bites of egg and then took an apple off the tray. "Plymouth is sort of like Mountain Heights. Most people think it's a regular prison, but it's actually high security specialized to contain mediums."

I took a deep breath. "I don't think I'd do well in prison."

Ander smiled weakly. "You're not going to prison."

"Good, because I've never shanked anyone before." I finished the last two bites of my apple and took a piece of toast from the tray. I looked over and saw the two teenage boys still staring at us. I narrowed my eyes at the both of them and they looked away. "How old are most of the kids here?"

"Uh," Ander rubbed his hand along his chin. "Usually new students are about thirteen."

"What?" I dropped my toast back on the tray. "Thirteen?"

"Yeah." He was looking across our table towards the rest of the room. "I think you might be the oldest extra credit we've ever had here. We had a guy two years ago who came to school when he was sixteen, but he had started seeing when he was twelve, so, he was a bit-" Ander widened his eyes and gestured the sign for crazy. "I think people will be surprised at how normal you are."

I could feel my face fall and I slumped back into my chair.

"It won't be so bad," he said.

"Whatever." I took a deep breath and looked away. "It doesn't matter. I don't have any friends back home anyways. For some reason, Ethan and everyone else took my sudden disappearance as abandonment."

Ander shifted uncomfortably, but after a moment of silence, he spoke. "Ethan will come around." His blue eyes sank into mine. "He's borderline annoyingly obsessed with you. He'll get over it."

"Yeah, well, I don't blame him for being pissed." I tried looking everywhere other than Ander, but I wasn't seeing much. Every so often, I would catch another student staring from another table, and I was reminded that they probably thought I was completely crazy.

"Let me see your schedule." Ander made a reach for the stack of papers I had next to me on the table. He flipped through until he found my schedule, and then he studied it for a minute while eating toast. He finished and slid it back towards me. "We have science together."

"Super." I looked at my schedule and saw that I had first period junior chemistry. "So, did you fail junior chemistry last year, or what?"

"Actually, I didn't take chemistry last year." He smiled briefly, recalling a pleasant memory. "I took biology, and I didn't fail, I was just asked never to attend one of Mr. Hang's classes again."

"What'd you do?"

Ander's wistful smile returned. "Something to do with a frog. You don't want to know."

I didn't.

"So, I guess I need to give you the heads up on some of the stuff that goes on around here," said Ander. "First, you probably won't be doing regular training with your class. Alex will have you watch the seniors since that's who he's teaching this year, and then he'll work on the basics with you afterwards. He takes his car down to the training site, so you can hitch a ride with him when you're done."

"Where's the training site?"

"There's a cemetery, about fifteen minutes away. Friday's field training day, so everyone gets on a bus that brings us down there. You have to wear gear, you should have that."

"Is that the black pants and shirt?" There had been a black outfit folded under my school uniform in my dorm.

"Yes," said Ander. "When you're down there, you'll be sectioned out and your group is paired with a trainer where you learn how to control and absorb...It's a hell of a boost. It's pretty much everyone's favorite day."

"What happens if you absorb too much energy? Do you explode?" I had pictured an overload of energy resulting in an effect similar to the blueberry girl from Willy Wonka.

"Most times you can't, there's no real dangerous limit from a normal spirit. If you get into absorbing Spooks, then you definitely get messed up." He scanned the room and pointed to a table behind me. "See those scrawny guys over there?"

I assumed he was referring to the skinny group of boys by the window. There were two small dark-haired ones with extra pale skin and bushy eyebrows; they looked like twins. The third boy was tall and blond with a rat face.

"The one with the lip ring, Jason." I looked closer and saw that the blond had two diamond snake bites under his lip. "My friend Trevor said his brother's in Plymouth for being a feeder." Ander was watching the boys with a look of distaste. "And that's why you don't get mixed up with that stuff."

I ripped my eyes away from the boys and turned back to Ander. "What's a feeder?"

"It's a medium that absorbs the energy of the living. It's only possible if you're already absorbing Spooks because the energy is so strong. You get addicted, and when you can't find a Spook to absorb, they go after humans."

"What happens?"

"It kills the person, and I don't know what it does for them except give them a boost. It's sick. Jason's brother killed a kid and two other people before he was found in a den and got locked up."

I raised an eyebrow. "Did he get neutered?"

Ander nodded.

"Wow."

As if seeing dead things wasn't enough, now I have to worry about getting absorbed by other mediums.

"Are there any other things I should know? Are werewolves and mermaids real too?" I sincerely hoped mermaids were real.

Ander snorted as if I had asked a ridiculous question. "We're mediums, not wizards."

"Same thing."

Ander looked at me, exasperated. "Not even close."

"Wait," I studied him a minute. "Are there wizards?" I said it a little too loud and the table next to us snickered. Ander shook his head, but I continued to prod. "Well, I don't know. Until a few weeks ago I didn't even know ghosts were real! I've probably walked through so many of them."

"You probably have," Ander said distractedly. He smiled at someone behind me and I turned to see a small crowd winding through the occupied tables of eating students.

At first, I thought they were coming to me. Molly was leading the group. There was the stocky boy with a beanie she was talking to earlier, a lanky blond boy, and a pretty Asian girl flanking her sides.

Ander stood and rounded the table to greet them. I felt awkward being the only person sitting, so I stood and went over to stand beside Ander. As he smiled and laughed with each of them, I silently wondered whether or not I should say hello to Molly.

Maybe she's already forgotten that I'm her roommate.

Molly didn't even seem to notice that I was there. She beamed at Ander with outstretched arms and embraced him in a tight hug.

Hey roomie, it's me. The girl you were so rude to last night.

I hovered awkwardly behind them. It was a long hug.

Annnd I'm air.

"Ander! How was summer?" Molly released Ander as he reached out to clap the hand of the blond boy.

"It was good, I uh-"

"What happened to your eye?" Molly interjected.

"Wow, bro," the blond boy reached over to flick Ander's face, but Ander slapped the boy's hand away. "You got yourself a real shiner."

"Did your idiot brother do that to you?" asked Molly.

"No," Ander shook his head and retracted slightly. Instead of answering, he just jerked his head in my direction, which was enough to send the Asian chick into hysterical laugher. *Great.*

"No way." The blond boy sidled over to me and grinned. "The extra credit did this to you?"

145

"My name's Lidia," I corrected him. "And I made the decision to come here...so I don't think I can really be labeled as extra credit." It was a lie, but I really didn't want to get stuck with that stupid nickname.

The blond boy turned to Ander with an eyebrow raised. I didn't see what Ander did, but the boy turned back to me and smiled. "You're extra credit," he said again.

"Lidia's my roommate," Molly said. "She only packed underwear and makeup in her bag, barely any real clothes." She smiled cruelly and continued. "I don't know what she thought Mountain Heights was supposed to be-" she laughed, "but now our entire room is covered in glitter. Might as well live in a strip club."

Ander tried to hide a smile as the others laughed openly. I could feel the heat rising to my cheeks and my heart start to hammer.

"I didn't pack my own bag," I said.

"Really?" Molly flipped her hair over her shoulder. "I thought you said you made the decision to come here on your own?"

I clamped my mouth shut and willed the back of my eyes to stop burning before hot angry tears could fall. I was grinding my teeth so hard I could feel pain shoot up through my jaw.

"Alright, be nice," said Ander with a halfhearted grin. "She's my friend's girlfriend, so let's give her a break."

"Was his girlfriend," I mumbled.

"Do you have to train her?" Molly asked.

146

"No, Alex does." They were talking like I wasn't even there. "I just have to tutor her with school stuff."

"That sucks." Molly's eyes shot toward me and then back to Ander. "We're helping Jeff unpack before classes, are you coming?" she said to him.

"Uh," Ander hesitated. "No, I'm going to give her a tour first, then I-"

"You know what-" everyone looked over to me, surprised that I had spoken. "I'd really prefer if you didn't take me on a tour." I reached over and snatched my things from the table. "Why don't you just go hang out with your friends, and maybe they can take you to the nurses office so you can get tested for the STD Whitney gave you after you screwed her behind the tool shed at camp." The STD part was a lie, but it had the desired effect.

The smile slid off Anders face like butter melting off the surface of a pancake.

"Might want to get that eye checked out too." I turned and stormed away. I would've loved for those to be the last words, but just as I reached the doors, I could hear one of the girls laughing and the blond boy shouted after me.

"See you later extra credit!"

Chapter 12

Since I never actually went on a tour of the school, I got really lost throughout the entire first week.

I was late to every single class on my first day. I knew people were going to stare, but somehow it felt worse when I stood in front of the entire room trying to apologize to the teacher for walking in mid-lecture. After a month, I had finally gotten used to the endless turns of the oak hallways that lead to large brightly lit classrooms, but I hadn't gotten used to the classes themselves. Mr. Dodger was putting it simply when he said they're academic program was rigorous. At my old high school, I could get away with decent grades if I simply did the work. Here, I was actually expected to learn the material, something easier said than done.

To make matters worse, I quickly discovered that absolutely no one liked the new kids. Most of them stared as if they were waiting for me to spontaneously combust, while others were just rude. Still, being completely ignored was probably the worse, and that happened a lot. Even Ander ignored me. It was like the person at camp had disappeared completely. Every time I saw him, he was either surrounded by his laughing clique of friends, or glaring at the space of air directly above my head to avoid eye contact when I passed him in the hall.

I thought my status as lone wolf would've worn off after the first month, but when I was still avoided like I carried a contagious disease well into the middle of October, I had completely given up on being social with my peers. Even with Ethan hating me, and Sammy thinking I was a terrible friend, I couldn't wait to pass my SETT and go home.

That is, if I passed.

On Friday mornings at eight, the junior and senior class got dressed in black gear and piled onto the Greyhound bus that gurgled smoke into the chilly morning fog.

I trudged behind the line of students hobbling onto the bus, laughing, yawning, and trash-talking their assigned trainer. I shuffled past the cramped aisles and made sure I got my usual seat in the back. I took my empty seat and watched as the rest of the students slowly filled each nook and cranny. Every seat was taken, except the one next to me.

Hello, my name is Lidia Powell, the lone timber wolf of Mountain Heights Academy.

Two girls in front of me were gossiping about boys and I listened idly as I twisted my hair back into a braid.

"Yeah, and then he kissed me, but I was like, whoa!"

"Levi? Isn't he gay?"

The other girl shrugged her shoulders. "I thought he was too, you know, but I guess not." There was a leaf stuck to the back of her head and it really bothered me. "I wonder if he'll ask me out, I would totally do it."

"You mean, do him," the other squealed.

"No," she laughed. "I'm still waiting for you-know-who."

You're waiting to be de-flowered by Voldemort?

"But, then again, I don't know. Maybe... you know? If it's right." She flipped her ponytail back, but the leaf still clung securely to her hair.

I reached my hand out to retrieve the little leaf from its hiding spot. The girl spun around and glared at me. I held the little piece of green up like a white flag. *Easy tiger.*

"It was stuck in your hair," I said.

"Thanks." She turned back to her friend to further discuss the love life of Levi Renton. I didn't bother telling them that I saw Levi kissing Will Cook not two days ago. He was clearly going through an experimental phase.

The lone timber wolf sees all things.

The bus started down the gravel road through the dark trees that sent us into shadows. Ander was sitting a few seats in front of me. Since I had a class with one of each of his friends, I could identify all of them by name. The tall blond guy that Ander was sitting next to was named Trevor. The small Asian girl talking animatedly to Ander from across the aisle was named Jessica. And the guy with the beanie super glued to his head was Jeff.

I hated all of them.

Ander shot a glance to the back of the bus and made steady eye contact with me for the first time in a month. I looked away quickly, pretending that the graffiti sketched into the back of my seat was far more interesting than it really was. It simply said- *Calvin was here.*

When the bus finally stopped, we piled out in one giant swarm of black. I stepped onto the cool dewy grass of Walden Cemetery and took a deep breath of the crisp morning air. It made a little cloud spill from my mouth as I exhaled.

Some of the fog had cleared, allowing the sun to create a sheen on the newer headstones across the manicured lawn and fallen autumn leaves. Walden Cemetery was by far the most beautiful cemetery I had ever been to, but it was also the creepiest. I had overheard some of the students talking about the history, and learned that most of the people buried at Walden were unclaimed bodies. It explained why so many of the headstones were blank.

I followed a group of students walking towards Alex and stood a few steps away from their circle formation. They laughed and talked animatedly as I chipped away a fresh coat of black nail polish. *Black. Like my soul.*

Trina would be so proud.

God, I wish Ethan was here...

Alex stepped forward and slung a black duffel bag onto the ground in front of us. "Dig in," he said.

The students bombarded the bag, grabbing a variety of different gadgets and knickknacks from its contents. Without really looking, I snagged a little black box that looked like a walkie-talkie with a speedometer installed in front.

"Today, we are going to work on extended energy transfer by levitation," Alex said.

I had a flashing image of myself hovering four feet in the air at the shack. A feeling of nauseous dread leaked through my stomach. I looked over at Ander, but he was busy playing with two metal rods that kept clanging together.

"But first," Alex continued. "We need to get ourselves a boost!"

The rest of the group cheered and set out towards the forest. Most of the students were so used to getting a boost, that this was the easiest part of training. The easiest part for everyone except me. I was the only person in my grade without years of experience, and a lingering fear of death. Every time I came close to touching a spirit, I had a flashing image of my grandma's bulging eyes and slack jaw mouth on my mother's creamy carpet. The worst part was the smell. Even an odorless apparition of a half-rotted lynch victim stung my nose with memories of death's sharp stench.

Nevertheless, I was learning. And though the prospect of being within absorbing distance of a spirit still scared the crap out of me, I could now identify the different types of ghost.

Type 1: Spooks. The strongest and most dangerous form of spiritual energy. Due to their recorded appearance as a dark mist without human characteristics, they have historically been believed to be demonic entities. They are illegal to absorb recreationally, and often times require immediate action if unintentionally absorbed.

Type 2: Poltergeist. A very strong spirit that is often characterized by their ability to move physical objects, and utilize other sources of energy from electronics in order to increase their own power.

Type 3: Phantom apparitions. The most common type of spirit, often found to be attached to a haunted object, or place, due to an untimely or violent death. Levels of spiritual energy fluctuate, though they are almost always found to be reliving the last moments of life. Some are not aware that they are dead.

Type 4: Anomalies. The weakest form of spiritual energy. They are categorized as any manifestation of a shadow, orb of light, or mist.

As usual, I lagged behind the group. It gave me the advantage of being ignored, while also preventing me from experiencing a lot of the boosting going on in the group. After half an hour of walking, my speedometer clicked and the needle went haywire.

"Oh hey!" Molly came up behind me. "The extra credit has something."

I stared blankly at the little device as a few other students came over. Molly twisted her head in the air like a sniffing bloodhound and crept around a nearby tree. There was a flash of light, followed by the distinct smell of ozone, and she returned a second later, grinning hazily.

"Booyah."

Trevor hurried to catch up with her as she stalked away.

"No fair!" I heard him say as they rejoined the group.

I shook my head and continued on. Every so often, a student would break away and run toward a light, a shadow, or a fully developed apparition replaying the memory of its death.

The group neared a small clearing in the trees and I followed. The clearing was thick with overgrown sword ferns and large rocky boulders that made each step uneven under foot. As I sidled over to a sliver of sunlight near the back, I saw that someone was standing on top of the large rock we were gathered around. He had caramel-colored skin and was wearing only scattered remains of leather pants decorated with a variety of white feathers and beads. It was the ghost of a Native American Indian, and he was stained head to toe in dark red blood.

I shuttered and a rush of cold dread leaked through my body, pooling uncomfortable at my toes. Alex stepped forward and gestured up at the spirit.

"Who hasn't found a boost yet?"

Only two students raised their hands. I wasn't one of them.

"Hmm…" Alex scanned he crowd. "How about the extra credit?" he asked, smirking over at me.

Oh dear God.

The other students all turned to stare at me, a few snickering. I could feel the cold nervousness move through the rest of my body, and I knew my nose had gone white.

"Come on, Lidia. Let's do this! It's all yours," Alex said.

Students parted like the Red Sea as I made my way forward. When I reached the front of the group, Alex pointed to the rock and allowed me to pass him slowly. The ghost was staring sadly over the cascading cliffs of the mountain, I didn't think he could see any of us.

I can do this, I can do this.

I forced my fingers to grip the side of the rock, and I hoisted myself up. The cool stone stabbed at my skin, but I kept climbing until I was on top. I steadied my balance and made sure I was firmly in place before raising my eyes to meet the ghost in front of me.

"You have to let it in!" Alex yelled as I stared into the dead eyes of the ashy Native American man. Feathers were intertwined with the remaining bits of hair that hadn't been scalped. "You have to want it!" Alex shouted again.

I felt the eyes of the other students stripping me down, but all I could do was stare at the soft fleshy red patch on the top of his skull that dripped blood down the side of his face. It trailed off the tip of his nose and the sides of his cheeks, striping his face in dark crimson.

"I-I-I don't want it!" I swallowed but my mouth was dry. I heard laughter beneath me. *Breathe Lidia.* I took a breath, but it was difficult to open my mouth when my heart was thumping so hard it was about to leap out of my throat.

Let him in.

The ghost turned to me. His eyes were dark and vacant, as if he was seeing me from far away. One thick arm raked with blood reached toward me. His skull oozed juices, now thickening the strands of his hair in wet sections, dying the white feathers red.

"Do It!" Alex yelled.

I twitched my fingers, but wasn't able to move my arm. It was like mustering the willpower to reach out and touch an electric fence.

The man's chest abruptly began to glow with a blossoming bubble of warm light. His bloody figure flashed once, twice, and then disappeared, leaving Alex glowering at me in his place. "Pathetic," he said. Alex turned and leapt off the rock. I watched him lead the group away before I slowly slid off the rock and followed.

I scolded myself as I trailed behind, feeling the hot flush of embarrassment sting my cheeks. *They can do it. Why can't I? All I had to do was reach out and let him in.* I sighed heavily as the group reached the open part of the cemetery again.

155

Alex told everyone to take a thirty-minute lunch break and then pair up. I took the opportunity to hide behind a tombstone and close my eyes. Since it was October, the blaring sun didn't provide anything more than light, and it was freezing cold in the mountains.

Alex called us back over to him a little while later, and the group was paired off. I sat down in the grass and watched the others use the energy from their latest boost to fling each other around like rag dolls while Alex sauntered around the dueling pairs.

Trevor was paired with a short redheaded girl who kept swinging him into the air and then flipping him upside down. He laughed and dangled his arms above, or, beneath his head. His fingertips grazed the grass, making him look like a blond orangutan on a set of invisible monkey bars.

When it was Trevor's turn to use his boost, he had a bit of dificultly. I silently laughed into the fabric of my gloves as he struggled to get her more than a few inches off the ground. She would levitate barely an inch and then somehow fall flat on her back. After his second attempt, the pile of autumn leaves next to his partner started to smoke and Alex told him he was done for the day.

Working beside Trevor and his partner, was Ander and Molly. She twirled him gracefully in the air as he casually lounged in the vacant space two feet from the ground. They were obviously better practiced than most of the students, and they both knew it. Ander seemed comfortable hovering in the air, in fact, he seemed to like it. I watched them for a long time before I noticed Alex.

Alex was watching Molly like a hawk.

His supervision of the other groups was navigated with a distinct path that led straight back to Ander and Molly, over, and over again. Each time he came close, he would take the opportunity to instruct her unnecessarily. After his third circle around the students, Alex snuck behind Molly and watched absently until deciding to reach for her arm.

"Like this, Molly," he instructed, altering her outstretched arm. Alex's touch startled her, and Molly lost focus on her subject. Ander crashed to the ground, swearing at the abrupt fall his relaxed position hadn't prepared him for.

"Jesus, Alex!" Molly slapped his arm.

Alex laughed at Ander as he slowly stood and tried brushing the dirt from his pants.

"Sorry!" Alex shouted, looking quite thrilled. "Here, I'll take over for you." He stepped over to where Ander was glowering. "Molly," Alex instructed. "You need to back up a few feet, and keep your concentration focused."

Molly rolled her eyes and backed up.

"What am I supposed to do then?" asked Ander.

"Go work with Lidia." Alex gestured without looking over at me. "She needs it."

"What the hell am I supposed to do with her?"

"Just fling her up in the air a bit." Alex replied, still focused on Molly in front of him. "Remember the shack? She's used to it."

Ass.

Ander sighed and took a few steps in my direction. I stood up from the grass, but before I was even on my feet, I was hovering. I yelped and began wiggling in midair. I felt myself tip in each direction as if I was balancing on a floating raft.

"What the hell, Ander? I don't even get a warning?"

"What do you need a warning for?" He smirked up at me. Ander twirled his finger, and consequently, me as well. "You're not doing anything. Just relax."

I swore and a few on looking groups laughed.

"Yeah, extra credit! Get some!" Yelled a kid from behind me. I made a mental note to figure out who it was, and to give him a fat lip at the next opportune moment.

As Ander brought me further into the air, I struggled to grab hold of a low hanging tree branch. I only succeeded in grabbing a hand full of sappy needles and a pinecone. Ander spun me toward him and I stretched my arm back to throw the little cone as hard as I could. He saw it coming and ducked, dodging the flying cone, and losing all his concentration.

I landed hard on the ground, making a soft thud as my body hit the cool grass.

"Ouch."

Ander made a hesitant attempt to walk over, but stopped himself. "You okay?"

"I'm fine!" I stood and brushed the grass off.

"Why'd you throw that at me?"

I didn't respond.

Ander shook his head and started to laugh.

"Well, I'm glad you think it's funny," I said.

158

He shrugged and leaned against a headstone to watch me. "You did it to yourself." Ander adjusted the long sleeve of his black gear. "If you would've taken that boost, you could've had a turn levitating me."

I so regret not taking that boost.

"Whatever." I folded my arms and sank back into my original spot on the grass. As soon as my butt landed securely on the ground, it was three feet in the air again. "Ander!" I shrieked.

"I have to practice!" Ander laughed as I drifted closer toward him. "I'm going to keep you away from the trees though."

■ ■

As I did every Friday, I stayed behind with Alex for our private training session while the rest of the students packed up to go back to campus.

"I'm going to do it this time," I told Alex as we watched the rest of the students pile onto the bus. They were all laughing, some even looked as disheveled as I did.

The sky behind us was turning grey with dimming light, and the air was so cold it stung my cheeks. I envied all the students that would be wrapped in warm blankets soon, and I was looking forward to taking a hot shower in an empty locker room when I got back later that night.

"Good." Alex watched the last student walk onto the bus sourly. "Maybe we can finally get something done today." He turned back toward the cemetery and started climbing the large grassy hill. I stuck my tongue out at the back of his head and followed.

Besides the distant roar of the buses over the gravel road, I could already hear nighttime sounds of calling owls over the moans of the wind pushing through the cracks in the mountains. The headstones became few and far between as we continued to walk. When we finally stopped, it was completely dark and we had entered a part of the cemetery that was filled with large statuesque grave markers. Most were tall crosses on large square stones, but others were statues that towered overhead with solemn faces and blank granite eyes.

Alex withdrew a piece of electrical equipment from his back pocket and switched it on. There were dotted lights on the front of the device that kept moving like a winning carnival game. I peeked over his shoulder at the dial moving from left to right on the little screen.

"What is that?" I asked.

Alex began to walk absently, one step in each direction, feeling out the energy. "It's an EMF meter," he said.

"What's EMF?"

"Electromagnetic Field Meter. It picks up on the energy frequency of spirits."

I heard a shuffle of leaves and looked around at the surrounding headstones. A little ways into the distance, I could see movement behind a large statue of a crusading angel.

"I think I see something," I whispered.

Crap... I definitely see something.

Even from this far away, I could tell that it wasn't a fully formed apparition. It was a staring black mass, ominous, but obscure.

"Where?" Alex asked.

"Over there, behind the angel." Guiltily, I felt a rush of relief that it wasn't a full apparition. Alex wouldn't be happy, but I knew I still wasn't ready to absorb a fully formed ghost.

"I can't see that far." Alex squinted his eyes. "I should've worn my contacts."

"You have contacts?"

"Yeah."

"Why don't you just wear glasses?"

"Because I like getting laid." He smacked the EMF meter. "I'm not picking it up on the meter." Alex smacked it again. "Stupid-" he gave up and shoved it back in his pocket. "Okay, you know what to do. I'll stay here."

I nodded and took a deep breath before I made my way over to the shadowed figure. My shoes swept over the thick blanket of dirt and fallen leaves that were piled against each of the headstones. The cold air bit at my skin painfully, but I could barely feel it as cold nervous dread started to make its way to my hands and toes.

You can do this, keep calm.

I weaved between graves and large twisted maple trees, until I was only a few feet away from the crumpling stone angel and the shadowed figure beside it. I stopped when I felt my bones itch from the searing burn that snaked its way through my body. I raised my arm, about to step forward.

"Lidia! Run!" Alex roared. I looked back to see him barreling toward me, then I turned to look back at the shadowy figure.

But it wasn't a shadow anymore.

It had taken the solid shape of a mutated human body. Its knees were bent backwards into an aggressive crouch at the base of the stone angel. Its bald head swiveled up at me, revealing glossy black eyes and a gaping mouth lined with rows of sharp pointed teeth that jetted out from black gums.

"Oh ga-!" I stumbled backwards and fell. I scampered away in the dirt like a frightened animal. The creature started to approach slowly. It stretched each leg out at an unnatural angle and I heard the sound of popping joints with the movement. The thing heaved a pained breath of air, its throat crackling with a foul stench. It smelled rotten, a mixture of sickness and decaying flesh.

The thing continued to crouch as it approached, hunched over, crackling, oozing its foul smell through the fleshy sheen of its bare skin.

"Run, Lidia!"

I struggled to get up, but just as I stood to my feet, the creature reached out and jabbed a clawed finger toward me.

"No!" I kicked back and stumbled against a headstone. "Ah!" I felt the hot searing pain as the creature leapt forward again, skidding its claws against the black fabric covering the back of my knees. I leapt over the gravestone and backed away, but with each step back, the thing crept forward. There were thick veins in the black eyes that watched me with malice. The gaping mouth with the crackling breaths of a drowned lung seemed to smile. I was so petrified by fear that my body wasn't working. Instead of running, I felt myself sink to the ground.

I reached down to the spot the creature had scraped. There weren't any tears in the fabric of my gear, but the spot burned my flesh like fire.

Alex hoisted me off the ground and threw me out of the way. "Run!"

I did.

My heart thrummed painfully against my chest and my lungs screamed in sharp pain, but I ran. I reached the clearing and saw the hill leading to where Alex's car was parked. I stumbled across the lawn and stopped when I reached a tree on top of the hill. I looked around and waited in the dark. Alex hadn't followed me.

Oh man, oh man, oh man, oh man.

"Alex!" I took a step forward and stumbled on a rock. My heart was still pounding in my chest and my mind was still wiped blank from fear. "Where are you?" I whispered.

There was no reply.

I kept walking forward and my breathing was so loud I felt like I was screaming in the silence of the night.

Keep calm Lidia, calm.

I scanned a tiny dark speck in the distance through the trees.

"Alex?"

"Over here!" I heard him call. The sound came from behind me and a rush of relief washed through my body as I ran towards him.

"We have to get out of here." I looked back and saw that the dark spot in the distance was getting closer. "Alex?" I half whispered, half yelled. I went over to the side of a large fallen headstone near a bare willow tree. I felt the plush moss under my fingers as I dipped behind the headstone. "Alex? I don't see you," I whispered.

God, I can smell that thing from here.

"Over here."

I stood and turned toward the voice.

A long crackling breath erupted from the silent darkness.

"Here I am." It was Alex's voice, but it came from the warped mouth of the creature crouching across from me in the dark. My body froze, even my pounding heart went numb. Everything was cold.

I stumbled back until I was pressed against the rough bark of the tree. *That's a Spook.* The backward bending knees jolted out from behind its naked body as it scampered toward me.

This is it.

"Ahhgg!" Alex leapt from the bushes and intercepted the creature. He thrust a fist forward and the Spook leapt toward it, melting into a puddle of silver smoke on the ground. Alex's fist steamed, and then began to smolder white smoke as the remains of the puddle snaked its way toward his out stretched hand.

What?

He...

164

There was thick silence as the smoke continued to rise off the ground toward Alex, feeding into his fist.

That was a Spook.

What is he doing?

I peeled myself from the tree and felt my knees buckle slightly. "Alex?"

"Shut up!" He watched hungrily as the smoke continued to rise off the ground. Alex stayed there, fist outstretch to receive the lingering remains of the creature that had vanished. He stayed until the puddle of smoke was gone.

"Alex?" My heartbeat hammered wildly as I watched his warped expression of tortured pleasure. "Alex, what was that?"

"Nothing," Alex said as he shook his head hazily.

What has he done?

"C'mon, let's go." He grabbed his keys from his pocket and tossed them to me as he stumbled on nothing. "You drive."

I walked behind him as he took uneasy staggering steps toward the car. Every so often, he would mutter something and laugh to himself. Alex snorted and stumbled against the passenger side of the car.

I walked over to him and tried to pull him straight.

"Get off of me!" He grabbed both my arms and flung me backwards. I stumbled back and looked at him, unsure whether to be scared, angry, or thankful that he had just saved my life.

"Alex?" I asked carefully. "What did you do?"

"It's hot." Alex pulled his shirt off and then started yanking at the door handle again.

"Are you insane?" I picked his shirt off the ground and tried shoving it back into his hands. "It's freezing!"

"No." He ignored the shirt, but managed to open the door. I stormed over, got into the car, and sat impatiently as Alex fiddled with his seatbelt.

"What happened?" I asked again.

"Nothing. Can we just go?" He pointed drunkenly toward the road like I was an idiot.

"No."

"I blocked the Spook. Okay?" he said. "I saved your ass."

"What did it do to you?"

"Nothing! It's not a big deal. I'll just transfer the energy tomorrow, and I'll be fine." When I didn't say anything, he sighed and looked at me. His eyes seemed to clear momentarily, but his words where still slurred. "It's called a block. Everyone has to learn how to do it eventually." He looked away, muttering something under his breath.

"What?"

"I should've taught you earlier," he said.

I nodded. I still couldn't tell if he was okay or not, I didn't know if this was normal.

"If you crash my baby, I'll kill you." Alex reached out to stroke the dashboard lovingly.

I turned the keys and the car started up. "I don't doubt it." I switched the headlights on and pulled onto the gravel road. I drove in silence through the dark for a few minutes before speaking again. "Thanks for saving me back there."

My gratitude hung in the air, unacknowledged by Alex who was half-unconscious in the seat next to me.

Is he okay?

My head darted from the road and back to him, trying to catch the rise and fall of his chest in the blackness. He wasn't moving.

"Are you okay?"

"I'm fine." He thumped his head back against his seat. "So stupid. The one time you open up enough to let anything in, it's a freaking Spook." My panic settled at his reply, but I still didn't feel right.

Thankfully, Alex had put his shirt back on by the time we reached the school parking lot. He rudely commented on my less than perfect parking job, but seemed to be returning to his normal self again.

"Do you need me to open your door, or can you get it?"

Alex responded by mumbling something rude, and yanked the passenger side door open. I got out and stood with my arms crossed as the cold night air whipped my hair in every direction. It had to be late, more than half of the lights in the dorm building were out.

"I can take you to the nurse's office."

"No, I'm fine."

"I really think you should go, you just blocked a-"

"Don't!" Alex whirled to stare down at me. "Don't talk about this with anyone, okay? It's none of your business, and I didn't really have a choice because you went and almost got yourself tied up with a Spook."

"Because you never taught me what to do!"

"When you see black smoke, you run." His condescending tone dropped and I thought I saw him mouth the word- *idiot* to himself as he turned away.

"Well, duh." I sneered back. "Now that I know what comes out."

Alex stopped. "Comes out of what?"

"What comes out of the smoke."

"What came out of the smoke?" Alex's expression had softened into something that looked almost frightened.

Is he playing dumb?

I couldn't tell if he was messing with me or not. I felt like I was talking to a mobster about a secret drug deal that I witnessed, but conveniently "forgot" to protect my family from getting whacked.

"Hey," Alex snapped his fingers in front of my face, the fearful panic straining his expression. "What did you see?"

"I saw you block a Spook."

His tension seemed to ease slightly. "I'll teach you next Friday, okay? For now, don't tell anyone. They'll get the wrong idea."

And why would they do that?

"Okay?" he asked again.

"Okay."

Alex nodded. "Good." He held a hand out for the keys, and I gave them to him like an obedient dog. "Goodnight," Alex said before he turned and strutted towards the dorms.

Chapter 13

On Monday, I sat at my usual table near the back of the cafeteria, eating my toast alone. I tore a piece off and dipped it into my mug. The butter melted and created a swirling oil stain that snaked across the surface of my black coffee. I stared at it for a moment, counting the floating crumbs.

I hadn't slept at all over the weekend. I was constantly torn between telling Ander about the Spook, and just keeping it to myself. The problem was that I wasn't sure if Alex really absorbed a Spook, or if he had blocked it. If Alex was meddling in dark spirits, I would tell Ander without hesitation, but I just wasn't sure and I didn't want to look like an idiot. The last thing I needed was another reason for people to make fun of me because I couldn't recognize a block from absorption if it danced naked in front of me wearing a neon cowboy hat.

I looked past the crowd of students to see Ander laughing with the rest of his table. The grey light leaking through the window on the far wall promised rain, but the gloomy forecast hadn't dampened the mood at their table. As I watched, Molly ran her hand through Ander's hair as he laughed and mirrored the gesture to Jeff. Feeling he was at risk of exposing a bare head, Jeff clung to the hat as Ander and Jessica tried to tousle it off him.

I sighed.

What would Ethan think?

My imagination conjured a dim image of Ethan sitting in the seat in front of me. *Wow, am I so lonely that I'm making imaginary friends now?*

Across from me, Ethan nodded in reply and took a bite of toast. *Lidia, I think you need to tell Ander. I mean, think about his family life as it is now.* Ethan chewed on the toast and swallowed. *Sister is fighting cancer, and now his brother is getting mixed up in dark energy...you owe it to him. If he knows about Alex before it's too late, maybe he can stop anything bad from happening.*

I don't owe him anything.

He practically saved your life. Ethan shook his head, looking back at the group, and then back at me. *You know you wouldn't have made it without him bringing you here.*

It's him bringing me here that has ruined my life. I mentally scowled at Ethan from across the table. *Plus, he has been a complete ass this entire time.*

After a few more seconds in my head, I concluded that imaginary Ethan was right. I just hoped Alex wouldn't get the chance to actually kill me for telling on him.

∎∎∎

When I got to chemistry later that morning, I took my usual seat in the back of the room. I noticed that each of the tables had a piece of paper with a number written on it. Mr. Radford took a sip of coffee at his desk before he stood up and started passing out more numbers to each student entering the room. When he passed by my desk, he gave me the number four.

"What are the numbers for?" asked Sarah Mitchell, a tall lanky brunette who played on the girls' basketball team.

"We are doing a fun class activity today in celebration of completing our first exam."

I groaned inwardly.

"Go ahead and find the table that correlates with your number," Mr. Radford said.

I got up and shuffled past a few other students until I reached the table marked four. As Mr. Radford greeted incomers from the doorway, I stared out the window. It was impossible to tell if the sun had already risen or not due to the onslaught of rain pounding the glass.

The seat next to mine slid back and someone sat down. I looked over to see Ander, ignoring me as usual.

"Great," I muttered. *Now I really have to tell him about Alex.*

"What'd you say?" he asked.

"Nothing." I reached for my backpack laying on the floor and pretended I was looking for something.

"Good morning class!" Mr. Radford's booming voice greeted the classroom. "Today we are going to have a little fun!" He walked over to his desk and retrieved a stack of papers. "But first, I'm going to hand back the test from last week."

My stomach sank as Mr. Radford made his way down the aisle. I watched solemnly as faces fell and rose in accordance to the test score etched onto the front page of their last chemistry exam.

Mr. Radford reached our table and placed a test face down in front of Ander. When Ander flipped it over a second later, I saw a large B written at the top. I sighed and reached out to take the test Mr. Radford passed my way. I already knew I failed, so I didn't even bother checking the score.

Mr. Radford crouched down and spoke in a loud whisper over the babble of the students. "Now, I understand that Mr. Dodger has set you guys up as a tutoring pair?"

"Yeah," I said. "Ander's my tutor." *He just never tutors me.*

"What days do you usually meet?"

Both Ander and I answered in unison.

"Tuesday."

"Wednesday."

"Right." Mr. Radford knew we were lying. "Well, based off these scores, I think the two of you would get the best use of your study time in the library during my office hours." He looked back and forth between us, daring a protest. "Does Wednesday work for both of you?"

We nodded and Mr. Radford stalked off to deliver the rest of the tests.

"So," Ander said without looking at me. "Every Wednesday?"

"I guess so."

"Sweet."

"Are you being sarcastic?"

"No," he said sarcastically.

172

I sighed and slumped further into my seat.

After Mr. Radford had finished with the test, he started passing out pictures of the human tongue. I hadn't ever given it a lot of thought before, but the tongue is really quite disgusting. The picture made it look like a thick pink slug surrounded by teeth poking out of shiny gums like a white picket fence.

Gross.

"Okay," Mr. Radford said. "Time for the fun part!"

A kid named Kyle cheered, but the rest of the classroom groaned in unison. Mr. Radford hushed the class and started passing out blindfolds and Tupperware boxes that were spray painted black.

"What we're going to do today is learn about the human sensory system," said Mr. Radford.

Dale Becker made an attempt to open the box but was intercepted by Mr. Radford's hand.

"Keep them closed," Mr. Radford said. "You and your partner are going to take turns using your senses to identify what's in the box, but you'll be doing it with a blindfold." He reached our table and gave us a box and a blue bandana blindfold. "Once you have smelled, felt, tasted, and even listened to the object in the box, I want you to write your table number, what the item is, and where on the tongue the flavor was most prominent." Mr. Radford reached the last table and threw up his now empty hands. "Have fun!"

Fun... right.

The moment Mr. Radford ended his speech, the classroom erupted into loud conversation. I looked over at Ander who was staring at me.

"So," Ander started. "Do you want me to blindfold you first, or-" he trailed off, fingering the piece of cloth in his hands and wearing a smug expression.

"You first." I snatched the bandana and gestured for him to turn. When he did, I draped the cloth around his eyes and tied it as tightly as I could. Secretly, I hoped cutting off the circulation to Ander's head would make him faint. Maybe then we would be excused from class.

"Ouch. Ah, Lidia." He swatted my hand away from the quadruple knot I was tying. "Is Ethan into this crap? I feel like you've done this before."

"Shut up." I reached over for the black box sitting at the edge of the table. A kid named Jay sat close to his partner at the table in front of us. Jay had his head towards the ceiling, trying to stare down his nose and view the contents of their black box from beneath the blindfold. Their box looked orange and mushy.

Sweet potatoes?

Ander's long arms stretched out into the space in front of him. "Hello? Is my partner still here?" He moved his arm so that it gently tapped the side of my face.

Ander couldn't see the cold stare I was giving him.

"Oh, there you are." He rested one hand on top of my head. "In case you forgot, I'm blind!"

I shook my head and his hand fell away.

Kidnapping, stuck up, smart ass, jerk.

I peeled back the lid of our box and revealed a giant glob of red jam inside. "Okay, here. Feel, smell, taste, whatever." I slid the box toward him and he reached out to find it. Ander's mouth curled down in confused horror when his fingers mushed into the gooey red substance.

"Gross, what'd you give me?"

"That's for you to find out."

"Yuck." Ander prodded it a few more times. "Should I taste it?"

"Sure."

He scowled with distrust, but after a second, he brought his index finger to his mouth and licked it. "Huh." Deciding the taste wasn't unsatisfactory, he sucked each finger clean. "Mm," Ander's lips broke into a wicked smile. "Raspberry jam."

"Right." I wrote it down on the paper.

"You sure you don't want any?" he teased. "Hey Lidia, remember the raspberry stand?"

You mean the day you kidnapped me?

When he chuckled to himself at my lack of response, a flash of hot anger flooded my cheeks. Without even thinking, I reached my hand into the tub of jam and smeared a thick red glob across the side of his face.

I immediately felt better.

"What the-?" Ander spluttered and tried to yank off the blindfold. The knot was too tight to undo, so he forced it off his head. When he finally got it off, his hair was a mess, but instead of flatting it like he usually did, he brought a hand to his cheek and felt the red stain of jam gently sliding down the side of his face. Ander's blue eyes jumped from his fingers to me and back again. An uncontrollable smile split across my face as he stared.

The tables surrounding ours saw his reaction to the surprise jam attack and started laughing, but Ander just continued to stare. "You just-"

I started to collapse into a fit of giggles. Something wet and squishy pressed against my left cheek. I looked up at Ander, his fingertips covered with a fresh patch of thick red goo.

"Hey!" I went to grab the jam again, but Ander slid it out of reach, laughing.

"What's going on?" boomed Mr. Radford as he jogged toward our table. I stole one more attempt to throw a glob of jam at Ander before turning innocently to Mr. Radford.

I blinked. "He started it."

"What? No way, you are such a liar!"

"Who started this?" Mr. Radford growled.

Both Ander and I pointed at each other as the rest of the class tried to stifle their snickers.

"Detention! Both of you!" Mr. Radford shouted.

Damn it.

The rest of the class fell silent.

"This is the last time we do a fun class activity! Both of you are excused to go wash up, but I will be making a visit to Mr. Dodger immediately to arrange detention. Ridiculous. I'm not paid to babysit children."

My good mood vanished as abruptly as it had come.

"Go! Now!"

I felt better after getting a lecture. Mr. Dodger was probably my favorite person in the entire school. He had attempted to be stern at first, explaining all the dangerous consequences of playing around with preservatives, but failed to appear disapproving as he soon lapsed into an hour long story of how his mother used to jam all sorts of fruits. Peaches were Mr. Dodger's favorite.

Unfortunately for us, it was Mr. Radford that chose the detention.

Which was horrible.

Ander and I were instructed to clean every stall in the girl's bathroom on the third floor of the main building. For the most part, we cleaned in silence, broken only by the squirt of a bottle and the scratches of the scrub brush.

My arm ached as I rubbed furiously over stall gossip about how much of a slut Mindy Johnson was.

She's a super senior?

She hooked up with Dale Becker?

Gross.

At least it was interesting to read. Since I didn't have any friends at Mountain Heights, I was constantly out of the loop on social happenings. I was surprised, and a little hurt that my name seemed to come up a lot too.

Lidia has four arms.

Lidia Powell talks to spiders.

Lidia knows what you did last summer.

They were all ridiculous, and none of them made any sense. Still, the fact that someone wanted to write about me in the girl's bathroom let me know that I wasn't as invisible as I felt. I would rather be invisible than made fun of, but at least they didn't say anything really mean.

Maybe it was Molly.

What really got my blood boiling was that Ander seemed to think they were hilarious. First Ander would scrub the stall walls, then I would come in and finish the job. He would clean the graffiti until they were faint markings in the wood, all the graffiti except the ones alluding to me. Then he'd come out of the stall and ask if he could see my other two arms, or ask me what my favorite spider word was.

I let my arm fall, unable to hold it any longer. I had just finished the second stall in the second to last bathroom on the third floor. I pushed a piece of fallen hair from my half ponytail, and sighed. It felt like detention had gone on for hours and I wondered how long it would take us to finish cleaning.

At least Ander had to suffer too.

"Are you done yet?" I asked.

"Yeah."

I pushed out of the stall just as Ander entered into the other. The new stall walls were freshly scrubbed and there was a faint lingering smell of Windex. Amongst the faded gossip was another line written in black pencil.

Lidia Powell eats bacon... and she likes it.

I stared at the wall.

"What?" I whispered. This lie wasn't even funny, and no one at Mountain Heights even knew I was a vegan except for-

"Oh my God," I said.

I stormed over to the next stall and saw Ander sitting with his back to the wall, a pencil in the hand that was leaving fresh graffiti across the vandalized stall door.

"Are you kidding me?" I shouted.

Ander jumped slightly, and turned. "What?"

For the second time in one day, I acted before I thought.

I hurtled myself toward Ander, dropping my scrub brush and cleaner as I crashed onto him. I was immediately wrestled to the ground. He swore in surprise, but after only seconds, he pinned me against the cold tile floor and secured my arms with his large hands above my head.

"Get off me!" I struggled against him.

Ander held me down. "No, you attacked me!"

"You were writing about me!"

"It was joke, lighten up."

"Uhg!" Infuriated, I actually growled. "I can't believe you! I was cleaning the stalls and you're over there making more mess for me to clean!"

"It was a pencil," Ander half smiled, half scoffed. It was a surprise smile, like the type that just happen when you're too shocked to react with anything other than humor. "God, you are seriously psycho," he said.

"I'm not psycho!" I wriggled, but his weight smothered me to the cold floor. "This. Is. So. Gross!" I gasped. "Let me off the floor you kidnapping-life-ruining-jerkoff!" I twisted an arm free, but before I could make use of it, Ander slammed it back against the tile.

I looked up at him hovering just inches above me.

Ander was pissed.

"What the hell is your problem, Lidia?" he said. "I get that-" Ander pushed harder against me as I writhed. "Just hold still!"

Exhausted, I gave up my struggle and settled for glaring at him instead.

"I get that this hasn't been awesome for you. I know you left Ethan, and that it sucks, but I thought you understood." Ander let out a gush of air as I wriggled beneath him again. He didn't let up. "I never should've brought you here!"

"Mr. Radford said we can't leave until each stall is cleaned!"

Ander rolled his eyes, exasperated. "He has to let us go by curfew, which is in five minutes."

I stopped moving.

"Why do you care anyways?" Ander continued. "You've got places to go?"

This floor is so nasty!

"Friends to see?" he prodded.

"No, I don't have any friends!" The back of my eyes burned and I tried harder to get out of his grip. "In case you haven't noticed, no one likes the extra credit!"

Oh my God, it smells like urine and bleach down here.

"Well, you haven't exactly been very friendly, what do you expect?" Ander's blue eyes stared straight at mine, and for a moment, I forgot to answer.

"I have been friendly. I've talked to a lot of people and everyone treats me the exact same way as you do."

"What are you talking about?"

"You've been ignoring me since school started, asshole!"

Ander stared down at me, incredulous. "You've been ignoring me! I was trying to give you space since you seemed to hate me so much."

Well, can't argue with you there.

"You can't blame a guy for trying not to get punched again," said Ander.

I realized he wasn't holding me in place anymore and I pushed him off. I stood quickly and brushed the invisible germs from my hair.

"I'm sorry you thought I was ignoring you." Ander was looking up at me from the spot on the bathroom tile where he was still crouching. His eyes were as intense as ever, more so with his gentle sincerity.

I shrugged. "Sorry for punching you... sort of."

Anders face split into a reluctant smile and his eyes focused on mine again.

I heard the creek of the bathroom door swinging open. "Okay, enough is enough. Get to your rooms before curfew." Mr. Radford's voiced echoed across the tiled bathroom.

Ander shot up from his spot on the ground. We exited the stall together, and Mr. Radford raised a surprised eyebrow as we passed.

181

"And if this happens again, I'll have you do the men's bathrooms!" Mr. Radford shouted for good measure as we scampered past him towards our separate dorms.

Chapter 14

Beeeep

The waffle maker sounded the alarm and I quickly retrieved my breakfast, moving aside to allow the next in line their turn.

The waffle wasn't my best creation. It was a little bit too crispy on the ends and bits of batter weren't cooked through which left holes in the middle. I decided the best way to rectify the damage was to fill the holes with as much syrup as possible. The result was a work of art. The waffle looked like a collection of square craters with lakes full of thick brown goo.

"Hey."

I turned and saw Ander standing behind me in the breakfast line. "Hi." I went back to my waffle. *Does it need more syrup?*

"Uh, what are you doing?"

"Art."

"I see," he said. "Do you have plans for breakfast this morning?"

I dripped a golden stream of syrup carefully into every other waffle square. "Besides eating?"

"No, uh, did you want to come sit with us today?"

I looked back at him, surprised. "Sit with you guys?" I turned back to the syrup and tried to relax my face. "Why are you so friendly all of a sudden?"

"Well, we were friends at camp." Ander shrugged with a smile. "I want to rekindle this friendship."

No point, I'll probably die in a week from the sixteen different bacterial viruses I contracted from the bathroom floor last night.

"I mean," he continued. "Unless you want to keep eating with all those seventh graders you sit with."

"I do not sit with seventh graders"

I sit next to them.

"Are you done yet?" The girl in line behind me was waiting impatiently for the waffle condiments.

"Oh, yeah, sorry." I set the syrup down and left the line to walk with Ander. "Are you sure they want me to sit with them?" I eyed his table with concern.

It was in a good spot. The light streaming through the window illuminated the plastic wood and bounced off the back of their heads to create soft halos. It was much better than the dark corner I hid in.

"It'll be fine. If I invited you, you're practically an official group member."

"You have to be a group member to eat at your table?"

"V.I.P."

"Wow, like a real club. Do you guys have a name?"

"The uh, Ghost... boosters."

"Ghost boosters," I laughed. "Very creative."

As we approached, Molly looked up and her brow furrowed in confusion.

"Good morning," Ander sat his tray down next to her. He gestured casually for me to take the seat across from him, next to Trevor. "I invited Lidia to sit with us today."

There was a beat of silence as everyone looked back and forth between the two of us, puzzled.

"Hi, I'm Jessica." Jessica waved. "That's Jeff," she pointed to Jeff who looked at me quickly before averting his eyes and smothering the beanie to his head. "And-"

"I'm Trevor." Trevor cut her off as he slid one arm across the back of my chair, extending the other for me to shake.

"Hello." I shook his hand, noticing that he really needed some lotion.

"Wow," Trevor said, leaning forward until he was dangerously close to popping my personal bubble. "You have beautiful eyes."

"Uh, okay. Thanks." I let out a short laugh and slid forward in my chair to gain an inch of space.

"She's taken." Ander took a bite of bacon and smiled warmly at me from across the table. "That's Ethan's girlfriend."

"Aw," Trevor removed his hand and backed away.

"Technically, we're on a break," I said. Molly rolled her eyes but I ignored her and nodded at Trevor in appreciation. "Not that I'm available anyways, but thank you."

"Yep." Trevor shrugged and took a bite of food, completely disinterested now that he knew I was off the market.

"Have you heard from Ethan?" Ander asked.

I shook my head. "Have you?"

"Yeah, he wrote a few days ago."

A little pang of hurt shot through my gut. "Did he say anything about me?"

"He told me to watch out and see if you were hanging out with other guys. I'm his spy."

Though the thought of Ethan ignoring me was hurtful, I was relieved that he was at least still thinking of me. If he wanted to make sure I wasn't with anyone else, then he obviously still cared. He wouldn't need a spy if he didn't care.

"What did you say?" I asked.

"I told him you were a hermit." Ander's blue eyes twinkled.

"Well, I guess that's accurate." I turned my attention to my waffle and started stabbing it.

The rest of the table turned to normal conversation while I continued to play with my food. I wasn't making a very good impression with Ander's friends, but I didn't really care. Their voices meshed into one lyrical stretch of sound through the collective chatter of the room.

Why does Ethan care if I'm with someone else? What does this break even mean? Does that mean we're still dating?

"Um, hello?" I looked up to see Molly staring at me. For once, she wasn't glaring. "Earth to Lidia."

"What? Sorry."

Everyone except Ander was watching me. "Are you nervous about your SETT?"

"Oh yeah!" Jessica clapped her hands. "You haven't taken those yet."

"No, I'm supposed to take them this winter... but I might push it up to the spring because Alex-"

I never told Ander about Alex.

"He uh," I continued. "I don't know if I'll actually pass." I wanted to blurt it out, but I wasn't sure if I should mention it in front of everyone.

"You'll do fine," Molly reassured me. "You've been training with Alex, right?" She turned to look at a table by the window where Alex sat. I was surprised to see that it wasn't the same trainer table where he had been sitting the first day. Instead, he was with three other students. Closest to Alex was Jason, the rat-faced blond kid whose brother was in jail for murder.

Great, now I really need to tell him.

Ander let out an aggravated sigh and took a few violent bites of food. "I don't know why he hangs out with those losers," he said. His eyes were fixed on the table. "Idiot."

"It's because they make him feel like a big man," Jessica reassured him. "They're the only people who think he's cool, so naturally, he wants the ego boost."

They continued talking until the bell rang, and breakfast ended. Everyone stood up, emptied their trays, and left the cafeteria. Trevor accompanied me and Ander on our way to chemistry for a few minutes before he veered off towards his own class.

187

"Ander," I reached out and touched his arm.

Ander stopped walking and students spilled around us as I pulled him over to the wall and lowered my voice.

"I need to talk to you."

"What's up?" he asked curiously.

"What does a block look like?"

Ander half laughed, as if I was joking. "What do you mean?"

"What does it look like? What happens when you do it?"

"Uh," he was still smiling. "Hasn't Alex taught you that yet?"

"No."

"Okay, well, it's just sort of a shimmer around you. If a Spook hits it, then they dissolve."

"Like, into a puddle?"

"What?" He looked confused. "No, they just disappear. Why? What happened?"

I felt my stomach sink and my heart rate spike as I geared up for the confession. "I think Alex absorbed a Spook."

Ander's face froze. He stood there looking at me like he hadn't heard, it made me uncomfortable so I averted my gaze from his intense stare. Students were filing into classrooms and the hall around us was nearly empty.

"What?" Ander finally spoke. "What happened?"

The final bell rang, the sound cut through the empty halls. Dale Becker jogged past us with his backpack hunched over his shoulders, and then we were alone.

"Last Friday at training a Spook almost got me. We were in the back of Walden, I went towards a dark shadow, then he told me to run, and when I looked back, it was just this- *thing*. So I ran, and then it found me again. When it was coming after me, Alex saved me by jumping in front of it. He turned it to smoke and it made this puddle, and it just went into his hand."

Ander's intense gaze was glued to mine despite the obscene hand gestures I used to retell the story. The sunlight that came through the windows lit half of his face, casting the other half in shadows. It made one eye look translucent and bright while the other was a stormy blue.

"Why didn't you tell me sooner?" His voice was just barely a whisper.

"I wasn't sure if I should. Alex told me that he blocked it, but, I'm not sure if he really did."

"He didn't," Ander swore. "I have to find Jeff... uh, can you not mention this to anyone. Please?"

"Yeah, of course."

Ander's stricken face nodded once and then he turned to walk away.

"Ander," I called out.

"Yeah?"

"I'm sorry."

Ander shook the apology off and waved absentmindedly as he sped down the hall and turned the corner.
■■■

As I sat in a corner of the library next to Ander, I was briefly reminded of a scary movie I had once seen. Empty library, shelves of forgotten paperbacks, and an ultra violet light blaring unpleasantly overhead that made the dark window to my left a mirror. Thinking of the movie, I kept feeling like a mummified Mr. Radford would come stumbling out of his office at any moment.

"Are you finished yet?"

"No."

"Well, focus." Ander had already finished his homework and was doodling on a piece of notebook paper as I tried to finish mine.

"Just let me copy yours."

"No way, I'm supposed to be helping you learn."

"It would help me learn."

"Just hurry up, you're taking forever."

I let out a long gush of air and my head flopped onto the desk.

Ander had extended the invitation to sit with his table at meals daily, until it eventually became routine. It was weird at first, but as the weeks went by, I finally felt like part of the group. Ander and I met in the library after dinner on Wednesdays to work on homework, Jessica sat next to me in English nearly every day, and even Molly was pleasant.

The only part of my schedule that had changed was Friday night training with Alex. After I had told Ander about his brother, he had gotten into a fight with Alex in the student lounge. The rumor was that Ander had inconspicuously pinned Alex to a chair using a boost as they spoke. When Alex retaliated by chucking a book at Ander's head, they were both sent to see Mr. Dodger, and Ander got detention. After that, Alex refused to train me for our private lessons, and Ander was constantly in a bad mood.

Ander had told the rest of group about Alex the next day as we sat in the plush couches of the student lounge. Besides the loud group of boys next to us using the pool table for what looked like a raunchy game of truth-or-dare, the room was empty, and we weren't overheard. I could tell by the way Ander spoke, that what I had watched Alex do at Walden Cemetery was a bigger deal than I thought. I knew it was bad, but I didn't fully understand how bad it was.

After that, the days seemed to blur together in a comfortable rhythm. I never mentioned it to Ander, partially because he already knew, and partially because he was already stressed out, but my nonexistent training lessons with Alex were making me nervous. Without the extra help, I wasn't sure if I would pass the SETT... not to mention chemistry.

"Here," Ander slid the textbook toward me. "Read this section, then try."

I sighed loudly before I read the thick chunk of black text. *To find the volume for Oxygenproduced, you are given pressure and temperature, so to determine vol-*

God, this is boring.

"How do you guys absorb spirits so calmly?" I asked randomly.

Ander looked up. "What do you mean?"

"How do you deal with it? When you see them all bloody and ripped apart, you can guess who they were when they were alive, and now they're stuck reliving the worst

191

moment of their life." I shifted uncomfortably. "Every time I see one, I feel like they're trying to tell me their story, and I don't want to hear it. Like, they want to take me with them, and have me dead too so that I can feel how sad they are."

Ander watched me steadily, seemingly impressed with my little outburst. "They are." He wrote something on his paper and looked back up. "But spirits don't want to kill, just communicate. They're stuck in the routine of their memory until they achieve what they needed release from, or something else disrupts the pattern, like us. We're an outlet. When we absorb their energy, we disrupt the pattern of memory and usually they're able to move on."

"So, every time I absorb a dead guy I help him go into the afterlife?"

"Sometimes, yeah." He went back to his doodling. "It's practically charity work."

"Where do they go after they pass on?"

Ander shrugged. "I don't know."

"How do you not know?"

"Nobody knows. Talking to a ghost is impossible. They just ramble."

"We talked to a ghost at the shack."

"Using a recorder doesn't count."

"Have you ever seen a Spook?"

"Yeah," Ander's gaze flickered up at me. "Once when I was on vacation, and once during the SETT."

My stomach sank. "They test you on Spooks?"

Ander nodded.

"Were you afraid?" I asked.

"Not really." Ander's head turned back to his paper. "But I am afraid of Mr. Radford giving us another detention if you don't get your homework done."

Darn.

I turned back to my book. *To find the volume of Oxygen, you must first mul-*

"No!" Ander hissed. I looked up and saw him squinting out the window. "He's so dead." Ander threw his notes and textbook into his backpack and stood up.

"What's going on?" I asked, packing my bag as well.

"I just saw-" he stopped himself and turned away. "I'll just see you tomorrow." Ander strode quickly away toward the double doors leading down the stairs.

"Wait!" I slung my backpack on and scurried after him. "What's going on? What's wrong?"

"Nothing." He glanced at a clock on the wall. "It's ten past curfew anyways. Go back to your dorm before you get caught out."

"No way!" This was exciting.

"Lidia," Ander growled.

"Just tell me what's going on."

Ander sighed, still running down the steps faster than I could follow. "I think I just saw Alex and Jason." We turned the corner and continued downstairs. "If you follow me, you'll get in huge trouble when we're caught." He raked a hand through his hair. "I can't believe this."

"Trouble's my middle name."

"Fine, hurry up." Ander sped up and I quickened my pace as we veered into the entry hall.

"Don't they monitor these things?" I asked as we pushed through the grand front doors and stepped out into the brisk night air. "Students could sneak out all the time."

"They mostly just monitor the halls leading to the dorms."

We jogged across the field toward the tall wall of trees in front of us. I took a gulp of freezing air and seconds later, we were in the woods. Somehow, everything got darker.

"Stay close," Ander whispered.

The gloom of the forest at night was palpable, and I kept within an inch behind Ander as we treaded quietly over tree roots and uneven mounds of dirt.

"You saw Alex and Jason?" I asked in a half whisper.

"And others."

"How many of them did you see out here?"

"I thought I saw four, including Alex."

"How did you know it was him?" I stepped on something that jetted out of the ground and grabbed his arm to steady myself. "Ouch, sorry."

"You're fine." Ander helped me up, and we continued to stagger through the broken pieces of nature in the woods. "I could tell it was Alex by his walk."

"He does walk like a rooster."

"Only when he thinks people are watching."

"What do you think they're doing out here?" A bug flew into the side of my face and I swatted it away. "Are they looking for a ghost?"

"No," Ander trailed off, listening to something.

"Do they even have ghost this far away from the cemetery?"

"No, they have Ultrasonic Spirit Meters out here. If they didn't, students would be in here for a boost all the time."

"Where?" I shot my head around in the dark to look for the little red light coming from a block hidden in the trees. "I don't see any red lights-"

"Shhh- listen..." There was shouting in the distance, and we followed it aimlessly.

"Where is it coming from?"

"I'm not sure." Ander scanned the trees. "Maybe this way," he took a few steps nearing the echoed woops and calls from the forest.

My foot caught on something hard, and I fell face first onto a bare patch of earth. Cold, moist dirt prodded the soft flesh of my cheek.

"You okay?" Ander's voice sounded from a few feet ahead of me. He crashed into something that sounded like a fern.

"Yeah, fine." The ground smelled like earth and... vanilla. My hands touched on something waxy and smooth, connected with something that felt like thick cobwebs.

195

"What the-" I scampered up from the spot to stare at a large circle carved into the dirt where I was standing. The moonlight was shining just enough so that I could make out the details. Amongst the twigs, leaves, and bark, I could see the faint shape of a spiked symbol, connecting five points of a circles edge. The waxy object I had felt was the burnt remains of a melted candle, and the cobwebs were real strands of black human hair.

"Ander," my voice broke. "You need to see this."

Ander stepped through the circle without noticing it. He searched my face in concern. "What?" he said, taking another step closer. "What is it?"

"Look," I pointed to the ground and his eyes went wide.

Ander leap out of the circle and stood at my side as we both stared. "It's a summoning circle," he said. "They were trying to call dark energy." He reached down and picked up something off the ground.

"What's that?" I asked.

The echoed cries of voices in the forest faded slightly.

"Spirit Meter," he croaked. Ander's face went slack as he stared down at the device in his hands. "They busted it. It's completely broken."

Ghost.

"So, there might be a Spook out here."

"Maybe."

I reached down to feel the candle wax. Most of the surface was hardened in the cold air, but my fingers met with one soft spot. "It's still a little warm, they were just here."

Ander cursed under his breath. "We have to go."

The sound of Alex and the others came again, louder, closer.

"We have to go now," he said and yanked on my arm, pulling me back through the forest. We made our way through the trees, blinded by the darkness. "Hurry!"

Branches snapped in the distance behind us, and the voices became coherent.

They're close.

"Ander!" I caught hold of his arm to stop him. "Shhh! If we keep running, they'll hear us."

Ander nodded as he scanned the woods. We crept behind a large cedar tree and tried to steady our breathing as we leaned against the shredded bark. A second later, I heard Alex and the boys approach. They crashed haphazardly through the dirt and bushes, breaking branches and kicking rocks.

Peeking out from behind the tree, I saw four dark figures stumbling toward us in the distance. Two were supporting each other's weight, singing a vulgar song drunkenly. The tallest, Alex maybe, was abolishing every living bush within six feet by blasting a long electric stream of blue energy from his palm. It left little smoldering piles of ash in its wake, and polluted the air with the scent of burning green.

My heartbeat thrummed.

"You, ha-ha, you're going to light the foressst on fire," slurred the boy next to Alex.

"Shut up, Jason," Alex barked.

I could see the outline of each face in the blue apex of Alex's energy beams. The scream of the electricity sounded again as it hit a nearby fern, incinerating it completely. The static in the air made each of my hairs stand on end and I shuffled closer to Ander.

Oh my God.

"Man," sighed one of the singing boys. "You're using up your entire boost."

I closed my eyes and pressed my back against the tree.

"I can't have all this power at training." Alex let out a short laugh. "Can you imagine if that little redheaded fuck tried pairing with Molly again, and then-" an explosive bolt of electric blue hit a branch overhead and exploded into a million slivers. I gasped, almost screamed, but Ander's hand flew over my mouth to stifle the cry.

"What was that?" One of the boys had stopped walking. "I heard something."

Their footsteps stopped and they stood silently, listening to nothing.

"I didn't heard anythin'... c'mon," slurred the other, giggling like a fool as he kicked something hard with a dull thud.

Ander's hand slowly withdrew and I looked up at him in the dark. His long hair danced across his forehead with the wind and he tilted his head to signal the direction we should move. I nodded and followed him a little nearer to the clearing. We stepped gently over soft bark and twigs with measured steps.

I could see it, the glorious grass clearing of the campus lawn through the thin layer of trees.

"Over here guys," one of Alex's friends said. "I heard something!" There was a stampede of breaking twigs as they all jogged closer.

Oh no.

Ander cursed softly and drew me close to him against another tree. I heard the unmistakable zap of electricity and a faint squeal as Alex electrocuted something that must've been alive. I tried to slow my breathing, but that only made it come out harder in a disjointed rhythm.

"Hello?" called Jason, nearing our spot in the dark. "Anybody out here?" I could see the profile of his pointed rat face only a few feet away. "Come out, come out, wherever you are."

He's going to find us.

"I've got a little surprise for whoever decided to follow us out here... you sneaky son of a bitch."

Ander whirled me so that I had my back pressed firmly against the tree, it's knobby bark jetted into my back. He ran his hands through his hair and looked at me with strained determination.

"Go with it, okay?" he whispered.

I nodded.

More footsteps neared as Alex joined Jason. It was completely inevitable that we would be found. *What's our excuse? They'll know we followed them out here and-*

Ander pressed his chest against mine and slid his hand down my leg until my knee was propped slightly against his hip. I pushed back, completely alarmed at his sudden closeness, but

Ander held my leg in place, and my skirt slipped to reveal a sliver of bare skin.

"Go with it," Ander hissed quietly in my ear. "Trust me." His cool lips brushed the skin of my neck.

Ander was kissing my neck.

I froze, but then my body relaxed, and I involuntarily sank into the compressed space between his body and the tree.

Stage kisses...Genius...Alex will think-

Ander's lips moved across my neck, slowing with each brush of contact. The hand he used to stabilize my leg to his hip tightened, and his fingers dug themselves into my skin. My breathing became staggered as the kisses against my throat deepened and...*was that his tongue?*

A gush of cool static ripped Ander away from me, and thrust him powerfully against a neighboring tree.

"Ander!" I cried out in surprise.

"No way!" Alex crashed through the trees.

There was a rupture of collective laughter from the group as one boy after another piled together to see the spectacle that Jason had exposed.

"Told you guys I heard something," he chuckled darkly.

"I c-c-can't believe it!" laughed Alex, doubling over to control his breath. "My brother with the extra credit!" He shook his head and his laughter died. "And have you told Ethan that you're banging his girl yet? I bet he'll be really happy to hear about that."

"Leave Ethan out of this!" Ander barked.

"Hey, whoa." Alex stretched out his hands in defense. "I won't tell him." Alex shook his head, chuckling, "I'm just surprised. Here I was, thinking my brother was some sort of goody-two-shoes, but," he shrugged. "I'm impressed Ander, and I don't blame you." He nodded in my direction. "Nice catch."

"Screw you, Alex!" I spat. Anger flared inside me like hot fire, but it only seemed to amuse them, and they laughed harder.

"What are you doing out here?" Ander asked coolly.

Alex shrugged. "Just trying to find a boost, not a lot of luck out of the cemetery apparently."

Liar.

"Anyways, you don't ask me questions, and I won't ask you questions." Alex eyed me pointedly. "Did you guys get out through the dorm doors or the front?"

"Front." Ander answered quietly, he was working so hard to keep the fury from his voice that it contorted his mouth into a lax scowl.

"Hmm...Yeah. I think we'll use the front. You should use the dorm doors whenever you, uh, finish up." Alex smirked and retreated with his group through the clearing. They crossed the lawn like a pack of hyenas, still hooting with laughter.

"They'll wake the whole school up," I muttered.

Ander slouched against the tree. His handsome features warped into an expression of helpless anger. I touched his arm tentatively, and he turned to me.

"Are you okay?" I asked.

"I don't know." His fingers pinched the bridge of his nose. "Alex can't figure out that we know until he's completely used up the boost." Ander sighed and stood up. "And then-" he suddenly turned and punched the thick bark of the spruce tree beside him. The sound made a dull crack. "Ahg!" Ander winced, cradling his hand in the cubby of his arm.

"What'd you do that for?"

Ander shot me a dark look. "I thought it might be fun." He shook his hand out a few times, and then sat down in the overgrown grass. He took a deep breath and stared at the nothingness that lingered in the shadows of the forest. "What am I going to do?" he asked.

I sat next to him and slowly reached over to withdraw his arm. Ander's hand had dark prickles of red blood protruding from breaks in the skin. He let me study his injury.

"I don't know," I finally said. "Can you tell Mr. Dodger?"

He was quiet for a minute before answering. "They'd kick him out of Mountain Heights, and then he would be charged."

"Charged?"

"Yeah, like arrested." Ander sucked in a hiss of air through his teeth as he removed his injured hand from mine. "Mediums have laws against this stuff. Being at a school while he was doing this-"

"Would he go to jail?" I didn't want to ask what I really wanted to know.

Would they neuter him?

"Yeah, I just-" he ran a hand through his hair again, pulling on the roots and looking back across campus. "I just need to think. We should head back."

I nodded and we made our way through the veil of trees and onto the open grass of the campus lawn. We parted ways as we approached the dormitories, but before he left, I spoke.

"Ander, let me know if I can help with anything."

"Thanks... uh, sorry," he gestured toward his neck. "About the-"

"Don't worry about it." I shrugged and tried to look like it hadn't affected me. "It was a good fake out."

"Yeah," Ander nodded a few times, almost rhythmically, reassuring himself. "Yeah, uh, well. Don't tell Molly, or the guys about Alex tonight, okay?"

"Okay."

Ander looked unraveled. I could almost see the string of concern spinning him in a twisted circle of knots and tangles. "I'll tell them," he said. "Just not yet. I want to figure some stuff out first." A broken smile curled his lips and he nodded in gratitude before turning towards the boy's dormitory for the night. "Goodnight, Lidia."

Chapter 15

On the Friday before Thanksgiving break, the usual mob of black and plaid at Mountain Heights had transformed into a glittering horde of school spirit. Everyone was wearing the Timberwolves raspberry red and evergreen in honor of our failing football team playing that night.

Molly and I pushed our way through the crowd on our way to the student lounge.

"Look at Mindy Johnson," Molly laughed.

I searched the room as we entered the lounge. It was usually a quiet place for students to come and hang out on big plush couches to do homework, or play board games. Today however, it was the central meeting place for the upper classmen allowed to attend the game.

Only the upper classmen- sophomores, juniors, and seniors, were allowed to attend the games. Molly and I had waited in a twenty-minute line to get checked into the lounge. When we reached the door, a tall woman with coffee-stained teeth scanned us with a weird beepy thing. I thought it was a metal detector, but Molly explained that it was a device that measures the static frequency of your aura. Basically, it could determine if you retained energy from a boost or not. We were supposed to be energy-free to prevent any tampering with the game, or tampering with other students from the opposing school.

I speculated for a minute on what sort of scenario had made this precaution necessary. Images of wayward footballs flying through the air in the opposite direction they were thrown, and opposing team members frozen in place came to mind. *Maybe our football team hadn't always been so bad.*

"I don't see her," I said.

The room was so crammed with people that the school spirit melted into a weird Christmas camouflage. Pieces of color would move, and that was how I deciphered a person from the crowd behind them. The only people that seemed to take human form were those huddled in front of the large floor-length windows overlooking the mountains.

"Green tutu, two o'clock."

I turned and successfully spotted Mindy Johnson's poor outfit choice. "Oh, ouch." She looked like a human Christmas tree.

Molly laughed again, and then turned towards me. Her fake eyelashes were only partially glued onto her eyelids, the corners popping up like hairy caterpillars trying to escape. Molly tried pressing them back down. "Is this okay?" She fluttered her eyes. "I can't tell. They feel like they're falling off."

"Just the corners. They look good though."

"Okay, good." She sighed and straightened her scarf. "They should already be here, it's impossible to see anyone in- oh, there they are!" Molly started speed walking toward a blond and something black hunched in a chair. As we neared, it became clear that the black figure was Ander, better dressed for a funeral than a football game.

"Well, aren't you festive?" I gestured to his dark denim and black jacket.

"Cute bow," he retorted.

I straightened the red ribbon holding my hair back in a high ponytail. "Thanks."

Things had been somewhat normal between Ander and me since the night in Walden woods. Ander was constantly brooding when he thought no one was watching, but apart from that, he was normal. If anyone was to blame for the awkwardness between us, it was me. Keeping eye contact was hard, and I frequently looked away mid-conversation. I couldn't help it. We would be talking, and then I would remember his lips on my neck, and I would have to think of antelopes, or fat men in little pink dresses, or something.

Jessica sighed, clearly annoyed. "Ander says he's not going."

"He's totally going!" said Molly definitively. "Ander, you're going."

"Look at him! He looks like the black plague." Jessica poked his shoulder. "He's just going to depress people."

"So, we'll get him to change."

Ander rolled his eyes and slumped back into the chair, watching the conversation between the two girls with a trace of amusement.

"Well, I tried to get him to dress up, but he just won't!"

"Here, he can have my scarf." Molly unraveled her scarf and flung it at him.

"I don't understand what the big deal is," Ander said as he donned the scarf and Trevor put a green striped hat on top of his head. "I rather stay here and work on the plan for the-" Ander dropped his voice, "A.P."

206

The A.P. was our code for the *Alex Plan*. After a week of silent consideration, Ander had confided in the group about what we had found out about Alex. Together, we were brainstorming ideas on how to eradicate his newest desire for dark energy. So far, or at least as far I knew, an exorcism was our best bet to get rid of any lingering Spook inside of him. The way they described it made it sound like a supernatural intervention, only a lot more complicated.

"Because Ander, it's our senior year. It's our last chance to experience high school for the rest of our lives." Molly threw her hands out like she was tossing fairy dust, which, considering the amount of glitter she was wearing, wouldn't be surprising.

"Where's Jeff?" I asked, looking around.

"Detention," Ander answered. "He mouthed off to Mr. Short in English."

"Since when does he mouth off?" I asked.

Trevor laughed. "Since when does Jeff say anything at all?"

The students around us all began shuffling toward the doors, jostling us together in a tighter circle around Ander's chair.

"Look," cried Molly. "It's time to go! Please come, Ander."

"I already know the end score. Fifty three to zero." Ander searched our faces from beneath the striped top hat.

"I hear they have pizza," I chimed in.

Gosh, I hope they have pizza.

"Oh, nobody said anything about pizza." Ander stood abruptly and Jessica clapped her hands. "The cafeteria stuff sucks, did you try it last week?" He made a face, and we all moved with the crowd in the hopeful pursuit of true American junk food.

The football game took place at Wallington Patterson Prep. As it turned out, Mountain Heights only played with other private schools, and only played away games. Since we were so isolated, and since most students could zap the ball away from any roided-out jock, it was a lot safer to play on another school's field.

I always wondered if the other private schools were hiding their own secrets. If the team at Wallington Patterson Prep were all aliens, it would certainly make the games more interesting. Watching Mountain Heights lose every time was a bummer, and it got boring after a while. Not that it would ever hinder our school spirit.

Without anything to lose, hope radiated through every face painted red and green. We filed onto the Greyhound bus that waited in the dying daylight. It felt excitingly backwards to get onto a school bus when it was about to be dark. Like eating breakfast at night, or dinner for breakfast.

The thrill of complete chaos.

I shuffled past occupied seats until I found a vacant one in the middle. I slid over to make room for Ander who was about to slide in next to me, but before he could take the seat, Jessica charged under his arm and sat down.

"Sorry," she lowered her voice to a whisper. "Maxx Jackson is stalking me." She shot Ander an apologetic look.

He nodded, annoyed, and continued down the line.

"Who's Maxx Jackson?" I asked.

"The guy right behind Molly." I looked up at the tall skinny boy with eyes that were so large they looked perpetually stoned.

"He's not so bad. I like his hair, he has really good hair."

"He thinks pirates are real, and he has a shirt that says - *only my cat understands me.*"

I nodded, appreciating the cat shirt at least. "He's quirky."

"Yeah. Whatever." She pulled a magazine from her bag and tried ignoring Maxx as he stared her down from two aisles away.

■ ■

Two hours later, we arrived at Wallington Patterson Prep sporting facility. We walked past a large brick building with a delicate architecture design in grey stone.

"That place is definitely haunted," someone whispered. I shuddered at the thought and hugged my thin sweater closer.

"You cold?" Ander strode up beside me. His hands were thrust deep in his pockets and his breath clouded like train smoke in the bright lights of the sports field.

"I'm okay." The crowd that was already assembled onto the bleachers were chanting a song, it sounded familiar. "What are they singing?"

"Jingle bell rock."

"Because we're red and green? It's not even Thanksgiving yet!"

Ander started humming along and I reached out to smack his stomach. "Don't encourage them."

"Ah," he laughed. "Give me a better song to sing." It was nice to see him laughing, Ander hadn't smiled a lot lately. "They're red and white, know any songs about that?"

"Uh... grandma got ran over by a reindeer?"

"I hate country." Ander thought for a minute. "And that's messed up."

"Looks like extra credit is really starting fit in with us mediums." Trevor swung an arm around Ander and me until he was sandwiched between the two of us. "It all starts with a wacked out, disturbed, twisted sense of Mormon humor."

"Morbid humor," Ander corrected.

"Yeah." Trevor smiled absently. "That's what I said."

The various grades of Mountain Heights marched into the bleachers overlooking the lime Astroturf washed with floodlights overhead. There weren't nearly enough students to pack the bleachers, so most clustered together in little bundles as stragglers drifted to and from groups, laughing and waving glittering scarfs in the cold night air. Adjacent to us were a stoic bunch of kids wearing nothing but white and red. A few glared at us under fuzzy hats, but most just sat watching the empty field with their breath clouding around their faces.

Jessica sat next to me on the bleachers while Ander, Molly, and Trevor sat a row behind us. Ander's long legs weren't meant to be confined to such a short space, and his knee jabbed me in the back. After I complained about it for the third time, he

210

remedied the situation by resting both feet on the bleacher next to me so that I was practically straddled between his legs. I became so distracted by the warmth radiating off the fabric of his jeans that I stopped paying attention to the game that had just started.

■■

"Uh, hi Jessica." Maxx Jackson sidled over to our group as the players started running across the field and the marching band sounded for half time. "Would you like to go to the concession stand with me? We missed dinner earlier, so I figured that maybe you were hungry."

"Umm." Jessica shot me a worried glance. "Yeah, I guess so." They got up and left just as a whistle blew from somewhere on the field.

Ander bumped me gently with his leg and leaned down to whisper. "What's that about?" I shrugged and was about to reply when everyone in red and green started cheering. I didn't know what was going on, but I started cheering too.

Jessica returned a few minutes later with a large soda. "What'd I miss?"

"No idea." I took the soda from her hands and helped myself to the coke.

"Hey." Ander's voice rang out behind me again, only this time his leg lingered against the sides of my arms as he spoke. The skin, though separated by multiple layers of fabric, burned at the contact.

I tried to ignore it.

"What happened to the pizza deal?" Ander asked. "I'm starving."

"There's no pizza." Jessica looked bored as she watched two players on the field crash together and then ricochet off each other like the dummies in seatbelt awareness commercials. "Maxx and I didn't see any at the stand."

"Oh, so now it's Maxx and I?" teased Molly.

"I say we ditch the game and grab a slice at Pikes." Trevor took Jessica's soda that I was drinking. "I saw one right across the street as we drove in."

We all agreed, and then slipped away from the cold metal bleachers in favor of the warm plastic seats at Pike's Pizza Parlor.

At Pikes, the walls were an unpleasant color of yellow that clashed with the vintage cushion booths lining the walls and windows of the tiny restaurant. It wouldn't have been my first choice, but it was the only restaurant within walking distance of the school, and I really wanted pizza.

As soon as we entered, I was instantly hit with a wash of warmth and the smell of melted cheese and garlic.

Oh Pizza. Where have you been all my life?

We huddled together to place our order with the pizza guy sitting at the front counter. He was hunched over reading a magazine. As we got closer, I saw that he wasn't so much reading, but mostly just looking at a picture of a bathing suit model featured in an outdated copy of Cosmo.

Molly cleared her throat at the counter. The pizza boy's blemished complexion paled when he looked up to see her smirking patiently.

"H-hi," he stammered. He shut the magazine quickly and slid it ungracefully off the counter. It landed on the tile floor with a soft smack. The pizza boy tried to smile casually, but his nerves gave his metal smile a warped strain. "What can I get you guys, uh... women, lady, uh, I mean, what can I get you... miss?" His smile had completely faltered by the end of the sentence.

Behind me, Ander and Trevor were stifling laughter.

"Is pepperoni okay with everybody?" Molly asked us.

We all nodded.

"One large pepperoni pizza please," she said.

"Oh. What a fine choice." He chuckled uncomfortably at his own humor. "Can't go wrong with the classic. Ha-ha."

I heard Jessica scolding Ander and Trevor, the three of them slowly backed away to a booth near the window.

"That'll be ten fifty seven."

Molly withdrew her card and handed it to him.

"Josh!" called a male voice from the back kitchen. "What was that last order?"

"Large pep." Josh finished the transaction and handed Molly her card back before he fled to the back kitchen.

Molly and I went to the booth where the others were already sitting, and I slid in next to Ander. He shot-put a sugar packet at me using a fork as I settled into my seat, so I threw it back, hitting him squarely in the neck.

"We have an idea for the Alex Plan," whispered Molly.

Next to her, Jessica clapped her hands. "Yes, okay, so we were thinking it should be done at winter formal."

"Winter formal?" spluttered Trevor. "That's, like, a million years away."

"It's in three weeks."

"Same thing."

"Anyways," Jessica peeled her napkin away from her fork. "Think about it, most of the school will be distracted and gathered in one place. Plus, it's a Saturday night, right after training which means if we can get Alex to use all of his boost the Friday before at training. Bingo! No powers! We do an exorcism, get rid of whatever has happened so far, and he'll see that we know, and unless he wants to get turned in, he'll have to stop."

A stifled argument sounded from the back of the restaurant. Since it was completely empty except for an older couple in the corner, and us, the conversation was somewhat distinguishable.

"I want to take it!"

"N-no!" squeaked Josh. "It's my job, I'm front counter today."

"I want to see her!"

"Shut up!"

There was a collection of muffled whispers that disappeared behind the roar of an oven and a telephone ringing. I laughed with Trevor and Jessica at Molly's mortified expression. Ander seemed fixated on the voices, and he craned his neck to peek over Trevor's head at the pizza boys.

A second later, a skinny boy with more eyeliner than Trina and a name tag that read- *Patrick,* came strutting out of the kitchen. Behind him, Josh was scowling from the front counter where he was taking a call.

Patrick carried the metal disk to our table and set a large pepperoni pizza in front of us. It steamed magnificently and smelled similar to how I hoped heaven would smell.

"Hey."

We all looked up to see Patrick still standing in front of our table.

Why is he looking at me?

"Enjoy," he said, tilting his weak chin upward.

"Thank you." It was my turn to feel mortified as the rest of the group beamed at me.

Patrick nodded again, still staring. "I hope it's extra delicious."

Ander scoffed. "Why? Did you spit in it?"

"What?" Patrick suddenly looked panicked, eyes darting to each of us at the table. "No. I just meant, like, you know, enjoy your pizza, its extra delicious, like always."

"Right," said Trevor.

"Hey. Trevor." Ander said to him across the table, mimicking Patrick's awkward chin tilt. "I hope your hot slice is extra delicious."

Patrick watched the two boys, his ashy cheeks blooming tomato red. I felt a guilty pang of empathy, suddenly disgusted with my table's behavior.

"Thank you, Patrick," I said and he scurried away from our silent giggles.

215

I jabbed my elbow hard into Ander's side.

"Ouch!" Ander rubbed the spot, turning a questioning face towards me while Trevor and Molly continued to giggle. "What?"

"That was mean."

"It was a joke!" he said incredulously.

"You embarrassed him."

Ander snorted. "Actually," he reached for a slice of pizza. "I think he embarrassed himself."

"I'm going to leave him a huge apology tip." I turned away to unfold my fork from my napkin and saw Ander's sour expression out of the corner of my eye.

After most of the laugher over Patrick's failed pick-up had subsided, five pairs of hands reached out and we all took a piece before continuing with our previous topic.

"Anyways, that sounds like a great plan Jessica, but-" Trevor stripped off a string of cheese. "How are we going to pull it off? If we all go together, it'll look suspicious. We never go to the dances."

"I do," said Molly.

"We can pair off in dates." Ander reached out and stole a pepperoni from my slice, popping it into his mouth with a sly smile. "Vegan."

"Semi-vegan." I reached over to steal an additional two pepperonis from his slice which he was about to take a bite of. "And even if we get everyone to the dance, how are we going to get Alex there? He's not a student."

"He can take Molly," said Jessica.

216

"Oh. Uh, no." Molly shook her head violently. "No thanks. I'm not going to a dance with either of the whore brothers."

"Hey-" Ander started but Jessica cut him off.

"Why not?" she asked, not bothering to correct Molly's insult. "He's in love with you."

"But it's over between us, we broke up."

Broke up?

"Doesn't mean he doesn't still like you, and besides," Jessica took a bite. "It's for his own good. It's Ander's brother, and we all love Alex." Trevor coughed pointedly, but Jessica continued. "If we can do something about it, we should," she said.

Molly nodded, looking up at me once before staring back down at the table.

Did I do something?

"Sounds like an awesome plan to me." Ander took a bite of pizza. "So," he turned. "How can someone be a semi-vegan anyways?"

■■■

"Uh hello, are you two done?"

I snapped my head up at Jessica, Trevor, and Molly who were all hovering out of the booth waiting for me and Ander to finish our conversation.

"Huh?" I slid quickly out of the booth and Ander followed. "Yes."

217

"How much time do we have left?" Molly asked, walking slightly faster than normal as I hurried to keep up with the group nearing the exit.

"We still have twenty minutes before we have to board the bus."

We burst out of the glass doors of Pikes and into the cool night air. It was freezing, and there were fluffy white particles of snow cascading in front of the streetlights as we walked.

"Anyone feeling, what I'm feeling?" said Trevor with a mischievous grin.

"I do," said Molly. The two of them turned and started speed walking down a dimly lit alleyway.

I followed while simultaneously attempting to catch snowflakes on my tongue. Ander laughed, jostling my side with a nudge.

Tonight has been good.

The awkward forced tension with Ander from the past week had faded, and things were how they should be. *Ethan would be happy to hear that his best friend and girl-*

I didn't even know if I was still his girlfriend. I wrote him a letter a week ago, but he never replied.

Stop thinking about it.

I closed my eyes, breathing in the air and decided to just enjoy the night.

"What are we feeling?" I asked as a cold bunch of ice melted onto the hot skin of my forehead. Warm fabric draped across my shoulders. It smelled amazing, a woodsy citrus cologne. It smelled like Ander.

"They feel a spirit," Ander said.

"You didn't have to give me your coat."

"I have an extra sweater on, and you have nothing."

"I'm wearing a sweater."

"That is not a sweater."

"Is too." I wrapped his jacket around my shoulders. It was much warmer than my sweater. "How can they tell there's a ghost around here?"

"It's just a feeling."

"Like your bones itch?"

Ander nodded as we turned into the alleyway. Now that I was aware of the spirit, I could feel it too. Trevor was standing alone under a streetlight as Molly and Jessica watched from the sidewalk. When Ander and I approached, both girls turned back to stare, and their eyes lingered on the jacket I was wearing.

Molly spoke first, her voice had become distinctively snotty. "Don't you have a boyfriend?"

I screwed up my eyebrows, trying to figure out if I should be insulted or just let it pass.

"Don't be a brat," Ander said to her. He shifted beside me, and suddenly I would've preferred the discomfort of the cold. I started to take the jacket off, but Ander reached over to pull it tighter over my shoulders. "Don't," he whispered. "She's just in a bad mood. You're fine."

I didn't feel fine.

219

"Wow, Ander," Molly sneered. "I guess there was more than one reason you chose Lidia for your extra credit." She turned back to watch Trevor. "Show some restraint."

Jessica gave Molly an exasperated look, but said nothing.

Did Ander tell them he kissed me in the woods?

Did he tell them it was so Alex wouldn't find out?

I glanced at Ander, but he was busy glaring at Molly. It didn't look like he had any intention of telling her anything, so maybe he hadn't.

"Damn it!" Trevor swore.

"What is it?" asked Ander, finally taking a step away from me.

"Poltergeist!" Trevor looked up at the empty space above him.

I shuffled closer to Jessica, ignoring Molly. "Uh, what exactly does a poltergeist look like?" I asked.

"It's-" Jessica started to explain before turning to shout at Trevor. "Just leave it alone Trev, let's just go back!"

"No way, bro! I'm gettin' it!"

Jessica sighed. "You'll see."

A trash can lid lifted into the air from the side of the building and hurtled toward Trevor. It caught him in the ribs and he fell to the pavement.

"Are you okay?" Jessica sounded bored.

Where is it?

I scanned the alley for an apparition, a figure, a ball of light, something. There was nothing but the gentle wet kiss of snowflakes as they fell to the ground.

"Yeah, fine."

Particles of trash rose from the dumpster bin and then plunged toward Trevor. He swore loudly as rotten mush splattered across various body parts. He swore again, and again. Trevor thrust his hands out in front of himself, muttering something incoherent as he did so. Blue light sparked from his fingertips and a wave of invisible static radiated off of his figure. It moved like a mirage, surrounding his body in a wave of glistening nothingness. The rotten food particles and trash that were hovering in the air seconds ago, fell and splattered on the ground.

Ander and Jessica started laughing. Trevor however, stormed angrily past them on his route back to the school buses.

Chapter 16

"Uhg, Trevor! Walk to your left, I don't want to be downwind of you... oh my God, ew," Jessica complained.

Trevor wore odor de-la-garbage, and he smelled awful. He continued to march in front of us until everyone had gotten onto the bus. Due to much protesting from other students, he was sent to sit in the back, while the wiser students, myself included, aimed to snag the first seats nearest the entrance.

"What's a poltergeist?" I asked Ander as he slid into the seat next to me.

"Just a ghost." He moved closer momentarily, his leg making contact with mine as he made room for the students stuffing themselves down the aisle.

It was a loud group, due primarily to the stink of rotting asparagus wafting from the back were Trevor sulked. The front doors closed and the bus started moving out of the parking lot.

"They can be kind of dangerous, just because they pack a little more energy than most, and they can choose if they want to be seen. But they aren't demonic or anything."

"You're sure?" I zipped his jacket up completely and hid my nose behind the fabric. *Sure smells demonic.* "Oh, I have a question," my muffled voice was almost indistinguishable through the jacket, so I unzipped. "About Alex."

"Shoot."

"Uhm," I scanned the bus. Molly and Jessica were in deep conversation a few seats away. "So, Molly and Alex dated?"

"Oh," Ander laughed. "Uh, yeah. That's how we became friends."

I raised an eyebrow.

"She started dating him three years ago, I liked her friend Jessica, so the four of us started hanging out and we all became great friends. Then Alex was an idiot, and cheated on her, and that was that."

"Oh." I thought for a moment. "You liked Jessica?"

"I did, but then I got to know her, and now I know she's too cool to date."

"Too cool to date?"

"I try and keep that stuff separate from the group." He shrugged. "It's a lot less drama."

"Have you dated any of them?"

Ander looked around the bus, seeming to take a mental head count. I let him get to four before I intervened.

"I mean, of the group."

"Uh," Ander smiled, bemused at my interrogation. "Nope, not Molly, or Jessica... or Travis, or Jeff either," he added with a smile.

I rolled my eyes and watched the back of the bus driver's head for a minute. The snow that zoomed past the windshield made it look like we were flying through stars in space at the speed of light. I leaned back into the cushion of the seat and listened to the chattering of everyone else on the bus.

223

"Do you think it'll work?" I asked.

"Think what will work?"

"The A.P.?"

Ander sighed. "I really hope so."

■ ■

I woke up.

The bus had stopped, and students were pushing through the brightly lit metal lane. I brought my head up and realized- *oops*.

I had fallen asleep on Ander's shoulder.

Great.

I rubbed the indented corner of my cheek. It probably looked like I had gotten run over by a tractor. Ander scanned my face casually as I continued rubbing the skin.

"You up?" he asked.

"Yeah, uh, sorry–"

Molly shoved past our seat, jostling us together as she stormed off the bus.

What is her problem?

"You don't have to go back to your dorm right away if you don't feel like dealing with that." Ander stared pointedly at Molly's retreating figure as she disappeared out the doors, then turned to watch my expression. "You can hang out in mine for a while. Jeff should be awake." Ander shook his head. "I swear that kid doesn't sleep."

224

Truth was, I didn't want to go back to my dorm, especially with Molly acting like I had vandalized her sock drawer with venomous snakes. I thought that it might be best to just leave, and deal with all the drama tomorrow. She usually went to sleep around midnight, so I had a few hours to kill before I could sneak back in without her being awake.

"You are a saint," I sighed.

With such a gigantic mob of incoming students, the sleepy professors that watched over our return were overwhelmed, unable to focus on each incomer. It made it ridiculously easy to sneak into the boys dorms. Ander helped fold my ponytail under the festive green striped top hat Trevor had given him earlier, and it was enough to blend in with the boys.

"I brought company," Ander announced as I stepped into his dorm and he clicked the door softly shut behind him. The dorm was dimly lit with the warm glow of a small desk lamp, and a bubbling blue lava lamp that sat in the corner.

"Aye!" slurred Jeff's deep voice as he swayed slightly in his desk chair. "Now it's a party."

Wow...he speaks...and from the looks of it, drinks.

"What's up?" Ander's eyebrows furrowed slightly in concern. "I thought we were saving that."

Jeff held up the half-empty bottle of Jack Daniels and shrugged. "Everyone was at the game."

"You're such a deviant." Ander's handsome face split into a smile. He shook his head and threw Molly's scarf onto the lower bunk of a double bed.

225

The small room was an exact replica of my own, only Molly's posters of shirtless men were substituted for posters of snowboarders and dirt bikes. Ander leaned against the bedpost, looking uneasy but pleased.

"Uh, make yourself comfortable," he said.

I took a seat on the bottom bunk, which I was assumed was his bed.

"Got it!" Jeff's baritone boomed from where he was sitting. He carefully set the bottle on the empty desk, and dove under the bed. He shuffled through an obscene amount of trash and old socks.

I laughed at his uncharacteristic enthusiasm and saw Ander grinning at me with a tight-lipped knowing smile. It was almost as if we were sharing an inside joke.

"Okay," Jeff remerged with a pack of cards. "We can play Banters."

"I don't think I've ever played that one before."

"Oh, you got to try it!" Jeff said. "It's the best drinking game."

"Okay," I laughed.

"I'll teach you," Ander sat down on the floor next to me, so I slid off the bed and the three of us huddled into a tight circle. "It's a game for mediums, it's like, an altered version of kings," he said. "We take turns pulling the cards, and whichever number you get stands for something."

"But, you have two seconds for a turn. And any sort of boost induced tricks are allowed," Jeff interjected.

"Lidia and I don't have any boost, we just went to the game."

"Sucks to be you," Jeff said. His head drifted slightly to the left as he spoke.

Ander continued with the rules. "So, two is for you – so you drink and you pick someone else to drink with you. Four is for whores – so girls drink."

I mumbled something about the rule of four applying better to other people in the room, but Ander either didn't hear, or ignored it as he continued to explain the rest of the rules. It seemed easy enough. I took the first card and presented an eight to the two boys.

"Eight is for I never. What's something you've never done?" Jeff asked.

"I have never-"

"Two seconds or you drink!"

"I have never slept with more than one person!" I blurted out.

Ander raised his eyebrows.

"You mean," Jeff continued. "Like, at the same time?"

Ander shot him a hard look.

"No... like ever," I said.

Both Jeff and Ander took a swig of whiskey.

"Just Ethan?" Ander watched me curiously without turning to face me head on.

"Yeah."

"Huh." Ander didn't elaborate of what *huh* meant, but it didn't matter because Jeff reached out and drew a four.

■■

The whiskey tasted like a sick combination of battery acid and furniture polish. I remembered all the old movies where the fancy men and women would sip on hard liquors in crystal glasses. They always appeared to enjoy the taste, but I soon concluded that they were all full of lies. It was disgusting, but it had the desired effect. We had barely gotten around the circle a third time when my head was swimming and my teeth had gone numb.

I lifted a finger to stroke my front tooth.

It feels smooth.

Ander's glossy blue eyes watched me, and he started to laugh a little too loudly. I could tell that he was also feeling the warming effects of the whiskey.

"What are you doing?" he chuckled.

"My toof fewls numb." I lisped through the obstruction of my finger.

"You're so weird." Ander reached over to hook an arm over my neck and pulled me towards him. I lost balance and collapsed, so we both lay giggling on the floor.

Jeff had passed drunk, and proceeded to pure belligerence. "I- go th munden," he mumbled, drawing a card and slapping it to his forehead.

We laughed harder.

"Is he going to be okay?" I asked.

"He'll be fine." Ander's warm arms were still entangled around me, holding me against his side where we lay. "He has a very unique personality. He's mostly shy, but as soon as it's time to let loose he comes completely undone."

"Work hard, play harder."

"Exactly." Ander's face turned to mine.

Movements almost seemed blurred, like the lag on my brain was registering the motion a second behind. I focused on his eyes to steady me... Ander really was handsome. His eyes were so blue.

There was a gag, and we both looked up to see Jeff slumped over. Jeff was gagging on nothing, his head swaying with the promise of vomit soon to come.

"Crap," Ander released me from his arms and crawled over to where Jeff sat. "How're you feeling, man?" He looked up at Jeff's unfocused face, shook his head, and looped an arm around Jeff's shoulder, hoisting him up to stand. "C'mon, I'll take you to the toilet... you better make it... If you puke in here, you're doing my laundry for a month."

Jeff groaned and Ander shot me an apologetic look as he hoisted Jeff out of the room. "I'll be right back," he said.

I nodded as they sidled out the door, then I looked around at everything dimly lit in the small room.

What a neat lava lamp.

For some reason, it made me laugh.

After a minute or two of waiting, I hoisted myself up from the floor. Everything spun slightly and I stumbled as I

229

walked towards the dresser on the far wall. I opened the top drawer and sifted through the junk inside.

Pens, graded homework assignments, a condom – *interesting*, gum wrappers, and, *oh-* a letter from Ethan.

Well hello, hello...

Ander,

Yeah, things have gotten better. Sorry for freaking out on the phone about it. I know you didn't have anything to do with how she acted, and I talked to her mom that day. Apparently she lied. They never told her she had to go, she just wanted to.

But whatever, I'm over it. It was immature of her, so to answer your other question...I don't know.....Maybe.

My fantasy football team is kicking ass! Some guys at school got me into it, and I'll have to show you when you come home for Christmas. Other than that, everything has been pretty much the same. Classes are fine, I'm starter on the team this year (that's pretty awesome), and I've gone to a few parties... Those have been...interesting. I hooked up with this one chick (Ashley) but I don't think it'll really go anywhere. Kind of a... to quote you "butter face" haha.

Keep an eye on Lidia for me. Not that it really matters, but it'd be nice to know if she's hooking up with any of the preppy privet school douche bags (no offense). Look forward to seeing you man.

Ethan.

A tight hot lump formed in the back of my throat.

Hooked up with Ashley?

My heart began to hammer in my chest. I was still drunk, and it was all so... confusing.

Ashley?

I tried to remember any and all Ashley's that I had ever known. Ashley Galveston was a junior in my P.E. class last year. She was blond, and had a belly button ring. I had never been jealous of her before, but somehow, I suddenly felt so overwhelmingly insufficient.

I scanned the letter again and felt tears blur my vision.

Apparently she lied.

"No!" I said to no one.

I didn't lie. I didn't have any choice...

I swallowed and tried to focus on the swarming buzz the alcohol had given me instead of the hot sickening anxiety leaking through my saturated emotions.

Ashley?

Ander knew everything and he was still letting Ethan hook up with other girls when he knows it's not my fault. Anger burbled over the hurt, swarming in my head mixed with the sweet alcoholic allure of unhindered self-control.

The door snapped open and Ander snuck back into the room smiling broadly. "He's out. I put him in a good position to puke his brains out in the toilet, but he's not going-"

I turned and Ander froze upon seeing my face. Slowly his eyes dropped to where my hand fisted the letter and the open drawer.

"Shit." Ander took a breath, looking suddenly scared. "Lidia-"

"Why didn't you tell me?" My voice was nowhere near as quiet as it should've been, but I didn't care. "Why didn't you tell him? This is your fault! This is completely your fault!"

"Lidia," Ander was already across the room, urging me to calm down with wide eyes. "Please, listen, I-"

"You what?" I was practically yelling, fighting tears that hadn't brimmed from my watering eyes. "You what?"

"I can't tell him that we took you!" Ander reached out to grab hold of my shoulders. "Lidia, I am so sorry." He looked like he meant it. "I'm so sorry, but think about it... what am I supposed to say? Me and my brother broke into your girlfriend's house at two in the morning and forced her into our car so that we could make her go to a school for kids who see dead people?"

"Yes!" My heart was still beating fast. Everything swarmed in confusion, anger, hurt. "He's with Ashley?"

"No, Lidia. God, no." Ander swallowed, looking down at me with eyes that struggled to project meaning. "He called your mom first thing, I couldn't do anything about it. I already sent the text saying they made you leave. I wrote to him, please-" Ander reached out for my face. "I told him you weren't with any other guys and that he was a fucking idiot. He was mad, it happened that first day getting to school."

"The first day?"

"Uh-" Ander realized it was the wrong thing to say. "He was pissed you left, so he found someone at a party. He's stupid, I told him that!"

Defeated, I let the tears fall. I saw Ander watch me through blurred eyes, his thumb still brushing tears away from my cheek as they fell.

I shoved him away. Hard.

Ander stumbled back and he looked at me with glossy bewildered eyes. I stepped forward to shove him again, but staggered drunkenly. He caught me just before I was able to slap his aiding arm away from my waist.

"Lidia, I'm sorry."

I reached out for a third time, but he trapped my arms, holding me stationary.

"You could've told me." I writhed sloppily, doing more to fall deeper into his embrace then further away. I couldn't move my arms and it made the swell of emotion burn my body in tense frustration.

"Stop." Ander held me still, his voice patient. "No, I couldn't."

I thrashed against my restraints, losing balance and I fell backwards. Ander's hold slowed my fall, redirecting me mid-motion so that I ended up with my back against the pillar of the bunk bed.

"Stop fighting," Ander's voice was stern. "You're going to hurt yourself."

Ashley.

"Stop!" He rattled my arms and the sharpness of his voice made me pause. "Stop," he said again, and I realized for the first time that Ander was very, very close. "Please," Ander breathed.

I stopped.

The fight left my body and his grip loosened, it allowed me the ability to sink onto the bottom bunk. "He's sleeping with other girls." My voice sounded weak. Pathetic.

The statement mulled in the air unpleasantly. After a minute, Ander sat next to me, and slowly reached over to grab the nearly empty bottle of whiskey. He handed it to me.

I took a swig and then he took a drink as well.

"He's just trying to cope," he said. "He does care about you. Ethan's just, I don't know, being an idiot."

"With Ashley Galveston," I continued, as if he hadn't spoken. "He's clearly enjoying the single life."

"Don't... don't compare yourself with her, or him. He's throwing everything away for *Ashley Galveston*." The way he said her name, as if it was something disgusting, made me feel only slightly better. "You deserve better than that." He ran a hand through his hair and looked down at the whiskey bottle in his hands. "You deserve way better."

I deserve better than that...

Do I?

I'm the one that left.

I'm the one who can see the dead.

"What we had to do to get you here was hard on you both... but if-" Ander stopped. "He should've talked to you. Ethan should've waited, at least long enough to write you a freakin' letter." A pained expression passed across his features, and I could see the guilt lingering at the back of his mind. "But, I don't regret it. You needed to learn how to deal with spirits. You needed to understand what you are. I'm just sorry about how it happened."

I stole the bottle from his hands and took a swig, refusing to comment. Deep down, I knew he was right. I had been surrounded by others like me for months, and I still wasn't handling spirits well. I never would've made it on my own.

"I'm glad it was you," he said. Ander moved closer, and one of his hands rested on the bed just next to my leg. His finger inadvertently brushed against the fabric of my jeans, and my heart lurched forward, mingling unpleasantly with the hollowness in my chest. "I'm serious. If you weren't here, you would've had contact with a Spook by now. At least you're safe." Ander's eyes looked intensely conflicted, but his voice sounded absolute.

"Did I ever say thank you?"

"No," he laughed. "Punched me though."

"Well, thank you," I smiled. "You're the one that has made me safe."

"I'll always keep you safe," he said softly.

Always?

I felt dizzy. "Ander?" I asked.

He seemed to wake from a daze. Ander shook his head and reached out, taking the bottle from my hands and bringing it to his lips. His hand still rested close to my leg.

"Are you going to kiss me?" The words were out of my mouth before I could stop them.

He sputtered, shock registering on his perfect features as he choked on the swig of whiskey. He slowly set the bottle down on the floor, then turned to me.

I can't believe I said that….

Ander's eyes smoldered as he leaned in close. He stared down at my parted lips, took a breath, then he smiled. It was a weird, half-restrained smile. A smile you give to someone when you're trying to be patient.

"If you let me," he answered. The smirk tugged at the corners of his mouth, as if he thought I was joking.

I wasn't joking.

"I'll let you."

The smirk disappeared. "Lidia," he sucked in a breath, his hazy eyes drifting towards my mouth again. "You don't need to do this."

"You don't want to?"

Of course not.

Don't cry.

"It's not," suddenly frustrated, he bore his gaze into mine. "You're... you can't just get back at him like this." Ander swallowed, and turned his attention back to my eyes, his concentration fading.

"Why not?"

"Because," he dropped his face until his forehead and the side of his warm body was pressed against mine. His breathing was short when he spoke. "What are you doing?"

What am I doing?

"It's just a kiss," I whispered.

With a strangled noise of resignation, he slowly leaned in, and then kissed me. My stomach dropped and swirled as everything but Ander's lips against mine spun around us. The gentle kiss came again, once, twice, again until it deepened and I parted my lips to let him in.

As soon as I tasted the whiskey on his tongue, everything melted. My mind when blank, but my body reacted intensely to Ander's tender touch.

This was a bad idea.

Ander's strong hands knotted in my hair, and clamped around my waist. Before I knew what I was doing, my body leaned back towards the mattress. Suddenly, I was beneath him. Ander pulled back, his face was dimly lit by the muffled light streaming through the snow splattered windows, and the soft blue glow of the lava lamp. He looked like he wanted to say something. To stop.

Don't stop.

I kissed him harder, drawing him to me and running a hand across the muscles of his broad chest and shoulders. Ander made a sound, and it jostled my hazy thoughts.

This was a bad idea...

"Ander, wait-"

This wasn't supposed to happen.

Everything but the swirl of his tongue felt numb from the alcohol, even my heart. I didn't care though. My blood was on fire, coursing through my veins and pooling heat wherever he touched.

This can't be happening.

I could feel the pounding of his chest. Our fingers laced together as he slowly stretched my arm above my head. His staggered breathing matched my own pounding heart.

Ander's other hand began to trail lower, and lower. He unbuttoned the top of my jeans and I gasped. Alcohol and lust had me intoxicated beyond anything I was prepared to handle.

"A-Ander." I choked between scattered breathes. "S-stop... Ethan." His name sounded like a blaring siren.

Ander froze.

He pulled back and looked down at me in raw desperation. There was so much hunger in his wounded expression that it made something in my chest pang uncomfortably as I stared up at him.

"I know," he said gently.

I didn't know what else to say. I was swimming, but his eyes- blue and steady, prevented me from spinning out of control.

Our kisses weren't gentle after that. They were a furious swirl of angry desire and need. Angry at each other for doing this to Ethan. Angrier at ourselves for wanting it so much.

Chapter 17

I could feel sunlight streaming in through the windows before I opened my eyes. I rolled to my side in the lower bunk.

This isn't my room...

A wash of memories and a hammering headache flooded my brain. Thoughts were slow, painful. I squeezed my eyes shut, willing it all to be dream.

Oh my God...

I opened my eyes again and searched Ander's empty dorm room. My shirt lay on the floor beside the bed, my jeans and panties had somehow managed to hang themselves haphazardly on the back of Jeff's office chair.

No. No. No. No.

My mouth was dry as I opened it to take a breath. It didn't ease the nausea that lingered in the pit of my stomach. Even in my denial, I could still smell the lingering scent of his cologne on the cotton bed sheets entangling my body.

No. No. No. No.

I leapt out of the bed, got dressed in my clothes from last night, and then staggered toward the door in a daze. I tripped on nothing, but managed to open it and dash out into the empty hallway.

I wanted to jump off the roof.

I wanted to bash my head into a brick wall.

But first, I wanted to get to the girl's bathroom.

I made it, just barely. I went into a stall, dropped to my knees, and heaved. I leaned my sweating cheek against the cool porcelain just before another wave of nausea overtook me.

What have I done?

Once I was finished throwing up, I crept to my dorm room. I opened the door quietly, hoping Molly wasn't there. It was mercifully empty. I grabbed a towel and headed back to the bathrooms to take the longest shower of my life.

Ashley...

My chest felt hollow at the thought of Ethan with another girl.

Ander...

It made the hollow cavity feel like it had been punched.

I took a deep breath, filling my lungs with fragrant steam. It was easier to cry in the shower. The tears weren't as noticeable, and sometimes when I didn't notice my own tears, I didn't feel as sad. I lathered my hair with shampoo in the hot water and tried unsuccessfully to wash away the memories of the previous night. It didn't work, but eventually I came to a conclusion.

It had been a mistake.

It was a huge mistake to sleep with Ander. The memory of his hands tracing along the curves of my body resurfaced and I smothered it. I forced the thought of him out of my head.

Ander was a decent guy, a good friend to have despite many of his questionable life choices, but he wasn't someone I wanted to trust with deeper emotions. Especially mine. I knew how he treated the women he slept with. I remembered how he ditched Whitney at Camp Tanka. I remembered waking up alone earlier that morning, and I knew that I could be no different.

I shook my head and spat out the suds of shampoo that had snuck into my mouth.

Worse of all, he was Ethan's best friend. I was still upset with Ethan, still hurt, but I couldn't believe that I had sunk so low. Even drunk, I wasn't that type of person. Ethan couldn't find out, and maybe then Ander and I could still be friends. All we needed to do was ignore it.

The thought made me feel gross.

I could avoid him for at least one day...couldn't I?

I switched the shower off.

Thanksgiving break started the next day. If I was strategic, I wouldn't have to see Ander at all before we left on holiday.

I brushed my teeth, dried my hair, and changed into clean clothes. As I came back to my room, I saw that Molly had returned from breakfast. She glared at me as I put away my makeup bag.

"Morning," she said.

"Morning."

I didn't feel like dealing with her, so I ditched the curling iron, grabbed my school bag, and escaped to the library where I planned to spend the rest of the afternoon. It would've been the perfect plan if it wasn't for stupid Jay Ronaldson and his delicious BLT sandwich.

I sat at my favorite table in the back of the library. The window next to me overlooked the snow covered ground where the sun shone bright and yellow across the forest of evergreens. I spent a few hours staring out the window, and another few studying. Everything was going perfectly until Jay, a quiet guy with short auburn hair and a lip piercing, came to sit in the desk across from mine. He looked up and smiled before he retrieved a sandwich from his bag.

As a vegan, I probably could've opted the bacon out, but as a teenage girl that hadn't eaten in the past twenty-four hours, the smell was beyond enticing. My mouth watered at the prospect of food. Golden crumbs of the fluffy bread cascaded across the table and the tomato poking out between the pieces of lettuce was a bright, juicy red.

Jay glanced up and saw me staring hungrily at him.

"Hi," he said.

"Hey."

He gave me a shy smile before returning to his book.

When I checked the clock again an hour later, I realized it was dinnertime. I convinced myself that if Ander and I were going to pretend like everything was normal, self-starvation wasn't going to work. I slowly gathered my things and made my way to the cafeteria.

I felt nervous, like I was going to throw up all over again.

What will he say? Will he even say anything? What if he told everyone?

As I turned the corner and looked at our usual table, a wash of relief flooded my body.

242

Ander wasn't there.

I loaded a tray with food and took my usual seat.

"Hey," Jessica said casually. "You weren't at lunch."

"No, I went to the library for a little while." Feeling like my excuse was inadequate, I continued with a lie. "I think I'm getting sick or something. My appetite is shot," I stared at my tray full of food, but I didn't feel as hungry as I thought I had been. Still, I took a bite of pasta and looked up to see Molly's narrowed eyes.

"Where were you last night?" she asked. "You never came back to the dorms."

Intrigued, the rest of the table turned to listen.

"Well, you were being so rude that I decided to hang out elsewhere."

Trevor snorted back laughter.

"I spent the night in Mindy's room, she let me sleep on the floor," I lied. I didn't really know Mindy, but I knew that her and Molly hated each other, so I figured my secret was safe.

Jeff caught my eye momentarily, then he looked away and smoothed the beanie on his head.

"Oh," Molly muttered. She took a deep breath and then craned her head to look around the cafeteria. "Where's Ander?"

Hopefully, the moon.

"He's probably packing." Trevor brushed some crumbs from the table. "You know it sucks for him to go home and see his sister for five days. He's always in a shitty mood during Thanksgiving."

A pang of empathy shot through me.

"Yeah," Molly sighed. "He seemed okay this morning though."

"No he didn't," Jessica countered. "He grabbed two bagels and booked it back upstairs."

My blood froze.

Is it possible one was for me…

"Speak of the devil," said Trevor as he looked at something behind me. "Here's our man!"

Crap.

Ander came up to Trevor's side and clapped his outstretch hand in greeting.

"Good of you to join us, bro," Trevor said as Ander's eyes darted around the table.

His gaze went from Trevor, to me, to Molly, to me, to Jeff, to me, to Jessica, to me. My heartbeat was unreal, a completely inappropriate speed for a school cafeteria. Unnerved, I turned my eyes downward and stared at the lettuce on my plate.

What a magnificent shade of green.

I heard a chair scoot out as Ander took the seat across from me.

Those tomatoes are super red.

The table fell into easy conversation as I continued to study my lunch.

"You look tired," Molly scrutinized.

"Yeah, uh, I didn't sleep much last night," Ander's casual voice answered.

My chest tightened.

"Me neither." Molly tapped a long fingernail on the table. "I kept waiting for Lidia to get back, but she spent the night at Mindy's, and apparently, got sick."

I wonder what Italian dressing is made of... what's the black stuff?

"You got sick?" Ander's voice sent an electric shock through my system, and I forced my eyes up. He was looking right at me.

Really looking at me.

"Yeah," I said.

A flicker of confusion flashed across his otherwise blank expression. "Rough night?" he asked.

Ha-ha, you're so hilarious.

"Yeah."

Ander smiled slightly, and a flashing image of the two of us swept over my vision. I turned away and tried to act normal, but I didn't meet his eyes again.

The next twenty minutes passed excruciatingly slowly. It was by far the hardest meal I never ate. By the end of dinner, I was anxious, still hungry, and all I wanted to do was curl up in bed and sleep through the rest of my life.

■■

"Hey! Lidia, hold up!"

I froze mid-step and turned. Ander came jogging down the crowded hallway, the dying sunlight beemed through the window gave the side of his face a soft glow.

"Hey," he said, finally catching up to me. He sounded out of breath, but I didn't think it was from the short jog over here. "Can I talk to you?"

I nodded.

This is going to suck.

Ander put an arm around my shoulder to stear me towards an empty fold in the hallway leading to a classroom door. I stiffened at his touch, and he seemed to notice because he quickly let his hand drop.

"Uh," he took a deep breath and ran a hand through his disheveled hair. "Sorry I wasn't there this morning, I was-"

"Oh!" I cut him off. My voice sounded high-pitched and fake. "It's totally fine. I was so sick, it was probably a good thing you weren't there. I'm so sorry about last night."

He stilled, observing me quietly for a moment. "For what?"

I can't believe he's going to make me say it.

"For everything... I can't believe we drank that much."

"Yeah." Ander's voice was flat, all humor seemed to vanish and it was replaced by a stoic silence as he watched me fidget under his scrutiny.

Black-clad students streamed through the halls in a noisy mob, but since it was a weekend, none of them were rushing toward class. A group of girls huddled together in front

246

of one of the windows and started laughing loudly at something outside.

"Are you okay?" Ander asked.

It was a loaded question.

"Yeah, fine. I'm totally fine. It's just-" I dropped my voice. Partially because I didn't want others to hear, and partially because I was ashamed that I had to say it at all. "I can't believe we made that huge of a mistake."

A flash of realization crossed Ander's face before his expression went completely blank. He was impossible to read and he just stood there, silently waiting for me to finish explaining.

"I mean, I know I have to see Ethan sometime over break."

Ander broke eye contact and stared stonily at someone down the hall.

"And with you guys, and him and me, I just don't think I should tell him."

Ander nodded a few times in agreement.

"But," I continued. "I still want to be friends."

At that, his gaze shot back towards mine.

"I know you prefer to keep these things separate from your group of friends." *Oh God... what number was I? Girl number eight? Ten? More?* "But, I promise I won't make it weird," I said. "Just friends. We just made a one night mistake, it doesn't have to happen again."

"Right." After a second of silence, Ander gave a short laugh without humor. "Yeah, we can be friends." The pit of my stomach dropped as his cold eyes turned towards mine. He gave a tight smile and a nod. "See you after break, Lidia," he said. Then he pushed off of the wall, and marched down the hall.

Chapter 18

It took six bus rides, and a very long walk, to finally get back to Roseville Oregon. When I had gone to the main office at school to retrieve my phone that morning, I first called my mom who informed me that she was busy with visiting family, and so I was responsible for making my own way back home. I wasn't surprised, but it would've been nice to have been picked up at least somewhere along the way.

I also thought I would've been happy to hold my phone again, but I wasn't. I spent most of the bus ride staring at it, wondering if Ethan would even pick up if I called, and if he did pick up, wondering what I could possibly say to him.

Eventually, I worked up the courage to call Sammy, and though she sounded a little hurt at first, she accepted my apology and we soon fell into easy conversation. I didn't tell her everything, but I did tell her about Ethan and Ashley. She spent twenty minutes verbally abusing Ashley while I watched a homeless man pet the stuffed animal he had on his lap in the seat across from me. It made me feel better.

I was dropped off at the edge of my neighborhood street, and I trudged passed a few dark houses towards my own home. When I got there, I saw that the driveway was full, which meant family was already there for a pre-Thanksgiving dinner.

I stood on my front porch and knocked twice. It felt weird too be back home again. I had become so accustomed to school and the lush vegetation of the mountain landscape that walking home in the suburbs felt like a weird sci-fi dream.

The door swung open and my mother's beaming mascara eyes focused on my disheveled travel-worn appearance.

"Honey!" She smelled like hairspray, perfume, and chardonnay when she hugged me. My mom drew back with a larger than life smile, and I spotted the half-empty wine glass in her hand.

Way to cope mom.

"Oh, there's our girl." My father came shuffling into the entryway and ushered me inside for a brief half hug. "Ryan!" he shouted down the hall. "Come help your sister with her bags."

Ryan slumped over to us and grabbed my duffel bag without greeting.

Hello sweet brother, how I've missed you so.

"Oh my Lord!" Aunt Isabelle trotted delicately over to where I stood exhausted in the doorway. Her glass of wine was twice the size of my mother's, and it was nearly gone. "Oh look at you! Have you gotten taller?"

God, I hope not.

"Oh, Cindy sweetie, look at her figure." My mother smiled as Aunt Izzy spun me around in a circle. "My Lord, if you aren't just blessed with the prettiest little toosh around!"

I abruptly stopped spinning and cringed a fake smile at my fake-fake-fake Aunt. She was, no doubt, my mother's sister. Unfortunate for them, they both hated each other...but they liked to pretend that they didn't. At least for the holidays.

"Hi Aunt Izzy," I said.

"Oh, come here you!" she squealed and hugged me. "You know you shouldn't call me Aunt. It's just Izzy." Aunt Izzy pulled me closer and fake whispered in my ear, her fake breast nearly broke my ribcage in her tight squeeze. "After all, I am younger than your mother."

My mother heard Aunt Izzy's loud whisper, and miraculously had to leave the room to get another glass of wine.

"You know," I said, mirroring the large plumped up grin she had strapped to her face. "I'm just so darn happy to see you, but, I had such I long ride that I think I need to get some beauty sleep."

"Oh sweetie, I don't think you'll be able to sleep yet!"

"Why?"

"Because we're right in the middle of dinner, silly!"

"Oh, that's okay, I'm not hungry. I'm just going to go to my room and-"

"No, no, no. Your mom let me have you're room for our stay. I have these back problems." Aunt Izzy rolled her eyes to emphasize how important her back problems were. "Uh, just dreadful. I need a bed to sleep in or I would be one Cranky Cathy in the morning!"

Is she saying what I think she's saying?

"Your mom and I have you all set up for the couch, but you'll probably want to wait until we're done with dessert and drinks."

You bed stealing thief!

"Come on, you! Let's get you some food! You're too skinny!"

251

As much as I hated to admit it, at that moment, I really wanted to go back to school.

■■■

There was a sharp bark of laughter from the kitchen. I rolled over in the covers, smothering the pillow over my ears.

Five more minutes.

There were more female giggles, and the timer to the oven screamed.

Five more minutes, please. I'll do anything.

"Lidia." My mother's shrill voice broke through the sound barrier that was my pillow.

I groaned, took the pillow off of my face, and stared up at the dimly lit ceiling of the living room. The entire house smelled like roasted turkey and burnt garlic bread.

"Lidia." My mother came into the room. "Honey, you've been sleeping all day. Dinner will be ready in another hour. Come socialize with the family."

You mean be a distraction for Aunt Izzy.

"Lid, hello?" She jostled the covers where I was buried.

"Just five more minutes."

"No. Get up and take a shower." She stopped harassing my blankets. "When was the last time you had one of those?"

Yesterday.

"Go fix yourself up. Up, up!"

252

I growled as I wrapped myself up in the covers like a burrito and shuffled upstairs.

■■

"Cindy, this ambrosia salad is just divine!" Aunt Izzy took another miniature bite and continued to gush at the surrounding table. "Isn't it Dale? Isn't it divine?"

Poor Uncle Dale nodded and cut another piece of turkey with his knife. His pale ashy exterior brightened momentarily as a plate of mashed potatoes were passed his way.

"Thank you," my mom said. "I used this new recipe I found, it was-"

I stopped listening. I went into a zone where I only focused on the green bean salad that sat on my plate. If I looked at it hard enough, my eyes would water, making it look like it moved.

The pocket of my jeans vibrated. Strategically, I retrieved my cellphone so that I could read it under the table. It was Sammy.

I think I gained ten pounds. FML!!!! Have u talked to E yet?

Mother was on her fifth glass of wine, busy reliving childhood memories with Aunt Izzy, and didn't seem to notice I had my phone.

Nope, not yet. So nervous. :-/

Don't be. E's been hang out with Bret Savage and is acting like a tool @ school. :-P Make him normal again!

Yeah...Me...Normal.

Normal if you didn't count seeing dead people as totally normal. I hadn't told Sammy about the night with Ander because I was still trying to pretend like it never happened.

"Lidia!" My father's gruff voice startled me and I jumped slightly in my seat. "What have we said about cellphones at the table?"

"Sorry dad." I shoved the phone back in my pocket, my heart panging uncomfortably in my chest with dread.

Should I go see Ethan? Even if he does hate me, I should at least look for closure- an official breakup. Ask him about Ashley.

There was a clatter and something wet leaked onto my lap.

"Oh shoot!" exclaimed Aunt Izzy as the wine glass next to her spilled white chardonnay onto my jeans. "I'm sorry darling."

"It's fine. It won't stain."

There was a jingling beep and my father got up from the table, cellphone in hand.

Hypocrite.

"I need to take this, excuse me."

In the twenty minutes following, the rest of the table made weak attempts at conversation while my dad's turkey dinner got cold. Soon, it was the only remaining particle of food left on the table.

"I think I'll go check on Hank." My mother excused herself and hurried out of the living room away from Aunt Izzy's scrutiny.

"So, Ryan," Aunt Izzy started as soon as she had left the room.

Ryan's head turned to gaze at Aunt Izzy, mouth stuffed as if he was in a chubby bunny contest. "Muh?" he tried to speak.

"Have you given any thought to that mission trip I gave you a brochure on?"

I could see the flexing muscles of his face, physically restraining himself from rolling his eyes as he chewed his food and nodded.

"You know, I just think it would be such a wonderful experience for you. There are lots of younger people going down to Mexico this spring, I think it would, just-" she sighed. "It would just be so powerful. They don't require any knowledge of the people down there-" Aunt Izzy dropped her voice to a whisper. "You don't even have to speak Mexican."

What did she just say?

"Lidia, if you're interested, I could probably find a spot for you as well."

"Mucho gracias, but no."

"Oh!" Aunt Izzy wrinkled her nose and slapped my wrist playfully. "Look at that, you already know the language."

"Yes, I'm quite fluent in Mexican."

Across from me, Ryan laughed and the too wide smile slid off of Aunt Izzy's face. She puckered up her lips and stared hard at me. "Do you have something you want to say, young lady?"

"Well, I would, but you only speak American." I pushed away from the table and walked down the hallway towards my father's den. Once inside, I sat there at his mahogany desk, listening to the silence and reveling in my solitude.

I could finally think.

I scanned the room and saw a collection of amber bottles sitting on a shelf. One of them had to be whiskey, and it reminded me of Ander. I took a breath, then dropped my head to cradle it in my hands. Muffled voices came through the air vent near the ceiling.

"*What will you do then Hank?*" My mother's shouts sounded. "*Is that what you want? Is that really it?*"

Without listening to the rest of the conversation, I bolted from the room, pausing only to grab a jacket before storming out of the house. I didn't really have an idea of where I was going, I just knew I needed out.

The cold air was refreshing. It washed over me in huge cleansing waves as the stuffy hot house full of unhappy people disappeared behind me. I continued down the street, guided only by the sound of pavement under my rhythmic steps and the orange glow of streetlights lining the neighborhood.

I only made it a block or so when I heard a soft whimpering. I stopped walking and stood stationary in the middle of the road, waiting for the sound to interrupt the haunting silence again.

It did.

It was soft, and high. Like a dog...

I took a step closer to the sidewalk where I thought it was coming from.

"Hello?"

This better not be a freaking ghost.

"Puppy?"

The whimper came again, and I stepped onto the cold grass, just enough to see the shape of something white lying motionless on its side.

"Bubba!" I hurtled down to where Bubba lay still in the grass. He whimpered again as I dropped to my knees, his tail wagging slightly in a painful attempt at greeting. "Oh, Bubba." Tears welled in my eyes as I looked down at his abdomen. It was completely caved in. His ribcage was deeply indented like he had been hit by a car. Bubba whimpered, his breathing pained and staggered. His eyes were wide in panic and he kept averting his gaze.

"It's okay. Good boy, good boy." I reached out hesitantly, not wanting to hurt him, and touched the bloodied dent on his side. His fur was soft and cold... really cold.

The spot of contact began to glow, heating up to an intense simmer of tickling electricity that snaked its way through my veins, swarming my brain. My bones started to itch before erupting with a seizing pain. I gasped and fell forward on the grass.

"Ah!" It was as if needles of ice were scraping themselves into each rib, something slammed into my chest with cold force.

The pain eased.

Then suddenly, it was like I had a million bees inside my brain that made my skull buzz with a blissfully vacant static.

Bubba's image flashed once, then twice on the grass.

He was gone.

I had just gotten my first real boost.

I turned away, sad that Bubba was gone, and watched the twinkling amber street lights shine with overwhelming intensity. The light stretched out with glowing beams, reaching for the velvet pavement sparking like glitter from a recent rainfall.

"Lidia...is that you?" Ethan stood in front of me.

Whoa... Has he always had so many freckles?

Ethan frowned and bent down to where I sat swaying on the damp grass of an unknown neighbor's lawn. "Lidia?" Ethan pulled me to my feet and looked at my face. His clear blue eyes shone like swimming pools, but I noticed faintly that the intense glow of the lights behind him were dimming.

Oh no.

"Are you drunk?" he asked, one side of his lip twisted upwards in a look of mild disgust.

"No," I was clutching the fabric of his shirt. The cotton felt soft, but the buzz- the boost, was fading quickly.

"I can smell the alcohol." Ethan pulled my hands away from his shirt. "Awesome, Lid. C'mon," he pulled me towards the sidewalk.

"I'm not drunk!" I yanked my hand free.

"Obviously, you are. Did you get into your mom's wine again or something?"

"No, it spilled on me."

"Then why are you out here acting like you're drunk?"

My first boost.

Bubbas dead...

The last thought shot a pang through my heart and what was left of the blissful static faded, leaving me completely sober...with Ethan.

"What are you doing out here?" I asked.

He shrugged. "Sammy called me and said you were home."

"Yeah? Did she say anything else?"

He didn't respond, so I knew that Sammy told him I found out about Ashley. He kicked his foot against the ground and looked at me angrily, as if he had a reason to be angry with me for finding out about Ashley. I stared back, because I knew that if he had a clue as to what had happened between Ander and I, then he'd be twice as angry as he looked.

"Did Ander tell you about Ashley?" he asked.

Hearing him say Ashley's name felt like a punch in the stomach. Hearing Ander's name made my heart squeeze.

"I saw your letter." I stared at him hard for a minute longer. "You're a dick." I added for good measure.

Ethan shrugged. "Can we talk?"

I also shrugged, and then we started walking toward the next neighborhood where Ethan lived. We walked in silence,

259

him in a sort of irritated determination, and me trying not to let my head explode in panic and anger.

Seeing Ethan, even seeing a mad Ethan, brought back a wash of familiarity. We walked across his driveway to the side door of his garage, and somehow, it felt more like coming home than my home did. I felt safe, despite the fact that I had just experienced my first boost, despite the fact that Bubba had died, despite the fact that I slept with his best friend, despite the fact that he wasn't even my boyfriend anymore.

I felt weirdly safe in the familiarity of it all.

Ethan still looked mildly annoyed as he dragged me into the garage and flipped on the fluorescent lights. The garage had been redone by his dad last year, now the part that wasn't occupied by the cars was a man-cave. There was a small fridge full of beers in the corner, a poker table to the left, and sports posters lining the walls. Ethan led me to the poker table where he pulled two disheveled camping chairs over and told me to take a seat.

"Wait here," he said and left the room.

It was cold in the garage, and even with all the manly décor, the combination of white light and darkness outside made me feel gloomy. A moment later, Ethan returned with an unnecessary glass of water.

"I don't need this," I said. "I'm really not drunk. I just had-"

"Lid, I've seen you drunk. Just drink it, okay?"

"Fine. I'll drink the stupid water." I took a sip, it tasted like plastic.

"What were you doing in Mrs. Peterson's yard?" he asked.

"What were you doing in Mrs. Peterson's yard?"

"Going to your house," he said. "My dad's in his office and my grandparents already went home, so, I thought I'd come see how Thanksgiving was going for you."

There was a beat of silence where Ethan watched me, waiting for my reply.

"Congratulations," I snapped. "You want a medal or something?"

"No, I just thought I'd-"

"Why didn't you just go see how Thanksgiving was going for Ashley Galveston?" I folded my arms tightly and tried not to think about Ashley, or Ander, or anything. It didn't work. "Now that you guys are such great friends."

Ethan sighed and looked away dramatically. "It happened once. I haven't hooked up with anyone else since you left."

"Yeah, and you did it as soon as I left. You did it that night, didn't you?"

He didn't answer.

"You did." I shook my head. "Wow."

"You just left!" Ethan's voice rose, but he looked at the garage door leading into the house and lowered it again. "Why did you do that?"

"I don't know." The thought knotted my stomach and I swallowed. I was more hurt than angry with Ethan. I felt worthless, second best, and the fact that I had acted so

261

impulsively and slept with Ander just made me feel cheap. A tear fell down my cheek. "I didn't know how to tell you."

I didn't know how to tell you that I see dead people.

"You should've just told me," he said.

"I know." There was a faint shimmer out of the corner of my eye. When I turned my head, I saw that there was an elderly man in a sweater vest gazing at some tools on a garage shelf.

He was dead.

Ethan didn't see the ghost wandering around the garage and for the first time, it didn't scare me. I didn't really feel anything at the moment, just numb. So I just watched the old man walk about the room, blissfully unaware of Ethan and I having a conversation only a few feet away.

"What are you looking at?" Ethan asked.

"Nothing." I took a deep breath and turned back to Ethan, pretending like the spirit wasn't there. "I already told you I was sorry that I left, and I still am."

Ethan's face softened and he stared at me for a moment. "How's school?" he finally asked.

"It's fine."

"Have you made a lot of new friends?"

"A few."

Ethan pressed his lips together. He looked at the wall as he spoke. "I've missed you."

"Doesn't seem like it. You didn't write back when I sent you a letter, and apparently you moved on pretty quickly...

Ethan, I didn't even know we were broken up. You said you wanted a break, not a break up."

"I don't want a break up!"

"Uh," I stared at him dumbfounded, trying to wipe away the few tears that had fallen. "It's a little late for that."

"Lid, I'm sorry." Ethan reached over and took my hand. I wanted to pull away, but I didn't. Part of me wanted to feel important to somebody again, to feel like I mattered. "I am. I swear, it didn't mean anything and I've missed you like crazy. Like, I'm sorry."

I pulled my hand away.

"Me too."

I was sorry I left, sorry I could see dead people, and sorry I had made so many mistakes. Instead of dwelling though, I took a deep breath and shut it all off. There was nothing I could do now. I was a medium, I had messed up, I had hurt Ethan, and damaged my friendship with Ander. All I could do now was nothing.

The thought of Ander shot a hot pang through my chest, but I ignored it so that my face would stay composed. Somehow, I felt like Ethan could read the secrets on my face if I thought about Ander for more than a second. If it wasn't a secret, then it would feel real, which would make it a much bigger problem.

"Lid, I really don't want it to be over between us." Ethan sounded almost desperate. "I'm sorry."

I didn't know what to say. Ethan kept silent and I kept my gaze focused on the fuzzy green fabric of the poker table.

"I've missed you too," I finally said.

Ethan took a deep breath. "I haven't even told my mom we broke up."

The knots in my stomach tripled, but my chest still felt hollow.

"I just, I couldn't believe you left like that. At Ashley's party, I was drunk and pissed off and, Uhg... Ander wrote to me and told me how much of an idiot I was, and he was right."

I was a few thoughts behind the conversation. "You didn't even tell your mom?"

Ethan shook his head then looked up at me from under his eyelashes guiltily. "Did you.... do you still want to go there for Christmas?"

"I-" I didn't know what I wanted. "I guess so."

Ethan's face split into a broad smile. "You do?"

"Sure... It can't be worse than things are here."

"Okay," his smile widened, and before I knew what was happening, he was leaning across the table to kiss me.

I let him, but it didn't feel like how it used to. It was familiar, and warm, and safe, but something was missing. After a few minutes, he pulled away.

"I know this doesn't mean everything is fixed, but I'm willing to try if you are."

"So, we aren't broken up?"

"Do you want to breakup?" he asked.

"Do you?"

Ethan shook his head. "No, I'll write you letters... I wish you guys had cellphones though."

"We wouldn't get good service anyways."

"Yeah, I guess not." Ethan's big goofy grin split his face and he reached for my hand.

Looking over, I saw that the ghost loitering around the garage was now sitting calmly in the passenger seat of the silver car parked next to a shelf of lawn fertilizer. The old man was gazing out the window at nothing, looking at the concrete walls as if he was seeing changing landscape. I shivered, uncomfortable, but not scared.

■ ■

"You'll miss me?" Ethan pulled me in for another kiss.

"Of course," I laughed against his lips.

"Good." He kissed me again. "You better."

We were entwined in each other's arms at the bus station. It was cold and grey, everything was cast in the gloomy promise of rain. A homeless man with twenty layers of worn clothes and a strange tick in his left eye watched us hungrily from the metal bench where he sat.

"Thanks for dropping me off," I whispered to Ethan. I eyed the bum wearily as he chewed on something that appeared to be very sticky in his toothless mouth.

"No problem." Ethan still had an arm draped over me, the other was responding to a text on his cellphone. He sent the text and put the phone back in his back pocket, then reached over to wrap me in the open folds of his jacket. "Hey," Ethan said with a half-smile. "Isn't that the girl from camp?"

265

I turned as the bus released a long line of bustling people into the cold wind. Amongst the new comers was Trina, but something wasn't right.

"What's her name again?" Ethan asked.

My mouth had gone dry. "Trina."

"Hey Trina!" Ethan shouted, waving her over.

Trina glanced over without expressing any amount of surprise at seeing us there. She had an aura of dark vapor emanating in the space around her. Wisps of blackness reached out from her head, they were almost indistinguishable from the long tendrils of her greasy black hair.

A strange heated tingle penetrated my bones as she approached.

That's not good.

"Hey Trina," said Ethan casually. "What are you doing here?"

"Hi." Trina sighed and rolled her eyes, inconveniencing herself to answer the question. "My parents, like, flipped shit when I didn't come home for Thanksgiving. So, we're doing Thanksgiving now."

"Have you always lived in Oregon?"

She shrugged. "Yes... but my mom is making it so lame."

I considered Trina's appearance as she spoke. With the exception of the smoking halo around her, she looked normal... sort of. The gothic makeup and black on black clothing was the same at least, but she looked dirty. Trina's hair was in tangles, she had large circles beneath her eyes, and she smelled like old laundry.

266

"I don't celebrate Thanksgiving slaughter. Which is what happened to the Native Americans," she continued, staring flatly at Ethan as she spoke. The wind blew, and the blackness wafted in the direction of the breeze. "It's so overrated."

"Right." Ethan said slowly.

"Well," Trina sighed again. "I have to go. The spirits are beckoning me to leave."

Can she see spirits too?

"They want me to go do some dancing at a club in Portland this weekend too. It's supposed to be, like, so cool."

Eh... Maybe not.

"But my cousin once ignored the spirits, and she died... so, bye." Trina turned, bumping drearily into the homeless man as she continued down towards the station. The black smoke lingered behind her like a shadow.

"What a freak... you okay?" Ethan asked.

I nodded.

"Hey, I think I see your bus."

I whipped my head back around to look at Ethan's easy grin. It faded slightly as soon as he saw my eyes wide. "Ethan, I need you to do me a favor."

"Uh, okay."

The bus was approaching, it would be in front of us fast.

"I need you to get Trina's address, or her phone number, and check up on her, okay?"

"Yeah, right," Ethan said as he eased the jacket he was wearing more securely around his shoulders.

"Ethan, I'm serious!"

The bus had stopped and the first set of riders flowed out from the doors.

"What? Did you just see her?" Ethan looked out into the distance at Trina's descending and disgruntled appearance. "I'm not messing with that much crazy." He scrunched up his face. "Besides, she got nasty."

"Ethan!" People were starting to step onto the bus. "Please, I think she needs help. She might be on drugs."

And possibly haunted.

"Fine. Whatever."

I reached up and kissed him on the cheek before running to catch the doors just before they closed. "Bye!" I waved with a thick gloved hand, blowing kisses as the bus driver grumbled something about sitting down.

Ethan waved back, looking sad and confused. The doors closed and I chose my seat by the window, I thought I saw him mouth my name as we pulled away from the station.

Chapter 19

After another long trek with six different bus drivers, I finally arrived back at school just as the sun was setting behind the nearby mountains. I trudged through the white powder on the ground, amazed that the buses had even gotten this far.

I had given myself a headache from stressing out about Trina. I knew I needed to ask the gang what they thought about the ominous dark mist that surrounded her, but first, I just wanted to rest. I hauled my duffel bag up to the girl's dormitory and tried not to think about anything other than sleep. Unfortunately, when I opened the door to my room, it was full of people.

Jessica, Molly, Jeff, and Ander were all huddled in front of my desk where a bunch of random items were arranged in neat lines.

"Hey guys," I said shrugging my duffel bag onto the floor.

"There she is!" squealed Jessica as she ran to embrace me in a hug. As I folded into her tiny arms, I saw Ander turn. His blue eyes froze over like glaciers before he returned his attention back to the assortment of objects on the table.

Great, he's going to make things awkward.

"How was your break?" asked Molly from Ander's side.

"Uh... it was okay. I got my first real boost by accident, but it was really sad because it was our neighbor's dog." The thought still pinched my insides. "I felt like I could feel him get hit by a car, is that normal?"

"Yeah," Jessica sighed. "How do you feel now though? Did you use your boost already?"

I shook my head.

"It feels good, right? I found two spirits hanging out with my mom's bible study group. I was like pow-" she thrust her fist forward. "But then she thought I was on drugs again, so she sent me to my room."

"Margret always thinks you're on drugs," Molly sighed.

"I know, right?" Jessica turned back to me. "The longer you wait, the more it will just fade naturally. You won't have as much to use when you do use it."

I nodded, undisturbed since I didn't have any demanding need to use my boost right away.

"I used my boost on Thanksgiving," Jessica continued. "My mom totally refused to cook the mackerel my grandma bought. It was disgusting, so I gave it a zap and it was like warm rubber." She made a face.

"Wait, you guys ate fish on Thanksgiving?"

"Yeah," Jessica shot Molly a look that said *duh*. "Koreans don't eat turkey. We ate duck and fish."

Molly pushed her lower lip forward. "Poor ducky." She reached over to Jeff who had just moved what looked like a bundle of leaves from the desk. "Don't touch that!"

Jessica ignored them and continued talking. Molly laughed, Jeff smiled, and Ander ignored us. He just sat there, swirling his finger in patterns on the table. Seeing him so unlike himself made me feel uneasy, like there was a heavy object pressing down on my chest. I wanted to tell him about Trina, but he didn't look like he was in a good mood. I remembered what Trevor had said about the holidays being so hard on him after going home and seeing his sister sick, and I didn't want to be the one to deliver more bad news. Still, I knew I had to tell him soon.

Really soon.

There was a knock on the door and a second later, a very pale Trevor came ambling into the room sniffling. "Sup everybody?" His voice was all nasally.

"Are you sick?" Jessica asked. She came up to him, her eyes narrowed in confused worry as her arms hovered in the air, debating whether or not she was going to hug him. At the sight of his tired eyes and runny red nose, she decided not.

"Yeah," he sniffled. "I timed it perfectly, just in time for school to start." He smiled proudly and wiped his red nose. "Hey Lidia, how was your break?"

"Good, I got my first boost."

Trevor gave me a high-five.

"How was your-"

"How's Ethan?" Ander's sharp voice cut through my casual inquiry like a knife.

"Oh yeah!" Molly chirped, oblivious to the shift in the mood. "Did you get to see him?"

Crap.

My pulse quickened momentarily. "Yeah, I saw him on Thanksgiving."

271

"How was it?" she asked.

"Um, awkward, but good."

Ander's eyes were like chiseled ice as he continued to watch.

"Did you guys make up?" Molly asked.

God, shut up Molly.

"Sort of... he invited me to his mom's for Christmas break?"

Jessica sucked in a breath, true excitement beaming from her face. "So, did you guys get back together?"

I shrugged, feeling fidgety under Ander's cool stare. When I met his eyes, his eyebrow raised, a taut smile lingered on his lips.

"You're not answering the question," Molly pressed. "He at least kissed you, right? Did you hook up?"

"No! I mean, yeah, we just kissed." My cheeks blushed. "We're back together," I said lamely.

Anders smile disappeared and returned to making swirling patterns on the desk.

"What's all this?" I pointed to the table.

"We're getting all the stuff we need for the exorcism ready." Ander's voice was flatter than a pancake that had been run over by a semi-truck, and it left my heart feeling drained.

This is not being friends. This isn't what I wanted to happen between us.

"Yeah," Molly sighed. "But Ander lost the most important part."

"I told you that I would get it tonight," he snapped.

Molly raised an eyebrow but didn't say anything.

After regaining control over his temper, Ander turned a casual smile to the rest of the room. "The trainer's are having a party tonight. It'll give us an excuse to sneak up there and grab something of Alex's from his dorm without anyone even knowing we were up there." He settled his gaze onto each of us, his eyes finally locking on mine. "It should already have started. I'm ready to go when you guys are."

"Uh," Jessica said guiltily. "I told Maxx I'd visit him tonight."

Molly catcalled as Trevor shook his head. "I'm not really feeling up for it, man," Trevor sniffed. "I think I'm going to crash."

Ander raised an eyebrow at me.

Is that an invite?

"I'll go," I answered.

"Me too." Molly flipped her hair.

"Yeah," mumbled Jeff quietly. He put a hand on top of his beanie as he spoke, as if the hat would fly off with the nonexistent breeze lingering in the dorm.

"Cool. Let's go." Ander straightened and swept past me towards the door.

The rest of us waved at Jessica and Trevor before we made our way out, following Ander's quick pace. The halls were packed with students hauling luggage and jumping from room to room in pajama pants. More than once, a girl in a fuzzy bathrobe, no makeup, and dribbling wet hair walked past Ander

273

in horror. Looking at the clock behind the girls, I saw that it was nearly curfew and boys weren't usually allowed in the girl's dorms this late. There weren't very many teachers patrolling the halls, but the few present would've sent us all to bed if they had seen the boys. Fortunately, Ander led us with the stealth of a ninja.

The four of us scurried through the dim staircases until we reached the trainer floor at the top of the boy's dormitory. It was a long stretch of windowless hallway. Small golden lit trophy cases where indented into the wall, displaying various ribbons and medals. *Do mediums have competitions? A gold trophy for whomever can get the strongest boost.* The thought twisted my stomach and brought something to mind.

"Hey Ander," I whispered.

"What?" He didn't look back at me.

"I think Trina's haunted."

"What?" Ander stopped, and this time, turned to me. I hadn't expected him to halt so abruptly, and I ran into his side, Jeff jostled into mine, and I heard Molly complain, so I imagined she did the same. Ander's sharp whisper broke the silence. "How do you know if she's haunted?"

"I saw her when Ethan dropped me off at the bus stop. There was a shadow following her, and it moved differently than–"

"Why–" Ander looked really annoyed. "In God's name, are you bringing this up now?"

"I just remembered... I asked Ethan to check up on her, but, I don't know if he actually will."

"You what?" His whisper lashed out in surprised anger, barely a whisper at all. "You asked Ethan to go check up on a dark shadow of a ghost? Half the time those things are demonic, Lidia!"

"That's why I'm telling you now! He won't be hanging out with her or anything," *I hope.* "I just wanted him to see where she lived."

"Are you stupid?"

"Screw you, Ander! She's in trouble!"

"Well good job, now Ethan's in trouble too."

"Hey," came Molly's voice as she shoveled past me. "You two- Focus."

After shooting me an accusing glare, Ander nodded. "We can talk about it later," he said.

A cold trickle of realization settled into the pit of my stomach. *Did I put Ethan in danger?* I made a mental note to write to Ethan the next day, hoping he could at least find Trina's address for me, but hoping more that he didn't have to come in contact with a Spook to do it.

There was the booming sound of music from somewhere around the corner, followed by a gaggling of mingled voices. Ander stopped, leaning his back against the oak paneled wall to look around the corner. I was standing closest, hesitantly waiting for his signal.

How does he always manage to smell so good?

Ander turned, gaze falling on mine until it flickered away towards the others, and he gestured us forward.

There were lights coming from an open door down the hall. Neon flashes of purple, blue, green, and the distinctly bitter scent of cheap alcohol flooded the hall. It made my stomach swirl in a mixed array of emotion and memories. I tried not to look at Ander, focusing my attention on the hallway surrounding us instead. Based off the sound and smell of this party, I was willing to bet good money that all of the trainers in attendance would be too hammered to notice four students.

Trainers went by a different set of rules at school. Not only were their "dorms" more like small apartments, but they also weren't restricted, or monitored, by the rest of the staff. Their responsibilities were to simply chaperone, train, and make sure none of the students were possessed by a Spook while at Walden Cemetery. They were still separated by gender, the girls at the top of my dorm, and boys at the top of theirs, but there was no curfew and the top level of the dorms was a sort of adult-free paradise. Not that I'd ever been, those were just the rumors.

"Whoa!" I halted, jostling Jeff who ran straight into my back again. "Why don't we have one of those?" I asked in a loud whisper. I was referring to the large stuffed wolf crammed into a huge trophy case in a petrified snarling growl. "That is so badass!"

"Lidia!" Molly's panicked expression turned to me. "Come on!"

Ander snapped the door to the first vacant dorm room open, took one look around, and then shut it again.

"Which one is it?" asked Molly.

"I don't know... not that one." Ander went to the next door; the party was right across the hall. "I know he has a Led Zepplin poster on the wall."

276

"Should we check the party?" she whispered.

"They'd notice."

"I'll do it," Jeff said.

"Me too," I said.

"Me too," Molly whispered.

Ander rolled his eyes. "Fine. Meet me back out here in two minutes, I'll go check the next room."

Molly clutched my arm tightly as I followed Jeff into the blazing neon light and hard music. Two tall guys near the door turned to watch us enter with red cups in their hands. The larger of the two put his arm out lazily to stop Jeff, but he eyed Molly and me with a grin that folded sloppily at the corners of his face.

"Hey man," he said to Jeff. "You can't come in."

"Uh, I'm looking for my friend, Catherine," I said casually. Sammy and I had snuck into a frat party once as a dare during Shannon Bittle's birthday party. I used the same line to get into the party, but two seconds later, someone pointed me out to a girl who actually was named Catherine. We ran back outside laughing like maniacs as we rejoined the rest of the girls waiting outside by the car.

"You know Catherine?" one of the guys asked.

Oh no, not again.

"Yeah," I lied. "Have you seen her?"

The two talked amongst themselves about where they had last seen the elusive Catherine, and I took the opportunity to look around the room. In the far corner by the window, Alex sat on the couch, his arm draped around Mindy Johnson, a student in my grade.

"There's no poster in here," Molly said. "Let's go." Her stricken face was focused on Alex in the corner, and it looked like she was trying to shoot him down with laser vision.

I heard the boys protesting as we turned to leave and rejoined Ander at the end of the hall. "I think I found it," he said. "It's this one."

We entered into the dorm and Ander pointed to the four posters of Led Zeppelin hanging on the wall above the couch. We walked down the hall and entered into a small bedroom with two twin beds, a desk, and a large closet.

"No one below the age of forty is this obsessed with Led Zeppelin." Ander withdrew a knitted hat from the top of the bed and turned it inside out. "This should work."

Jeff grinned and came over to give him a high-five.

There was a sudden shriek of laughter outside, and unsteady footsteps came tromping toward the open door. Molly sucked in a gasp of air and ducked under the desk. Jeff dove towards the far bed and covered himself in the sheets, looking like a heap of blankets.

Oh... shoot. We're hiding.

My brain finally kicked in and I spun around the room, looking blankly around for a hiding spot. Ander's hand grabbed my wrist and he pulled me into the darkness behind the closet doors. I stumbled back against a sheet of hanging clothes. The blackness surrounding us was striped with dim light through the wood panels. Ander reached out, pulling me straight just as two voices blasted into the silent space.

There was a girl giggling and an unfamiliar growl of appreciation as the two fell onto the bed neighboring Jeff. It was impossible to see anything besides the bulky shadow of movement through the sliver of an opening, but the sound of shifting sheets and laughter was enough to derive the general gist of what they were doing.

"Oh, Catherine," the guy muttered.

Joy.

I finally found Catherine.

My breathing became shallow, sounding impossibly loud in the silence broken by the faint moans and creak of the bed. I was suddenly aware that Ander's steadying arm was still resting on the small of my back. His gaze was fixated on the sliver of light illuminating his eyes, but as I turned, his gaze shifted and his arm immediately dropped. We looked at each other, unable to speak in our forced silence, but his expression was saying something.

"What the-" the male voice boomed out in shocked dismay, and there was the sound of sheets shuffling. "Who the hell are you?"

Ander whipped his head back towards the door, and then pushed it open. Jeff was thrashing out from under his tangle of covers and Molly was already sprinting for the door. We burst from the closet to see the shocked expression of the couple half dressed in bed. The girl looked particularly pissed off.

Sorry Catherine.

We ran from the room, joining Jeff and Molly as we raced towards the stairs, stifling giddy exaltations of frightened laughter. The tall trainer with bushy eyebrows came waddling after us down the hall, sheltering his manly bits with a pillow and sliding across the smooth floor in tall tube socks.

279

"Hey!" His foot slid beneath his body and he face planted on the floor. "You perverts!"

We kept running through the halls and stairs until we were just outside the student lounge.

"Oh. My. God." I gasped. I couldn't figure out if I wanted to laugh or breathe first. My body was trying to do both and it was painful.

Jeff was grinning wildly, and Ander was already curled against the wall in hysterical shoulder shaking laughter.

"That was so great." Molly slid down the wall, collapsing against Ander with a flash of white teeth.

He looked down, still smiling with an eyebrow slightly raised at her sudden proximity. A small burble of heat filled my stomach, but before I could analyze it, I spotted a man that looked almost exactly like Albert Einstein pass through the hallway in front of us.

"Professor Short," Jeff murmured.

The Professor had wild wisps of white hair that stormed above heavy eyebrows. He turned at the sound of Molly's giggles and his brows shot strait up, disappearing into his cloud of hair.

Jeff swore and started down the hall at full speed, I followed, Ander and Molly close behind. My heart felt like it was going to burst. My ribs were suddenly a cage for the throbbing organ inside of me. Jeff dodged down a dark corner and I followed, pressing my back against the wall as Ander and Molly ran straight pass.

No! Wrong way! Wrong way!

Not two seconds later, Professor Short went speeding in their direction. I looked a Jeff who silently communicated-*they're screwed,* with a single look before nodding toward the stairs.

"Should we just leave them?" I asked.

Jeff shrugged. "If you want a detention you can go find them, but they're caught either way."

He was right... and I definitely didn't want another detention. Feeling a little guilty, I agreed to return to my empty dorm. Molly came in an hour later, looking disgruntled, but not unhappy.

"Hey," I said from the top bunk. "What happened? You ran right past us."

"Mr. Short cornered us in the Janitor closet." My stomach did a weird twist of revulsion at the imagery. "We got detention, but it actually works out perfectly."

"Why?"

"We have to water the greenhouse this week." She smiled happily and crawled under the covers. "I love the greenhouse, so, it won't be so bad. It's just kind of perfect."

Chapter 20

I didn't even know Mountain Heights had a greenhouse. It was tucked behind the school gym in a cluster of trees that hid most of the exterior from view. The outside had mysterious brown streaks creeping down the plastic paneling, but inside, everything was vibrant and alive.

After Molly and Ander had finished their detention, they invited us all to join them in the greenhouse to help me practice for the SETT, which I had signed up to take the following week. Professor Short watched warily as each of my friends took turns teaching me how to levitate leaves near his favorite potted shrub.

For the most part, I did okay. Ever since I had absorbed Bubba, the mystery of a boost had been diminished, and I realized that it wasn't as frightening as I had first anticipated. It still created an intimate connection between the spirit and medium due to the death-memory-flash experienced during absorption, but the resulting boost almost made it worth it.

The humid air and soft natural light leaking in through the ceiling of the greenhouse was soothing enough for me to actually concentrate as I practiced. That is, until Ander started commenting on the way my face scrunched up when focusing on the leaf or how the leaf shook in the air. After his third insulting prod, I got so frustrated that all my energy was expelled at once, leaving Professor Short's favorite shrub nothing more than a tangle of twigs. We weren't allowed to practice in the greenhouse after that.

To make matters worse, Ander kept jumping from making sarcastic remarks disguised as humor, to being downright rude. It was driving me insane. I couldn't tell if his irate mood swings were because I had put Ethan in danger, because he was stressed about preforming an exorcism on his brother, or because we slept together. Whatever his reason was, our friendship was far from friendly.

I had even started waking up earlier in hopes of being the first person at breakfast. Being first meant that I was able to avoid eating with Ander since he usually slept in.

And go figure... I try and avoid him, and he's already here.

I took an excruciatingly long time in the waffle line, making a piece of sugar-art that would rival even some of Picasso's work. Knowing I couldn't avoid Ander forever, I finally sighed and walked over. I set my tray on the table gently, hoping my silence would somehow make me invisible. Ander took a sip of coffee and looked up.

"Did you write to Ethan yet?" he asked.

"Yeah, he should've gotten the letter today."

Ander had cornered me in the student lounge the day before to discuss how stupid it was to ask Ethan to check up on Trina. He had yelled. I had yelled. People had started to watch.

It was anarchy.

In the end, I agreed that Ethan shouldn't try and talk to Trina in person, but only after making it clear that Ander had a bad attitude, and it wasn't appreciated. Besides, I had already written to Ethan the night after going to the trainer's dorm.

"Great," Ander nodded and continued to watch me while I cut into my waffle.

"What?" I asked.

He didn't say anything.

"You want some? The waffle line is that way."

He raised an eyebrow, as if I had been the one creepily staring a minute ago.

Okay Lidia, calm down… If we aren't going to be friends, it won't be for lack of effort.

"How's your breakfast?" I asked, trying to keep my voice light.

Ander continued to stare as he took another sip of coffee. "Excellent." His voice was flat and sarcastic. "How's yours?"

"Good."

"*So good*?" he moaned.

I froze mid-bite.

Ander made another moan, louder this time, as he took a bite of his own breakfast. "*Oh yeah.*"

"Shut up," I hissed. A few people from nearby tables turned to look over at us. "What is wrong with you?"

"Nothing," he smirked. "I thought I was doing a pretty good impression."

"Screw you, Ander!"

"Again?" He ignored the heat rising to my cheeks and continued eating, as if nothing unusual had just been said.

"Don't you ever get sick of having waffles for breakfast every single day?"

I was just about to shove the waffle into his smug little face when the seats around us scooted away from the table and four people sat down.

"Okay," Jessica chirped. "This is getting ridiculous. The dance is this Saturday, and I'm still the only one with a date." Jessica had announced her decision to take her stalker A.K.A. Maxx Jackson to the dance yesterday.

"Not true." Trevor winked at Jeff. "Jeff and I are taking Rose and Kristin."

"Oh," Jessica rolled her eyes. "Yeah, you guys will have fun with those two... I don't understand why they don't just come out of the closet and go together."

"I'm not complaining," Trevor eyed the two girls from across the cafeteria.

Rose and Kristin were best-friends-forever with borderline lesbian-like qualities to their relationship. They were both pretty brunettes that were practically joined at the hip. Most of us speculated that they either wanted to be each other, or be on each other, no one could really tell.

"Maybe they'll let us watch them make out," Trevor said with dreamy eyes.

"Grow up," Jessica sighed. "That's good though." She clapped her hands. "We're all set up! I'm going with Max, Jeff and Trev have the weird sisters," Jeff made an inaudible comment but Jessica ignored him and continued. "Molly is going with Alex, and then Lidia and Ander can go together. That works out perf-"

"I'm not going with her!" Ander set his coffee cup down with a little too much force. The hot liquid splashed the sides and ricocheted onto the table in dark steaming droplets.

"What?" Jessica exclaimed. "Why not?"

Ander chewed the inside of his cheek as he glared into the dark abyss of his coffee mug.

"I haven't even asked Alex yet," said Molly, taking a hesitant glace at the table where Alex and his delinquent group of friends sat. Alex was sitting, not in a chair, but on the actual table while he entertained the boys with a story that required a lot of crude hand gestures.

"Well," Jessica looked aggravated. "Tick-toc."

"Right now?"

"Yes! Go ask him."

Molly rolled her eyes and stood up. She smoothed a hand over the folds of her blouse before taking a deep breath and marching across the cafeteria toward the group of boys. They eyed her like a piece of meat as she approached. Molly tapped Alex on the shoulder. After what looked like a short, but heated exchange, Molly turned abruptly and stormed back to the table.

"I won't do it. I won't!" Her voice was at a normal volume, but somehow it still sounded like she wanted to scream. "He's such an asshole!"

"Did you even ask him?" asked Jessica.

"No!"

After a moment of silence, Ander let out a breath of air and eased an arm across the back of Molly's chair. "Well, that solves that problem," he grinned. "If you guys aren't going together, we'll just lure him there. I needed a date anyway, he'll *hate* it if I go with Molly."

Molly looked as surprised as I felt, and a lot happier. Behind them, Alex's brooding zeroed in on Ander's arm around Molly.

"I like it!" Jessica said. "I think this will work."

I felt like the last picked for the dodge ball team. "What am I supposed to do about a date?"

"Guess you can't go," Ander said.

"Thanks," I shot him a look, but he just smiled and took a sip of coffee, his arm still slung around Molly's chair. "It's fine," I said. "I have the SETT to worry about anyways, and I don't even want to go. I can just meet you guys somewhere."

"Cool," Ander said. "There isn't anyone for you to go with anyways... unless you asked the thirteen-year-old boys you used to sit with."

"I didn't sit with them."

"You sat with them."

"Sat *next* to them."

"I bet they'd go with you," Ander continued, ignoring my glare. "The redhead was extra credit last year, you'd have something in common." I swore at Ander, but it only made him chuckle. "Whoa," he put his hands up. "Not my fault you can't get a date."

"Actually, Jay Ronaldson has a fat crush on Lidia," Molly said. "He was talking about you in Trig the other day."

"Jay Ronaldson?"

BLT guy?

I recalled the auburn-haired boy with a lip piercing from the library, and I looked around the cafeteria. I found him sitting with a group of kids I'd never met.

"I don't think he's ever actually talked to me," I said.

"Really? He sounded really into you," Molly shrugged. "I know he's shy, but he's really nice."

"He's an idiot," Ander scoffed. The collective group at our table turned to look at him. "What?" Ander said, his voice rising an octave in false innocence. "I'm sorry, but I thought you were back together with Ethan?"

"I am!"

"So, does that include messing around with-"

"I'm not messing around with anyone!"

"Oh yeah, that-"

"Dude," Trevor cut in. "We're doing this for your brother, cool off."

"I know Ethan's your friend and all, but I seriously doubt she'll run into any trouble with Jay," Molly said. "Jay is kind of a wienie... you'll have to lay on the charm."

"Will do." I started mashing what was left of my waffle with my fork, picturing it as Ander's head.

■ ■

Apparently, I was really bad at "laying on the charm" and as the dance approached, I was becoming more and more nervous. I had tried talking to Jay several times throughout the week. I purposefully dropped my books in the hall in front of him- which he ignored, tried borrowing a pencil in class- he only had pens. I even smiled like an idiot every time I caught him staring. I felt so stupid.

Unfortunately, whatever charm I lacked, Ander made up tenfold in his quest to lure Alex to the dance via jealousy. It seemed to be working.

Throughout each meal in the cafeteria, Molly miraculously ended up on Ander's lap while Alex glared moodily over from his usual table. In the hallways, Ander would play with her hair, and whispered sweet nothings into her ear. *Disgusting*. I knew it was all fake, but it still made me feel sick. Probably just because Ander made me feel sick in general... all the freakin' time.

In a way, I was lucky he had other duties to perform because it let me study for the SETT uninterrupted. Ander was so busy playing touchy-feely with Molly that he had little to no time to insult or embarrass me. Not that the new situation was any less annoying.

I had been especially annoyed on the day of my SETT when they decided to join me for study time in the student lounge after lunch. Since the two off them took up the entire couch, I sat cross legged on the floor, hunched over unattractively at their feet. I was trying to stare sense into the sentence I was reading, but my concentration was continually interrupted by Molly's laughter. One of her books slipped off the couch and smacked the text I was reading.

"Okay," I picked the book up, and shoved it hard into the small patch of Ander's stomach that I could actually reach. "Can you not?"

"Ouch," Ander chuckled, one arm still intertwined around Molly. "Jesus, Lid."

"Don't call me Lid."

"Why?"

"Because."

"Ethan calls you Lid."

"So do my parents."

"Then why can't I?"

I didn't respond. I looked over and saw Alex reading a small paperback novel with a fainting damsel on the cover. It was obvious Alex hadn't looked at the cover before he pulled it off the communal bookshelf. He was already half-way done, and it was upside down.

"What time does the SETT start?" Molly asked.

It was finally time to take my SETT, and I was freaking out. I hadn't slept in what felt like days, and my eyes had gone blurry from so much reading. The gang had told me it was all a practical, but since field training was my weakest point, it only made me feel more nervous.

All through the school day, I had watched as teachers and three men in suits that I didn't recognize, set up a large wire fence in the field out front. Molly told me it was electrified, making it possible for even the weakest spirits to appear as full apparitions within the confines of the wires while surrounded by Ultrasonic Spirit Meters around the rest of the campus. By the time they had finished midafternoon, the fence resembled a caged boxing ring. The black wire fizzed and sparked from all angles. The sides and the top, even the rubberized metal rods made a high voltage checkerboard on the grassy floor.

"The signup sheet said it started at four," I said, highlighting a line of text on my paper.

"It's three fifty seven!"

My heart stopped. I whipped my head at the clock, saw that Molly was right, and scrambled to my feet. I haphazardly gathered my things and raced out of the lounge without a goodbye. I thought I heard Ander wish me good luck, but I didn't have time to figure out if he was being sarcastic or not.

I ran down the hall with papers flying out from behind me. Busting outside, I finally made it to the line forming in front of the sign-in sheet. After I had slowed my breathing, I realized it was incredibly cold and I had completely forgotten my jacket.

Most of the snow had melted, leaving only small white patches that hid from the sun in the shadows of the trees. The rest of the field had turned a marshy yellow, all of the dead wet grass lay flat against the ground. Only the evergreens of the forest had maintained their usual color.

"Lidia Powell," a tall teacher I had never met called my name.

"Here."

She nodded and made a note on her clipboard. She called a few other names, and each student raised their hand. The other students were all thirteen or younger, and I towered above them. It was nerve-racking gearing up for such an important test, but mostly it was embarrassing to be surrounded by such young kids outside of Psychic 101. Now that class was out, the embarrassment was amplified by the swarm of older students that had gathered around the testing arena to watch the SETT. There were even kids inside the school that pooled around the large windows and pointed down at us.

The woman that had called my name cleared her throat. "Now that everyone is here, I think it's time to start. My name is Mrs. Harkling, this is Professor Short, The Dean of Admissions, Mr.Dodger," she gestured to each of them gathered in front of the arena.

Mr.Dodger was wearing what looked like a bearskin over his usual attire. He waved cheerfully at me from across the crowd, and I cringed a smile back. He had the fashion sense of a blind hobo, but the fuzzy bear coat looked warm.

"From The Federal Department of The Gifted, we have Mr. Carlson, Mr. Walker, and Mr. Benton."

Mr. Benton, the eldest of the three men in black suits, nodded at someone in the crowd watching. I looked over and saw that Ander, Molly, Jeff, Trevor, and Jessica were all huddled together in the cold. Jessica smiled at me, and Jeff nodded back at the man in the suit. I remembered that Jeff's last name was Benton, and I wondered if they were related.

Maybe he can put in a good word for me if I don't pass.

Why didn't I bring a flippin' jacket?

"We are going to be assessing you on this three part test. This is the Standardized Energy Transfer Test, the purpose is to clearly identify how capable you are at using your abilities, and to decipher whether or not you require further training. The first part of this test is the absorption of energy. This will allow us to see how well you deal with spiritual apparitions."

I gulped. I already knew that I was not good with spirit apparitions.

"The second part of the test is expulsion. If you complete the first stage of the test, you will be using the energy to levitate an inanimate object at least six inches off the ground.

292

The third stage of the test will be defense. This is a very dangerous step, but necessary in the process of deciphering your ability. You will be required to block a manifestation of dark energy."

Oh no.

"There will be onsite trainers in the cage with you during this stage of the test to assist you if you need it." Mrs. Harkling then went into a long list of rules and expectations while I shook from both fear and cold. Eventually, she started calling names and the first stage of the test commenced.

Each student entering into the cage stopped in front of the first of two tables located near the entrance. The tables were lined with what looked like a bunch of old junk, stuff you would find in a flea market. Mrs. Harkling explained that each object was haunted. The spirits were mild, but in the cage they would become full apparitions. The student was allowed to choose whatever object they liked, so long as it didn't have a red sticker, and were then instructed to step into the cage.

Most of the apparitions weren't too horrific, but the students looked appropriately terrified as they stretched their fist into the abdomen of choking phantoms reliving the last few seconds of life. A small kid named Tyler McCoy brought a rustic axe into the fence with him. When a wailing apparition of a bloodied man choking on his own crimson spit appeared a minute later, Tyler had bolted towards the doors and received a jolt of electricity as he clawed at the exit. He wasn't allowed to go on with the rest of the test.

When my name was finally called, I forced my legs forward. I heard my friends calling my name from the crowd, but I felt queasy, and I didn't think I could fake a smile their way. Without really seeing the table full of haunted objects, I chose at random and entered the wire cage with a white ribbon in my hand.

"Clear?" asked a trainer from outside the cage.

I nodded and she yanked the handle down on the door. The wire around me started to hum and I was suddenly hit with an intense chill that went further than skin deep. My bones seared as if they had been doused in dry ice and I winced, surprised by the sparking pain in my body.

"D-d-d-d-d-don't do- do this," sobbed a woman from behind me.

I turned and found myself face to face with a gorgeous young girl, only a few years older than me, dressed completely in white. She had a veil that hung haphazardly from a tangled mess of hair, and her wedding dress was torn and speckled with blood.

"Ssssstop." Tears streamed from her eyes as her face crumpled. One cheek had a dark circling bruise and a small red cut. "I-I- lo-lo-love him." She was begging with me, shaking from head to toe. "Please, please, le-let hi-"

She reached out towards me, but before the woman could touch my shirt, I thrust a fist forward and it sank into her chest. It glowed, soft and warm. I felt a wash of overwhelming sadness take my body and I fell to my knees, hard spikes of pain shot through my face, my groin, my arm, and then I felt a crack at the base of my neck.

Everything went hazy as I watched the women's face relax. Her figure flashed once, twice, and disappeared. My brain exploded with sparks of buzzing pleasure. Woozy, I carefully stood up and smiled. I heard my name like a distant echo through the rumble of the crowd.

"Woohoo! Good job Lidia!"

There were flowing veins of blue electricity that traced around the black wire cage. They were intensely vibrant, sparking neon. I blinked, feeling the warm buzz through my body fade, and then suddenly the sparks stopped, and the wire went back to a flat matte black.

"Miss Powell," called the trainer from the open cage door.

I gave her a hazy grin and waltzed forward. By the time I left the cage, the remainder of my boost was gone, but I was still smiling because I had passed the first stage.

The second stage was boring to watch.

There was a table set up in the middle of the arena with a square box resting on top. A trainer stood by with a ruler and measured the length of air under the box as it was levitated. Nearly everyone passed this stage of the test, including myself.

Unfortunately, by the time the third stage of the test rolled around, my palms were covered in sweat despite the dropping temperature and fading daylight. As night dawned, the testing station was lit up by a large fluorescent light that gave everyone inside an eerie white glow. It was like being under a never-ending camera flash.

The third stage of testing started like the first. Each student was able to choose a worn object from an assortment of junk on top of the table, marked clearly with large red hazard stickers. The students held their haunted objects like ticking time bombs.

"Simone Pratt," called Mrs.Harkling.

Simone Pratt left the line and walked toward the table. She picked up an old guitar, almost as big as she was, and stepped inside the cage with a trainer close at her side. The trainer nodded at the teachers, and the test began. Not two seconds after the electricity was turned on, Simone drop the guitar as if it had bitten her. A dark oozing mass erupted from the strings twisted around the neck of the instrument and pooled together on the opposite side of the cage.

"Just let me know if you need help." The trainer, I think his name was Cody, poised his stance.

Simone's wide eyes watched the darkness warp itself into a human form, before something else stepped out.

I felt a hitch in my breathing.

The Spook resembled the monster I had seen at the graveyard with Alex, only this one was smaller. Dark flat plates of skin covered most of its body like scales, but there were still oozing red blotches of raw flesh in patches. The Spook looked like it had been burned alive.

I looked back at Simone, she was worried, but nowhere near as terrified as I felt.

The Spook's mutilated body knelt forward, bones and joints cracking into an unnatural lunge. It moved like an insect, sudden jerking motions propelling the twisted limbs forward. Just as it was about to reach her, a burst of shimmering air clouded around Simone, and the Spook was gone.

The crowd clapped politely and she exited the station. No one looked shocked, and when the next student took her turn to calmly block the black-eyed monster racing forward, I began to panic. Even Tyler McCoy, who was terrified of his bloodied apparition, watched the rest of the students testing with a glazed-over expression of disappointment.

"Lidia Powell."

"Go Lidia!" called Jessica.

"Woop Woop!" Trevor pumped his fist.

I took a deep breath and made my way towards the table. I chose a large metal rod with the red WARNING sticker wrapped around the side. I wasn't sure why anything would be haunting such a boring piece of metal, but figured I could at least use it as a weapon when the Spook came after me.

The trainer, Cody, walked me to the center of the cage, then stood with hands folded in front of him by the exit. He looked far too relaxed. If Cody knew how I felt about the whole situation, he'd already be pulling me out of the cage. He nodded once at Mrs. Harkling outside, and the electricity was turned on.

The metal rod seared hot in my hands, but I forced myself to hold on as black vapor streamed from the end. I reached my arm out as far as it would stretch. It was like shooting off a roman candle, but instead of colorful sparks, blackness trickled from the tip in a heavy cloud.

Don't let go, don't let go.

It wafted upwards until it was right in front of me, reaching out with tendrils of black mist that moved like ink polluting clear water. After a long minute, the darkness had diluted, and the rod felt cold again.

A low guttural growl sounded in my left ear. I whirled around and saw the Spook hunched over on the opposite side of the cage. It twisted its face sideways, neck breaking with soft pops under the skin until the black eyes were lined atop of each other.

You can do this.

I tried to slow my breathing, but the scent of decay emanating from the Spook's slack jaw made it hard to concentrate. It made another low growl. I had to force myself to breath.

You just watched thirteen other students do this, you can do it too.

The Spook turned its head a little further to the side, bone scraped against bone. It leapt forward.

I swung the metal rod as hard as I could against the rotting flesh that thinly veiled its disgusting face, but instead of a hard crack, it felt like I had hit water. The resistance was nothing, my rod cut through the Spook easily, and I fell to the ground.

"Do you need assistance?" Cody asked, a hint of confusion in his voice.

"N-no," I gasped. "I got this."

You can do this, you can do this.

I dropped the rod and turned to see the Spook staring intently at me. It was half standing in an ill attempt to appear human. The broken ribs jutting out of its abdomen shifted and the Spook stepped forward, staggering slightly due to the unnatural structure of his build. It opened its mouth in a snarl, but over the guttural noise, real words came out. It almost sounded like- *You can see.*

I forced my eyes shut and exhaled.

Blocking felt like a migraine. I forced so much energy, so much tension and focus, into the back of my eyes that my head pounded unpleasantly. It left a cool static on my skin and a deep throbbing in my brain.

The sound of hesitant clapping is how I knew it was over.

I opened my eyes fully and looked around the cage. With the exception of Cody, it was empty. A wash of relief flooded my body and I smiled back at the crowd. Jessica gave me the thumbs up, Jeff looked intensely puzzled, and Ander clapped with one eyebrow raised.

I had passed.

Chapter 21

The next day was the Friday before the dance, and I still didn't have a date. During lunch with Jessica, Jeff, and Trevor, I tried not to throw up on my sandwich as I watched Molly and Ander feed each other chips on a nearby tombstone.

"It's disrespectful to the dead... I wouldn't want crumbs on my grave." I bit off a piece of my sandwich with a scowl.

"I would if they were BBQ ranch," Trevor said. "The flavors would seep through the ground and into my open mouth." He did a disturbingly good impression of an opened-mouthed corpse in rigor mortis.

Jessica laughed, but I was too busy watching Molly lace her fingers between Ander's while they looked deeply into each other's eyes. I threw my half-eaten sandwich back into the bag, suddenly sick.

"Hey, extra credit!" Dale Becker called to me from his gang of friends. "Are you signing up for the team this year?" He pretended to swing an invisible baseball bat in the air. His impression, albeit a poor one, made his friends and a few onlookers laugh.

"Hey Dale," Ander called, his hands still attached to Molly's. "Are you actually going to make the team this year?"

Dale grumbled and turned back to his friends who were still laughing. I pulled chunks of dead yellow grass out of the ground and ignored them both.

"That was pretty funny," Jessica said. "Seriously, I have never seen anyone try and hit a Spook before."

"Spooks are scary!" I threw a blade of grass at her, but it only floated to the ground. "I'm surprised everyone passed that part."

"Yeah, but for new mediums, apparitions are usually way worse." Trevor had finished his lunch and was crinkling the paper bag into a tight ball. "Maybe we've told you too much about Spooks."

"No, they're definitely scarier."

"Well, we aren't going to smack the Spook out of Alex tomorrow, so you better get used to the block." Trevor was talking about the A.P. set to take place tomorrow night. We were all nervous, but none of us wanted to admit how unsure of success we really were. "Though-" Trevor trailed off as he watched Alex glare in the direction of Molly and Ander. "If you wanted to try it, I could probably find you another piece of piping."

"Is that what it was?" I asked.

"What did you think it was?"

"I don't know. Why was a pipe haunted?"

"Maybe a group of devil worshipers dumped all their voodoo juice down a toilet," Trevor said. "And the Spook was all- *Oh, I think I like it here.*"

"That's gross," Jessica rolled her eyes.

Trevor laughed. "Lidia's the one who took the piping from a haunted John."

I reached over and smacked Trevor in the stomach and he started giggling like a little girl.

"What did you see when-" Jeff stopped himself as the rest of the group turned to watch. It was such a rare moment when he spoke, that it usually received undivided attention. "Never mind."

Alex's blaring whistle sounded the end of lunch.

Jess nudged my leg as Jay Ronaldson trudged by, completely oblivious to my presence. "If you don't ask him to the dance today, I'm asking him for you."

I sighed, got up, and stomped over to where Jay was slouched against a tree. "Hey," I said.

Jay's eyes widened momentarily before his mouth split into a crooked grin. "Hey."

I waited...

Is that it?

Apparently it was.

"Uh, do you want to be my partner for the training today?" I asked. "We could practice at that tree over there?"

"Yeah, sure."

"I have to warn you, I got a mean boost earlier." I had absorbed two orbs and I was extremely proud of myself.

"Ha, okay."

"Yeah, so... watch out." I plastered the sweetest smile I could muster onto my face.

"Okay. I will."

I had already discovered that Jay wasn't a talker, though I was still consistently surprised at his ability to bring any sort of conversation to a halting stop. In a way, I felt like bringing Jay to the dance would be comparable to just carrying around a pet-rock. I had a suspicious feeling they would offer the same amount of social stimulation.

It was probably for the best though. I hadn't told Ethan the full truth about the dance, he wouldn't have understood an exorcism, and mentioning I would need a date would've really pissed him off. Since I didn't want to lie completely, I told him I was going with a "group of Ander's friends" and planned on leaving early, which was essentially true.

As the rest of the students paired off, Jay and I sauntered off toward a patch of trees on the forest edge. Jay walked so close to me that our shoulders kept brushing and I nearly tripped on his feet more than once.

Alex blew his whistle again.

"Just like last week, we're doing electrical force and directional expulsion." Alex's voice was loud and confident, though his eyes kept wondering towards Ander and Molly who were at the tree next to ours. "You need to focus on getting all the energy in one area." He wiggled his fingers in the air. "With these," Alex pointed an outstretched hand toward the nearest tree, and a strong blaze of electricity burst through the air. The beam shimmered like a mirage as it leapt up and down with seizurous jerks. When Alex withdrew his hand, there was a burn mark on the rugged trunk of the oak the size of a CD disk. "Okay, losers!" Alex said. "Get to work!"

Jay may not have been great with words, but he wasn't bad at his energy transfers. I watched him blast energy through the air with some admiration.

"You're so good that this!" I called out to him.

"Yeah," he said. "I know."

I tried not to roll my eyes as I hugged my black jacket closer to my body. The air was sharp this high in the mountains, and the smell of snow and smoke stung my nose. Somehow, it reminded me of the campfires at Camp Tanka.

So much had changed since then.

Out of the corner of my eye, I saw Molly walking over to Alex and I felt a twinge of pleasure. Instead of making babies, Ander and Molly were on A.P. duty. Molly was responsible for having Alex show her how to use the boost, and in doing so, charm him out of all his own pent up energy. Ander was left to practice cooking trees with a mean-faced boy that barely came up to my elbows.

Jay zapped the tree.

"I think it might snow again," I said, turning away from Ander with a smirk.

"Yeah," said Jay. "I love snow."

"Me too." I waited for him to finish and then stepped uncomfortably close to his side to take my own turn.

"Good job." Jay smiled encouragingly at my lame sparks that shot a foot in front of me and then disappeared with a pathetic fizzle.

"Uh, no, I suck."

"No, you're really good." Jay stepped closer and rested a hand on my lower back.

Whoa buddy.

"Thanks," I smiled warmly, but turned just enough so that he was forced to drop his hand. "Your turn."

Jay let a burst of brilliant electricity explode from his fingers and blast into the side of the trunk. When it ended, I cheered, and reached up to give him a high-five, which he decided to bypass. Ignoring my hand hovering in the air, he leaned down and wrapped his arms around my waist in a tight hug.

"Oh," I cringed and forced my arms to fall around his neck. "Uh, I guess your boost beat mine."

Ew, ew, ew. He's touching me.

Jay leapt back. He cursed and waved his foot around in the air. I watched him jump around in a weird dance for a minute before I was suddenly hit with the smell of burning rubber and noticed the stringy bits of black tar trailing off one of his boots.

"Ah!" I heard Ander shout from beside us. "Sorry man, my aim sucks."

"Ander!" I shouted, fury boiling inside of me. "Knock it off!"

Ander laughed, raising both hands. He turned back to his partner, and gestured back toward the tree.

Molly was on the other side of the cemetery with Alex who was smiling like an idiot. She kept asking him to show her how powerful his beams of electricity were. Over, and over, and over again. Through the thrashing spark of his electric beam, I kept hearing Molly say *"Like this?"* and *"Wow! Show me again!"* It was really pathetic, but it seemed to be working.

Jay swatted at the smoking globs melting off his boot. When he had finally stomped it out, a little patch of melted rubber lay frozen in the grass at his feet.

"Are you okay?" I tried to look concerned and not just like I wanted to laugh, which I sort of did.

"Yeah... asshole just got my shoe," he grumbled.

"Awe, your date for the dance will be disappointed. How are you going to dance in those?"

Somewhere to my left, I heard Ander snort a laugh.

"What do you mean?" Jay asked. "I wouldn't wear these shoes to a dance, these are my training boots."

Well, thank you captain obvious.

"Oh good. Then I guess your *date*," I emphasized the word for clarity. "Will be able to dance with you after all."

"I don't have a date." He screwed up his face and looked at me a minute, putting the pieces together. "Do you?"

"No," I shrugged sadly. "No one has asked me yet. I'm looking for someone to go with me as friends though."

Come on... ask me, you dingus.

"Uh, do you want to go with me as friends?"

"Sure." I smiled like a star struck fan-girl and his whole face split into a broad smile.

It sent my insides crawling.

■ ■

Molly looked over at me from her station in front of the mirror in the girl's bathroom. "You look really upset," she said.

She was right.

I had on the fancy nature-green formal dress I had worn to sophomore homecoming. My hair was curled and pinned to one side, leaving a bronzed shoulder bare. My eyes were bright, accented with a shimmering shadow and smokey liner. My lips, currently pouting, were a deep crimson.

Altogether, I was gorgeous. It was my warped facial expression of absolute dread that really undid all the hard work that went into my attire.

"I don't want to go."

"It'll be fine," Molly said, arranging the sparkling golden rose that held up her high bun. With her bright yellow dress and blond hair, she looked like a sunbeam. "We've been planning this for weeks. Ander said, that Alex said, that he would be coming, and I got Alex to use up, like, all of his boost yesterday." Molly shook her head and sighed. "So pathetic." A fake sparkly eyelash started to come undone and she leaned closer to her reflection to fix it. "Anyways, Jessica put all of the stuff in her ginormous tote, and Alex isn't going to suspect a thing because we all have dates. It's going to be great." She smiled at herself, looking a little too excited, and a little too pretty to be preparing for an exorcism.

"Well, if I'm being honest. My date is what I'm dreading the most."

"Why? I think Jay's really cute."

Then why don't you take him?

"Talking to him is like talking to-" I picked up a jar of face gunk from her cosmetic bag. "This moisturizer." I held the jar face level. "Well good evening Neutrogena, tell me, how do you feel about exorcisms?" I listened for the response. "Fascinating."

Molly snatched the jar away from me and stuffed it into her bag. "You're so weird."

"Hey, I was having a conversation!"

She giggled, rolling her eyes as she finished packing up. "Come on, everyone's probably waiting by now."

We teetered down the stairs toward the main building where we were supposed to meet everyone in front of the gym. The extra inch of height the heels had given me made it hard to walk, but I tried to keep good posture as we turned to enter the hall.

It was flooded with students. Girls in silky candy colored dresses, and boys in smart tuxes were all huddled in various sized cliques around the gymnasium entrance. There was already booming music deafening the conversation in the hall and the velvet curtain covering the gym entrance kept moving as students made their way into the dance.

Molly and I shuffled past a few kids, and finally found a group of familiar faces. Molly grabbed my hand to drag me forward. "Hey guys," she had to shout her greeting over the music as we approached.

The circle formation broke and the two boys facing the gym turned towards us. Ander's eyes immediately locked on mine, and he stared without the usual smirk of sarcasm for the first time in weeks. The momentary parting of his lips reminded me of our night together, and I swear I could feel heat radiating off his body in waves. I faintly registered someone saying something from the circle, but didn't turn to see who spoke.

Ander ripped his eyes away from mine and bowed toward Molly. "You ladies look lovely," he said, mimicking a posh accent as he leaned down to kiss her hand.

Right...

Why is he kissing her hand? Alex isn't here to see that yet.

"Lidia, I love your dress!" Jessica swooshed over to me in a flurry of turquoise silk.

"Ah!" I gushed, making her spin as I admired the fabric. "Look at you! You look like a mermaid!"

"Thanks," she giggled. I noticed that she already had one hand around Maxx's arm. "Has Jay showed up yet- oh."

I felt a lanky hand wrap itself around my midsection. I jerked forward and whirled around, all in one motion. Jay looked a little surprised at my sudden 180, but overall very pleased with what he was looking at.

"Hey," Jay's eyes were slightly unfocused. I couldn't tell if he was drunk, stoned, or if it was just his usual mental speed that was resulting in delayed facial expressions.

"Hey," I said.

"You look like an angel," he said.

Uhg. Vomit.

"Thank you." I wiggled free from Jay's half embrace. Unfortunately, Jay wasn't familiar with the concept of personal space, and he reached out to grab hold of my hand, intertwining the fingers. "Uh, ha-" I tried to pull my hand free, half laughing. "Friends don't hold hands."

"Yes they do," Jay grinned.

I seriously might vomit.

I looked up to see Ander watching us, but he looked away as soon as I made eye contact.

"Well, I don't know about you guys, but I'm ready to bust a move," Trevor did some sort of ridiculous heel kick coupled with jazz hands, much to the admiration of his beloved audience- Kristin and Rose.

Kristin and Rose were dressed in two different, but nearly identical lavender dresses. Their hair was the same, their makeup was the same, and their underwear was probably the same. If it wasn't for the fact that they had different faces, they'd be twins.

"Same," Jeff said, looking extremely bored despite the fact that Rose was clinging to his arm while she mouthed something incoherent to Kristin.

"Yeah. I want to go in." I was still trying to yank my hand free from Jay. "I could really use some punch."

The dance was just like every other dance I'd ever been too, only maybe a little more put together. The gym had been decorated with long sheets of emerald velvet that hid most of the athletic banners on the walls. Ginormous speakers were set up near the back by the stage with flashing lights. Dj-what's-his-name was up there, taking song requests and looking longingly at the small table of refreshments on the back wall. It was nice, but there was still the scent of old gym socks that lingered in the air. We first walked towards the table covered with an assortment of soggy desserts. It was in the back, facing the wallflowers that watched our group as we huddled together.

After we had our drinks, we all sat at one of the many vacant tables circling the dance floor.

And that's all we did...

Just sat.

For a good twenty minutes.

"So this is fun." Jessica's sarcasm was palpable.

"Sure is." My voice was just as sarcastic.

Molly and Ander didn't say anything, probably because they *were* having fun. As usual, Molly was in Ander's lap. This time she was whispering a very long secret into his ear as he sipped on punch.

I felt the burning desire to dump my own cup of punch on Molly's perfectly curled bun. I hadn't had a lot of experience with sleeping around, but I had always heard the stories about how it makes you emotionally involved. I didn't want to be emotionally involved with Ander at all, but I didn't want anyone else to be involved with him either. I swallowed hard and tried to push my irrational feelings away. It was all for the exorcism after all, they were only faking it, and after tomorrow, things would be back to normal.

Jay stretched a long arm behind me and then leaned forward. I felt the cold tip of his nose touch the skin of my cheek as he spoke directly into my ear. "You're not having fun?"

I tried not to pull away as I shouted my reply in his ear. "NOT REALLY."

He winced and pulled back. "I know something that will make it better," Jay said to the table. Jessica turned to him inquisitively, and he withdrew a small silver flask from his coat pocket.

Oh... so he was drunk when I first saw him.

Sad how I couldn't even tell.

Jessica shook her head, mouthing *A.P.* to me as Jay turned to offer a drink to Trevor. Everyone except Rose and Kristin said no, and Jay looked a little sad as he turned back to me.

"You sure?" Jay asked, trying, and failing to gain my sympathy in a pout.

"Hey, yeah," Ander sneered. "What's the matter Lidia, I thought you loved to party?" He was looking at me from over Molly's shoulder. She straightened as the conversation turned.

I didn't reply.

"Or was it just games you liked?" Ander jeered, turning to Jay. "Lidia's *boyfriend* told me how much she likes drinking games. They really loosen her up. You could probably get her to do anything."

"Ander!" Molly and Jessica gasped, but Jay just turned to me, looking more confused than ever.

"You have a boyfriend?" Jay seemed to be working out whether or not it bothered him.

It was my out, I could've ditched Jay right then and thereby apologizing and telling him that I was taken, but Ander's smug look was just too much.

312

"It's complicated." I twisted a piece of my hair and glared at Ander before turning back to Jay. "We broke up and have been seeing other people... well, he's been seeing other people."

"Oh," Jay thought about it. "You haven't been seeing anyone?"

"Well, there was this one guy," I exhaled. "But that was a complete mistake and now I regret it."

"Why?" asked Jay.

"Because he likes sleeping around with other girls anyways," I said. "Plus, he's a huge jerk." Out of the corner of my eye, I noticed that Ander's smirk had turned into a scowl.

Good.

Jessica had been following our conversation a little too closely. "Who-"

"Hey!" I said excitedly. "Let's dance!" I took Jay's hand and dragged him to his feet. I pulled him past couples and onto the dance floor a safe distance away from Jessica's inquires.

I can't believe I said that.

I looked back over at the table and saw Jessica deep in conversation with Trevor. Jeff was looking at Ander, who was talking with Molly. Apparently, my love life had started a whole damn conversation.

It was hot and muggy on the dance floor. I was moving among the bodies swaying in time to the swirling bass, attempting to dance and watch Ander at our table simultaneously. The dancing students seemed to move as an entity of their own, one undulating mass of hands and feet.

I regretted bringing Jay out there almost immediately. Amongst the gyrating and sensual grind of the student body surrounding us, there was no way to escape Jay's roaming hands. He was behind me, leading my hips in a deep sway to the roll of the bass. Jay was a decent dancer, but his hands never stayed in one place for long, and more than once I had to do some quick maneuvering to prevent them from landing anywhere too inappropriate.

Ethan would not be okay with this... No wonder Ander was pissed.

After the first few songs, I noticed the rest of the group had joined us. Trevor was, if anything, dancing next to Kristin and Rose. The two girls kept circling each other, moving their hips saucily as they took turns bending over to twerk. Trevor attempted to be a part of the dance, but really, he was just the third wheel.

There was a swoosh of turquoise silk next to me. Jessica and Maxx started to do a strange bouncing grind, and I would've laughed if it wasn't for seeing Ander and Molly dancing not too far away.

The sight almost made me sick. Their movements were in-sync as they entwined their bodies to the twisting rumble of the music with nauseating sensuality.

Alex must be watching...

I scanned the room, finally seeing Alex, arms crossed and brow furrowed while he stood amongst the wallflowers. A little wash of relief went through me, but then I remembered it wouldn't be the last I'd see of him tonight.

We still had an exorcism to perform.

I shook my head and turned away so that I didn't have to panic about what could, or would, happen in a few short hours.

What if it doesn't work?

What if it makes him worse?

I willed my heartbeat to slow and I turned to Jessica who was watching Alex from the corner of her eye as Maxx brushed sweat away from his forehead and continued to bounce.

"Ladies and gentlemen!" The DJ announced, his voice echoing like God through the gymnasium. "We're bringing it down for a little romance. Guys, find that lucky gal and let's bring it down for a slow dance."

Couples turned to face each other, murmuring and laughing as a gentle guitar strum sounded from the speakers. Jay skillfully spun me in his arms so that we were face to face.

Uhg.

He smiled down at me. It would've been a nice smile, but since it was coming from him, it just felt creepy. Thankfully, all he did was smile as he held my hips firmly to his own waist. We swayed and it was almost nice-

Oh hell no!

Jay moved his left hand so that it cupped my butt.

"Uhm," I pulled back, but he didn't move. "You know... This just isn't working."

"What do you mean?"

I reached behind me to pull his hand up, and lo-and-behold, his other hand went straight down to take its place.

315

This kid cannot take a hint!

"Yeah. I'm going to need you to let go of me."

"Why?" Jay was still smiling like an idiot, and it was then that I noticed the sharpness of alcohol on his breath.

"I said let go," I pushed against his chest, but he had me in a death grip by my butt cheek.

A familiar face suddenly appeared, and I looked over to see Alex towering next to us. He had dark circles under his eyes, and he was still dressed in his black training gear from yesterday. His hand shot forward and pushed Jay back.

"Excuse me dweeb, she said let go." Alex turned, and without looking at me, took one of my hands in his and set the other on my waist. "Fuck off," he said to Jay and whirled me away.

We started to dance.

If it was possible, my jaw would've hit the floor.

Jay stood in the spot where Alex had shoved him, looking slightly upset that his dance partner had been commandeered. After a second of concentrated thought, Jay turned and walked back toward the tables.

I looked up at my savor who was busy glaring at something not too far away.

"Thank you," I said to Alex, eyes still wide in shock.

My hero... who I will later rid of dark spirits.

Oh, the irony.

"Whatever." Alex continued to dance without actually looking at me. He seemed very focused on whatever it was he was staring at. As we swayed to the music, I couldn't help but notice he was guiding me conspicuously through the dance floor.

I understood as soon as I saw the yellow dress glittering from the corner of my eye.

"What's up baby brother?" Alex's eyes shot daggers at Ander as we swayed next to where he had Molly wrapped in his arms. "Enjoying the dance?"

"Go ruin someone else's night, Alex," Molly sneered over her shoulder.

Alex's wicked smile broadened. "Always playing hard to get... Here-" Alex let go of my waist and gave me a push towards Ander and Molly. I stumbled and they broke apart as Ander reached out to catch me before I fell. Alex swept in to take his place with Molly. "Trade," Alex explained, smiling like a lunatic as he whisked a distraught looking Molly into the crowd.

For a long minute, we stood there, completely still as the bodies swayed around us.

"Well," I said. Ander's hand lingered on my arm. "He seems cheerful... think he knows how the night will end?" I turned, Ander was gazing down at me, his eyes were ocean deep and a darker shade of blue than normal. "Uhm," I took a breath. "If we're just going to stand here we'll draw attention."

I was about to suggest we go back to the tables, when Ander's hands wrapped around my waist. My stomach jolted and I stiffened, surprised. He seemed to notice my reluctance, but instead of making the rude comment I had come to expect, he gently took both of my arms and hooked them around his neck.

"Did you mean it?" he asked. His voice was low, but I could hear it through the blaring music perfectly clear.

"Did I mean what?"

Ander was very close and it made my heart stutter in nervous excitement. I remembered our night together, and then I thought of Ethan. It made the guilt settling on my insides heavy, as if they were coated in thick grease.

"What you said about me to Jay just a few minutes ago."

"Sort of."

Ander sighed, and surprisingly, drew me closer. It made my stomach whirl, and his eyes dropped to my mouth for a moment. He seemed lost in thought. I wasn't going to ask if he would kiss me. I had already done that once, and I couldn't do it again.

Ander swallowed, and brought his eyes back to mine. "Are we ever going to tell Ethan?" His brow furrowed as he watched me process what he had just said.

"No."

"Yeah." He nodded a few times, in agreement. "Yeah, uh," he pulled back so that he could look at me, we were still swaying, but just barely. "It's just...I just don't like the idea of you saying that what happened between us was a mistake, when you're willing to mess around with Jay Ronaldson." He grimaced like the name left a bad taste in his mouth. "Especially after you tell everyone that you're back with Ethan."

"Nothing is going on with me and Jay! I didn't even want to have him as a date!" I looked over to the table where Jay was sitting next to a girl wearing fashionably large glasses with the lenses popped out. They passed the flask. "He's just a little grabby, that's all. I was only doing it for tonight, and I told him it would just be as friends, but he didn't get it."

"You're not-"

"God no!"

"He's all over you."

"He's drunk. I've literally talked to him twice. You were right, that kid is dumber than a rock."

That seemed to lessen the storm brewing behind Ander's eyes.

"How could you think I would do that?" I regretted the question as soon as it left my mouth. I wasn't sure I wanted the answer.

Ander just shrugged. The couple next to us started making out with a disturbing amount of PDA. I turned my eyes away and tried to focus on something else as the music strummed on.

"What do you mean, you didn't like me saying it was a mistake?" I asked.

"I just meant-" One of Ander's hands left my waist and he raked through his hair. "That Jay is a tool, and I know Ethan would rather rob a bank wearing a miniskirt than have Jay take you to winter formal... and since I really don't want to see Ethan go to jail, especially in a mini skirt-" I tried to hide my laugh but couldn't, and Ander smiled gently at my warming exterior. "I was just looking out for both of you," he said.

"I didn't actually tell Ethan," I added guiltily.

"Yeah, I figured." He took a deep breath and looked down at the barely-there space between us. "And, I'm sorry I've

been a dick. It's been a lot to deal with, and, I don't know-"
Ander's jaw clenched, working to find words. "I shouldn't have
gone for it."

"Gone for what?"

"You." Ander was looking directly at me now. I think we
might've stopped dancing. "I took advantage of you."

"No, you didn't."

"Yeah I did, I took advantage of the situation. You were
upset, and even though I knew it was messed up, I still did it."

"No, it was my fault." My voice was barely above a
whisper. "Ander, I asked you. I was the one who started it. If it's
anyone's fault, it's mine."

"It's not completely your fault." Ander almost smiled,
but it was washed away by something else. "Either way, it still
happened."

"Yeah, but it doesn't mean we can't still be friends. Just
don't let me drink around you." I forced a laughed. "Apparently
it turns me into a mega-slut."

Ander looked at me sternly. "You are not a slut."

I half smiled, only half believing him because sleeping
with your boyfriend's best friend is exactly something a slut
would do. "So," I cleared my throat. "Is that why you've been so
mad at me lately?"

He shook his head and looked away. "I wasn't mad at
you." Ander's voice was flat, and he was staring at Molly and
Alex. As he watched them, the lines of dread slowly etched
themselves into his face. Ander looked stressed out, but
considering everything going on, I couldn't blame him.

"The A.P. seems to be working." I tweaked my head around so that he was forced to look at me instead. "We have everything planned, and ready to go." I sounded more confident then I felt. "I think tonight will work out, and Alex will be back to normal- so, he'll still be a jerk, but, he'll be Alex again."

"I really hope so."

We swayed together in a moment of silence, broken only by the hum of music. Even Ander couldn't save us against something demonic if things were to go wrong later that night, but somehow, I felt peace in the moment.

One way or another, everything would be okay.

"Does this mean you'll be nice to me again?" I asked.

Ander laughed, a real genuine laugh that I hadn't heard in what felt like forever. "Within limits," he said, intentionally, or unintentionally drawing me closer. "I'll still make fun of your ridiculous waffle art."

I smiled so big it felt like it was going to break my face. "Is it weird to say I've missed you?"

His eyes went sort of unfocused as he looked down at me in his arms. "I've missed you too."

Jessica appeared out of nowhere in a whoosh of turquoise silk. She grabbed at my arm and started pulling me towards the gym exit. "I just ditched Maxx, and I saw Jeff follow Molly and Alex into the hall... come on!" She whispered, tugging harder. "It's starting!"

Chapter 22

Ander's face went pale, but he successfully steered Trevor away from Kristin as they danced a few feet away. Trevor quickly realized what was going on and clapped Ander reassuringly on the shoulder as we followed Jessica into the hall. We ran as quietly as we could through the empty corridors, but the sound of clicking heels still echoed in the stairway as we climbed further and further up the main building.

"She said room A 403," Jessica whispered as we took another step upward.

The walk felt like forever in the dark. We navigated through the shiny oak-paneled halls with only the dim moonlight to guide us. I kept shooting worried glances at Ander, noticing that his face hadn't change from the sickened expression of dread. He kept his eyes forward at all times as Jessica led the way.

Eventually, we reached the top level of the school. There weren't any floor-length windows on this level. Most of the rooms seemed to be janitorial closets or storage space reserved for the drama club. It even smelled different than the rest of the school. Unused and clean, like dry chalk and lemon soap.

"Psst!" A figure in a black tux and a knitted beanie gestured us toward a door at the end of the hall. "Do you have everything?" asked Jeff.

"Yeah," Ander's voice was breathless and his eyes were almost too wide.

My heart thrummed in my chest.

We can do this. We've been planning for weeks.

Jeff put his ear to the door and listened. "Okay, Trevor, are you ready?"

Trevor's fingers sparked an electric blue, illuminating his face from beneath like he was holding a flashlight under his chin. "Ready," he whispered.

Here we go.

Jeff thrust the door open, and just as I registered two silhouettes intertwined together in a sliver of moonlight, everything erupted in a flash of light. Trevor zapped an electric beam so powerful it blinded Alex and Molly on the opposite side of the room. The lighting fixture overhead cracked and sparked before there was a loud pop and the entire thing came crashing to the ground.

Ander bolted past me and tackled Alex. I only saw flashes of it happing, jolts of movement in the light making it appear slow motion. They wrestled together on the floor, knocking against the metal legs of desks that screeched across the tile.

"Go!" Jessica and I followed Trevor and Jeff into the room.

When the lights stopped, white spots danced across my vision as I stared at the complete blackness. I tripped on something, but kept moving. Jeff and Trevor fell onto Alex's writhing form. I saw Jeff press something white against Alex's mouth as Ander and Trevor held him to the floor. After another minute of thrashing, Alex's body went limp.

Ander stood up shakily. "Alright...that won't hold him. Let's tie him up."

I helped Jessica retrieve the rope from her tote that she had flung to the floor. Trevor set Alex upright in a chair and I ran over to help wrap the thick coils around his hands. The rope was tight. There were little red marks around the cuffs of his wrist where it had already started irritating the skin.

"Lidia, help me light these." Molly tossed a pack of matches my way, and I trailed behind her as she arranged large white candles so that they encircled Alex's chair. With the growing warmth of candlelight, I saw that the classroom was noticeably larger than the ones downstairs. The flickering light didn't quite reach the vaulted ceiling, but it bounced off the patches of stained glass that made up a large arching window on the far wall.

"Are we in a chapel room?" I asked.

"Yeah, this is where I have my bible study every Wednesday," said Jessica, setting the last candle and gesturing me towards it.

I dipped my head down and lit the candle. When I was finished, I looked around at the uneasy faces surrounding Alex. The parts of him that weren't tied to the chair slumped and hung in weird angles, as if the bones of his body were missing. Orange light danced across his vacant features and I felt a twinge of nostalgia as I watched him sleep. Only a few months earlier he was normal.

How long has he lived with dark spirits inside of him?

None of us said it, but all of us were thinking it...

This better work.

A loud *clump* sounded as Jessica set an old book down on the desk that had been scooted a few feet away from Alex's drooping form. The silver moonlight leaking in through the window made the silk of her turquoise gown look liquid, and her usual smiling face had turned hard in set determination.

"That hat," Jessica said to me. I crawled over to the spilled contents of her purse and retrieved Alex's hat.

"Put it right in front of him."

I did.

"Dude, are you sure you know what you're doing?" asked Trevor. He was crouching near a sideways desk a few feet away from Alex, ready to pounce if need be. "It's not too late to play this off as a joke or something. If it goes wrong-"

Jessica's face faltered.

"We have to try," interjected Ander. His voice was strong, as determined as Jessica had looked. "This will work." Ander strode over to me and reached down, his arm brushed across my shoulder as he grabbed a bundle of dried sage leaves on the floor. "Are you ready?" Ander held out his other hand and drew me to my feet.

"Yes," I breathed. "Let's get it over with."

We can do this.

We can do this.

Ander nodded, looking worried but resolute. He held out the bundle of leaves. "I need a light."

I struck a match and set fire to the tips of the withered green leaves. The flame licked at the tips of the sage gently, then consumed it entirely. Ander blew the fire out, and a long twisting stream of smoke snaked its way through the stagnant air. It was silent except for the gentle fizzle of the hot smoke.

The silence was broken by a loud screech as Alex's head jerked back and he jolted his chair across the floor. Alex swore quietly, twisting his head left, then right, trying to look at the crowd gathered behind him. The only person in front of him was Jessica, watching his struggle silently.

"What's going on?" Alex spat. "Molly!" he barked. "What are you doing?"

Molly made a move to step forward, but Ander held her back, taking her place beside his brother.

"Ander? What's going on?" Alex struggled against the rope again. "I swear, this isn't funny. I'm going to kill you!" Sweat wetted the disheveled hair on the back of Alex's neck as he started to thrash more violently in his chair. "Untie me! Where's Molly?"

"Alex," Ander's voice didn't sound as strong as it had a moment before. "We know what you've been doing with Jason and Connor in Walden woods. The night you saw me and Lidia-" Ander swallowed hard and continued. "We saw what you were doing. We saw the ritual spot in the woods when you summoned dark spirits."

"What are you talking about?" Alex scoffed. He tried smiling like it was a joke, but his eyes were wide, wild. He looked like a frightened animal.

"How long have you been doing this?" Ander barked. "How long?"

"I haven't done anything."

"I'm not stupid, Alex!" Ander raked a hand through his hair, trying to stare sense into his brother. "How could you do this? We already have enough to deal with worrying about Sarah. I saw you in the woods with Jason, and you had such a strong boost over Thanksgiving that you almost lit mom's oven on fire! Where'd you get that sort of boost?"

Alex kept his mouth shut in a tight, ugly line, but his nostrils flared from his heavy breathing.

"Lidia saw you absorb a Spook."

"Lidia doesn't know what she saw! I blocked it!"

There was a beat of silence. The only sound was Alex's heavy breathing and the gentle lick of fire on candlewick. As the seconds ticked by, panic seemed to radiate off Alex's entire body. He started squirming, fidgeting uncontrollably.

"Alex," Ander finally said. "This is an exorcism, we're going to help-"

Alex hissed. "Are you joking?" He struggled more violently.

"I told them what you did with that Spook in the cemetery, Alex." The words tumbled out of my mouth as I walked forward to stand next to Ander.

Alex's face was slick with a sheen of cold sweat. "You're such a little liar!" He sucked on the inside of his cheek, and spat at me. The spit hit the floor in front of my feet.

Ander's face hardened and he withdrew a small metal flask from his pocket.

"We're trying to help you," I said.

"Ander," Alex coughed, then cleared his voice, forcing it to remain calm. "She's trying to turn you against me." Alex was speaking to his brother, but he kept his eyes on me. "Remember what I ran into that night in the woods?" Alex said. "You and Lidia were like two sexually frustrated little bush bunnies." Alex's voice had turned sweet, a sicken molasses that didn't match his twisted smile. "Poor Ethan. She's just a-"

"Shut up," Ander snapped.

"Oh, come on," Alex's eyes raked back and forth between us. "You know it."

"I know there's something inside of you." Ander swallowed hard. "And we're going to get it out."

"You don't know what you're talking about."

"Yes, I do."

Alex's face softened momentarily, and his head tweaked to the side with an irritable twitch. Molly covered her mouth, but a sob escaped.

"Molly?" Alex tried to look behind him to where she was standing. He cussed, and then started rambling, the words tumbled from his mouth faster than their meaning could register. "Let me go, Ander. Come on, it's for Sarah," he breathed. "I only did it that once for Sarah."

Ander didn't reply. He was watching Alex with a mixed expression of confusion and horror.

"It's for her! She's getting better. I can get rid of the cancer, every time I push some of the energy into her, it strengthens her immune system. She has more ener-"

"YOU WHAT?" Ander's fist balled up at his side as he took a step forward. "You put that Spook inside of her?"

"No, Ander, listen to me," Alex said as Ander leered over him. For once, Alex looked genuinely afraid. "It's helping."

"It's demonic! What do you think that'll do to her?"

"You saw what it's done to her! When was the last time she's been this active?"

Ander didn't answer.

"It's healing her. She has more energy, she's eating again. In a few months they said they might even take her off chemo." He yanked against his binding. "Come on! You're going to let her suffer and die?"

Ander flinched.

"I know, it was bad-" Alex tweaked again. "But it was all for Sarah. Besides, I-I only did it once. Okay? I swear, it was one time and I'm fine. Okay, Ander? Can you let me go?"

Ander didn't say a word. He just watched as his brother stared up at him.

"LET ME GO!" Alex's temper spiked.

Ander's hand shot out to splash whatever was in the flask onto Alex's face. Alex screamed in a bloody gush of rage as the wet flesh sizzled, sending wisps of steam into the sage-soaked air. There were no burn marks when the sizzling stopped, but the whimpering noises coming from Alex told us he was in pain.

It was torture.

No...I shook myself free of sympathy. *Not until it's over.*

"Jessica, do it now!" Ander roared.

Jessica snapped out of her horrified daze and turned to the text in front of her. She started to murmur, almost incomprehensible, verses from the book in lyrical rhythm. Alex screamed again, thrashing more violently.

He's going to break out of the ropes!

I leapt forward, trying unsuccessfully to hold onto his arms and keep them from wriggling free.

"Help me!" I shouted. Jeff came up behind me, then Trevor, and we gained a sturdy grip.

Alex's face twisted backwards abnormally far and he snapped at my arm holding his shoulders. His teeth missed my bare flesh by an inch. I fell backwards.

It wasn't even Alex anymore.

There was a translucent veil over his face, twisting his features until they resembled something both unnatural and evil.

"What's happening to him?" My voice trembled and I looked up to see Jeff's equally horrified expression. Our eyes locked. Alex snarled, the blurred veil of a monster continued to stretch his features.

Jessica read from the book and Alex pulled harder. Jeff had taken a step back, horrified by what he saw in Alex, but Trevor continued to hold him down, undisturbed.

I looked over to where Ander stood, and at seeing Ander's face as it watched his brother's body writhe in a sickening twist, my heart broke. I stood up on shaky legs. "Ander!" I shouted.

Come on, snap out of it.

Ander continued to stare down at Alex, the sage in his hand had almost completely burned out.

"Ander!" He wasn't even seeing what was in front of him anymore.

Jessica's voice continued to chant, and her voice wasn't alone. It echoed, as if joined with a choir of lost souls. It reverberated around the room until everything felt static and alive with an energy of its own.

It was thick.

Alex's thrashing became more violent until suddenly, it all stopped. Alex's head flopped forward and his body collapsed against the ropes.

Nobody moved.

Nobody spoke.

Molly sniffled from the corner where she had been crying. After a minute, Ander took a step forward, but Jeff held out an arm to stop him.

"Wait," he said.

The sound had gone. The room was empty of the voices, Alex had stopped moving, and there wasn't a lingering tingle of static... but something felt wrong. I expected the atmosphere to clear, but the air still felt heavy, pregnant with the weight of dread.

Alex's shoulders began to shake, and small noises came from his limp figure.

He's crying.

We all watched Alex intently, but when he tilted his head and I saw his face, I stepped back.

331

The face that veiled his own was gone, but Alex's appearance was morphed with an expression so menacing the handsome features were contorted into alarming unfamiliarity. His mouth, so like Ander's, was twisted in a smile of silent laughter.

The exorcism didn't work.

I remembered Alex's moody scowl from Camp Tanka, and I would've given anything to see that instead of the sick smile playing across his mouth at that moment. His lips parted, revealing a string of saliva and a twitching tongue flickering restlessly behind his teeth.

"Oops," Alex jeered at his brother. "It's too late to be a hero, baby brother."

A radiating pulse of force shot through the room like an electric bomb. I flew through the air, the feeling of static wind bit at my skin before I registered screaming and a loud crack. I toppled over a desk. The metal legs screeched, and the hard plastic wood dug at my back and forearms. I struggled to catch myself mid-fall, but pain erupted from my shoulder and forehead as I fell further through the tangle of chairs and tables before hitting the cement floor.

My head felt like someone had taken a baseball bat to my skull. As I lay there, I registered something warm trickling down my cheek. It was blood. I looked up, focusing beyond my spotted vision.

Alex had freed himself from the chair and ropes. He stood fixed, heaving angry breathes as he looked around at the destruction he had caused.

Two bodies were slouched against the far wall. Jeff and Jessica had landed near the door. They were crumpled together in a mess of turquoise silk on the ground.

They weren't moving.

Alex took one more surveillance of the room. Beside me, I heard Ander struggle to his feet, pulling at a desk to support his weight.

"Back off, Ander!" Alex roared.

Ander crashed back into a desk.

"All of you!" Alex boomed again. He leapt toward the window, his usual swagger replaced by long powerful strides. He thrust his arm forward and it shattered. Through the shower of glass that fell around us with a delicate clatter, I saw Alex disappear into the night.

A second ticked by when there was nothing but silence and the gush of cold wind.

"Alex!" Ander's desperate howl rattled my senses and I tried to stand up.

Oh my God.

My legs shook and I felt off balance.

He jumped out the window.

Ander neared the window. Pieces of stained glass jutted out of the frame like the sharp teeth of a gaping mouth. He cautiously approached the ledge, and then his ashen face went snow white.

"Ander, don't-" I didn't know what else to say. "Ander," *I'm coming, don't move, please don't move...* I fumbled through splayed desks and over turned chairs. My heels crunched shards of glass as I staggered towards him. I reached Ander and looked out the window to the ground.

It was empty.

Icy wind whipped through the room, sweeping away the warm musk of smoking sage. A slate of white powdery snow blanketed the lawn and shrubs below. There was no body. There was no blood. There weren't even footprints.

"No," Ander whispered.

I looked over to see his shock replaced by a despairing rage.

Ander snapped.

"NO!" His voice was so loud that I stumbled backwards. "NO!" He picked up the nearest object, a chair, and threw it against the wall. His shouts thundered with the clattering of plastic against wall as the chair tumbled to the ground. His fist slammed into the wall with an audible crack.

Trevor was suddenly behind me, pulling me away from Ander. I tried to pull forward, to go back towards him, but Jeff motioned us to move farther away as Ander's fist made contact with something that sounded sharp.

The haze that vibrated within the walls after Alex had jumped, started to clear. I registered more noises. Molly was sobbing uncontrollably in the corner, and Jessica was taking pained breaths through clenched teeth as she cradled her leg.

He jumped out the window.

It didn't work.

It didn't work.

Trevor nudged me, and I think he asked me to check up on Jessica. I staggered over to her and sank to my knees. The sharp glass that littered the floor poked through the thin fabric of my dress and pricked holes in my skin, leaving little bloody spots on the green silk. I asked Jessica if she was okay, but she didn't answer, she just kept breathing, kept her eyes shut.

My body felt heavy and my head throbbed, so I told her that I was tired. There was shouting, from Ander probably. The door next to us busted open, and a white-haired man leapt into the room. He looked surprised. I started to speak, but decided to lay my head against the floor instead. I didn't even notice the blood pooling around the pillow of glass as I closed my eyes and drifted to sleep.

■■

Everything smelled like latex and disinfectant. I shifted the side of my body on the crinkly paper bed, but my shoulder screamed with sharp pain so I gave up.

What happened?

I blinked.

The room wasn't very big, and the first thing I noticed was the baby-blue curtain encircling me, illuminated by a comforting lamp light on the nightstand. I looked up at the paneled oak ceiling and guessed that I was still at school.

Heavy footsteps shuffled on the other side of the room and I closed my eyes just as the curtains opened. The footsteps stopped. I listened to the breathing of the person watching me for a moment, and then another person, female, walked past. She said something quiet to whomever else was there, then left. A moment later, I heard her muffled voice soothing someone

335

else not too far away. The person in my room came closer and sat down on a chair scooted close to the bed. There was a long sigh.

I chanced a peek at my visitor.

It was Ander.

He sat with his head buried in his hands, hair messier than usual. One of his hands was wrapped in an uncomfortable-looking brace, and the other was wrapped in blood-stained gauze. I tried to sit up, but winced at the radiating pain. It felt like a sharp hammer was attacking my head.

"Careful," Ander's voice was raspy and gentle. "Don't sit up. The nurse wants you to relax."

"I don't want to." I mentally screamed a cluster of curse words at my aching body as I tried to bend forward.

"Just stay down." I felt mild pressure on my uninjured shoulder, Ander was holding me down. Not that it took a lot of effort. "You need to rest, Lidia. Tomorrow you're getting interrogated about Alex by Mr. Dodger and some guys from The Department, and trust me, it uh, it'll suck less if you feel better."

"What?"

He must've seen the panic on my face because he answered in a rush. "It's okay, just tell them the truth. I've already had my turn." Ander's croaky voice was flat, impassive with the strain of keeping emotion out. "We're all in trouble, but mostly just me. Even I got off the hook easy. I told them I didn't realize Alex was this far gone. None of us expected it to be this bad."

I let out an aggravated breath and scrunched up my face. *Since when do I use my shoulder to breath?* "What happened? Where am I?"

"You're in the school clinic right now." Ander's eyes studied me. "They want to take you to Louisen Medical Center for a CAT scan. You might have a concussion."

I groaned and shook my head. *Great, that hurts my shoulder too.*

"Jessica and Trevor are here," Ander said.

I closed my eyes and sunk into my memory. "Alex left?" It wasn't a question.

His face collapsed, and the bleak pain Ander was trying so hard to hide was now visible. "Yeah," he said.

"What happened to him? Did you ever find where he went?"

Ander shook his head. "They have a search party out right now." He swallowed as if he was going to be sick. "They put a warrant out for his arrest."

"What did they charge him with?"

"As a medium, they charged him with possession... My parents don't know about that though." Ander's mouth, usually so vivid and animated hung slack. The words drizzled out slowly like poison. "They- they don't know about mediums anyways, because of our privacy policy, but, The Department created a federal charge to use in case anyone outside of the community finds him. So that's the one they'll hear about."

"And what would that charge be?"

"Assault under the influence."

337

"Assault of who?"

"They made up a student profile and said that Alex attacked him when he was high on- I don't remember what it was." Ander raked a hand through his hair. "Meth, I think... It's the closest related charge to the truth that the general public will understand, so, that's what the police file will say." He stared hard at the ground. "That's what my parents will hear."

"What will happen if they catch him?"

"He'll serve his sentence in Plymouth."

My breathing caught in my throat. "Would they-"

He knew what I meant.

Would they neuter him?

Ander shrugged without meeting my eyes, silently conveying that they probably would.

"That's a little harsh, isn't it?" My chest rose and I felt an indignant flush of heat. "I mean, he never actually used his boost against people until we tried to perform an exorcism. He hasn't technically done anything wrong... except mess up my shoulder."

Ander was silent for a minute. "It's not Alex." He stared at the corner of my bed. Looking down I saw that I was still wearing my green dress, only now it was spotted with blood. "It's not even him anymore. You saw it. That wasn't him. They don't know what he'll do, and he's already pushed that energy into Sarah." Ander ran a hand through his hair. "No one's heard of anything like that before. Feeders suck it out of the living, not push it in."

"What did she look like when you last saw her?" I asked, thinking of Trina and the misting black tangles of smoke that circled around her.

Ander shrugged. "She looked better than she had in a while."

"No black smoke?"

"Black smoke?" Ander squinted at me, confused. "No."

"Good." I nodded, thinking. "Do you think it'll still hurt her?" I tried not to imagine the catastrophe of horror that could happen if worse came to worse.

I had learned about human possession in my Psychic 101 class. Usually it's brought on by a weakened state of mind or an especially open one. People could become easily possessed after seasons of extreme stress that make them emotionally vulnerable. Another way is entering into a "hot zone" such as a haunted house intentionally or under the influence of drugs.

Even humans can become addicted to a certain something in the dark energy of Spooks, but often they don't survive possession. Still, a human possessed is more likely to be successfully exorcised than a medium. Mediums have the genetic makeup that binds with spirit energy. The Spook imprints itself, and from there, it's easier for the medium to fall deeper into the addiction than to erase what's still living on the inside. A medium possessed is infected with a dark spirit that acts like a tapeworm. It feeds off the energy they absorb until that energy isn't enough, and they need to find a more potent source- the living. That's how feeders are made.

"I don't know if it'll hurt her," Ander said. "I mean, she has gotten better since Thanksgiving."

"Yeah but, Ander, how can you be healed by something so dark?"

"Mr. Dodger said that if she hasn't been showing signs of possession, that she might be fine. He said Alex might be pushing all the energy into her, but keeping the darkness inside, and basically, acting like a filter. Just like how it would be if he used his boost. The energy would be gone, but the- the other stuff stays inside. That's why Alex must've gotten so bad so fast, something like this never happens in just a few months... and I swear Lidia," Ander was looking at me now, "I swear he wasn't like this when we started school. All throughout summer, that was completely Alex-"

"It still is," I said. "Sort of."

"It's not."

"But he still had a connection to everyone, he's still in there...I just don't understand why it didn't work."

"It's not him," Ander choked.

"Yeah, but-"

"Lidia," Ander shook his head, still not looking at me and I saw the pain in his features. My heart felt like it was being ripped apart. *Oh Ander...*

I reached out and took one of his hands. Ander stared at our fingers for a moment, winding and unwinding together. I could feel his skin, warm and smooth through gaps in the gauze.

"I'm really sorry." Ander was so quiet I almost couldn't hear. "I thought it would work."

"We all did, it's not your fault."

He smiled, a broken, fake, half smile. "How are you feeling?" he asked. Ander's smile faded and his gaze turned studious as he analyzed my every flinch.

"Not too bad," I shrugged. *Ouch! Mistake.* My eyes squeezed shut. "My shoulder's the worst."

"Let me see," he leaned across me, peering over at my shoulder. I hoisted myself up as best I could and felt Ander's fingers trace the bruised flesh and sweep away my hair. He swore and sat back down in his chair. "How's your head? It looks even worse." His eyes lingered on something bulky above my eyebrow. I couldn't quite see it, but I assumed it was some sort of bandage.

"It's fine. Is everyone else okay?"

He looked away again. "Jessica broke her leg, Trevor got stitches... Uh, Jeff is okay, just some bruising. Molly's a mess," he sighed. "She's fine, just, really freaked out." Ander had returned to cradling his head in his hands.

"How are you?"

Instead of answering, he lifted his head to give me that broken fake smile again, and stood up. "I'm going to go check on everyone...I'll be back later. Can I get you anything? Do you want some water?" I shook my head no, and watched sadly as he brushed past the blue curtain and into the rest of the room.

Chapter 23

When I walked into Mr. Dodger's office for the "interrogation" the next day, I felt, and looked, like death. I still had a lingering headache from the night before, and the nurse had put my arm in a temporary sling. Black flakes of mascara were scattered under my eyes, completing my *I'd-rather-be-dead-than-awake* look.

Jeff, Jessica, Trevor, and Molly were all seated on the hall bench outside when I joined them. They looked just as bad as I did. Jessica, with her left leg wrapped in a bright blue cast, looked the worst.

"Hi," I said.

"Hey." Though she had broken her leg less than twenty-four hours prior, Jessica had still managed to get one signature that said-*Trevor is the bomb. Get better.*

"Where's Ander?" I asked.

"He's in the office talking to Jeff's uncle," Trevor said as Jeff hung his head and stared meekly at the ground. "He's from The Department." Trevor made a cut-throat gesture.

I exchanged a forlorn look with the others and took a seat next to Molly, but none of us spoke. After what felt like an hour, the door to Mr. Dodger's office opened, and he called all of us inside. Ander was hunched in one of the chairs facing a grey-haired man in a neat suit. I recognized him as Mr. Benton, one of the men sent from The Department to oversee the SETT testing.

"Thank you everyone, for arriving on time," Mr. Dodger sighed, bridging his fingers in a steeple in front of his face. It was the first time I had seen him completely serious, and it was a little unsettling. Even the mangled polyester suit that he wore wasn't funny. "Mr. Benton," Mr. Dodger gestured him forward. "May I introduce you to Mr. Cusp, Miss Yeom, Miss Rollness, Miss Powell, and you already know Mr. Jeff Benton here."

Mr. Benton nodded curtly, his long protruding nose pointing at each of us directly.

"Will the five of you please take a seat," Mr. Dodger pointed us towards the plush green couch near the window and a few folding chairs that had been brought in. We sat. "Now," he sank into the chair opposite. "Mr. McCullen has told me a little about what happened last night, but I was hoping I could get a recap on the events."

Trevor spoke first. He gave an honest report of what happened as the rest of us twisted our fingers and shuffled our feet. When he was done, Mr. Dodger nodded seriously, and Mr. Benton came to stand behind him.

"To get involved with someone possessed by such a dark entity is extremely reckless for mediums of your age and experience." Mr. Benton's voice was so deep that he somehow managed to sound loud and quiet at the same time. "All of you should be aware of the legal consequences if one of you were to inadvertently become affected by this dark entity."

We all nodded, though, I was only partially aware. Possession, being arrested, sent to jail, getting neutered. Whatever the exact consequences were, I knew they weren't good.

"I thought so. Unfortunately, considering the strength of energy Alex possessed, and the way in which the exorcism was performed," Mr. Benton said as Jeff sank deeper into his chair. "I'm going to have to make sure that the energy in the room wasn't absorbed, and that it *did* remain with the host body."

Hearing Alex referred to as the "host body" made my stomach turn. Out of the corner of my eyes, I spotted Ander. He was staring hard at the corner of the table with eyes that were so tired they looked bruised. Mr. Benton retrieved a flask and napkin from his coat pocket and took a step back.

"Miss Yeom," he said. "Will you please approach?" He dribbled a little liquid from inside the flask onto the cloth. "It won't hurt," he said softly. "I'm only going to determine whether or not you've developed an allergic reaction to holy water. If you are possessed, the skin has a physical reaction."

Jessica hoisted herself off the couch with the help of Trevor's aiding arm, and wobbled over to Mr. Benton on her crutches. Mr. Dodger's eyes shone with worry as he turned his head around to watch Mr. Benton press the soaked fabric to her forehead.

Nothing happened.

"Thank you Miss Yeom, you may take a seat."

Jessica's shoulders slumped in relief. Mr. Benton motioned her over to where Ander sat, and called Molly forward. She passed the test. So did Trevor and Jeff, though Jeff received a very stern look and a harsh whisper before he went to sit next to Molly.

"Miss Powell." I pulled myself out of the couch and stepped over toward Mr. Benton. His nose was very shiny, and everywhere Mr. Benton turned his head, his nose went first. It was like the axis of direction for the rest of his face. "Will you please push your hair out of the way?"

I did.

When Mr. Benton pressed the soaking cloth to my forehead, I gasped. "Sorry," I said. I tried to pull my head away from his cloth, but Mr. Benton kept an aggressively firm amount of pressure against my skin. "It was just really cold."

Mr. Dodger let out a huge sigh of relief and Mr. Benton removed the cloth with a wry smile. "So long as it doesn't burn," he said and gestured for me to join the others.

Ander had ripped his eyes away from the table as he watched me approach. He raked his eyes across my forehead in concern, but after he finally realized holy water hadn't turned me into a soul-sucking monster, he turned away.

"So, Miss Powell," Mr. Dodger came over and took a seat at his desk. "Mr. McCullen tells us that you witnessed some suspicious activity in Walden Woods before Thanksgiving break."

"Uh, yeah." I nodded.

"And that only a few weeks prior, you believe that you might've seen Alex absorb a dark entity at Walden Cemetery during your routine training session?"

I nodded again.

"Could you please tell us what happened."

"I was trying to absorb an anomaly, it was a shadow." Being put in the spotlight made me squirm in my chair, so I readjusted a strap on my sling as I continued. "But then it turned into smoke and a Spook came out. It started coming after me so I ran-"

"The smoke came after you?" Mr. Dodger asked, his brows furrowing slightly.

"No, the Spook did."

"And how did it come after you?"

"It, uh, it crawled?" I couldn't tell if I was answering the question right. "I don't think it could-"

"Thank you, Miss Powell." Mr. Benton cut me off by raising his hand. When Mr. Dodger gave him a puzzled look, Mr. Benton simply shook his head and turned his nose back towards me. "When you were in the woods with Ander, could you identify the other students Alex was with?"

"I don't know all their last names, but uh, Jason Singer, Connor, and Jeremy. They sit together at lunch."

"Yes, I am already familiar with the Singer family." Mr. Benton suddenly looked very tired. "Mr. Dodger, I think now would be an appropriate time."

Mr. Dodger nodded and left the room. A few minutes later he returned with three police officers in uniform, and three scowling boys- Jason, Connor, and Jeremy. The boys were hunched forward, hiding their faces in curtains of unwashed hair as the officers stood behind them like intrusive shadows with good posture.

"Are these the boys you saw in Walden Woods, Miss. Powell?"

I gulped, "yes." The word felt like a death sentence.

Jason shot a furious sneer my way, but Mr. Benton looked thoroughly unsurprised. "Mr. Singer, please step forward."

"Why?" Jason's lip curled in confused disgust, his snakebite jewelry flashing silver with the movement. "What's this for?"

"Due to an unfortunate incident last night, we have discovered that one of the student trainers, Alex McCullen, is possessed. You are an alleged acquaintance, and so The Department must take precautions to ensure the safety of all students. This is a simple test." Mr. Benton had already drenched his cloth in holy water. It dripped onto the office floor, leaving little dark spots on the carpet.

Jason's eyes skated nervously around the room, but before he could take a step forward, Jeremy grabbed his arm and pulled him back. "Don't," he muttered to Jason before turning back to Mr. Benton. "We haven't done anything wrong!" The long strands of his old-fashioned bowl haircut shimmied as he shook his head.

"Yeah!" His protest seemed to spark Jason's own indignation. "Is this just because of my brother? Because that's messed up. I can't be persecuted for his mistakes!" Behind him, Connor was eyeing the officers warily. Measuring them up.

"Please step forward, Mr. Singer," Mr. Benton said, sounding bored.

"I don't have to! It's my right to refuse!"

"You are legally obligated to oblige."

"Not until I see that paperwork."

"There is no paperwork needed for a simple test." I could practically hear Mr. Benton roll his eyes. "The other students have all taken turns, and are sitting over there." He gestured toward us. "They can attest that this test isn't painful."

After a minute of strenuous consideration, Jason pushed past Jeremy's outstretched arm, and reluctantly stepped toward Mr. Benton. Jason's eyes squeezed shut at the sudden contact of the wet cloth on his skin, and his mouth pressed into such a tight line that the skin around his lip rings went white. After only a second, there was the sound of sizzling skin, and the cloth started to steam. "Ahh!" Jason tore his head away, but the officer who had trailed behind him was already prepared. When Jason turned blindly, the side of his face made contact with the officer's chest. The officer whirled him around, gripping both arms, and slammed Jason against the back of the couch. With one hand, he retrieved a shiny pair of handcuffs and clipped them to Jason's wrists. Jason screamed, his mouth gaping wide in a silent cry of pain. I looked down at the cuffs, which were padded with a wet material. His mouth continued to stretch like a fish out of water as the officer escorted him to the opposite side of the room.

"Mr. Walstone?" Mr. Benton called.

Both Jeremy and Connor took a step backwards.

The officers leapt onto the boys without hesitation. Connor screamed when handcuffs clipped around his wrists. He crumpled to the floor, kicking weakly at the ankles of the man lunging towards Jeremy. The officer stumbled, and Jeremy was able to scoot out of reach before he thrust his hand forward. It shot the policeman back against the wall with the force of a small bus.

"Enough!" Mr. Benton roared.

Jeremy flew into the air, his entire body encircled by a mist. He shot a fist this way, and that, but Jeremy's energy was blocked by the air around him. Even his scream seemed muted.

348

"Roger," Mr. Benton nodded toward the officer who was finally able to peel himself off the wall. "Please," Mr. Benton smoothed his hair back, pointing up at Jeremy in frustration.

"Sorry, sir." Roger reached through the mist and pulled on one of Jeremy's ankles. The boy drifted down, trying, and failing to lash out at Roger before the handcuffs were securely clipped, and he crashed to the carpet of Mr. Dodger's office with an ear-piercing cry of pained rage.

Everything felt too surreal, too private, too horrible for us to be watching as bystanders. I noticed Trevor was clutching the back of his chair, Jeff was open-mouthed, Molly was silently crying, and Ander's face looked as if it was made of stone. I tried to swallow the hint of guilt that flooded my stomach as I watched the officers and Mr. Benton haul the three boys out the door.

What would happen to them now?

"What's going to happen to them?" I asked nimbly once the door shut.

"They will have a trial, and they will go through a series of cleansing rituals." Mr. Dodger smoothed the folds of his mustache, looking sadly down at his hands. "Let us all pray for their treatment to be a success, and that their families survive this tragedy."

We were all quiet for a long moment. Mr. Dodger had his eyes shut, and he was muttering softly under his breath. I wasn't sure if he really meant we should pray, so I just looked down at my hands sheepishly and tried not to think about what the process of treatment might entail. Next to me, Ander stared wide-eyed at Mr. Dodger. He barely looked like he knew where he was at. I wanted to reach out to take his hand, offer some comfort, but just as the thought crossed my mind, Mr. Dodger finished muttering and turned his gaze back to us.

The next hour was spent listening to Mr. Dodger explain the legal process in which Alex and the others would be prosecuted. He didn't mention anything we didn't already know, but as I sat there listening, I felt the reality settle in.

Where was Alex now?

Eventually, Mr. Dodger dismissed the group and we got up to leave.

"Uh, no, Miss Powell," he stopped me before I left with the others. "I need to have a word with you."

"Okay." I went back inside his office, waved at the others, and Mr. Dodger pulled a seat out for me. It felt out of place next to all the empty ones my friends had previously occupied. Mr. Dodger took his usual spot at his desk across from me and withdrew a manila envelope from his top desk drawer. "Miss Powell, will you please finish your account of your experience in Walden Cemetery the night Mr. McCullen absorbed the dark entity?"

"Sure," I said slowly. "Do you want me to start from the beginning?" I couldn't think why it would be relevant now.

"No, no. Please, just start from where you left off. I would like to hear your description of the Spook."

I did my best to explain. It required a lot of hand gestures, which were hard to do considering I only had the use of one of my arms. "And, well," I finished lamely trying to describe the darkness behind black veined eyes. "You know-"

"Yes, Miss Powell," Mr. Dodger nodded, a sympathetic smile playing across his face. "I do know. However, I am only a third of the medium community that is familiar with what a dark entity looks like."

I scrunched my forehead. "What about the SETT? Doesn't everyone have to block a Spook?"

"Yes, we are all exposed to dark entities during testing, but only a few mediums are able to see beyond the usual spectrum... mediums see human spirits, but entities are essentially," he paused, "demonic."

Well duh.

"Only one in three mediums are able to see angelic and demonic energy as it intermingles with the energy of this world. It is fairly uncommon, but it does happen. We have an extended sight."

I let his words sink in. *So that's why the SETT was so hard for me.* I not only had *the sight,* I had *the extended sight.* It was like ordering a sandwich and getting the super-combo. Drink and all.

I didn't want the super-combo.

I didn't even want the sandwich.

"Uh," my voice was faint. "So, uh, there are angels?"

"They are extremely rare."

"Have you ever seen one?"

"No."

What. The. Fudgecake.

I did a mental rerun of each time I had ever seen something. *No one saw Spooks?* It made sense. If Alex or any of the boys could see what they were absorbing, I doubt they'd touch the thing, let alone let it inside of themselves.

"Why haven't I heard of this before?" I asked.

"We are called, for lack of a better term, exorcists," Mr. Dodger said calmly. "An English man named Author Bride came up with the name during the 1860's. Our ability to clearly see the demonic entity allows us to identify human possession with ninety percent accuracy."

Trina.

"Mr. Bride said he was even able to speak with entities, directing them by name to leave the host body. He saved one hundred and thirty seven lives from possession." Mr. Dodger nodded, mostly just to himself. "Exorcists have an incredibly rich history, Miss Powell. Scholars have dated mediums with extended sight all the way back to the fourteenth century when Joan of Arc spoke with angels. The unfortunate mediums who suffered from incurable possession, and are what we now call energy feeders, are directly linked to eighteenth century vampirine folklore," he pointed to one of his many large bookshelves. "And all the literature associated with it," he said drolly. "Our influence is also found in various witch trials throughout the world. Some of the earliest cases of witch-related hysteria was simply a medium developing their sight... it is a tragic history, but it is also a gift. Out of all the psychic mediums in this world, only those that are able to focus on the embodiment of evil energy that possesses a person, are successfully able to exorcise it out of the body."

Is he saying I could've helped Alex?

My question must've been obvious from the look on my face, because he continued in a rush. "Not that it is common for an exorcism to end successfully, especially for someone so unexperienced. There is very little chance, had you played a more significant role last night, that you would've been effective, and we are very lucky that you and Mr. Benton didn't play a larger role because if you were able to exorcise the spirit, it could've attached itself to another body in the room."

"What if it was blocked? What- hold on... can Jeff see Spooks too?"

"No." Mr. Dodger bit his lip. "I have absolutely no way of knowing," he cleared his throat. "When I was in my early twenties, I worked at The Department in the first stage of cleansing at Plymouth." I couldn't picture Mr. Dodger as a twenty-something-year-old. With his polyester suit and boyish smile, I couldn't see him amongst the orange jumpsuits at a prison either. "I, along with a priest and five other exorcists, were responsible for cleansing new inmates. It's the first stage of action Mr. Singer and his friends will experience when they arrive at Plymouth."

My stomach sank. "Will it work?"

"It is unlikely. Only one in forty cases end successfully."

"Oh."

"Miss Powell, it's because of our abilities that we become the natural enemy for demons." He leaned in closer, his voice suddenly stern. "When a medium suffers from possession, the spirit within becomes all consuming. It has access to everything, including our memories, feelings, thoughts... it's very important to keep your ability private. If you confided in someone, even a close friend, and they become possessed, then you run a great risk of being targeted by the dark entity inside. Demon's will always attempt to eliminate a threat to their host body."

Oh great.

I felt my facial expression warp into a slack look of defeat. *Demons will target me.* I pressed a hand against my eyes. The pressure was meant to be comforting, but I only managed to smear my already ruined makeup. *Another secret to keep.*

"It isn't something to fret about." Mr. Dodger reached over and patted the limp hand resting in my sling. "You are the only exorcist identified by the SETT this year, but last year we had three!"

"Oh. Wow," my voice was drained of emotion.

"Due to our secrecy, we tend to feel very alone, but I assure you, that you are not. Mediums, such as Mr. Benton, have been serving our community as some of the most powerful exorcists for over twenty years," he smiled gently.

"Why did you tell me you were an exorcist if we are meant to keep it a secret?"

"As an educator, I must take some small risk for the sake of my students. After all, I have training, and good health insurance if anything was to go awry. "

"Well," I took a breath. "Thank you."

"You should go get some sleep, my dear. You have had a long day. Thank you for taking the time to speak with me." He stood up and led me towards the door. "Oh, and before I forget," he gave me the envelope he had been holding throughout the duration of our conversation. "This is from The Department, recapping everything I've just discussed with you. They also include your results to the SETT. Very well done."

"Thank you," I folded the envelope and stuck it in the sling before making my way up to the dorm. When I got there, I collapsed onto my bed, hoping I could just sleep for the rest of my life.

Chapter 24

Apart from the meeting with Mr. Dodger, none of us were in real trouble, but our meal hours in the cafeteria became uncharacteristically quiet. The table where Alex used to sit with Jeremy, Jason, and Connor was empty. As for our own table, things were strained. Molly's eyes were constantly red, and all of us with our various battle scars and bruises, were gawked at like zoo animals... everyone except Ander.

Ander had stopped coming to breakfast, lunch, and dinner. He had also stopped going to classes.

We each took turns bringing food and homework to his room, but Molly was there the most. They were both close to Alex in their own way, and I bit back the sting of jealousy that came when he seemed to prefer her comfort over my own.

The teachers didn't seem to mind his absence, I'm sure they all received a notice about the situation. A sibling possessed was treated like death in the family, which in a way, it was. Even if Alex stood next to me, it wouldn't really be him. Alex was gone for good.

By the time winter break came along, I hadn't seen Ander in over a week. The halls were crowded with students bundled up in winter gear, hugging goodbyes with rosy cheeks and knocking into each other with overstuffed luggage like bumper cars.

"Ander!" I knocked on his door.

I had my thick plaid jacket and tall snow boots on. My duffel bag, packed and ready for a long winter vacation, was sitting by my feet. Inside Ander's dorm room, there was a soft rhythmic thumping on the wall.

"I know you're in there, we should've left an hour ago." I knocked again.

Before the A.P. fallout, Ethan had written to me saying that Ander would give me a ride to his mom's house in Lake Chelan for Christmas break. At the time, I would've rather taken a hot bath in barbeque sauce while eating an entire ant-farm than spend two hours in Ander's company. Still, I wrote back to Ethan and let him know it was a good idea, and the plan was set. Now that Ander and I had made up at the dance, two hours with him didn't seem so awful. I was even looking forward to having a chance to see him, talk, and make sure he was okay.

"C'mon Ander," I whined, knocking again. "I told Ethan we would be there at three."

The door cracked open and through the sliver of an opening, I saw a figure in basketball shorts and a white T-shirt shuffle across the room. I took this as an invitation and pushed the door open all the way. Ander flopped himself back onto his bed and threw a neon tennis ball against the wall. It bounced back and he caught it with ease.

"Hi," I said, taking in his disheveled appearance. "Don't you think you might get a little cold in shorts?"

No reply.

"Did you see that it's snowing again?"

"Yep, that's what windows are for."

I took a deep breath. "Can you just get dressed, please? We're going to be late."

"I'm not going." He threw the tennis ball again. "You'll have to take the bus out there." Ander paused. "Sorry," he mumbled.

I strode over and snatched the tennis ball from his hands just as he caught it again.

"Hey!"

"Get up! There's no way you're just going to sit here over Christmas."

Ander scowled in response and looked away from me.

"Come on," I snapped. I went to his closet and started throwing clothes at him. *Jeans, shirt, jacket...*

"Lidia, I'm not going, okay? Take the damn bus, it won't kill you."

"I'm not leaving you here!"

Ander looked at me like I was speaking French and then spoke very, very, slowly. "I'm. Not. Going. Home."

"Fine." I crossed my arms. "Then. I'm. Not. Either."

Aggravated, he sat up. "Ethan is expecting to see you."

"Yeah," I shrugged. "He's also expecting to see you."

Ander's scowl deepened.

"And so is your mom, and your dad-" I pressed.

His features softened.

"And your sister," I said. "I know it's hard after what just happened with Alex... and, I'm really sorry, Ander. I know how

358

hard this for you." He wasn't looking at me, but I could tell he was listening. "But you need each other for support during times like these. Christmas is like, four days away. You guys need to be together. It'll be good for you."

I waited as Ander continued to brood. After a minute, he finally spoke. "Yeah," he nodded. "Yeah, okay." He looked around his room. "I haven't packed."

"I'll help!" I jumped up and started rummaging through his closet again. Ander got dressed quickly, and hauled an empty suitcase from under the bed.

Within twenty minutes, we were packed and trudging toward the student parking lot through the snow. It was weird being in the old Chevy without Alex behind the wheel. My heart panged as I watched Ander take his place. He looked exhausted.

As I buckled in, he started the car. A loud guitar screamed. It was Alex's Led Zeppelin CD blaring from the stereo.

Ander froze.

I reached over and shut the music off. After a second of silence, Ander cleared his throat and backed out of the student parking lot, snow crunching under the tires as we turned from campus and drove away.

It was a long drive, made even longer by the cars in front of us driving slower than Mrs. Peterson in a school zone. Not that we would be speeding anyways. The Chevy wasn't made for traveling through the mountain pass, but even with the smell of burnt plastic seeping in through the air vents, we crept along the winding cliff roads faster than most.

I spent most of the drive thinking about angels and demons, and other students at school who might also be exorcists. I was almost positive Jeff was, but I hadn't asked him yet. I also thought about the afterlife. Though some people stayed on earth as spirits, the existence of angels and demons meant there had to be some sort of heaven and hell.

I looked over at Ander. Driving through the snow seemed to lull him into a comfortable daze. I turned back toward my own window. If God knew as much as I thought He did, my afterlife was going to be very warm.

Eventually, the giant banks of dirty snow on the sides of the roads lessened to small mounds, and the tall evergreen forest faded into rocky hills with scattered leafless trees.

We descended the mountain, and entered into a Christmas-white hilly landscape. The only trees around this deserted area were the haunted-looking orchards. I had never seen so many wineries in one place. The knobby skeletons of hibernating trees lined the hills in rows and rows, warriors protesting the elements of ice and snow.

The sky sank into a darker shade of purple as we drove through the small town surrounding Lake Chelan. It consisted of only a few streets where the cluster of restaurants, shops, and hotels overlooked the giant lake. There were even a few tourists walking the streets, bundled up in obscene amounts of snow gear. I felt a little jolt of holiday cheer as I watched them shop. I could practically smell pine and sugar cookies.

When Ethan had said he lived in a small neighborhood, I had pictured an isolated house out in the boonies of hick country. However, as we continued to drive, I realized that all the neighborhoods around the lake were small, if you could even call them neighborhoods. Most houses were scattered amongst the hills, two or three acres between each neighbor. The houses themselves looked fancy, twice the size of the suburban cookie-cutter homes in my own neighborhood.

"We're almost there." Ander spoke for maybe the fifth time through the entire trip. We were driving up a twisting road on the side of a hill overlooking the lake.

The view was amazing.

"Did you want me to drop you off at Ethan's, or is he picking you up at my place?"

"Uh…" I wanted to see Ander's house. I was curious what his room looked like.

Ethan's expecting me.

"Probably Ethan's," I said.

Ander turned into the driveway of a magnificent Tuscan-style home.

I sucked in a breath. "Whoa."

"Have you seen his house before?"

"No," I half laughed with excitement. "Not this one."

The car slowed to a stop and I climbed out. To my surprise, Ander also got out. He opened the trunk and handed me my duffel bag.

"Thanks," I said. "Are you coming in?"

Ander shook his head. "No, I'll uh, let you guys get reacquainted. I'll see him later."

"Okay." My good mood deflated slightly. *Stop it.*

Ethan's waiting.

"Bye." Ander gave me a little salute and walked back towards the car as I made my way to the front door. The engine started but Ander didn't pull out of the driveway.

Is he waiting for something?

I knocked on the door and a freckle-faced blond woman wearing a pastel pink sweater answered with the biggest smile I had ever seen.

"Lidia?" she asked.

I nodded and the woman wrapped me in a hug. She smelled like baby powder and hairspray.

"Hi! It's so good to finally meet you, I'm Deborah."

I laughed awkwardly and tried to hug her back, but my arm was still holding my bag. Deborah released me and waved at the Chevy over my shoulder. I saw Ander wave back and slowly, it pulled out of the driveway.

He was waiting to see if I got inside safe.

"He's a good kid," Deborah sighed.

Something in my chest clambered uncomfortably.

"Come on inside sweetie, it's cold out here."

The house was beautiful and cluttered. The combination of sungrass yellow walls and various antique lamps spurting light made everything bright. As Deborah led me through the hall and into the kitchen, I saw that the wall decorations were a mix of china plates and Rocco paintings in obscenely thick golden frames.

"Ethan should be heading back over soon, he went over to Ander's house to wait for you."

"Oh no, I thought he was meeting me here."

"That's okay." She smiled and shrugged. "How was the drive?"

"It was okay." I struggled through a list of mental conversation topics reserved for meeting important adults. "It was snowy."

Ah, the weather. So cliché.

"Oh, I bet. Ethan will be here soon, he was just excited to see you." Deborah's smile reminded me of Ethan's own goofy grin. "If you want, you can start unpacking. I have you all set up in the guest room upstairs."

"Thank you, yes, that would be great."

"I'll show you the way." She led me upstairs and into a small room with a beige dresser and a twin bed covered with a horribly old vintage quilt. "I'll send him up when he gets back." Deborah smiled again and I felt like I should say something important, but I couldn't think of anything.

"Thank you," I said.

"Of course. We're very excited to have you." As soon as she shut the door, I flopped onto the bed. It smelled like lilac fabric softener.

And now we wait…

I didn't bother unpacking as I preferred the adventure of living out of a backpack when on vacation. It was the one time I could have my clothes spilling onto the floor without it being considered a mess, and I planned on embracing that privilege completely.

Ethan where are you?

∎∎∎∎∎∎∎∎∎∎∎∎∎∎∎∎∎∎∎∎∎∎∎∎∎∎∎∎∎∎∎∎∎∎∎∎∎∎∎

Ethan came home only ten minutes later. He swept into the room and scooped me off the bed in a giant bear hug. Ethan's winter jacket held the cold, little particles of snow melted against my body as he swung me around. I laughed.

I've missed this.

Everything suddenly felt so comfortable.

We stayed in the guest room for a while, talking briefly about his quick visit with Ander, his friends at school, and his favorite sports team. It was nice listening to his rambling about normal life. No mention of Spooks. No mention of the SETT. No mention of dark energy. Everything was just normal, and I envied him for how easy it must be.

Ethan's mom eventually called us downstairs, and we chatted with her in the warm kitchen over a plate of sugar cookies shaped like snowmen and reindeer.

"Oh! What time is it?" Ethan asked.

Deborah looked at her white wristwatch. "Ten past six."

Deborah was super nice, almost creepily nice. She was the polar opposite of Ethan's bland, workaholic father. She seemed to do nothing but smile, bake, and shop for antiques. Her and Ethan obviously had a good relationship, but I noticed how quick she was to coddle him when there was a hint of any negativity or disappointment in his voice. Even when he simply mentioned that the Seahawks had lost the Super Bowl, she instantly started reassuring us that they would win next year. I doubted she even watched football.

"It's ten past six?" Ethan swore and Deborah shot him the dark look only mothers could make. "Amy invited us over for dinner tonight," Ethan said. He bit into a cookie, decapitating the frosted snowman.

"Are you sure they want company?" Deborah asked. "I thought they would like a more private Christmas this year."

"Yeah, she said seven."

"Who's Amy?" I asked.

"Ander's mom."

Something in my stomach squirmed and I shivered. My sudden chill was brought on by either the presence of a spirit, or Ander. I hoped it wasn't Ander.

"It's a welcome-home dinner for Ander."

"Even after what happened with Alex?" Deborah suddenly gasped and put a delicate hand to her mouth. She looked at me guiltily. "Was I not supposed to say that?"

"Oh," I said quickly. "I already know about Alex."

I was there.

Ethan bit his thumbnail. "Has Ander talked about it with you at all?"

"No. He hasn't really talked to anyone."

Ethan tapped the rest of his cookie against the table, it dusted white crumbs onto the dark granite like snow. "I just can't believe it," he said.

"You can never really know someone." Deborah started the sink and began running hot water over the dishes. "Even your closest friends and family can turn out to be complete strangers."

"Don't bring dad into this, mom."

"I wasn't. George is a different case." Deborah and Ethan continued to bicker, but I stopped listening as soon as I noticed the man in short-shorts and a neon purple tank top sitting on the white sofa in the living room.

He tapped his foot as he stared at me. Half of his face was missing, bashed in, a deep bloody cavity where his left eye should've been. The raw flesh looked wet with blood, little pieces of white bone visible amongst the soft squishy matter bulging from the indented wound. The afro of permed hair covered most of the damage that had removed a portion of his skull, but it still made me feel sick.

He kept muttering something that sounded like- *I don't have the money.*

"Lidia?" Ethan watched as I stared at the couch. "You okay?"

I turned to Ethan. "Yep. I'm fine." I struggled to swallow.

"What should I bring over? It's kind of last minute." Deborah started bustling around the kitchen, but I could still hear the ghost over her clatter.

"I don't have the money."

"Chicken salad? Wine?"

"I don't have the money. I can get it to you man, C'mon man... Be cool."

"They have an entire wine cellar," Ethan said lazily. His hand snaked under the table to hold mine.

"I'll call my friend Ralph, he owes me. I can get it to you... Please. I don't have the money."

I looked over to see Ethan's pale blue eyes still watching me. "You have goose bumps," he said.

"It's cold."

366

The ghost kept tapping his foot on the floor. *Tap, tap, tap.*

"*I don't have the money. Be cool.*"

"Oh!" Deborah clapped her hands and trotted over to the fridge. "I'll bring some dessert! I have a pumpkin pie- Ah ha!"

I couldn't take it anymore.

I got up and pretended to stretch. "This is such a nice couch." I approached the man slowly.

He whipped his head up to look at me.

"Oh that?" Deborah grinned. "I got it at an estate sale."

As I approached, I saw that the man's eyes were the darkest shade of brown, almost black, and the whites of his eyes were streaked with red veins. His bloodstained shirt clung to his chest and stomach. His hands clutched his knees and his foot continued to tap.

Tap, tap, tap.

"It once belonged to Charlie Milton. You're probably too young to remember him, but he made those water aerobics videos where everyone was dressed in leotards."

"Oh yeah!" Ethan laughed. "I remember those."

I sat down on the couch next to Charlie Milton.

"Hey Lid, do you remember seeing that show on TV?"

"Yeah, those leotards were awful," I said absently.

Charlie suddenly leered towards me. He was so close I could count the hairs on the stubble of his chin. *"Where's yo leotard,"* he snarled, a little dribble of blood ran down his cheek.

I shot my hand forward. There was the sharp painful sensation of ripping tendons behind my left eye, and then the dull crack of my skull as if beaten in. Warm static erupted from my hand and raced through my veins. After the pain was gone, Charlie was gone too, and my head erupted in a fuzzy fit of blissful electric static.

Whoa...

The room was almost blinding, each lamp glistened with outstretched rays of yellow light bouncing off the yellow walls in shiny beams.

Ethan and his mom were still discussing Charily Milton, their voices sagged and slowed. I curled my fingers on the leather cushion of the couch. It was smooth, but also a little bumpy. Each little miniscule bump shifted under my gentle stroke, and moved on its own accord. Slowly, the blissful haze cleared. The lamps stopped shining like burning suns. The leather stopped moving beneath my touch.

Then the confusion set in.

Charlie Milton spoke to me as if he had heard me say something about his leotards.

That wasn't normal.

Even though spirits often addressed the medium, they never really saw us. They were reliving the last moments of life, a medium could take the focus of the spirit's energy. They'll turn and talk to us as if we are their murderer, their spouse, their child, but never as ourselves. They don't really see us, let alone hear what we say.

Maybe it's an exorcist thing.

"Why don't you guys go change into something nice for dinner," Deborah called from the kitchen.

"Mom," Ethan groaned.

"Ethan," Deborah mocked.

"Yeah, I'm going to go change," I said.

Can I stand up? Oh good, I can.

I shimmied my shoulders, wincing slightly at the lingering pain from my fading bruise. "I'll be ready in ten!" I raced up the stairs.

Chapter 25

I smoothed my shirt absently as Deborah reached forward to ring the doorbell of the beautiful house. Like Ethan's, Ander's house was also a Tuscan-style stone.

"You look beautiful, Lidia." Deborah patted my shoulder.

I cringed a smile, "Thanks."

I hadn't brought too many dress-up clothes, and the best I could do was a black cardigan over a silky white blouse and dark denim jeans. I had attempted to throw on some fashionable earrings and lip gloss, but it didn't really make a difference. I was still nervous.

Why? I wasn't sure I knew why I was so nervous. I did know that having Ethan and Ander in the same room, pretending like everything was just how it was at Camp Tanka, made me sick.

The door swung open and a tall woman with a billowing ponytail of dark auburn hair opened the door. She smiled and ushered us inside.

"Hello!" She cooed her greeting softly. "I'm so glad you guys could come."

Deborah reached out to give her a hug, and I noticed that the woman had dark circles beneath eyes that looked a little glossy, as if she had recently been crying.

"I wanted Ander to be able to see Ethan sometime over break," she sighed and then lowered her voice to speak directly to Deborah. "I thought it might make things easier, they always miss each other… but you know they'd never admit it."

"Boys," said Deborah.

Ethan looked a little embarrassed. He took a step away from his mom, and reached out for my hand just as Deborah turned back to Amy.

"How are you doing?"

"Oh, you know." Amy gave a weak smile and I noticed that she looked a lot like Alex. They had the same chin. "We're holding up okay. We just want to try and keep the holidays as normal as possible for everyone."

Deborah nodded. "Well, we are more than happy to see you." She turned towards Ethan and I for introductions. "I don't think you've met Ethan's girlfriend yet, this is Lidia."

Amy beamed at me and stretched out a hand for me to shake. "I've heard a lot about you," Amy said. "It's nice to finally meet one of Ander's school friends."

"Nice to meet you, too."

"I think Ander's in the living room. You guys can go find him if you want."

Ethan pulled me forward, but just as we turned the corner, I heard Amy's loud whisper to Deborah. *"She's gorgeous."*

My cheeks flushed. If Amy knew more about me, I don't think I would've been getting any compliments.

I felt sick.

Ander's house was warm and it smelled like rosemary bread, and other buttered herbs. The walls were painted in a

371

darker color scheme than Ethan's house, mostly browns and burgundies, and the decorations were tasteful.

Against the far wall of the living room was a huge Christmas tree, expertly decorated with a glorious array of red and gold. It twinkled like the perfect trees surrounding Santa's photo booth in the mall this time of year. There wasn't any snow, but boxes wrapped in gold paper already littered the base of the tree.

Oh God, there he is.

Ander was slumped in the large puffy couch facing the fireplace. He was wearing a long sleeve shirt that he didn't have on during the drive over. My heart started to thrum uncomfortably at the sight of him as a trickle of guilt soaked my innards, sticking to the sides of my stomach and weighing it down like thick oil.

"What are you drinking?" Ethan asked.

Ander's head turned, he looked a little surprised and a little disappointed to see us both standing there. As we neared, Ander's eyes jumped to Ethan's hand conjoined with mine before shooting back to our faces.

"Hey," Ander smiled. "What's up guys?"

Ethan led me to the couch where he sat down. There really wasn't enough room for me, so I tried leaning against the side table, but Ethan pulled me over to sit on his lap. Ander's smile faded as he watched our movements with a blank stare. Ethan didn't seem to notice. He leaned over to sniff the snowman-shaped mug Ander was holding.

"Whew!" Ethan leaned back, his arms twisting around my waist

I'm going to be sick.

"That is some strong coffee my friend... What is that? Did you put Jack Daniels in there?

Ander's panicked eyes shot to mine, and it felt like a bullet pierced my heart. My pulse skyrocketed.

"Yup." Ander looked back at Ethan and smiled again. "Happy holidays."

It'll be fine.

Then why don't I feel fine?

Ethan half smiled, sympathy lacing his voice. "Any word on Alex yet?"

Ander shook his head and took a long swig from his mug.

"Ander," Amy's voice called from the other room just as her head peeped out from the corner. "Why don't you show our guests the house? You'd like a tour wouldn't you, Lidia?"

"Yeah, I'd love one. Your house is really pretty."

Amy's smile wrinkled her nose. "Thanks." She disappeared back into the kitchen.

Ander pursed his lips together and raised his eyebrows at Ethan's chortling laugh.

"Do you want the grand tour?" Ander asked me, insinuating, and probably hoping that I obviously wouldn't.

"Ethan said you have a wine cellar."

He nodded, barely looking at me.

"Is it like the Cask of Amontillado?"

373

"No," Ander sighed and hoisted himself off the couch. "Okay. First stop, wine cellar."

Ethan and I followed Ander to the hall where he led us down a tight and short flight of stairs. It ended abruptly at another door with a little key-in pad above the doorknob.

"Fancy," I said.

Ander hunched over to press a few numbers. "I'm not technically supposed to know the code, but-" he shrugged.

"We've had some good times down here." Ethan squeezed my hand. "Dude, remember that time we snuck in and stole those two bottles for Robbie's fourteenth birthday party?"

Ander's face broke into the first real smile I'd seen in days. "Oh yeah," he chuckled.

"We, like, didn't know how to use the bottle opener so we smashed the tops off on the fence outside and-" Ethan made a broad gestures with his hands, "the entire bottle just exploded. I got my hand cut, and then we did it again! And got cut again!"

"You didn't stop after you got cut the first time?" I asked him.

Ethan shrugged. "We were fourteen. Do you still have the scar?" he asked Ander.

Ander opened the locked door with a little pop, and led us inside. "Yeah," he held up his bandaged broken hand. "And then some," he added dryly.

"Dude, how did you not get suspended for punching a hole through a desk?"

Is that the story Ander gave him?

374

Ander shrugged. "I guess they just like me."

Ethan laughed. "I think you got ripped off. If it was going to break my hand I would've at least bet fifty."

"The next time I bet someone I can punch through a desk, I'm betting a hundred."

The wine cellar was awesome. A small cedar room with shelves holding various red and white wines, most of which seemed to be from local vineyards.

"This one is my mom's." Ander came up behind me.

I swear I could feel him stand there before I heard him speak. I felt hyper aware and completely on edge.

"She owns one of the vineyards on the other side of the lake."

"Oh," I turned the bottle in my hand, admiring the delicate lacey writing over a logo of a wolf wearing a top hat. "Is it good?"

"Eh," Ander took the bottle from me and set it back on the shelf. "I don't know. I hate wine... are you ready to see the rest of the house?"

I nodded and turned to the door. Ander followed me up the steps, and seeing that the wine gazing was over, Ethan followed us. Ander showed us the granite counters in the kitchen, the eloquently decorated table overlooking the lake in the dining room, and the small laundry room. Ethan veered off to use the bathroom, so Ander took me upstairs.

"That's the master bedroom." Ander let me peer into the doorway. "Alex's room, and Sarah's room, but she's sleeping right now. And my room's this way."

The room was very… Ander.

The full bed was made with pearl white bed sheets, and a charcoal grey comforter. There were a few posters of his favorite snowboarders on the walls, a band poster featuring a group of guys doing something questionable in rubber duck suits, and a few trophies on the dresser. I went over to the trophies. "You play soccer?" I asked.

Ander cleared his throat. "No, I, uh, did. Those are old." He hadn't made eye contact very much during the tour, avoiding both Ethan and I by looking at the walls and floor. "I think I got the last one when I was eight, and I pretty much just picked grass."

"That's what I did in soccer," I laughed. "My dad would get so mad because I'd make those daisy crowns instead of actually play."

Finally, our eyes locked and Ander smiled. A warm thrill shot through the core of my body, but I looked away, trying to distract myself. Something shiny caught my eye, and I went over to the side of the dresser. It was a giant ninja sword.

"Oh my God!" I giggled as I pulled it out of its sheath. "Wow." I practiced swinging it, making great slashes of silver in the air. Ander stepped forward, unsuccessfully attempting to persuade me to put the weapon down. I poised the tip of the blade against his chest. "Is there something you'd like to tell me?" I grinned. "Are you a ninja?"

Ander's smile was amazing. "I don't need to be a ninja." The sword suddenly flew from my hands sideways and floated in the air next to me. The blunt blade turned to point towards my head. "I'm a psychic."

"Speaking of," I watched the blade uneasily as I spoke. "Have you ever had a spirit talk to you?"

"What do you mean?" The sword drifted like a feather back towards its hiding spot as Ander leaned against the dresser, watching me.

"Well, Ethan's house is full of antiques." At this, Ander's face broke into a knowing smile.

"Yeah, his mom practically collects spirits."

"I've already absorbed Charlie Milton today."

"The leotard guy?"

"Oh yeah!" Ethan came striding into the room and within two seconds, one of his arms was around my waist. "My mom has his couch." Both Ander and I stared blankly at Ethan's sudden appearance. "So, did you get the grand tour?" he asked.

"Yeah, I think I've seen it all." I took his hand and started downstairs. "Did you know that your best friend is a ninja?"

"Oh yeah?" Ethan laughed and looked back at Ander who was trudging slowly behind us, eyes on the floor.

■■■

Amy called us into the dining room for dinner soon after the tour had ended. The entire dining room looked like something off Pinterest. I honestly couldn't figure out how she got so many pine cones to balance the way they did as a centerpiece. There were even little name cards on each place setting.

377

Amy saw me searching for my name as everyone started refilling wine glasses, and taking their seats. She pointed me to the end of the table where I was to sit next to Ander, across from Ethan so that "the boys" weren't able to leave me out of the conversation. After I found my place, she warned Ander and Ethan that if either of them started a repeat of the food fight that happened last Easter, they would both be banned from the adult table, and have to eat on the back porch... in the snow.

I smiled over at Ethan sitting across from me as Amy started hauling a variety of dishes onto the table. Deborah was chatting with Ander's father, Mark, an extremely tall man with Ander's high cheekbones and expressive mouth. His silver hair and white teeth were exotic and dangerous looking against his tanned skin, and he was kind of scary at first. However, after he asked how I was doing in school, and what I thought about their Medieval phone policy, I could laugh easily with Mark.

It was strange, and unexpectedly comforting to talk so effortlessly with Ander's and Ethan's family. It made the cold distance between my own family painfully obvious. Everyone at the table treated each other with respect and genuine interest. They listened. There wasn't the structural hierarchy of adult and child that I was so used to at home.

Amy returned to the table and sat down with the final dish. "Okay everyone, dish up while it's hot!"

The conversation lulled as the food was passed around the table like clockwork.

"Is Sarah coming down?" Ander asked his mom.

Amy frowned, but managed to keep her voice cheery. "No, she's not feeling well today." Her face aged ten years as she spoke that one sentence. "But in honor of Ander's... and Lidia's homecoming," she added my name thoughtfully. "I made your favorite." Amy smiled and passed a large dish to Mark who awed as he loaded a glob of vibrant orange gook onto his plate.

Ander's blue eyes widened in excitement and I almost laughed. "Mom makes the best macaroni," he said to me, shoveling a huge portion onto his plate. Cheese stringed together in the sludge. Red spots of spices were mixed in amongst the orange that oozed from every noodle.

Gross.

"Oh, wow." I tried to make my face look hungry, but I was secretly hoping Ander would finish the bowl so that I could bypass. "Mm," I said. "It looks really good."

It looks like it came from another planet... Is it breathing? I swear its breathing.

"It is," Ander said. "Here." Without asking, Ander spooned a giant glob onto my plate. "You have to try it."

Ethan laughed across from us. "Lid's a vegan, dude."

"You're a vegan?" Amy sounded concerned.

"She's a semi-vegan," Ander said, still focusing on piling the mound of macaroni and cheese as high as was humanly possible. "She'll eat it." Seeming satisfied with my portion size, he handed the dish to Ethan.

Ethan was looking at me like I had sprouted antlers.

"Are you sure?" Amy asked.

"What's a semi-vegan?" Ethan asked, loading his own plate with orange goo. "Is that even a real thing?" he muttered.

"It means she's vegan ninety nine percent of the time," Ander answered again. "Until there's temptation, and she doesn't feel like it anymore." He added blandly, more to himself than anyone else.

My gut turned.

Are we still talking about food?

"Try it." Ander pointed with his fork.

I did.

"Oh muh gawd." I tried to speak, but my mouth wouldn't stop chewing. It was like cheese heaven exploded in my mouth. "This is so good!"

Amy beamed. "Sarah came up with a special name for it. What was it, Mark?"

"Moon food." Mark said, sipping a glass of red wine in-between bites. "Since the moon is supposed to be made out of cheese."

"So, Mark," Deborah started. Her eyes were getting glossy, and I think she was on her third glass of wine. "How's the job search going?"

Mark took a thoughtful sip of wine before answering. "Not so great, to be honest. There aren't a lot of opportunities in this area." He reached out to take hold of Amy's hand and she looked at him lovingly.

Parents that actually like each other... weird.

"Amy and I have been thinking about downsizing in the city."

"Really?" Deborah poured herself another glass, not seeming to notice that she had just added white to the last remaining drops of red. The result was a glass of baby pink liquid, the exact shade of her sweater.

"Well," Amy injected. "Alex is-" she took a breath. "Well... Ander's away at school. We make enough with the vineyard right now since we already own the house, but it's just hard to float with Mark's unemployment, especially with the cost of Sarah's treatments. It's a long drive for her hospital visits too, so, it might just make it easier for everyone if we were closer to Seattle."

My heart went heavy. To say the least, Ander's family was going through a lot. Yet there they were, loving, warm, and inviting neighbors into their home to eat Moon Food.

Something gnawed unpleasantly inside of me.

Feelings.

Not only for the trouble of these good people who smile despite their worries, but also pity for the misery of my own family who suffered from nothing at all, but were still some of the most miserable people I knew.

What does that say about me?

The biggest problem in my life was when the cafeteria ran out of waffle mix- well, that and seeing dead people. For so long I fought against becoming a medium. I thought it was an unmanageable burden, and yet Ander's family had gone through the same thing- twice. Hell, Alex went to an institution after trying to commit suicide when he was only twelve.

It was like a light bulb went off in my brain, and I was suddenly so ashamed of myself. I looked down at my empty plate and listened to the rest of the conversation absently.

How did I become so... selfish?

"Where do you plan on going to college, Ander?" asked Deborah. "Ethan hasn't even started applying, but I keep telling him that now is the time."

Ethan rolled his eyes.

"Uh, I haven't gotten my acceptance letters back yet, so, I'm not sure," said Ander.

My already low-hanging heart plummeted like an elevator that had gotten its cables cut on the top floor.

"I think I might hear back from California pretty soon, but, I also applied for the University of Washington."

"Do you know which one you want to go to?" Deborah asked. "Or what your major will be?"

"Uh, no, not yet. I like the weather in California more, so hopefully I get in there."

Ander's going to college.

Of course he is.

I won't see him after graduation.

I looked at Ander and realized that after June, I might not ever see him again. My stomach was in ropes and I felt myself start to panic. Ethan was staring, but I didn't care.

The doorbell rang and Amy got up with a quizzical look on her face. "Excuse me."

Ander's going to college.

Her heels clicked down the dark hall, I could hear her unlock and open the door over the quiet chatter at the dinner table.

He's leaving.

Amy gasped from the entry way. "Alex."

Chapter 26

Mark pushed his chair back from the table and jogged down the hallway toward the front door. I looked over at Ander, his face had frozen in an expression of shock.

"Alex?" Ethan asked, looking questioningly around the table.

I stood up and started toward the hall. I heard two other chairs scoot out from the table behind me, but just as I was about to turn the corner, I ran into someone that smelled like stale smoke and copper.

It was Alex.

I stumbled backwards.

It had only been a few weeks, but Alex didn't even look like the same person. His face was sunken and hollow, making his high cheek bones jut out sharply against the starved cavities of his face. Cool blue veins trailed along the flesh of his neck, stopping abruptly at the protuberant collarbone.

"More company than I expected." Alex looked at Ethan and Deborah before turning his hazy grin back at me. "Did I scare you?"

"What are you doing here?" Ander sounded breathless.

"Alex, does Amy know you were coming?" asked Deborah, her feeble attempt to sound motherly faltered with surprise and fear. I could see her out of the corner of my eye as she kept looking back toward the hall. "Maybe, maybe I'll go grab her and we can all sit down for dinner? She made your favorite. I'm sure there's-" her panicked expression deepened as Alex strode towards her confidently. "There's some... left in the fridge."

Alex stood behind Deborah's seat, smiling down at her with sick sincerity. "Sure, let's have a nice dinner." Alex let his hand drift onto Deborah's forehead. As Alex held it there, Deborah closed her eyes and her face went slack.

Once Alex took his hand away, Deborah's eyes opened again. She was staring at the ceiling, her eyes rolled so far back that all I could see was the milky white peeping out from under her drooping eyelids.

"Mom!" Ethan pushed past a chair toward his mother, but as he reached forward, Alex's other hand clamped across Ethan's forehead. The light extinguished from Ethan's pale blue eyes and he stopped moving completely.

"Stop it!" I heard myself shout, but I didn't move.

Ethan closed his eyes, and swayed in one spot. A moment later when Alex removed his hand, Ethan's eyes sunk so far back in his skull that it looked like he was about to have a seizure.

"What did you do to him?" I stepped forward, but Ander's arm shot out and he held onto my wrist.

"Ah, ah, ah," Alex tisked. "They'll be fine. I don't need to mind-wash you two." He shrugged, looking around the room as if he was bored. "No point since you already know everything... it doesn't work on other mediums anyways."

Ander's fingers dug painfully into my arm.

Alex smiled, and then called down the hallway. "Mom, dad, you can come in now."

Amy and Mark walked into the dining room. Their eyes were lifeless, white.

"What are you doing, Alex?" Ander half growled, half shouted. "What have you done?"

"I already told you, when you and your stupid friends tried an exorcism on me." Alex spat. "I'm helping Sarah get better, and I'm not letting you, or anyone else stop me because it's working." Alex's tongue flickered across his teeth, and his jaw twitched with enthusiasm.

"You stay away from her!" Ander let go of my arm and leapt across the table toward Alex. Bowls of green salad, the bread basket, and the orange Moon Food crashed around him as he scraped through the silverware toward his brother.

A wave of hot static washed through the room and Ander, along with all the plates, were swept from the table and fell to the floor. Food splattered and dishes broke around Ander in a deafening ring of sharp noise. I ran over to Ander, Moon Food mushed underfoot along with the crunch of broken plates. Ander swore as he took my hand and let me help him to his feet. His sweater was covered in dangling bits of the destroyed dinner. Globs of orange goo soaked into the fabric of his shirt and greasy clumps clung to his hair.

Alex stared at his brother with narrowed eyes, daring him to make another move. "I don't want to hurt anyone," he said. Alex's mouth moved silently in-between sentences, struggling to keep up with his wandering mind. "Mom and dad's current state will last as long as I'm over, and it's going to stay this way. Sarah won't even know I'm here, and when they wake up-" he gestured to his parents. "They won't know I'm here either… If you, or you-" he looked directly at both of us in turn. "Screw this up, and try to turn me in- Sarah will die."

"She's already dying," Ander said.

"Without me, she would be gone within a month. I am the *only* thing keeping her alive right now! The treatment isn't working." Behind Alex, Deborah and Ethan continued to sway, looking at nothing.

"You and your girlfriend are going to do exactly what I say, when I say it." Alex's bulbous eyes flashed in my direction, then back at Ander. "And right now, I'm saying that you're going to keep your mouths shut, and your noses out of my fucking business."

We stared back, silent.

Seeming satisfied with our silence, Alex nodded at Ander. "Clean this mess up." He turned to Deborah and Ethan. "Take Lidia home. When you're there, everyone will go straight to bed and forget that I ever showed up. It was a lovely dinner party."

Deborah and Ethan walked over to me. Ethan took my hand in a death grip, and dragged me mechanically towards the front door.

"Ander!" I dug my heels into the floor and reached for Ander who started towards me.

"Don't help her!" Alex boomed.

Ander's body froze mid-reach, and I knew that Alex had him completely immobilized.

"Ander!" My voice was faint, pleading. "Alex, please don't do this. Please." Ethan's hand was crushing my own. I could feel the bruises blooming between my knuckles and wondered if he would break it. "Ouch," I pulled away but he just pulled me harder, eyes focused on the ceiling. "Ander!"

Deborah turned back to address the table before we exited the hallway, surveying the mess without actually seeing anything. "That was a lovely dinner." Amy and Mark swayed in the corner, the ruined dinner lay on the floor, and Ander's spoiled attire clung to his frozen outstretched body. Deborah smiled at the disaster. "Thank you." Her voice was robotic. Empty. She spun, and walked directly toward the front door as Ethan drug me out of the house by my throbbing hand.

■■

"What happened to your hand, babe?" Concern sprang from Ethan's voice. We were sitting at the kitchen table, eating breakfast. Deborah was fiddling with the coffee pot, and Ethan was digging into his scrambled eggs with vigor, stopping suddenly when he saw the blotches of blue and purple on my left knuckles.

"I punched the driveway," I said nonchalantly, taking a bite of cereal.

Deborah muttered something about kids these days, and left the room with her coffee.

It was the sixth time he'd asked me about my hand within two days. The first time I had told him I fell, but after a while, I realized it was pointless, and just started making up ridiculous stories. Being mind-washed had left his memories jumbled and scattered, and both Deborah and Ethan were having a hard time remembering a lot of things. Neither could remember the day of the week, where they set something important, what they had done the day before, or even what they had just said moments before. Over time, it had gotten better, and I suspected the effect of the mind-wash would fade away soon.

Ethan's eyebrows scrunched together. "When?"

"Yesterday, don't you remember?"

"Oh," Ethan nodded. "Yeah."

In a way, having Ethan with a short-term memory had been useful. I snuck away to Ander's house more than once in the past forty-eight hours, and though I was always honest about where I had been, Ethan was usually mad, but he forgot about it within an hour. Even if Ethan had remembered everything, I still would've gone to Ander's because Alex disappeared again.

Ander said he was gone an hour after he showed up for dinner, and he hadn't seen him since. We searched the attic, the wine cellar, even the bedroom closets, but Alex never showed up.

He was there though, lurking around the house like a ghost. There were always footsteps a few rooms away, sometimes a door was locked for no reason, and Sarah continued to get stronger. Ander watched her like a hawk, nervous Alex would hurt her, or worse, she'd hurt herself if she became possessed.

I had brought up the idea of turning Alex into the police, but Ander shook his head and said he was torn between two wrong decisions. I understood. Even I wasn't sure what the right thing to do was, if there even was a right choice in this scenario. Every time we saw each other, Ander and I just talked ourselves in circles before I finally noticed the time, and hurried back to a disgruntled and confused Ethan.

"What are we doing today?" I asked. "It's Christmas Eve, we should do something fun."

Ethan screwed his face up, trying to count the days. "Well," he said finally. "We can go to the movies tonight." He seemed to realize something. "But, I need to finish a little Christmas shopping."

"I thought we said we weren't doing presents?" I said. "I didn't get a chance to do any shopping at all this year."

"Yeah, I know–"

"Ethan, I literary got you nothing."

"I know, it's cool. You can come shopping if you want?"

"I don't even have any money. Please, don't get me anything."

Ethan gave me a goofy grin and pinched my cheek. "I won't."

"I'm serious."

"Okay." He rolled his eyes.

I felt a little twinge of anger, and for the first time ever, his smile annoyed me. "Look, I really appreciate it, but I would feel really bad if you got me something."

"That's what all girls say."

"What other girls have you been buying Christmas gifts for?"

Ethan's smile disappeared. "Lid," he said softly. "I thought we were over that?"

"I'm over it." I let my spoon drop back in to the cereal bowl, and I pushed it away. "It was a fair question."

"Why are you in such a bad mood?"

"I'm not." I crossed my arms, but after a minute of silence, I sighed and got up. "I'll just see you when you get back from shopping, okay?"

"Fine." Ethan watched me walk upstairs to the guest room, and fifteen minutes later, I heard his car pull out of the driveway. I dawned my thick plaid jacket, a scarf, and gloves before trudging into the cold. The thick snow made a muffled crunching sound as my foot sank into the ground with each step. By the time I reached Ander's house, I was sweating beneath my snow gear.

I ambled up to the empty driveway and was just about to knock on the door when I heard a faint radio playing from the back porch. I turned and headed toward the back. Classic rock trickled from the speakers of an old stereo sitting next to a small figure bundled up in a magenta coat.

Sarah sat on a porch swing that overlooked the white sloping hill of her backyard and the smooth surface of the lake.

"Hi Sarah," I said as I approached the covered awning.

"Ander's not here."

"Oh," I continued on, peering behind her through the glass double doors into the dining room. Amy sat at the table with a computer while she sipped a steaming mug. "Where is he?" I asked.

"He's getting the mail."

"Okay, I can just wait for him." I took a seat next to her on the bench.

Sarah was only fourteen, but her youthful features had been depleted by the cancer. Sarah was very pale, and

391

unnaturally skinny. She had no eyebrows, or eyelashes, and most of her head was covered in a thick purple hat with jewels sewn along the brim. A sparkling pink scarf was wrapped around her neck. As we sat, she gazed at the lake with large blue eyes, the exact same shade as Ander's.

"I like your scarf," I said.

"Thanks...I like your boots."

I had met Sarah a few times, and each time I couldn't help but notice how her eyes seemed to stick to my clothes, hair, and makeup. Between cancer treatments at the hospital and recovery at home, she didn't get a chance to hang out with a lot of other girls. I think I made her a little nervous. Once, I had mentioned that I could paint her nails, but she refused with a shy smile.

"What are you listening to?" I asked. It was Tom Petty.

"I don't know. It's one of my dad's CD's." Sarah shrugged, embarrassed.

"Ah... You and your dad have good taste. These are the best of the best," I said. "It's where all the modern stuff comes from." Sarah turned to watch me as I fiddled with the stereo. "Can I see what's on here?"

She nodded and I started to switch songs. I stopped on the soft melody of a piano and harmonica. "Oh! Bruce! This is Thunder Road, do you like this one?"

"Uhm. Yeah."

I turned the volume up a notch.

"*The front- screen door slams, Sarah's dress sways,*" I sang along with the music, altering the lyrics slightly since I didn't know it word for word. I wasn't a vocal talent, but Sarah's face split into a wide smile. *"She's dancing across the porch as the radio plays."*

I smiled and pointed playfully at the porch and the radio. Sarah giggled, which encouraged me to stand and do a saucy dance, swinging my hips animatedly to her delight. I probably looked like my grandma dancing during bingo night after one too many wine coolers, but Sarah was laughing so hard that I kept going.

"Don't make me dance alone!" I reached forward and pulled Sarah to her feet. Her frame was so delicate that I thought she might break, but we held hands and swayed to the music. Sarah half laughed, half sang as she spun around and around. *"You ain't a beauty but eh, you're alright."*

I looked up and saw Ander inside, frozen behind the glass door. He was looking directly at me the way he had that night at winter formal. He had a bundle of mail in one hand and the other on the door handle, but he didn't open it.

Bruce's rocky voice mingled with Sara's as the music spilled from the radio. Our eyes met, and for a second, everything else seemed to stop.

"Lidia?" Ethan's voice came from the side of the house coupled with heavy footsteps crunching across the snow. Ethan rounded the corner and saw Sarah laughing, still spinning in front of me. "I thought I heard you back here."

"Ethan!" My voice sounded surprised, guilty. "I thought you were going shopping."

There was a click behind me and Ander stepped out onto the porch. "Hey," he greeted me casually without meeting my eyes. "Sarah, your pen-pal sent a letter."

Sarah clicked the radio off and took the letter from Ander. She sat back down on the porch swing, tearing the blue envelope open with small white fingers.

"Hey man!" Ander waved at Ethan who was already climbing up the porch.

"Hey," Ethan's voice hitched momentarily upon seeing Ander. Ethan turned to me, looking slightly hurt. "I didn't know you were going to Ander's house."

Busted.

"Yeah, I just had to come over here... to ask Ander what time we're leaving next week. What happened to shopping?"

"Oh." Ethan didn't look mad, but he didn't look happy. "I changed my mind. I got a call from my friend Vern, and he has his girlfriend over, and I didn't want to be the third wheel. So, I came back home to see if you wanted to hang out with them."

No, I don't.

"Oh, uh, yeah, okay."

Ethan turned toward Ander. "You can come too-"

"Vern Smith?" Ander asked, making a face. "No. That guy always smells like soup... you guys have fun."

We waved goodbye and left to go hang out with Vern Smith. The soup kid.

Chapter 27

Vern did smell like soup. Tomato, to be exact.

Hanging out with Vern's girlfriend, a bag of chips, and a disrespectful wiener dog who kept biting my shoelaces led me to conclude that it was the worst Christmas Eve of my entire life. Not just my life either, it was probably the lamest celebration in the history of celebrations.

While Ethan and Vern seemed to get along swimmingly, Vern's girlfriend, Amanda, and I were forced to enjoy each other's company. It was extremely difficult to do considering Amanda had the personality of a wet blanket. Her face seldom showed expression, and her voice droned on and on about things I could've cared less about. She didn't even notice her wiener dog, Putsy, was trying to eat my boots. I kept pulling the ends of the shoelace out of his mouth every time I heard a gagging sound somewhere near my feet.

The evening eventually came to an end, and Ethan took me back to his house so that we could drink cider and gaze at the lake through the living room window. We sat together, curled up in a warm blanket on Charlie Milton's couch. It was nice, but at the same time, it felt wrong. Every time Ethan touched me, my skin crawled, and I couldn't figure out why.

He wrapped an arm around my legs. I didn't like it. "I'm really glad you came over for Christmas, Lid," he said.

"Me too." My voice was weak as I stared blankly out at the sky. You couldn't see the stars, there were too many snow clouds that stormed past the moon in waves.

I wonder how long Alex will stay around...

"Can we talk about something for a minute?"

What if Alex gets caught?

"Sure, talk away," I murmured.

Will we be in legal trouble for not turning him in?

Ethan planted a soft kiss on my forehead. "Are you mad at me?"

"No, why?"

"Well, like, you've been so distant lately. Is there anything wrong?"

Yes.

Ethan was warm as he held me, and I tried to speak but I couldn't swallow. My mouth felt sticky and my jaw felt tired. Too tired to even open and give Ethan an answer.

"Do... do you still want to be with me?"

"I don't know."

The words just came out. I didn't think, I didn't feel, I just sort of spoke. I felt Ethan's body tense all around me, but I just didn't care. I looked back at his face, everything I had once found so endearing just bothered me now. His smile, his freckles, his goofy sense of humor.

"What do you mean, you don't know?" His voice rose an octave. "You just- Christmas is tomorrow. I invited you to Christmas with my family." His mouth twisted down in confusion. "Why did you come, if you don't know if you want to be together?"

Because of Ander.

I answered his question in my head, and the response sent a shock of horrible resolution through my body.

Oh no.

I wanted to be with Ander this Christmas.

"I don't know." I could feel my hands go cold as I spoke. I knew this was not the time nor the place to breakup, but, I couldn't stop. "I'm really sorry, Ethan... things are just so different now and we're trying to make a long distance relationship work after- after everything, and it's not working."

I looked over to see him watching me intently. His freckled face was so familiar. Ethan was like home. Ethan was security, safe, and normal. He was looking at me like I had shot a kitten, and I felt the heat of tears build behind my eyes.

I'm so selfish.

Ethan's voice was strained. "We can make it work."

I don't want to.

Ander's face flashed through my mind. Just imagining his smile made me melt. I loved Ethan, but this was different. I knew I would do anything for Ander. Anything- and that terrified me.

"Lidia," Ethan's eyes pleaded. "Say something."

"I want to break up," I choked.

"Wow." Ethan let out a half sob and frisked the back of his hand over his eyes. There was a moment of silence as everything sank in, then he said it again. "Wow."

"Ethan, please. I'm so sorry." Tears had spilled from my own eyes, but at the same time, I felt like a weight had lifted from my chest.

Ethan pushed me away and got up from the couch. "Thanks for ruining Christmas, Lid," he said. Then he stormed upstairs.

I sniffled, wiping the tears from my eyes and turned back toward the window.

Now what?

A few houses in the distance had their Christmas lights blinking in flashes of red and green. A plastic depiction of Santa and his reindeer shone from the rooftop of a house near the lakeshore.

I'm so stupid. Do I really think Ander and I will ever work?

My chest panged in answer. *No...*

I got up and walked upstairs towards the guest room. After getting into a pair of sleeping shorts and a T-shirt, I crawled under the thick quilt, wishing I could drown in the bedding and never reemerge.

What will I do about Christmas tomorrow?

A silver misty shadow pooled in the corner of the room near the nightstand. I sat up a little to watch the spirit, wondering if it would take full form and turn into an apparition. The mist hovered for a second, then sank into the wall.

It was gone.

"Crap," I let my face crash into the pillow. *Maybe I should just leave.*

Can I run away with no car?

Everything in my body felt queasy, sick.

Ander's leaving for college anyways.

I was glad I let Ethan go. It wasn't fair for me to string him along for personal comfort and my own insecurity. The thought of him hating me though- that sent me into a depression. Thoughts of Ander gave me anxiety, and thinking about facing Ethan and his mom tomorrow on Christmas made me feel nauseous.

What have I done?

▪ ▪

Something hit the side of the house, then my window. I sat up and looked across the room to where the moonlight shone through the panel of glass.

The sound came again, and then there was a long, sharp scratch that scraped along the side of the house. I turned the bedside light on and peered over at the window.

Scratch, scratch...

Scratch.

Thump.

Slowly, very slowly, I climbed out of bed and glided toward the window. I switched the latch and pulled it open, letting a blast of icy wind splash my face as small white particles of snow drifted inside.

A dark figure jumped from above and landed in a crouching position on the windowsill. "Hey."

I gasped, and without realizing it, stretched my hands out in front of me. Blue sparks flared from my fingertips and shot forward.

My aim was way off.

I blasted the window frame instead of the person.

"Jesus, Lidia!" Ander swore.

I stopped zapping and stared, horrified, at the black burn mark on the otherwise perfectly white wood trim.

Now Deborah will really hate me.

"It's just me, cool it." Ander swung a foot over the ledge and stepped inside. "Ah, you almost got my jacket."

My hands fell to my sides, but the window continued to smolder.

How am I supposed to explain that?

"Ander!" I hissed, legitimately pissed off. "What are you doing? I thought you were Alex."

"I was leaving you a note." He stood upright and looked at me. The side of his face was lit up in a soft glow from the Christmas lights lining the gutter outside. I couldn't help it. My anger quickly faded, replaced by a fluttering sensation in my stomach.

"Why didn't you just call, or ring the doorbell?" I imagined myself swallowing acid to kill the butterflies dancing around my stomach, but it didn't work.

"I didn't know you were awake," he said. "I guess I can just tell you." Ander ran a hand through his hair, a sign of stress. "Alex left."

"What?"

"He left, only an hour ago, and I'm going after him. I saw him get into a car with that kid, Jason. I didn't know they were still hanging out." Ander sighed, fidgeting slightly. "I just wanted to let you know...I didn't want you to think I ditched you."

"Okay," I said lamely.

"Well," Ander looked like he was waiting for something, but after a moment more of looking at me, then at the floor, he turned. "I'll see you later, Lidia."

"Wait!" I grabbed his arm. "I'll go with you!"

"No way."

"I'm not letting you go alone."

"Lidia, Alex is dangerous and illegal."

"I know."

Ander considered me a minute. "Fine," he said. "But we need to go now."

I leapt over to my duffel bag and the clothes strewn across the floor. I found a pair of jeans and a jacket and shrugged them on over my pajamas. Within two minutes, I was packed and ready to go. "Okay, let's go."

Ander watched me, looking confused but not completely reluctant as I climbed in front of him onto the roof.

This is probably a bad idea.

Ander crawled out beside me and ambled over to the ledge just above the gutter. His chest swelled as he took a deep breath, and leapt into the air. Instead of plummeting to the ground like a rock, he drifted down like a feather.

This is such a bad idea.

He landed with a muffled crunch in the snow.

"I don't know how to do that yet!" I whispered down at him. Snow entangled itself in my hair and eyelashes. The wet weather was already soaking through my clothes, leaving a deep cold that sunk through my skin.

"You know that feeling after you hold your breath and then let it out? That dizzy feeling? Do that, and I'll help you down, just keep your focus on me."

Not a problem. That seems to be all I can currently focus on. I sucked in a breath and held it until my lungs felt ready to explode from the pressure. I let it out, staring down at Ander and willing myself toward him.

"Jump!" he said.

I did.

My body sank into the air like I had jumped into a pit of thick foam. I wobbled uneasily, balancing on nothing as Ander's outstretched arms guided me toward the ground.

"Good job." Ander was beaming as my feet made contact with the ground. "C'mon," he gestured toward the front of the house, and we raced over to where his car was parked.

I got into the passenger side of the smoking Chevy idling in the driveway, and I rubbed the cold wet fabric of my jeans. It didn't seem to help my body get any warmer, so I reached out to blast the heat. The warm air burst through the vents and made my cheeks hot and red.

"Do you know where he went?" I asked, ringing out my hair as Ander backed out of the driveway and sped onto the winding road toward the main highway.

"I don't know, but I know that Jason's brother lives on the other side of the mountains in Everett. They might have a group hiding down there."

"Where's Everett?"

"It's about thirty minutes north of Seattle."

"Oh," I nodded. "That's far away."

"Only four hours." Ander was hunched over, struggling to see the road through the blizzard brewing in front of the streaming headlights.

I swallowed.

I can't believe I'm doing this right now.

I tried to think of something to say, but it didn't seem to be the time for conversation, and Ander was busy trying to drive.

"Can I turn on the radio?" I asked.

"Yeah, go for it."

Every station was broken static. After a few minutes of surfing, I gave up and just turned it off. We drove in heavy silence.

Should I say something? What should I say?

Ander hadn't been wearing a hat and the snow had drenched his hair. It hung in thick tendrils that dangled across his eyes and dripped beads of cold water onto his nose.

"Can..." Ander's eyebrows knitted together. "Can you feel that?"

Feel that? Feel what? Feel the awkwardness between us? Can he tell that I like him?

"What do you mean?"

"Spook," he said.

I stopped, focusing on the sensations around me. I was already cold from being soaked with melting snow, and the heat blowing from the vents kept the chill away from my skin, but I noticed my bones had startled to tingle. I thought it was just nerves.

"I don't see any?" I looked at the back seat. It was empty.

Thank God.

"Did we just, like, drive past one?"

"Maybe." Ander was still focused on the road. He drove, but after a minute, his face got serious and he spoke in a stern voice without looking at me. "So," he said. "What about Ethan?"

The question permeated the air with an unpleasant weight.

"What do you mean?" I asked.

"You know what I mean." Ander turned, his eyes boring into mine.

"Uhm," *Don't ask me Ander, please don't.* I turned forward to avoid looking into Ander's eyes. White spots pelted the windshield before melting to watery slush.

There was a man standing in the middle of the road.

"Ander, look out!" I screamed. I reached over to grab the wheel but Ander had already jerked the car in a hard left.

The tires squealed on the wet pavement. The Chevy flew off the road, jostling us inside the car with violent jolts of movement. It felt like the worst sort of carnival ride, and in less than a second, it was over. The car smashed into something solid with the deafening crack of broken metal.

Everything stopped.

Smoke burbled up from the hood, polluting the inside of the car through the air vents with the sharp stench of burnt rubber and gasoline. I moaned and rubbed my head.

"Lidia?" Ander's voice was panicked. "Oh my God." There was a click as Ander undid his seatbelt. "Lidia?"

"Ander?" I croaked, my voice was horse and I was at a weird angle, still in my seatbelt, but practically laying with my head against the passenger door. My shoulder hurt again, but that was it.

Ander let out a breath and reached forward. One of his hands brushed against my cheek and he held my face steady.

"Are you okay?" His eyes were dark in the dim light of the car. One of the inside lights had started flickering. He looked at me with a pained restraint that I had never registered in his face before. One of his hands left my cheek and pushed back a stand of hair. "Are you okay?" he asked again, softly this time.

"I'm okay. Are you okay?"

Ander's eyes were so dark blue. "Yeah," he was practically panting. "Yeah, I'm okay."

The light that came from outside changed as a shadow passed by. Ander looked up at the window behind me and then undid my seatbelt, shifting his weight until his body was flush against mine.

Something slammed into the side of the car with force. Ander jerked back, turning towards the noise. It felt as if we had been hit by a car, though there wasn't the sharp crunch of metal on metal. The thing that hit our car sounded like flesh and bone.

It came again.

Thwack!

Something was running into the car, rocking us inside.

Ander reached up and clicked the light off.

"What?" I whispered, but Ander's hand gently fell to cover my mouth.

"Shh." He fell back onto me until we were completely horizontal against the bench seat of the car. His weight sank into me as he sheltered our bodies from view.

Thwack!

The car rocked again. A loud animalistic screech pierced the air. It was a slow, hungry noise, unlike anything from this world. It was demonic. My heart beat spiked, my breathing came out fast and harsh through my nose, Ander's hand still held my mouth shut.

Something landed on the roof with a hard *Thump*. The joints of the car creaked with metal resistance under the weight. *Thump...thump...* Whatever it was, it was right above us.

Blue snow was slowly blanketing the windshield. *Please let it not see us, please let it not see us.* The movement on the roof stopped, and the only noise was my harsh breathing and the sizzle of the smoking engine.

Ander closed his eyes and pressed his forehead against mine. I could feel his heart hammering against my chest and his breathing was as sporadic as my own.

Thwak!

"Baby brother," Alex's voiced cooed from outside the car.

Thwak!

I whimpered in surprise as the passenger door vibrated from the intensity of the hit, but Ander's hand pressed more firmly against my mouth.

Thwack!

We rocked again, the heavy armor of the car swaying with the brutal assault.

"I told you not to follow me. I told you, I didn't want to hurt you." Alex's muffled threat sounded outside, closest to the passenger side window. "So, Anderrrrrrrr-"

Please let him not see us, please let him not see us.

"DON'T FOLLOW ME!" Alex shrieked, the sound going beyond his voice and warping into something else. It was nails ripping from fingertips as they carved themselves into a chalkboard.

Thwack!

I was trembling beneath Ander's weight.

Please, make it stop.

We waited, our scattered breaths sounded like screams in the deafening silence.

Alex didn't say anything else. There were no more footsteps on the roof. No more noises outside. Slowly, Ander removed his hand from my mouth, his face inches from mine. Our hearts were still thrumming insanely against each other.

Neither of us spoke.

Something blue and red outside the window caught my eyes. Beyond the blanket of snow, were flashing police lights. I pushed against Ander's chest.

"Look!" I whispered.

He twisted to look up, just as someone started yanking the contorted passenger door open. I fell out and landed onto the soft snow. A set of dry warm hands yanked me into a standing position, and a flashlight was shone into my eyes, blinding me.

"Are you two okay?" The officer's voice boomed, it sounded like my father. "We got a call, someone saw the accident." The hands drug me away. I blinked, trying to decipher images as white spots danced across my vision. "We need you two to move away from the vehicle. That smoke doesn't look promising... We don't want anything to blow up."

I was led toward a cluster of patriotic lights. I leaned against the side of the white cop car as Ander was guided by a second officer to stand next to me.

"Are you two okay?" The flashlight was back so I scrunched my eyes closed.

"We're okay," Ander's firm voice answered.

"What happened here?"

My eyelids flashed pink, then black, then pink again with the changing light. "Has there been any drinking tonight?"

"No, sir." Ander's voice again. "We were hit by a family of deer. I tried to swerve out of the way, and that's how I crashed... There are dents all over the side of the car."

The officer grunted, then sidled over to the car. I opened my eyes, watching him inspect the damage a safe distance away from the smoldering hood. He came back shortly. "I don't see any blood," the officer protested. "Or deer."

Ander shrugged. "We were hit by something."

Yeah. A demon...your brother.

"Okay," seeming satisfied, the officer pulled out an electronic note pad. "I'm going to need your information... let's see if we can't get you kids home safely tonight." The other officer, a few years younger, spoke something into the static of his walky-talky.

Ander gave the officers all of our information accordingly as I stood in shocked silence and watched the smoking engine with bloodshot eyes.

What was I thinking?

A little while later, a silver SUV pulled up to the wreck and both Mark and Amy climbed out. They stared, horror-struck at the black fuming Chevy crunched into the side of a small tree. Amy's hand flew to her mouth as her eyes welled with tears, and she searched the small gathering for Ander. She came forward, crying, wrapping him in an embrace. Mark's face was stony, but more frightened than anything else. Amy let Ander go and grabbed me, sobbing into my hair. Mark had an arm around his son in a firm hug, though it looked like some very stern words were being spoken. Amy released me and walked towards the officers, dialing a number on her phone.

Ander and I assured everyone that we were okay, but we had to repeat it a million times before the officers finally presented a deflated looking Ander with a ticket, and let us climb into the back of the SUV.

We drove back to Ander's neighborhood in stark silence. Just as we entered onto the winding road of the hill, Amy's voice sounded. "Lidia. We're going to drop you off at Deborah's. I already called her, she's very worried."

I blanched.

This is so bad.

"Mom, you already called Deborah?" Ander protested. "We're fine!"

"Ander!" Amy's voice was shrill and angry. "Lidia is Deborah's responsibility. She should know when her son's girlfriend is in a car crash with the neighbor boy!"

Neighbor boy.

The words hung in the air, silencing all further protest.

I'm such an idiot...

Chapter 28

We continued to drive, slowing down briefly as we neared Ethan's house before continuing on the road. They didn't stop to drop me off.

I looked over at Ander, he was staring at his parents, just as confused as I was. Minutes later, we pulled into Ander's dark driveway. The sudden stop of the car seemed to jolt Amy from her thoughts.

"Mark!" she hissed. "We were supposed to drop Lidia off."

"What?" Mark turned to her, then looked back at me. He seemed honestly surprised to see me sitting there. "Oh," he fumbled. "I'm sorry, Lidia." Mark turned back to his wife. "Where are we dropping her off?"

Amy's anger faded as she struggled to remember where it was I was supposed to be going. "She was-"

"You said she could stay with us for a little while," Ander interjected hurriedly.

"Oh," Amy nodded. "That's right." Her warm smile flooded the icy tension. "C'mon in then, I'll make everyone some hot chocolate."

Thanks to Alex's mind-wash, Mark and Amy's memory was still out of whack. It was so convenient that I almost didn't trust our good luck.

What about Deborah?

411

I had the awful feeling that Ethan and his mom wouldn't be so quick to forget. Their memories had nearly made a full recovery from Alex's last visit.

We kicked the snow off our boots at the front door and filed into the warmth. My heart thudded nervously. I wouldn't know what to say if they suddenly remembered what had just happened. Ander took my jacket with a raised eyebrow. It said- *play along.* Butterflies jostled my stomach.

"Uhmm…." Amy prattled fingers across her temple. "What was I doing, we just said it."

"You have to call Deborah," Ander rushed to answer. "I prank called her, and she thinks Lidia and I got in a car accident."

Shock register on Amy's face. "Ander, why would you do that?" She stared at him sternly, but then sighed. "Right, there was something else."

"And make hot chocolate," Mark added.

Amy smiled, "and hot chocolate." She shuffled into the kitchen and Mark followed.

"Oh my God." I covered my face with my hands. "We got so lucky," I mumbled through the fingers.

Ander gave a shaky laugh. "Yeah, we did."

I walked over to the living room fireplace, flipped the switch, and sank onto the couch to watch the flames roar against the glass and artificial wood. "I can't even-" I shook my head and fell back against the cushion. "I can't believe that just happened."

A loud pounding sounded at the front door. Someone was knocking. Ander switched the top lock and opened it. Ethan burst into the entryway, bringing a flurry of snow with him.

Crap.

"What the fuck happened?" he demanded. Ethan was wearing a jacket but no hat, and the snow had completely drenched his copper-brown hair. It lay flat against his skull, making his ears look more prominent than usual.

"Ethan!" I scrambled off the couch.

Ethan strode past Ander and into the room towards me, ferocious anger contorted his face into an ugly scowl. "What happened?"

"Nothing, we're fine."

Ander approached. "Ethan, we-"

"I wasn't talking to you!" Ethan turned back to me. "What were you doing? Why were you in the car with Ander at two o'clock in the morning?"

Crap.

"We were- " *chasing Alex.* I stared at Ethan like a deer caught in headlights. "We were going into town."

"Town's in the opposite direction," Ethan scathed.

"We- I was going-" my insides were mush. Useless, stupid, mush. There was nothing I could say to defend myself against the truth, and a part of me didn't want to.

And he knew it.

Ethan turned back to Ander. "What were you doing with my girlfriend, in your car, in the middle of the night?"

Ander didn't say anything, he just stared at the floor.

"What were you doing?" Ethan asked again, angrier, louder.

When Ander still didn't respond, Ethan walked up and shoved Ander, hard. Ander took a step backwards, finally meeting Ethan's eyes. "Back off, Ethan," his voice was dangerously low, and tension radiated off his taut body like a heat waves.

Ethan shoved Ander again. "I asked you a question!" He pushed him harder and Ander fell back against a small table, rattling the assortment of picture frames. "What were you and Lidia doing at two in the morning?"

Ander's eyes flared and he stepped forward. "Don't push me!"

"I'll do whatever I want to any guy trying to screw my girlfriend!" Ethan shouted into Ander's face, his cheeks red and a vein popping from his temple.

"Stop!" I tried to push them apart. "Stop it!"

They didn't listen. Didn't even seem to hear.

Ander didn't back away from Ethan, but he spat his next words like poison. "She's not your girlfriend."

Ethan's nostrils flared.

"Ander, stop it," I pleaded.

Ethan lunged forward, knocking me out of the way. Ethan threw a punch, but Ander caught his arm and swung it around, thrusting him to the ground. After a second, Ethan sprang to his feet again, his ears flaming red.

"You can't let me have one thing, can you?" Ethan bellowed. "You have everything, and you have to go after Lidia!" Ethan was in Ander's face again. "You have a perfect family, perfect friends, that perfect prissy school, and you had to take her with you- you didn't even tell me! You never told me it was the same goddamn school!"

"You don't know what you're talking about!"

"I know exactly what I'm talking about! The only problem in your life is that Sarah is dying!"

Ander looked livid.

"Even at camp, you flirted with her right in front of me! And I-" Ethan half smiled, his face still an angry red. "And I trusted you, because I thought you were my friend."

"I was your friend! I was looking out for her while you were acting like a jackass!"

"Everything would've been fine if she hadn't gone to that stupid school with you. You could have any girl you want, but you just had to have her, didn't you?" Both of his palms pushed Ander back again. "Because she's mine, and you can't let me have one thing better than you."

"Lidia's not a thing!" Ander snarled. "She's not a trophy, you piece of shit!"

"Oh, shut up." Ethan barked. "Is this what you do? You act all righteous until they sleep with you."

Ander's mouth pressed into a hardline, but he didn't say anything.

Ethan glared at him, and then it clicked. "You already did it, didn't you?"

415

Ander bit the inside of his cheek. Even with one of his hands in a cast, I could see his white knuckled fist clenched at his side.

"Did you?" Ethan's eyes widened and he took a step back. "Go ahead," he said with his arms raised. "Tell me, how were my sloppy seconds? Huh? How was it?"

Anders jaw clenched and unclenched, but after a second he spat out words. "It was worth it."

Ethan leapt forward, his fist colliding with Ander's mouth. Ander swore loudly as they both fell backwards, crashing against the table, and knocking picture frames to the floor. They rolled in a blur of fists, their thrashing forms scuffling against the furniture. I could hear the loud claps of knuckles colliding against flesh.

"Stop!" I ran forward, tugging at Ethan's shoulders as he threw one punch after another at Ander's furious face. Ander yelled and pushed Ethan back, knocking me to the floor as they switched positions.

"Hey!" Mark appeared in the doorway. He ran over and pulled the two boys apart, yelling something at Ander.

Ander pulled back, holding his swollen lower lip while he glared at Ethan from hooded brows. Mark was still shouting at Ander, but Ander didn't seem to care. His chest rose and fell slowly with deep intakes of air. After a minute, Ethan shoved himself to his feet, not looking at anyone. His mouth was nearly as red as has face, each tooth coated in a slimy red film of blood from where Ander's punches had broken the gums.

I stood up on shaky legs, struggling to maintain a composed expression.

What have I done?

As Mark continued to scold the two boys, I slowly stepped backwards down the hall.

What have I done?

I rounded the corner, went into the bathroom, and locked myself inside. I pressed my back against the cool wood. After a minute of heavy breathing, a sob broke free and I covered my mouth with a shaking hand as I slid down the door, trying to smother my own crying with a fist. There were a few muffled voices from the entryway, then the front door slammed.

I could imagine Ethan walking home in the snow. Angry, alone, betrayed.

What have I done?

I bit harder onto my hand, screwing up my face as wet tears streamed down my cheeks. I took a few sloppy breaths and tried to focus on something else. The bathroom was painted a warm brown and the fabric shower curtain was a pastel blue with Moroccan swirls. Amy had put a dish of blue hand soaps on the counter. They were shaped like snowmen and made the entire bathroom smell like "ocean breeze" room spray. Anything that said it smelled like ocean breeze never actually smelled like the ocean. I doubted they would make a bathroom scent that smelled like rotten seaweed and salty shellfish.

"Lidia?" Ander knocked on the door, his voice raspy and low.

I wiped away a few tears and tried to compose my voice, but it still sounded watery. "Yeah?"

The doorknob turned and I pushed myself to my feet as Ander came in. He closed the door and I forced myself against the far wall. He leaned against the counter opposite me, an ice pack pressed to his mouth. The small bathroom suddenly felt too small with both of us in there. He had washed the blood from his lip, but when he took the ice away, I could see that it was still swollen and red.

I knew he was watching me intently, even though my own eyes skated around the room. I couldn't even look at him.

"You okay?" he asked.

No.

"Yeah, I'm fine." I caught a glance of myself in the mirror. Crying had made my face blotchy, and most of my eye makeup was smudged.

"Lidia," Ander set the ice pack on the counter and ran a hand through his hair, it had gotten so long over the winter months that it just fell back into place. "I know you didn't want him to find out. I-"

My chest tightened and I felt an overwhelming wave of nausea sweep over the pit of my stomach. Ethan must be half way home through the snow by now.

"I couldn't do it anymore," Ander said softly. He stood up straight and took a step forward. There was already so little space between us that his one little step closed the gap. He was standing an inch in front of me.

I pressed myself back against the wall, hoping it would just open up and swallow me whole.

"I can't keep hiding it." Ander never looked nervous, but he looked nervous now. His eyes were all over my face, and I could see the vein in his throat throbbing.

"I'm sorry I made you lie to Ethan," I said. "I thought it would make things better, not worse."

It looked like he had gotten stung on the lip by the largest bee in the world. Still red from where Ethan smashed his fist, it looked even worse now that the icepack was gone.

All because he had told the truth. I was the sloppy seconds.

A flashing image of Ethan and Ander greeting each other at Camp Tanka came to mind just before it was replaced with the vision of the two of them crashing into each other with nasty snarls on their faces.

"It's not worse," Ander said.

"Yes it is." I wiped a tear that rolled down my cheek. From outside the bathroom I could hear someone knocking on the front door. Both Ander and I shot glances in the same direction, as if we had x-ray vision and could see through the walls. "Do you think that's Ethan?" I asked.

Ander wasn't looking at the wall anymore, just me. His features were soft, almost sad. "Probably."

"I, uh," I sniffed, trying, and failing again, to hide my crying. "I better go talk to him this time."

Ander nodded and stepped back to let me leave.

Amy was walking down the hallway as I exited the bathroom. She looked surprised to see me in the house, then worried to see that I had been crying.

"I've got it," I said gesturing toward the door.

She nodded, still looking a little confused before turning and going back toward the kitchen.

419

I sniffed again, trying one last time to wipe away all the tears. There was no hope in saving my makeup. Go figure, the one time I actually bother putting on eyeliner and it ends up all over my face. Maybe it was a good thing though. Maybe Ethan would be less mad if he saw how bad I felt about everything.

I peeped out the side window of the entryway and saw a corner of Ethan's Jacket, then I unlatched the lock and opened the door. Ethan stood there, eyes white, face slack.

"Oh sh-" I felt the words stick in my throat as I registered what I was looking at. "Ethan!"

"Hey, Lidia." Jason Singer stepped out from the shadows of the house. Like Alex, the past few weeks hadn't been kind. He stood behind Ethan, a smile playing across his thin lips. He looked like an emaciated raccoon. "Is Alex home?" he asked.

"Ander!" I called as loudly as I could, but my voice quivered and I'm not sure if it carried. "An-" a pair of strong clean hands clamped over my mouth and I was hurled backwards against a large body that smelled like Old Spice cologne. I caught a glance of silver hair behind me and knew it was Mark. I didn't need to see his eyes to know it must've looked like he was having a standing seizure.

Jason smiled more broadly as he watch me struggle, then he turned his smile to someone descending the stairs. "Hey Alex... I found someone."

Alex cussed loudly. "What the hell? I said someone random!"

Jason cocked an eyebrow and tilted his head down to look at Ethan. He considered him like a vulture, trying to figure out if he wanted to play with the mouse, or eat it. "He is random," he finally said.

"No, that's the neighbor. I've known him my entire life. He thinks fantasy football counts as a real sport."

"How was I supposed to know that?" Jason sneered. "I've never met your neighbors."

"Where'd you find him?"

Jason looked a little guilty. "Over the hill."

"By the neighbor's house?"

"Yeah."

"You're an idiot." I heard Alex's angry footsteps behind me. Then there was the rattling of a doorknob and Ander's muffled voice came from the bathroom.

"Lidia?" Ander shook the door. "Lidia, I'm locked in. What's going on?" He banged on the wood with his fist.

Alex gently knocking back. *Knock, knock.*

Bang!

"Baby brother, for your own safety I need you to stay calm."

Jason snickered from the doorway as I tried breaking free of Mark's grip, but I couldn't. He was way stronger than I was, and with his hand clamped firmly over my mouth, I couldn't even open it to scream.

"Mom, Dad, and Sarah will all be safe-"

"Let me out!"

"Oh, come on," Alex cooed through the door. "You tied me up, got my friends expelled. I think fair is fair."

"If you touch her, I swear to-"

"I'm not going to do anything to Lidia," Alex sounded annoyed. "Everyone is going to be fine." He paused and reconsidered this statement. "Well, everyone you know is going to be fine. I'll be gone by morning, and you won't ever see me again." The last of his statement fell flat, the words falling from his mouth without his usual vigor.

Jason pushed Ethan inside and pointed him towards the dining room. Ethan turned abruptly and strode down the hall, walking straight past Ander as he shouted from inside the bathroom.

"Jeremy and Connor are on their way," Jason said as he shut the front door behind him and pulled a cigarette out of his pocket. He lit it with a cupped hand and pulled a long draft. When he exhaled, the stench polluted the warm homey smell of the house. "I think Peter is almost here too."

"What?" Alex didn't sound happy. "I thought you said they'd be here in an hour? I still need to find someone."

"Why?" Jason blew smoke in my direction. "If you don't want to use him, then just use her."

"I can't use her! I told you I wanted someone random!"

Jason just shrugged and ambled past us, still smoking his cigarette.

"Lidia!" Ander's fist jolted the door, but it was still shut. "Lidia, can you hear me?"

I tried squirming out of Marks arms, but I still couldn't move. My heart was thrumming like crazy and I was sweating

422

from trying to break free and run. It was like trying to move a brick wall.

Alex strode over, he glared at me, a muscle in his cheek twitching in random intervals. "You are the stupidest girl I have ever met," he hissed. "Why can't you and Ander just stay away?"

"Lidia!" Ander bellowed.

"Oh, hey-" I heard Jason call casually from the hallway. "What if Peter wants her?"

"Peter can't have her, or him!"

Jason laughed. "I wouldn't want to tell Peter that."

Alex pushed air through his flared nostrils like a bull. "You're dead."

Chapter 29

Alex had his father drag me into the dining room. Ander was still shouting and banging on the door, and I tried kicking one of my legs out to knock against it as we passed by, but I only managed a tap.

"Jason, get the lights."

Jason turned to Ethan. "Kid, get the lights."

Ethan turned and flipped the switch that turned off every light in the dining room.

"Seriously?" Alex sneered.

Jason laughed. I could smell his cigarette in the darkness that suddenly engulfed us. The Christmas lights around the windows let in an eerie red haze that kept flashing green, and blue. The light made everyone's silhouettes glow, and it clung to the wisps of smoke that drifted from Jason's mouth.

I took a deep breath and tried to think. I needed a boost, but I had expelled all my energy zapping the window frame at Ethan's house.

What do I do?

There were still only two of them, and four of us-excluding Ander who was caged in the powder room. If Amy, Mark, and Ethan weren't mindless zombies, we'd have them outnumbered. We could escape.

I need my phone.

My cell was in my back pocket, but I could barely move. Luckily, Mark had my arms pinned to my sides and if I twisted my arm slowly, I might be able to retrieve it. Alex was having me restrained, not watched, and he was too busy whispering to Jason to notice me. I moved my elbow outward, as slowly as I could. I shifted my weight onto one hip and Mark squeezed me tighter. It felt like my ribs were about to stab through my lungs. I took a tiny breath and just moved my hand.

I got it.

What's speed dial for 911?

Being away from my phone while at school had made me clumsy. Once, I had been able to punch out a text under the school desk without even looking at the screen, but now, I just hoped it was on. I had no idea what I was doing.

"Hey!" Alex's head whipped around when he saw the lime light of the screen flash against a shadow on the wall. "Give me that." He snatched it from my hands, looked at the screen, and then threw it as hard as he could against the wall. It hit with a hard crack before skidding across the floor in pieces.

I screamed at him through Marks hand, but the sound only came out as an angry hum.

I need to get to Ethan's house and have Deborah call the police.

Jason and Alex were bickering quietly in the corner, their conversation inaudible due to Ander yelling in the background. All I could hear were fragmented sentences and random words.

"Brotherhood."

Bang.

"Not enough time for that."

Bang, Bang. "Let me out of here!" *Bang.*

"Get over it."

"Peter."

Bang, Bang, Bang.

There was a knock on the door. The front door, not the bathroom door Ander was still pounding. Alex cussed and Jason went into the hall. I heard a collective greeting of male voices and then a stampede of heavy footsteps as Jason and three new guys entered into the room.

"Is that Lidia Powell?" Connor, one of the boys Alex used to sit with at lunch said. He still had bushy eyebrows, and a mean smile, but he had lost weight. As he came closer, I saw that each tooth was lined with yellow plaque and his breath was stale. He spoke right into my face. "You and your friend's got me expelled, and if it wasn't for Peter, I'd be in Plymouth right now."

Good.

I knew Connor didn't expect a verbal answer, but I tried giving him a physical one. I kicked my right leg out, pushing myself against Marks body for support. I got him right in the groin.

"Ah!" Connor doubled over, oohing in pain as the rest of the boys laughed.

Jeremy, the one with dark hair in an old-fashioned bowl cut, was smoking next to Jason as they watched me from the shadows. I assumed the redheaded stranger was Peter. His body was rail thin, but his face looked oddly round, though I couldn't tell if it was because of his full beard or not. Either way, he wasn't in high school.

When Connor recovered, he lurched forward with a fist raised, the way bullies do in movies when they threaten to punch. I didn't flinch, and despite the blood pumping hard through my veins, I'm convinced I would've stuck my tongue out at him if Mark hadn't been holding it shut.

"I like your choice for first feed, Alex," Connor said, scowling at me.

"She's not my feed," Alex said. "Jason screwed it up and grabbed the wrong person."

"Then who's in the bathroom?" Connor asked.

"Ander," Alex sniffed. "I have to grab someone since Jason decided to pick the neighbor-"

"Whoa, whoa," said Peter, his voice sounded like gravel. Based off the scratch in his voice, I guessed he had been smoking cigarettes his entire life. "We don't have time for this. I see a room full of people that could work."

"This is my family," Alex said defensively.

"She's not," Connor sneered at me.

"Let me see her," Peter gestured Mark to bring me forward. "She's pretty," he said. Peter studied me like a Picasso painting. He even stroked his beard.

I shot daggers at him through my eyes, but that's all I could do. He was too far away to kick.

You evil redheaded feeder.

"If you're going to choose between her and the neighbor, I would definitely choose her," Peter said.

"I don't even think she passed her SETT," said Jeremy.

Yes I did.

"Really?" Peter raised an eyebrow and chuckled. "How sad." Up close, I could see he had the same strange tick Alex had in his left cheek. His eyes, dark and thoughtful, still held something evil inside. You could see the emptiness behind his curious expression.

"No." I could hear Alex breathing behind me, and Peter raised his eyes to look at him.

"Why not?"

"I won't do anyone I know," Alex said. "That wasn't part of the agreement. I didn't sign up for that shit."

"It's too late," Peter snapped. "You have two choices, hurry up and pick."

"Choose the girl," Jeremy said beside him. "She's hot."

"Yeah," said Connor. "Jeremy picked a dude for my first feed."

"That's because I knew you'd like it."

"Shut up, Jason!"

Jason was about to respond when Peter cut them off. "Both of you, shut up. We need to get this over with. Alex, pick one." He smiled, false kindness polluting a smile that was already ruined by grey teeth. "Choose the girl, or the guy," his smile broadened. "We won't judge."

The boys laughed and I heard Alex let out a gush of air. "Fine," he practically whispered.

"Lidia!" Ander was still knocking against the bathroom.

"Excellent choice." Peter nodded to Mark. "Let her go."

428

Mark let go, but as soon as his hands left, I crumpled into a heap onto the floor. I wasn't immobile, I wasn't even unconscious. It just felt like every bone in my body had melted away leaving nothing but my mushy insides.

"When are you going to teach us that one?" Connor asked. I couldn't see his face.

"I'm not," Peter said. "It's my trademark."

My lips could still move, but I wasn't able to get a large enough intake of air to make much of a sound.

"Alex," I whimpered, just barely above a whisper.

Alex stared down at me like a dog he both pitied and despised. His left eye kept squinting, and his mouth worked hard in a deep scowl.

"Alex, please." I sounded like I had been lost in the desert for days. "Alex don't do this. You don't have to."

He bent down and picked me up. My head lulled backwards in his arms, I already looked dead, and soon, I would be. Cold sweat left a sheen on my skin and I felt my heart in my throat. I have never wanted to move so badly, but I couldn't. I was completely useless. My heart pounded in my ears, louder, and louder, as Alex gently set me down on the dining room table.

All I could see was the ceiling, but the boys were still talking in the room, Ander was still pounding at the bathroom door, Ethan was still swaying silently in the corner.

I felt tears leak out of my eyes and spill down my face, collecting in my hair and ears. "Alex," I choked. "Please." I had to stop talking and tried to breath. It was hard. "Alex."

429

"And the knife-" Peter continued talking. "Blood is life, and ours to take." They were in the middle of a conversation but I hadn't heard a word. "Welcome to the brotherhood."

The pounding in the bathroom finally stopped, but the blood rushing through my ears was so loud I could barely tell the difference. When Alex leaned over the table a minute later, I could see it wasn't him anymore. Even with only the dim light coming from outside, I could see the mask of a monster swirling around his face with flesh-colored smoke. It left black holes where eyes should've been.

What have you done to yourself, Alex?

Alex's hand shook and he brought it to my neck and pressed the cold silver tip of a knife against my throat.

"I'm sorry," he said, before I felt a sharp sting. The blade pierced my skin with a slight pop. He drug the knife further, opening more flesh and creating a sharp dull pain that prickled as air brushed past. I could feel a trail of warm blood trickle down my chest. It pooled around my head and made my hair wet.

"Ah," I was still choking on tears. "Ouch."

Someone on the other side of the room laughed.

Alex pulled the knife away, through the mask, I saw his mouth gape as he stared at what he had just done. He hadn't cut deep enough to kill me, just bleed.

Is this how I go?

I pictured myself as I must've looked then. A seventeen-year-old girl with a limp body, still half dressed in pajamas with mascara trailing down her face. I was just lying there, helplessly submissive, on the dining room table as my killer watched blood run down the sides of my neck and soak my hair into dark wet tangles. If I died and became a spirit, I'd be stuck in this moment forever.

I had to make it a good one.

I couldn't use my body, and I had never tried using a boost without the physical motions associated with the transfer and focus. Plus, even if I could do it, I was pretty sure I didn't have enough energy in my body to move a leaf.

I still had to try.

I gurgled, and a gush of blood spurt from my neck. It stung with a deep ache.

Ignoring the pain, I stared hard at Alex's shirt and clenched my teeth until pain shot up through my jaw. I felt the heat in my mouth first, and willed it forward. There was a spark, and then the hem of Alex's shirt caught fire.

Alex screamed and jumped, swatting the flame until it was completely gone. Behind him, all the boys started laughing loudly.

"I don't think she likes it, Alex," Connor teased.

Alex's face whipped back towards me, the wash of smoke growing thicker around his mouth and thinner around his eyes. I saw Alex's real eyes through the fog, and they were terrifying.

"Just do it and get it over with," said Peter. "Before she tries lighting a candle next."

The boys laughed louder.

Alex leaned forward slowly, eyes wild, and he pressed his open mouth against my fresh wound. I wanted to pull back.

The smoke mask licked out to touch me, and I wanted to pull away so badly, but couldn't.

Alex's mouth was the same temperature as the blood and the two mingled against my skin in a wet, soft, painful mess. At first it hurt, I could feel his sucking, pulling the blood from my veins and sharpening the sting of broken flesh. Then it felt nice. The sharp sting became a dull discomfort. Even when Alex reached forward and pinned me against the table unnecessarily, it didn't hurt. He bit down, teeth scraping tendons together. My eyes drifted backwards and my body felt easy. I sighed.

Is this dying?

I couldn't muster fear, only pity for the boys with the masked faces of demons around me. I wondered how they could even look at each other. Though, not being exorcists, they probably didn't see the horror in the mask that they wore. *How could anyone volunteer for this?* Ethan's eyes were still pointed toward the sky. He would never know any better, which was probably for the best.

There was suddenly a flash of light and something loud crashed against the wall. I heard the boys shouting, and Ander yelled my name.

I opened my eyes. I had bones in my body again, but I felt too heavy to move. I didn't want to move. Ever.

"Lidia!" Ander's voice cracked. "Lidia, get up! Lidia!"

I let my eyes fall on him. Ander was struggling against Jason and Connor, swinging widely as the two boys held him tight. I wondered why they didn't just immobilized him. Maybe they had to keep too much focus on Amy, Mark, and Ethan. Maybe they can only control so many people at once.

"Get off of her you sonofabitch!" Ander looked so scared and angry. Both of his hands were bloody. "You're killing her!"

Jason told him to calm down and Ander took a swing at him. Across the room, Peter watched me hungrily, he didn't even seem to notice Ander.

"Hurry it up," Peter said.

Alex sucked more furiously at my throat and I felt a sudden jolt of lightness take my body. It was the good part of the roller coaster, the part when all your insides float up for a second before they catch up with your fall.

"Lidia!"

I flipped my eyes open again at Ander voice.

A Spook was hovering in the air just above me. It was like waking up from a nightmare into another nightmare. The Spook's hazy black eyes were locked on mine.

It smiled, revealing a broken row of sharp teeth that oozed globs of black tar. The spit strung the gums of his mouth together like black cobwebs.

"Lidia!" Ander cried.

The Spook crackled, a long croak of pleasure, and I suddenly felt another jolt of lightness. The demon started to reach forward toward my head- just as I did when I was about to absorb a spirit.

I felt a short burst of fear, but once I accepted it, the fear was replaced by determination. I pressed all my focus into my front temple to block.

"No." I didn't even hear my voice, so I wasn't sure if I even said it out loud. "You can't have me."

The Spook's mouth snarled, and its dark eyes narrowed, but it didn't stop reaching. Someone on the other side of the room asked who I was talking to.

"No... go away," I said.

I don't know how I felt so confident that I wasn't going to be taken by the Spook, but I was. I was still blocking, and the Spook was still reaching. Its stench permeated the smoke-stained air. Just as a long demented hand with thin veins and oversized knuckles reached my forehead, I closed my eyes, and prayed.

It was something I had done before, but not often. I decided right there and then, that no matter what happened, how I died, or how much it hurt- the Spook wouldn't be let inside. When I had prayed, I simply asked for help in doing just that.

Alex ripped away from my neck. He fell on all fours and started heaving, bile mixed with blood spewed from his mouth.

"What happened?"

"Lidia!" Ander yelled.

A few of the boys started talking again as Alex wretched. My eyes drifted closed. My neck stung and my body felt cold, and heavy. I was exhausted and just wanted to sleep.

Someone swore loudly and shouted.

"Police!"

"He stole your phone?"

"I told you to put him back in the bathroom."

There was the sound of a fist against flesh.

"Leave him."

I heard the shuffle of feet, and someone hoisted Alex from the floor, still puking. A few minutes later, Ander had me in his arms.

"Stay with me, Lidia," he said. "Stay, c'mon, stay with me."

Something fell to the floor across the room, it sounded like a broken vase. I might've even heard a woman crying. There was knocking on the front door.

"Stay with me," Ander continued to chant, half rocking me.

First, there were voices, then hands, and then more hands. I was wrapped up in something warm and soft. Beeping and the smell of weird astringents became more powerful as time went on.

"Stay here."

"Stay with us, okay?"

"I want you to stay awake."

Everyone kept asking me to stay, so I did.

To Be Continued...

Acknowledgments

I never really thought I could write a novel. It was something writers did, and as a misfit college student who couldn't even settle on a major, I was no writer. The idea for BOOST came to me when I was nineteen (which is also when I started writing it), and without the help of so many readers, editors, family, friends, and even coworkers, I never would've been able to make it happen.

To Maxx Powell, thank you for loving me throughout all my crazy "zoning out" moments, and bringing me tea even when I was hunched over my computer like an ugly troll.

To my friends and family, thank you for taking the time to read the ARC copies of BOOST. Your enthusiasm gave me so much hope and confidence.

To Kristine at The Schwartz Reviews, thank you for your kind words and help getting BOOST ready for the public.

To all my ARC reviewers, thank you so much for your interest in BOOST. To Sibella, you made me cry tears of joy at Olive Garden... it was awkward.

To all the Authonomy readers, your help editing BOOST in the early stages made such a tremendous impact. Thank you.

To all of you reading this now, thank you so much for taking the time to read BOOST. It's hard to describe the immense feeling of gratitude I have for anyone giving my book the time of day, so thank you. If I could buy you all gift baskets, I would.

About D.A. Paul

Since graduating from the University of Washington in 2014, Desiree has tried adhering to a more "adult" lifestyle. It didn't work out. Undisturbed by her aversion to domestic and professional work, she has decided to pursue a more creative career and become a writer instead. Her first novel, BOOST, will be the first of two books in the Haunted Addiction series.